Praise for the work

The Lady Adventu

If you enjoy your romance mixed with a rip-roaring adventure, then this is the book for you. Karen Frost allowed her characters to become more than they ever could as individuals. By joining together as the Lady Adventurers Club, they found strengths they could never have imagined. For some, they found a love that they never knew existed. I was swept away with them.

-*The Lesbian Review*

I loved the women of *The Lady Adventurers Club*, it was such a great read. It had what I was looking for in a historical novel and from this genre of book. The characters were interesting, and I was invested in the adventure that was going on. I really enjoyed reading this, and I hope the women have another adventure.

-Kathryn M., *NetGalley*

Fun beginning of what I hope is a new series. This is an adventure to read, think Indiana Jones but with a team of talented women.

-Kaye C., *NetGalley*

For those looking for an action/adventure story and a little romance, this is the book for you

-Cheryl W., *NetGalley*

I had a lot of fun reading this book. If you love adventure, intrigue, romance, and a bit of the paranormal in your historical fiction novels, then give this book a try.

-Betty H., *NetGalley*

The Demon's Guide to the Apocalypse

Karen Frost

Other Bella Books by Karen Frost

The Lady Adventurers Club

About the Author

Karen Frost is an LGBT fantasy author whose works span a range of sub-genres. Her Destiny and Darkness young adult high fantasy quartet, published by Ylva Publishing, explores what happens when strong young women are thrust into the politics of a kingdom at war while monsters from another world are baying at the gates. *The Lady Adventurers Club*, published by Bella Books, follows four accomplished women in the early 1920s as they race across Egypt in pursuit of antiquities thieves...and they're not alone. Karen is also a pop culture pundit and blogger who writes about sapphic representation on the big and small screen. You can find out more about her on her website karenfrostbooks.com.

The
Demon's Guide
to the
Apocalypse

Karen Frost

BELLA
B O O K S
2023

Bella Books, Inc.
P.O. Box 10543
Tallahassee, FL 32302

Printed in the United States of America on acid-free paper.

First Edition - 2023

Editor: Heather Flournoy
Cover Designer: Kayla Mancuso

ISBN: 978-1-64247-486-2

PUBLISHER'S NOTE

Acknowledgments

This book is both about and not about several things—first and foremost of these, religion and identity. It takes the former and fictionalizes and reduces it down into something commercial. It is not about any particular sect or belief system. While it builds on Christian ideas, that's only to offer it some sort of framework with which many readers will be familiar. Thus while some of the ideas are real ("Does the majority of humanity deserve to be sent to Hell during the Apocalypse, as the Book of Revelation claims?"), others ("Angels are selfish jerks") are merely for literary convenience.

The issue of identity and belonging is much more complicated. While I used sensitivity and beta readers in an effort to craft as genuine characters as I could, there is no doubt that I have failed to capture the full and nuanced experience of women of color, even in a fictionalized, urban fantasy setting. For that, I hope that readers will show patience and recognize it as a good-faith effort. During the sensitivity reading process, I was educated in a new and much more effective way about a particular trope that has long been applied to some women of color. The lesson here is that all of us can unwittingly reinforce stereotypes and tropes even when well-intentioned. All we can do is try to learn from others and move away from these negative portrayals, which I hope I've done here. Writing a book is a long process, and it is benefitted at multiple points from the contributions of others. I'd like to thank my wife, my beta readers, and my editor for being part of the shaping process. As with every book I write, I hope there are readers whom this book speaks to. And if not, maybe the next one…

Dedication

For my wife, who likes this one the best.

CHAPTER ONE

Andromalius's instructions had been clear. "Kill that fucking shit stain Merihem and text me when it's done." Andromalius wasn't the sentimental type. Nor was he the forgiving type. Whatever Merihem had done, it was enough to get him a one-way ticket straight back to Hell, courtesy of the three women currently crouched in the hallway outside his door.

Theodora didn't care what the demon had done. She never did. All she cared about was that in a few minutes, he was going to rejoin all the other miserable excuses for demons who couldn't keep it together on Earth and were now going to be stuck in Hell for the rest of eternity.

She hefted her shotgun, snugging the butt into her shoulder and aiming over the black barrel at the pallid green door in front of her. The paint was peeling at the edges, and decades of hands had left dirty, blotchy stains around the knob. Demons like Merihem always lived in seedy, run-down apartment buildings like this. Roaches liked the company of other roaches.

"He better not be a fire-breather," Annabeth muttered under her breath behind Theodora. The small woman was kneeling with her shoulder against the wall, her fingers wrapped tightly around a medieval-looking thick black morning star. If the demon stared out his peephole, the hallway would appear empty. He wouldn't see them coming. "This is my favorite cardigan. I don't want holes in it."

Theodora rolled her eyes but didn't say anything. The aforementioned black cardigan made Annabeth look like an elderly Latina librarian, an effect reinforced by her large, thick glasses. In Theodora's opinion, Merihem would be doing her a favor if he torched it. She was too young to look like a grandmother. But then again, Annabeth had a closet full of cardigans. The loss of this one wouldn't dent the collection.

"I bet he runs," Harriet said. She was leaning casually against the railing, watching the door with deceptive casualness. Although her hands were empty, the black handle of her katana was visible over her shoulder. She could draw it in under a second, more than enough time if Merihem somehow caught on to what was waiting for him and decided to go on the offensive first.

"He better not," Theodora growled, annoyed by even the prospect of it.

The first problem with hunting down insubordinate demons was that each of them had some kind of demonic ability or talent they inevitably tried to use to defend themselves. Andromalius had a fucking terrible habit of not mentioning what their targets' supernatural abilities were when he sent the women to revoke them, so it was always an unwelcome surprise to see what waited for them on the other side of a door. And fire-breathing, as her wardrobe could attest, was an annoyingly common talent. As was venom-spitting.

The second problem was that their targets never went quietly. Those turdgurglers may have come from Hell, but they absolutely didn't want to go to back there. Nothing was worse than Hell, even for a demon, so predictably, they either fought or ran.

Theodora hated when they ran. She was too old to go chasing after demons. Even thinking about running was exhausting. She might have chased demons when she was younger and had stamina and lung capacity, leaping over garbage cans and parkouring down stairwells, but she was too old for that shit now. Now she'd rather shoot them in the face and go from there. Less cardio was more.

She kicked the door to Merihem's apartment a few times with her heavy black boot, the leveled shotgun barrel not wavering an inch. The sound echoed hollowly, like the distant boom of a cannon firing. No one inside could miss hearing it. Nor could the neighbors, although none of them would care or dare to investigate who had come knocking at this hour. In a place like this, the three women could be anything from undercover police to drug dealers to gang members. No one, in short, you wanted to meet face-to-face unless you wanted trouble.

Silence. For a moment, Theodora wondered if Merihem was out. That would be aggravating. One visit to this shithole was enough. She didn't feel like making a repeat visit. And they weren't exactly going to camp out for a few hours. She had shit to do at home, like laundry.

Finally, she heard muffled shuffling inside. The lock clicked. She looked down at Annabeth and nodded. They didn't need to exchange words. Everyone knew what would happen next.

The door started to open, creaking noisily.

She didn't wait for whoever was on the other side to finish. Her finger pulled gently on the trigger. The weapon roared in response. She gritted her teeth as the butt of the shotgun kicked into her shoulder so hard it made her collarbone burn. Her ears rang.

In front of her, a dozen small holes appeared in the door, perfectly round and black. She pumped the slide, ignoring the shell that ejected beside her, and fired a quick second round. Then, without pausing, she raised her knee and drove her foot into the door. The chain keeping it closed gave way easily, the thin metal links snapping without even a hint of resistance.

The door didn't open very far. After only a few feet, it hit whoever was standing on the other side and came to an abrupt stop. She grunted and kept pushing, forcing it open until whoever was on the other side moved, creating a gap she surged through. In the sickly yellow light of the apartment, she saw that the buckshot had caught Merihem—she recognized him from the grainy, black-and-white picture Andromalius had sent—in the left side of his wide face. It made him look like he was suffering from a particularly bad case of chickenpox.

As he stumbled backward, he listed into the wall, one hand rising to his face and the other hand reaching weakly out as though to stop her. She glanced past him, confirming he was alone. She'd only made that mistake once. She could still remember the shock of watching her own teeth fly out of her mouth like rice at a wedding when the second demon inside sprang into action. Lesson learned.

Satisfied, she looked back at Merihem. She wasn't surprised to find the demon was as unsavory as everything else in the apartment building. His white wifebeater had yellow-brown stains at the armpits and in a vee down the front. His greasy black hair was spiked like he was in an alt-rock band from the early 2000s, and between the purple under his eyes and the paleness of his skin, he looked like he hadn't seen the sun in weeks. Most likely, he hadn't. He didn't seem the type to do anything more ambitious than stay home binging on Cheetos and bottom-shelf liquor, but he had done *something*, and whatever it was had been bad enough that the Daemonium, his own people, had wanted him revoked. That meant he was dangerous in some way. Probably. Or else an excessive embarrassment to his kind.

The third problem with hunting demons was they healed quickly, even when the bullets were blessed by a priest. In a minute, the buckshot Theodora had blasted into Merihem would begin to squeeze out of his healing skin and fall to the carpet like metal rain. Then it would be game on. She pumped the slide once more, ready to dispatch him back to Hell, but before she could pull the trigger, he grabbed the barrel, redirecting it just in time. A lamp exploded as the tiny apartment's living room was sprayed with buckshot.

She grunted, annoyed. It was normally at this point, after the door had been kicked open and the demon caught sight of who was on the other side, that every demon they'd ever hunted either tried to run or fight. Merihem, it turned out, was a fighter. And he was not only strong, but fast. Before Theodora could react, he grabbed higher up the barrel with his second hand and yanked hard. Since she hadn't expected it, the maneuver sent her staggering past him into the living room.

Annabeth, who had followed her into the apartment, swung at him with her morning star, trying to finish what Theodora had started with a crushing blow to the skull, but he was again too fast. He blocked her swinging arm, redirecting the weapon so that it slammed into the drywall behind him with a soft thud. She struggled to wrench the spikes free, finally tearing them out with a chunk of drywall still attached. Before she could wind up for another blow, however, he sucker-punched her in the stomach with a fist the size of a softball. She immediately doubled over with a squeak, her face twisting into a grimace of pain.

Theodora reseated her gun in her shoulder, looking for a shot, but it was too dangerous. Not only would she almost certainly hit Annabeth, but also Harriet, who was standing in the doorway. She growled, shaking her head. She would have to wait for a better opportunity. In the meantime, Annabeth was on her own.

Merihem raised his leg to kick Annabeth in the stomach, taking advantage of her injury, but before he could, she straightened, twisting her upper body at the same time. The morning star swung in an arc that—if successful—would have run from his hip to his chin. Instead, the spikes met only air. Surprisingly agile for a lowlife, he had dodged at the very last minute, backing away from her and toward the living room and Theodora.

"Come on," Theodora growled, pumping herself up.

She glanced around the apartment. Since it was too risky to use her gun now that Annabeth had joined the fray, it was time to get a little creative. She threw the weapon down on the tan shag carpet and grabbed a frying pan conveniently located on the kitchen counter. It was the heavy, cast-iron kind, with egg still burned on from whenever he'd last used it—which, based on his overall level of hygiene, could have been weeks ago. Holding it like a baseball bat, she crossed the few steps to the demon then swung it at the back of his head, taking advantage of his distraction to deliver a sneak attack.

She was surprised to hear a soft metallic clang as it connected. "What the—?"

She didn't have any more time to think about the unexpected acoustics as Merihem bellowed angrily and rounded on her. He grabbed for her, thick white fingers like overstuffed sausages topped by blackened nails stretching toward her neck. This close, the bright yellow irises and slitted, snakelike pupils of his eyes stood out even in the apartment's low light. If she hadn't already seen eyes like that a thousand times, she might have been shocked into stillness by their inhumanness. But this was just another day at the office, and he was just another dumbshit to take care of.

She leveled a front kick into his groin. He grunted as it landed, his body bending almost in half as he was pushed back a step. Before he could recover, she followed up with a spectacular blow to the face with the frying pan, swinging for the fences. This time, the sound was more like a quiet gong. He spun to the right, his body limp as a rag doll, and crashed into the wall next to the dirty green couch.

Annabeth was on him in an instant. She may have been a solid foot shorter than him and a hundred pounds lighter, but she could throw a punch that could fell an ox. Her small brown fist shot like a rocket toward his nose. Theodora could almost hear the crunch of bone as it connected. Then Merihem's nose exploded, gushing blood everywhere. His head slammed into the wall behind him, then bounced forward. This caused his brain to pinball inside his skull, triggering an immediate, involuntary hard reboot. Although he was technically still standing, it was with the woozy half-consciousness of a boxer.

Now Harriet stepped into the living room, joining the fray at last. With an effortless elegance, she drew her katana and took Annabeth's place in front of the demon. Next came the important part, the part that guaranteed Merihem wouldn't be renewing his lease on this shithole apartment, this year or ever. With grim solemnity, she intoned, "In the name of the Daemonium and the demonic hierarchy, your permission to dwell on Earth is officially revoked."

She said the words in Latin, the language of the celestials. It was the language that cast curses and made all covenants binding, demonic or angelic. Just in case the unconscious demon wasn't up on his dead languages, Theodora added helpfully in English, "Enjoy your eternity in Hell, fuckface."

With a smooth, single cut that would have made a samurai cry tears of joy, Harriet severed Merihem's head from his body. His head fell to the carpet with a dull thud. The rest of his body followed a second later, a heap of limbs and flesh. Theodora stepped back several paces—arterial spray could be unpredictable, and she *hated* having to clean it off her clothing—and set the frying pan back down where she'd found it.

Annabeth looked away from the blood rapidly pooling in the carpet, nose wrinkled. Theodora could read her mind. Someone was going to have a sucky job cleaning it all up later. Merihem's body would exsanguinate before his heart finally stopped pumping, and it wouldn't take long for that gallon and a half of blood to seep through the carpet and carpet pad into the subfloor. It wasn't the type of thing you could just get up with some hydrogen peroxide. On the other hand, a newly formed pond of blood was the least of the carpet's problems—the whole thing smelled like sour milk in the middle of a heat wave.

Theodora wiped the frying pan's handle clean of fingerprints using the bottom hem of her white tank top.

"Next time, you get to come in first," she grumbled to Harriet. "That sleezeweasel's breath could've knocked down a muskox."

Harriet shrugged, unfazed. "Okay." She retrieved a black piece of cloth from her pocket and used it to quickly wipe the blade of her sword. Satisfied, she resheathed the weapon. Theodora couldn't help feeling a twinge of jealousy at how smooth Harriet made it all look. The one time she'd tried fighting with a sword, she'd gotten it stuck in a doorframe and had almost been forced to abandon it. She hadn't tried again.

She cast a glance at Annabeth. "You okay?"

"Yes. I'm fine." But the other woman wasn't quite standing straight, indicating Merihem's blow had taken more out of her than she wanted to admit. Theodora shrugged. The pain would wear off in another minute or two. Moving on, she began to scan the room, eager to be out of the filthy apartment. "Okay, let's see what this fucker did to get himself revoked."

They always checked the apartments of the demons they were sent to revoke. Sometimes they found nothing, but occasionally they found things the demons weren't supposed to have on Earth. When they found those illicit items, they had to bring them back to Andromalius and the Daemonium. Although she couldn't prove it, Theodora suspected the Daemonium had a room somewhere of confiscated items, like a police station evidence locker. She began pulling up the fading green couch cushions, tossing them carelessly onto the carpet. There was nothing beneath them but years of lint, crushed potato chips, and an empty gum wrapper.

She squinted at the walls. Sometimes demons liked to hide things on the backs of pictures or in safes. Not Merihem. The yellowing walls of his apartment were as smooth and bare as a prison cell. He definitely wasn't hiding anything there.

Annabeth stepped into the tiny galley kitchen, opening the few cabinet doors and peering inside. "Nothing here." She opened the refrigerator. "He liked Chinese food." Pause. "Oh God, is that... Is that a maggot?"

"Dinner?" Harriet suggested.

As Annabeth made muffled gagging noises, Theodora moved on to the bedroom. The floor was littered with clothing the demon had been too lazy to pick up, detritus that would soon find its way into garbage bags as the apartment was prepared for the next occupant. She stepped on it guiltlessly, her boots crushing new wrinkles into the shirts and yellowing underwear. The only furniture in the bedroom was a bed and a dresser, both of which had seen better days. She pulled the dresser drawers out one by one, dumping their contents onto the floor and checking their bottoms for anything that might be taped beneath them. Nothing. Kneeling, she ran her hands along the inside and back of the dresser, feeling for concealed compartments. Still nothing.

"Come on, you muppethead, I know you've got something here," she murmured. And it was true. She had a sixth sense for sniffing out what the rogue demons were hiding. If it was here, she would find it.

Standing back up, she turned her attention to the bed. She slapped the thin, lumpy pillows, feeling for anything he might have hidden in a pillowcase, but they collapsed with sorrowful, silent sighs. Huffing her annoyance, she got on her hands and knees to look under the bed, carefully scanning for any slits cut in the box spring, but aside from a few socks she had absolutely no fucking intention of touching, there was nothing there either.

She sat back on her heels, ignoring the crinkle in her knees, and considered the open closet door. Merihem would hardly be the first demon to hide something under a fake floor, behind a hidden panel, or even in a shoebox on the top shelf. Before she could get to her feet to go look, however, Harriet called out.

"Oooooh boy. Found it."

Her tone—surprise mixed with something else that sounded oddly like awe—instantly put Theodora on alert. She unfolded herself, ignoring the soft grunt of protest from her lower vertebrae, and headed for the source of Harriet's voice, arriving at the same time as Annabeth.

Over the years, the women had seen a lot of shit. They definitely hadn't seen *this* kind of shit. Theodora gaped, then immediately covered her nose with her hand, fighting to avoid retching. "What the fuck is that?"

In the small bathroom, Harriet was standing between the toilet and the bathtub. The latter was a relic from older times, white porcelain with heavy iron claw feet. While it would have been considered chic and trendy in an upscale house, in this apartment it was both outdated and dilapidated. And it was filled with blood. Blood and entrails and Theodora was pretty sure at least one eyeball. It smelled one hundred percent as awful as one would expect of a bathtub of decomposing body fluids.

"So that's why he was revoked," Annabeth said. There was a note of recognition in her voice that indicated this wasn't just any old bathtub full of blood.

Without thinking, Theodora crossed her arms, frowning. Of course Annabeth knew what it was. Annabeth was a walking dictionary. Then another wave of stench hit her and she immediately uncrossed her arms, returning the hand to her nose and gesturing to the bath with the other. "Well, what is it?"

"It's part of a summoning spell. He was trying to summon something from Hell."

"Like what?"

The petite woman looked around the bathroom, taking in the grody sink stained with streaks of brown calcium deposits and the smudged, streaked mirror. Her eyes fell on a small pile of what looked like dog teeth mixed with black fur sitting on the metal soap dish. She pointed to it with a nod of certainty. *"Oude Rode Ogen."*

"A what?" Theodora said.

"A hellhound."

Harriet raised her thin black eyebrows. "That's a big no-no."

Trying to manifest something from Hell without the express and extremely bureaucratic permission of the Daemonium was definitely more than enough to get Merihem revoked. No wonder the Daemonium had called for a rush job. But it was stupid as shit. What did he want a hellhound for? Even if he had successfully summoned one using his forbidden tomato soup, he would have been caught the second he took his new pet for a walk. Demons that dumb deserved revocation, and Theodora was happy to be the one to carry that out.

"Good thing we got to him before he completed the spell," Annabeth observed, adjusting her glasses with her thumb and forefinger. "Otherwise, Andromalius probably would have sent us after the hellhound as well."

Theodora considered the idea. She wasn't sure if it would be easier or harder to kill a hellhound than a demon. Probably harder. They were likely smarter than their summoners.

She heard something in the distance and snapped to attention.

"Time to get out of this roach motel," she told her companions.

"We can't just leave this." Annabeth waved her hands toward the bathtub.

Theodora furrowed her eyebrows. "Why not?" They weren't a cleaning crew, nor did the Daemonium pay them enough to be.

Annabeth gave her a stern look that suggested she had said something dangerously close to stupid. "A decapitated body and a bathtub full of blood is noteworthy even for this city."

The implication was clear. They didn't want the police—or, just as bad, the press—investigating. The women never worried the city's humans would discover they were unwittingly living side by side with angels and demons—there was no chance of that. The celestials were too good at covering their tracks, and what wasn't covered could be covered up or written off as delusion or misinterpretation. But the women did have to worry that if they got sloppy, someone might come knocking on *their* door. The Daemonium protected its own, but they weren't part of the Daemonium; they were just contractors. And as far as any human knew, they had just murdered the shit out of someone.

"So drain the tub and let's go," Theodora said. Her feet itched, restless. Her skin was starting to feel too tight. Apartment buildings like this were unpredictable. There was no telling what might be gathering outside Merihem's door at this moment. Most of the time when the women carried out a revocation, the residents stayed inside their apartments, afraid of the sound of fighting. But every once in a while, they came ready to brawl, not knowing what was happening but prepared to defend their own. She didn't feel like fending off angry humans all the way down nine flights of stairs. They should be thanking her for removing a terrible demon from the world, not trying to shank her with a paring knife.

Harriet ran her hands over her pristine white dress shirt as if to smooth invisible wrinkles. Somehow, she had avoided the dreaded arterial spray despite standing right in front of Merihem. She said firmly, "I'm not touching that."

The eyeball in the tub stared at them balefully, floating in the biological equivalent of an oil slick. Theodora looked at Annabeth, who wrapped her arms around herself tightly and refused to make eye contact.

"This is my favorite cardigan!" she squeaked, shaking her head. "Besides, I cleaned up the mess last time."

Theodora glared at both of them. *She* didn't want to touch it either. She flexed her jaw, preparing to argue, but then she remembered Annabeth was right—it was her turn. Growling to show she didn't appreciate what was about to happen, she shook off her leather jacket and shoved it into Harriet's hands. At least since she was in a tank top, she didn't have sleeves to roll up. Although that meant more of her skin would be touching the blood directly, which wasn't much better.

She took a deep breath, held it, and got down onto her knees next to the bathtub. Harriet and Annabeth owed her for this. Big time.

Steeling herself, she silently counted to three, then plunged her arm into the tub. Her eyes shut reflexively, blocking out the sight of what she was touching. The blood was lukewarm and uncomfortably viscous. It reached all the way to her elbow, and she had to fight the urge to gag. She began to slide her hand along the bottom of the tub, feeling for the drain as quickly as she could while moving smoothly enough to avoid sloshing the liquid either higher on her arm or out of the bathtub. The last thing she needed was blood on her pants and shoes.

With her eyes still closed, she could almost pretend she was touching regular bath water. Until her hand brushed against something large and body-part-shaped. She instantly dry heaved.

"Are you okay?" Theodora could hear the concern in Annabeth's voice.

She opened her eyes and glared at the other woman. "*You* want to feel around?"

Annabeth shook her head.

"Thought so."

Theodora's fingers brushed against the stopper. She yanked it gratefully. The drain made a loud, awful gurgle, then, slowly, the blood began to run down the building's plumbing. She immediately pulled her arm out and rushed to the sink, frantically rubbing her dusky skin with the thin white bar of soap next to the faucet. She couldn't wash the resulting pink lather off fast enough.

"Gross." She checked her tan palm for any remaining flecks of blood that might have gotten caught in the creases. This was definitely the grossest thing she'd had to touch during a revocation, and that included the time she found brain matter in her hair. Fuck Merihem and his dumb ass for trying to summon a hellhound.

"Uh, Theo…"

From the tone in Harriet's voice, Theodora knew she wasn't going to like what came next. With dread, she turned back to the tub. And felt her stomach sink.

It looked like someone had poured half-set raspberry Jell-O all over the inside of it. Patches of blood, both dried and gelatinous, clung to the sides and slid slowly toward the drain. But that wasn't the problem. The blood would come out with a simple rinse, especially if they used the scraggly toilet brush to scrub the porcelain. The problem was the eyeball that was too big to go down the drain. And the arm lying on the bottom of the tub like it was on a goddamn silver platter.

"Shit." A beat passed as she stared, mind blank. "What the fuck do we do with those?"

They couldn't just throw them in the garbage. The whole idea was to hide what Merihem had been up to, not move it to the first place the cops would look. The police wouldn't spend too much time investigating a dead lowlife, even if he had been decapitated. They *would*, however, go all Sherlock Holmes over an eyeball and an arm. That would make the scene a double homicide, not just a regular old homicide, and that was infinitely more interesting to bored detectives.

"We can stick them in a trash bag and walk it out," Annabeth suggested. "We can toss it in a dumpster along the street."

That idea might have worked had no one been around to see it, but that ship had sailed a few minutes ago. Theodora heard the low murmur of voices outside, indistinct gossip punctuated with exclamations indicating concern and shock. The residents had come to investigate. They wouldn't forget seeing three armed women walking out with a trash bag slung over their shoulder like Murder Santa.

She jerked her head at the small, narrow window above the bathtub, thinking fast. "Get that open."

"What? Why?" Annabeth asked.

"Just do it," Theodora growled.

Obediently, Annabeth set her morning star down on the tile floor and started to wrestle with the rusty latch, standing on her tiptoes. It took a moment, but eventually the window opened outward with a sharp squeal of protest. The room was immediately filled with fresh air and the sounds of the city below them.

It was then Harriet realized what Theodora was planning. "You've got to be kidding."

"You got a better idea?" Theodora snapped. "I'm all ears."

Harriet frowned and shook her head.

"That's what I thought."

Clenching her teeth and holding her breath, Theodora grabbed the bloated white arm, trying to ignore the way the skin wanted to slough off, and tossed it out the window. The eye followed a moment later, sailing through the air like a bloody golf ball. If someone was walking below, they were about to have a very, very bad day.

The evidence disposed of, she motioned to the tub. "Get that blood off. Fast."

She grabbed the yellowing toilet brush and shoved it at Annabeth, ignoring the bristles that fell off like dandelion seeds. While Annabeth knelt and reluctantly began to scrub the tub, she washed her hands a second time, compartmentalizing her revulsion at what she'd just touched. If she thought about it, she might vomit, so she refused to think about it.

She finished right as Annabeth did. The tub looked a little better, but it still wasn't anything someone would want to get into for a nice soak. Good enough. They weren't the landlord. She grabbed her leather jacket from Harriet and shrugged it on. "Let's get out of here."

Back in the living room, she grabbed her shotgun from the floor. A cluster of round faces peered in through the doorway—at her, at the torn-up apartment, at Merihem's body and detached head. They formed a gauntlet the three women would have to pass through in order to get out. She threw her shoulders back, undaunted. The best way to get through a situation like this was with confidence. You could get away with anything so long as you were confident about it—even decapitate a demon with a samurai sword and leave its headless body in a puddle of blood.

She marched toward the rubberneckers with the gun cradled in her hands, daring them to stop her. They did not. Like the Red Sea before Moses, they parted, giving way silently. Head held high, she started down the stairs. Another night, another dead demon. Revocations could get messy, but at least business was always good. The three constants in life were death, taxes, and some demons being absolute fucknuggets that needed permanent time-out in Hell.

CHAPTER TWO

At three in the morning, the diner should have been as quiet and empty as the city streets around it. It was during that dead hour, Harriet always thought, that time seemed suspended and the world shimmered with surreality—a facsimile of the waking world that evanesced with the rising sun. The diner should have been part of that quiet dreaminess, the yellow industrial lighting shining out from its windows transforming it into a lighthouse in a sea of tall, dark buildings. But somehow, the diner never was empty, and reality seeped in relentlessly through the window seals and the occasional opening of the door, refusing to be kept at arm's length. As a result, what could have been an impressionist's romantic imagining of a diner became, instead, a realist's grimy reproduction. But then, there were few things in the city that were beautiful, at least for long.

After months of coming at exactly three every Thursday, Harriet knew the kinds of people she would see when she walked in: a drunk passed out next to a cup of cold coffee, two or three graveyard-shift workers on break, and even the occasional gangster types with shifty eyes and lumpy brown suits talking business in the corner booth. She slid into the first booth, the one closest to the door, a rip in the vinyl long ago patched with duct tape, and waited, her palms pressed lightly against the table and her back straight. The lighting above her flickered, enough to be noticeable but not quite enough to be annoying. Her eyes took in the room, from the half-filled coffee pot near the register to the man in a rumpled suit at the counter eating what looked like scrambled eggs. It was a quiet night. Or morning, depending on one's perspective.

Seeing her, the only waitress working set down the permanently gray-white rag she'd been using to wipe down one of the tables and made her way over, pushing a stray lock of her dirty-blond hair back behind her ear. Harriet's eyes scanned the white name tag on her pink uniform automatically, although she knew the name. Summer. It was far too cheerful a name for a place like this. It was a paradox, like the woman herself.

Summer put her hand on her hip and cocked her head, taking Harriet in with kind blue eyes. Normally, Harriet had a talent for not being seen. She was unmemorable. A ghost. But Summer seemed to see right into her. It was a disconcerting feeling.

"The usual?" Summer asked.

She had a pretty face. In the many times Harriet had come to the diner since her first visit, she had reached the conclusion that it wasn't just her name that didn't fit Summer. *Nothing* about her belonged in a diner in one of the city's most dangerous neighborhoods, three in the morning or otherwise. Perhaps that's why Harriet was so interested in her. It was like finding a beautiful white orchid blooming in a trash dump. There had to be a story behind how a seed inadvertently dropped here had somehow found a way to take root and blossom.

"Yes, please." Harriet spoke politely, almost meekly. With her narrow face and short black hair, she could have been mistaken for a beautiful Asian man or an equally beautiful, rather androgynous woman. Her voice, however, was unmistakably feminine.

Summer nodded, not bothering to write in the order pad at her waist. "You got it. One slice of blueberry pie coming up."

She turned away, her blond ponytail swinging across her shoulders, and Harriet's attention briefly drifted to the street outside the window. As long as she could remember, she had felt that the city was a living, breathing animal—it had its own personality, its own moods. When it was angry, the murder rate went up. When it was sad, the suicide rate. Because she knew the city so well, could almost feel its heart beating deep below the ground, she recognized trouble was brewing. In the last few months, she'd noticed that crime was increasing, anarchy growing. Merihem and his hellhound weren't a random coincidence. They were a symptom of some deeper disease.

She rubbed the muscle of her palm at the base of her left thumb. Last week, a demon had stabbed straight through it with a screwdriver during a revocation. The wound had healed within a few hours, but the pain had lingered as a phantom sensation for longer. She wasn't as young as she used to be. A few years ago, the injury would have been little more than a temporary nuisance. Sighing, she pulled a knife and fork rolled together in a paper napkin from the utensil holder beneath the window and carefully placed all three elements perpendicularly in front of her. Social entropy: the natural decay of structure in a social system. If entropy was increasing in the city, something had to be driving it, but what?

She must have been lost in thought more deeply than she realized, because when a small, round plate hit the table and slid in between the utensils, knocking the knife slightly off-kilter, she startled.

"Blueberry pie, coming in hot," Summer said.

The slice was perfectly triangular, the dark-blue filling so gelatinized that it maintained its form even after the application of tepid microwave heat. It wasn't food, it was rubber. But that didn't matter. She fixed the knife and looked up with a flicker of a smile. "Thank you."

Summer nodded. She started to turn away, then stopped, conflicted. Unlike Harriet, hers was not a face that could hide emotion. After a moment's hesitation, she said, "It's from a box, you know. Frozen pie from a store. We put them out on the display like we make them here, but we don't really. If you like it that much, I'll look at the box and tell you what it is. I'm sure you can buy it somewhere nearby."

Harriet didn't react to this proffered insider information, valuable as Summer seemed to think it was. "That's all right."

The other woman's mouth twitched into a brief frown. "I don't think it's that good anyway. I tried it once." The comment was more for herself than Harriet, and it likely encompassed *all* of the diner's offerings. People didn't go there for the quality of its food. They went there because it was the only thing open at that hour.

Harriet watched her without responding, waiting to see how this situation would unfold. Sometimes, she had learned, it was best to stay quiet and let others talk.

Summer's thin arms convulsed, filling with restless energy. "I just…" She twisted her fingers together and looked around the diner, taking its measure. "I don't know why you come here. At three in the morning. For pie that's honestly just—" She broke off. Her eyes widened and her hands flew to her mouth as she realized what she was saying, the scornful judgment of her customer's taste in pastry. It was a major customer service faux pas. "I shouldn't have said that. That was rude. I'm sorry."

It was the most conversation they'd ever had. Harriet spoke softly, her calmness contrasting with Summer's liveliness. "Maybe I just like pie."

"Yes." Summer nodded, too vigorously. "Of course."

But that wasn't why Harriet came, not in reality. No one would walk thirty minutes through some of the city's most violent, dangerous streets for pie with a crust that tasted like wet cardboard and filling that would make a child's teeth fall out. But it was a convenient answer, and so Harriet used it.

After a pause, Summer asked tentatively, "Do you work nights?" She was trying to recover from her misstep—making conversation as a way to smooth any ruffled feathers. But it wasn't necessary. Harriet wasn't the type to be easily insulted.

"No."

"Then why—I'm sorry, it's not my business."

She took a step back, and Harriet realized her short, brusque answer had discouraged any further conversation. In an attempt to salvage the moment, she hastily followed up with, "I have insomnia."

That was true, although her insomnia was mostly unrelated to her repeated visits to the diner. Summer shifted her weight, looking over her shoulder to check on the man at the counter. Harriet could feel the opportunity to learn more about the waitress slipping between her fingers. Once it was gone, she wouldn't have the chance again for another week. Longer, if she couldn't find a way to coax Summer into talking next time.

"I work in a pawnshop. During the day," she said, reaching for some way to keep Summer's attention. She felt like a machine turned rusty with disuse. She needed to get out more.

Her effort was successful. Summer looked back at Harriet and raised her pale eyebrows. "Really? You don't look like—I mean, you're so pretty and well-dressed. I always pictured pawnshops as being…shady." She wrinkled her nose, her eyes glazing as they gazed upon an invisible image of a stereotypical pawnshop. Then she blinked, dashing the image away, and hastened to add, "But you don't seem shady."

Harriet allowed herself a small smile. "I hope not."

The pawnshop was another variation of the truth. She did technically work in a pawnshop, but the business was a front. The shop had never loaned anyone money, and all of the "pawned" items hanging on the walls and displayed in the counter case were attentively curated props that Annabeth had gathered to provide cover for their actual business, which was carrying out revocations on behalf of the Daemonium. But Summer didn't need to know that, nor would she have believed it if Harriet had told her. All the human world needed to know was that Harriet was the one-third owner of a small, marginally successful pawnshop. One with a very unusual and specific clientele.

"I mean, sometimes you can't tell, you know? But you seem like a good person," Summer rambled.

Harriet understood more than Summer could ever know. The lines between good and evil weren't what they once were…if they ever had been clear. That's why she saw the world as shades of gray. With a few exceptions.

"Is that where you got that bruise a few weeks ago?" Summer pointed to Harriet's left cheekbone.

Harriet's hand automatically lifted toward the spot. It had been a very late revocation, and she'd left in a hurry to reach the diner on time. She hadn't even realized the demon's flailing fist had left a bruise until she got home, by which time the purple smudge was almost gone, transmuted into a pale yellow. She wasn't surprised Summer had noticed the mark, but she was quietly pleased the other woman had cared enough to remember. Perhaps Summer didn't see her as just another faceless customer.

"No, not there." Harriet grimaced, annoyed the demon had managed to land the blow, even if glancing. But that was part of the job—someone was always getting punched or kicked or stabbed. Sometimes she was the one on the receiving end, sometimes it was Annabeth or Theodora, but it was rare they revoked a demon without the demon getting in a few shots first. At least this one hadn't managed to gouge her with his claws. There was little she hated more than being stabbed in the stomach and then having to limp home and wait for the tissue to regrow. She continued, "It was an accident."

"I know how that goes. I broke a toe once when I accidentally kicked my couch." Summer smiled and shook her head almost fondly. "I told people I broke it in a bar fight."

Harriet was amused by her proud bravado. She could imagine Summer throwing a punch in a bar to protect herself. But…she would likely break her hand in the process. It was dangerous to fight without experience. The waitress was more likely to hurt herself than someone else.

Harriet's eyes skimmed over the Pepto-Bismol-pink pleather booths and stained white linoleum around them. The time had come to ask the question that kept her coming here. "Why do *you* work here at three in the morning?"

Summer looked down at her matching pink uniform, white cardigan, and white half apron as though the answer was written there. "It's the only time I can. I'm in nursing school." Her smile turned wry as she looked up. "This helps pay the bills, you know?"

Harriet blinked, surprised by both this information and its implications. "When do you sleep?" The math didn't seem to work out right.

"Any time I can find a free second."

Summer rubbed her forehead, and for the first time Harriet noticed the fine lines around her eyes and the shadow of purple beneath them that showed the toll her schedule was taking on her. "I fall asleep on the bus coming back from the hospital pretty often. I've gotten good at finding my way home from halfway across the city when I miss my stop." She sighed. After a moment, she put her hands on her hips and tilted her chin at Harriet's pie. "Can I get you anything else?"

Harriet looked down at the slice. It was so alone on its little plate, a tiny ship adrift at sea. "No, thank you." She was still processing this new datapoint. So Summer was a nurse, or at least on her way to becoming one. It made sense. She belonged in a hospital taking care of people, not serving objectively terrible pie in a diner whose health rating would have made a fruit fly shudder.

"Well, if you don't—"

Harriet reached out without thinking, looking to stay her. Whether she'd actually meant to touch Summer or whether Summer moved her arm at that moment, Harriet's fingertips brushed against the skin of her wrist just below her cardigan sleeve and above her watch. Instantly, Harriet's breath was snatched out of her lungs as time lurched, pulling her with it. The diner disappeared in a flash, replaced by thick darkness.

Immediately, she was on alert. Where was she? The blackness around her offered no clues, nor could she move to find any. Hands touched her and she propelled herself into the dark shape in front of her, hitting with enough momentum to rock the other person back. But it wasn't really *her*, neither her body nor her actions. Harriet recognized this was a vision of the future—Summer's future. She herself was only a spectator, watching through Summer's own eyes.

Summer wrapped her arms around the stranger's neck with frantic need, clutching tightly. She panted, her mouth near the stranger's ear, heart beating fast. From the thin frame in her arms, Harriet realized the other person must be a woman. She felt short hair tickle Summer's cheek. Then, a brief flash of light cut through the dark from behind, illuminating the side of the stranger's face just enough for her to make out who it was.

It was her, Harriet. She stared at her own face, shocked. Then it was all over. Time regurgitated her back into the present so fast it made her head spin. She curled her toes in her loafers—stylish yet athletic enough to be worn during revocations—rooting herself to the present and trying not to give any outward sign that anything had happened. For everyone else in the diner, time had continued to move linearly. Only she had been affected by the temporal hiccup.

The problem with the random, unpredictable visions she received of the future was they never lasted longer than a few seconds and they were always without context. Sometimes it was obvious what was happening. Other times it was not. This time, she thought she had a pretty good idea of what she'd seen. Darkness and heavy breathing tended to only mean one thing. And it answered another question she had about Summer.

"Yes?" Summer looked mildly surprised that Harriet had touched her.

Harriet recoiled, trying to recover her composure. The words that spilled out of her mouth were truthful, but not necessarily what she would have said had she been in full control of her senses at that moment. "You have kind eyes." Then, feeling this was uncomfortably direct, she quickly added, "I bet you're a great nurse."

It was a good thing Theodora wasn't here. Theodora would have howled at her awkwardness. Harriet was better at dispatching demons to Hell than talking, and it had been a long time since she'd tried to flirt with someone. She was beyond out of practice. But Summer didn't seem to notice. She smiled brightly. "Thank you! It's a lot of work, but I think it's worth it."

"I'd...like to hear more about it sometime." If there was such a thing as the verbal equivalent of two left feet, Harriet felt as though she had it in that moment.

Summer's chin tucked as her eyes turned coyly bashful. "Are you—?"

Harriet rallied all her charm and gave her most encouraging smile. "You're right. This pie is terrible. And there's got to be someplace nearby that has better coffee. Maybe we could find it sometime."

She had an unexpected ace in the hole. Because of her unexpected vision, she already knew where this exchange would eventually lead, even if she didn't know the exact sequence of events in between or how long it would take to get there. It gave her a shot of confidence. She slid out of the booth and stood, feeling in the pocket of her extra-long blazer. Pulling out a pen, she wrote with quick, neat strokes on the white paper napkin, taking care not to rip the fragile material with the nib. She handed the result to Summer. "If you want that coffee sometime, text me."

Somehow, it all came out much smoother than she could have imagined. Suave, almost. She didn't want to risk messing that up by talking more. She had done enough for one night. Turning, she headed for the exit, leaving the store-bought pie untouched on the table.

She had barely made it two strides out the door when Summer caught up, eyes wide and cheeks slightly flushed. Harriet turned when she heard the slap of Summer's shoes on the pavement behind her.

"It's a quiet night," Summer said. "I could close up until the next shift starts and you could walk me home. It's a rough neighborhood. Strength in numbers, right?"

Harriet found the idea appealing, but... "Won't you get in trouble?"

Summer shrugged. "Yeah, but what are they going to do? Fire me? No one else wants to work these hours. And it's not like there are a ton of customers right now anyway. Wait a minute. I'll shoo that guy out and we can go, okay?"

Harriet glanced back at the diner, uncertain. "Are you sure?"

Summer looked her up and down quickly. Whatever she was searching for, she must have found it, because she nodded with firm certainty. "Yeah. It will be fine."

As she disappeared back inside, Harriet considered her vision, turning it over in her mind. Had it been a preview of what might happen in an hour or two? Perhaps. But there was no use getting ahead of herself. She knew the future's destination, just not the path. It was enough.

She took a few steps back and leaned against the diner's stainless steel siding, watching the occasional car roll past in the night. She kept her left hand in her pocket, fingers wrapped around the hard, oblong handle of a switchblade. A year ago, she would have been much less on guard. Now, even the shadows around the diner were full of potential menace.

Three minutes later, the man who had been sitting at the counter stumbled out, wrapping his tan jacket around himself and glancing around with unfocused eyes. Summer followed, buttoning her cardigan against the chilly air. The door jingled as she shut and locked it, then she turned and smiled brightly at Harriet. "Ready?"

Harriet bobbed her head, and with Summer taking the lead, they began to travel south. Around them, the city lights glimmered, fighting valiantly to push back the dark. Theodora had laughed when Harriet had presented her anthropomorphic theory of the city. To Theodora, the city had always been a hopeless cesspool. Annabeth, at least, had been more open to the idea, even if she didn't immediately agree.

"So, is picking up waitresses your thing?" Although Summer asked the question playfully, there was also sincerity in her voice.

"Maybe. When I'm not checking out the single moms taking their kids to day care." Harriet smiled a half-smile. It gave her a playful, almost cheeky look. "Do you always ask strangers to walk you home?"

Summer raised a single eyebrow. "Maybe."

"It's dangerous, you know." Harriet wasn't joking. The city was full of bad people who would happily do bad things to a trusting nurse-in-training. Summer was safe with Harriet, but she didn't know that. Blind faith in the goodness of others could easily get her killed.

Summer brushed the warning off with a toss of her head. "I have mace in my purse. Besides, you don't know where I'm taking you. Maybe *you're* the one in danger. Did you think of that? I could be a serial killer."

She was about as intimidating as a kitten, and Harriet knew she could be overpowered well before she could get to anything in her purse, but there was no use mentioning that.

Summer added after a pause, "And anyway, is a random hookup app any safer? I mean…" She shrugged, a gesture of helplessness and acceptance. "Nothing in this city is safe."

Harriet hadn't thought of it that way, but Summer had a point. Spending time with a stranger was inherently dangerous, whether the introduction was made online or in person. And friends and family weren't always safer, according to the statistics.

She appraised Summer from the corner of her eye. "So how did you end up in the city? You're definitely not from around here."

"Is it that obvious?"

"Yes." There was no use sugarcoating things. She was too bright and sparkly to have been in the city long. The city hadn't dimmed her shine yet, but if she stayed here long enough, it would. The city couldn't help it—corrosion was in its nature. It was the seat of Daemonium, the demons' ruling authority on Earth, and that meant corruption, rot, and violence spread into the ground and air like radiation in Chernobyl. If Summer was smart, she would get away as soon as she could, before it twisted her into its own image. For now, there was still time…but it would run out eventually.

Summer looked at Harriet flirtatiously from under long eyelashes. It made butterflies flutter in Harriet's chest. "I suppose it's too cliché if I say I'm just a small-town girl who came to the city with big dreams?"

Harriet huffed a chuckle and smiled. "Not if it's true." She had figured as much. "How's that working out for you?"

Summer's face fell immediately. Her light tone turned wry. "I'm working in a diner at three in the morning in the part of town with the highest murder rate. How do you think?" She rubbed her arms as though cold, her mouth twisted unhappily.

Harriet regretted the question. She hadn't meant for the conversation to turn serious. Now she didn't know how to lighten it again. After a moment, however, Summer rallied. "How about you? What's your story?"

There were any number of stories Harriet could tell her. How her mother's side of the family had emigrated from Thailand back when it was still called Siam and had somehow ended up here, of all places. How they had ostracized her mother after Harriet's birth and left her to raise this unwanted child on her own. Why she had never left the city despite her fiercely ambivalent feelings about it. But those were not stories for a walk like this, so she simply said, "Born and raised here." Truth was like a diamond: what someone saw depended on which facet they were shown.

"How long have you been working in a pawnshop?" Summer scrunched her eyebrows together in an adorable wrinkle of confusion. "And also, why a pawnshop?"

Harriet's eyes briefly fluttered shut as she calculated how many years ago she had met Theodora. The Theodora who materialized from the mists of her memory, fierce eyed and lanky, with cheekbones sharp as knives and an even sharper tongue, was twenty-five years old—seven years older than her—with a chip on her shoulder that might as well have been a boulder. On the day they had met, Theodora had been sitting at a bar throwing back shots, glaring at anyone who dared look at her. Theodora was older now, but not much else had changed about her. Even her face was the same, defiantly refusing to wrinkle or gray. (As Theodora said, "Asian don't raisin.") It had been Theodora who told her about the Daemonium's unusual job offer. And then convinced her they should take it.

At the time, they had thought they were the only two people in the world that shared their striking, unique commonality. Then two years later, they met Annabeth. And it was Annabeth who had eventually suggested they open the pawnshop.

"Eighteen years," Harriet replied after a quick delay. She shrugged, considering Summer's second question. "And I guess why not? Work is work. Plus, it's easier if you're good at it."

Summer looked at her quizzically. "You can be *good* at working in a pawnshop?"

Harriet thought about her katana and the other weapons in their arsenal. Yes, she was good at her job. She was a better fighter, in fact, than either Theodora or Annabeth. And of course, it helped that they healed much faster than any human could. All in all, the three of them were perfectly suited for their job as revokers.

She bobbed her head. "Sure, why not?"

Since there wasn't much else to say about a pawnshop front company, the conversation lapsed. Harriet was comfortable with silence, but silence, she knew, bred boredom for most people, and she didn't want Summer to be bored with her. She grasped for some way to disperse the silence filling the narrow space between them. "I guess you left behind a string of immature, angry exes in that small town of yours? A few guys with big muscles and bigger trucks?" It was a joke, but also an intuitive inference. A hunch.

Summer laughed. It was a delicious, warm sound. She reached up and pulled out her hairband, letting her hair loose from its ponytail. When she shook her head, it fell freely past her shoulders, full of thick, wavy body. She adjusted it by running her fingers through the hair at her scalp. Harriet watched, captivated.

"You're reading my life like it's an open book," Summer said.

"Yeah?"

Summer nodded. "A bunch of rednecks who sit around drinking beer all afternoon and shooting off firecrackers. I couldn't get out of there and away from them fast enough. I spent every dime I had to get here and never looked back." She smiled. "How about you and your single moms? I'm guessing you have to change your number once a month to duck their calls?"

Harriet could have played along, making up an elaborate story about dodging desperate housewives, but instead she decided to answer honestly. Putting her hands in the pockets of her black slacks, she shook her head. "No. The truth is, I don't get out much." Unlike Theodora, who regularly spent her nights in bars and went through men like Kleenex. Harriet couldn't remember when she'd last gone on a date. It had probably been years. She didn't often find women who caught her eye. That's how she knew there must be something special about Summer.

Summer raised her eyebrows, and Harriet sensed genuine surprise. "What? A catch like you? You're kidding."

Harriet held in a smile, pleased. Summer continued, "So do you live around here? Is that why you come to the diner?"

Although she should have seen the question coming, Harriet grimaced. The truth was she didn't live anywhere near it. The first time she'd gone there had been by coincidence. Revocations didn't always end as cleanly as they had with Merihem, and she had just experienced a particularly messy one. The demon they had been sent to revoke had taken human children hostage to protect herself. After, Harriet had wanted to forget what had happened, so she'd walked out of the apartment and found the nearest diner. And Summer. She didn't believe in fate, but coincidence, yes.

"It's…a long story. So why did you decide to move *here*?" Of all the places in the world Summer could have gone, why had she come to the center of all evil in the world?

"I guess it was kind of by accident. I got in my truck, started driving, and this was the first place I ended up."

"And you stayed." Harriet couldn't keep the quiet disbelief out of her voice.

Summer scoffed. "You make it sound like it's hell here."

"More like some of the people here are from Hell."

And some of that special category were sent back kicking and screaming, by Harriet's own hand. They overstepped the rules about interfering with humans, for example, electing to torture and murder their mortal neighbors instead. A few particularly stupid demons even tried to challenge the Daemonium's control, which was a guaranteed way to be booted. And then of course there were the demons like Merihem… The Daemonium accepted that its demons were lawless, but there were limits even for it. The demons who crossed the line got permanent time-out in Hell.

Summer tossed her head, sending her hair rippling. "I won't argue with that. The other day I had a customer throw coffee on me because he said it wasn't hot enough." She rubbed the back of her left hand with her thumb, agitated by the memory or else reliving the injury. "At least he was right that it wasn't scalding."

Harriet was first appalled, then furious. If she'd been there, she would have smashed the man over the head with the coffee pot and then dunked his nose into the nearest hard surface to teach him a lesson about manners. She opened her mouth to say as much, but at that exact moment, she sensed movement out of the left corner of her eye. Danger. Immediately, she was on guard, her senses tingling. Adrenaline flushed her system, readying her for whatever was about to happen.

As her heart started to beat faster, she scanned the street around them covertly, keeping her head down. She didn't want to alert whoever was there that she had noticed them. Nor did she want to alarm Summer. Not until she had assessed the situation. Casually, she put her hand in her pocket, fist closing around the handle of the switchblade. It wasn't her katana, but it was something.

The block around them was silent and empty. Not even a light flickered. As far as she could see, they were totally alone. Everyone in the neighborhood was sleeping. Instead of relaxing, however, this evident absence of danger put her even more on edge. Even if she didn't see anything, she knew something was out there. She could feel it.

Her scalp prickled. She didn't like being stalked. She'd rather be the one doing the stalking.

Summer held up her battered, brown leather purse, oblivious to the shift in Harriet's mood, and continued her story. "Anyway, it's times like that it's a good thing I can't reach my mace while I'm working. Otherwise I might have been tempted to spray him in the face."

Her voice drifted over and around Harriet, who listened with one ear. Harriet was assessing, looking for clues. Was their surveillant human or demon? Alone or a spotter for a larger group? She would fight if it came to it, but she'd rather not. If it was a group, it would be difficult to both fight and keep an eye on Summer. The two of them would have to run and hope for the best, and that was never a good plan.

Summer stopped abruptly. Harriet had been so distracted that she almost kept walking. She caught herself at the last moment and turned back to face the waitress. Summer gestured to the brown, ten-story apartment building in front of them. It was one of the nicer ones on the street, with a black fire escape that ran up the front like climbing ivy. It was quaint, or at least as quaint as the city could offer in this part of town.

"This is me. Do you…want to come up? I might have some coffee. You could tell me more about growing up in the city." Her fingers played with one of the buttons on her cardigan, somewhere between coy and genuinely shy.

Unbidden—and despite the unseen danger around them—Harriet's mind replayed the vision she'd had in the diner. Tomorrow morning, it would be gone, erased from her memory as though she'd never seen it, but for now, it sent an electric thrill all the way through her. For a moment, she forgot everything but the desire to slowly strip Summer's uniform off and kiss a line down her stomach. She licked her lips and took a breath to answer.

More movement, this time close by. Harriet whipped her head around to find it, all thoughts about Summer and her apartment gone in an instant. Her eyes panned over the street, searching openly. The threat was close. She had to find it and stop it.

"Get inside. Now," she commanded. Her voice came out a low, terse growl.

"What?" Summer didn't move. She was frozen in place, her eyes wide.

Harriet's switchblade was out of her pocket in an instant. The blade snapped into place as she stepped to the door, eyes still watching the neighborhood around them for the source of the danger. Her senses were on full alert, her nerves screaming. With her right hand, she yanked the door open. It was heavy. Good. Bracing it open with her body, she grabbed Summer by the biceps. Her fingers bit into the other woman's arm, rough and impolite. She would apologize later, but not now. Right now, the priority was keeping her safe.

She shoved Summer inside, pushing so hard that Summer almost lost her footing. At least she was past the threshold. Without waiting to explain, Harriet spun and strode away from the building as fast as she could without running. Whatever form the danger was about to take, she had to lead it away from Summer. She had to make herself the target. Predators loved a good chase.

As she moved, her eyes fell on something. She was positive it hadn't been there half a second ago. Approximately fifty yards away, too close for her to have missed noticing, a man in a long black coat and a matching black hat was walking away. Her feet stilled into motionlessness as she realized what she was seeing. Although they were so transparent they were almost invisible, she could just make out the wings on his back.

CHAPTER THREE

Then I saw in the right hand of him who sat on the throne a scroll with writing on both sides and sealed with seven seals. And I saw a mighty angel proclaiming in a loud voice, "Who is worthy to break the seals and open the scroll?"

I watched as the Lamb opened the first of the seven seals. Then I heard one of the four living creatures say in a voice like thunder, "Come!" I looked, and there before me was a white horse! Its rider held a bow, and he was given a crown, and he rode out as a conqueror bent on conquest.

Theodora shook her head and crossed her arms, her expression closed. "No way. It must have been a trick of the light. An optical illusion. No way there was an angel that close."

Annabeth gently set the metal tea tray down on the counter, humming so softly it was almost inaudible. She poured a cup of black tea and handed it to Harriet, then poured one for herself and sat down on the free stool behind the counter next to her. As Theodora didn't drink tea, she offered her nothing. Peering into the brown water, she considered Theodora's words. Because of her astigmatism, sometimes when light hit Annabeth's glasses just right at night it created a visual distortion. Although Harriet didn't wear glasses, it was possible that a streetlight had cast an unusual shadow, or that the man Harriet had seen had been wearing some kind of a backpack, making it appear as though he had wings. She wasn't attributing Harriet's experience to that, but it was a possibility worth considering.

"It was an angel," Harriet insisted, wrapping her hands around the cup but not lifting it. Her face was puckered into a scowl of annoyance and frustration.

The alternate hypothesis to Theodora's visual distortion theory was, of course, that Harriet really had seen an angel. There was no third option, at least that Annabeth could see.

"How long has it been since we last saw one?" Annabeth wondered aloud. The question wasn't rhetorical. She really couldn't remember, and that was saying something given her prodigious memory.

"Fifteen years." The quickness of Harriet's response suggested she had already asked herself the same question and found the answer.

Annabeth took a sip of her tea, thinking. Between the three of them, they had only ever seen a half a dozen angels. Even then, it had always been by accident, and all but once from a great distance. However it had once been, this city now belonged to the demons. It was no place for angels. So while it wasn't out of the question that Harriet had seen an angel, it certainly was curious.

Annabeth let warm steam tickle her face as she held her cup close to her chin, the bottom edge of her glasses fogging white. "Do you think he wanted you to see him? That he was trying to lead you somewhere?" Her mind churned methodically through scenarios and hypotheses, looking for a logical solution for why an angel had not only appeared after all these years, but so close to Harriet. Surely it wasn't coincidence, not if there wasn't anyone else on the street.

Harriet drummed the fingers of her right hand against the counter while she ran those of her left through her short hair. Her agitation was palpable. "No. I tried to follow him, but he disappeared."

Annabeth nodded, understanding the unstated implication. "He glamoured."

Glamouring was a special ability that some celestials had, like donning a cloak of invisibility. They had only met one demon with that particular party trick, but according to Andromalius, all angels could do it. This was of particular annoyance to the demons because it meant the angels could pass among them completely unseen. It also meant the three women might have been near dozens or even hundreds of angels throughout the years and never known it, a fact that had frustrated Theodora to no end.

"Fucking angel bastards." The fingers of Theodora's right hand curled, full of tension.

Annabeth resisted the urge to reach out and touch her in reassurance and sympathy, and held the mug more tightly instead. The angels were more than just a touchy subject for Theodora. Thirty-seven years ago, her father had been killed by an angel. She had never forgiven them for it. If it were possible to revoke an angel, she probably would try, but she'd never gotten close enough to one to attempt it. None of them, in fact, had gotten within twenty feet of an angel.

"Then what do you think he was doing?" Annabeth asked Harriet, hoping Theodora wouldn't become too distracted. Unlike Harriet, Annabeth hadn't spent time in that particular part of the city. She didn't know what the angels might be interested in there.

Harriet shrugged, frowning. "I have no idea."

Annabeth took a sip of her tea, then stared at the dark purple lipstick stain left on her white mug. One thing to be said for the demons was that at least they were semipredictable. After years of working for Andromalius, the women had a basic understanding of what the demons did and why. Or at least, as much as could be understood from the outside of chaotic, occasionally anarchic celestials. The angels, on the other hand, were an enigma shrouded in mystery. The women had no idea what they did. Or why. Or where. Whatever Andromalius knew, he hadn't shared it with them. And they weren't foolish enough to ask.

Annabeth sighed. There was no solution to the question of what Harriet had seen. The angels would just have to remain a mystery.

The phone in her pocket vibrated, startling her. She pulled it out and scanned the incoming text message, smiling unconsciously.

"Jonathan wants to know if we should expect you at dinner tonight. It's been a while since the boys have seen Aunt Theo. They miss you," she told Theodora.

The other woman still looked tense, her face drawn tight as a drum, but she shrugged and forced herself to relax a little. Her hand relinquished its claw form.

"Fine, but no more two-on-one water-balloon fights," she grouched. "Especially if I don't get a forewarning. Otherwise, next time I'm coming with a water cannon and your spawn are getting it in the face. I don't care that they're children."

Annabeth chuckled to herself at the memory of a *very* drenched Theodora standing in the doorway, water dripping down her hair and face. And then the image of Theodora showing up with a water cannon on her hip, Terminator-style.

"I'll pass that along," she promised. As if her young children would listen.

"And tell Jonathan to make those little dessert hamburger things," Theodora added.

"Macarons," she corrected.

"Yeah, those."

Just then, the small bronze bell above the door jingled. Annabeth looked toward the sound, surprised. As the thick layer of dust on the shelves could attest, it had been years since someone had last walked into the shop. Although from the outside their office looked like a legitimate pawnshop, she had done everything she could to make it as uninviting as possible. For the most part, her efforts at covert discouragement had worked, but every once in a while they got visits from unwitting would-be customers.

She set down her teacup and adjusted the black frame of her glasses, sweeping her bangs to the side and preparing an apology for why they would be unable to do business with the man who had walked in. Normally she blamed it on computer troubles, but sometimes she got creative. Perhaps today would be one of those days.

"May we help you?" She tried to sound helpful, but not *too* helpful. It was a delicate balance.

The would-be customer was short and painfully thin, with round, clear-framed glasses and sparse white hair like the head of a Q-tip. Wearing a black blazer over a gray sweater-vest, he looked like a kindly, bookish grandfather—not the type of person who would need a loan from a pawnshop. He peered at the three women at the counter owlishly, his warm brown eyes made larger by the magnification of the lens. "Greetings, daughters of the *egrégoroi*." His voice was thin and reedy, as though he didn't often use it.

Annabeth cocked her head, confused. Her smile drooped a little. Huh? She didn't want to be rude however, so she asked, "Do you need a loan, sir?"

The smile he gave her in return was an awkward, thin-lipped expression that made him look like an ostrich. "No, no. That's not why I'm here."

Then why he had come?

Theodora stepped casually around the corner of the counter so she was partially behind it. From the corner of her eye, Annabeth saw her reach for the aluminum baseball bat on the second shelf. Subtle as Theodora was, the man must have somehow intuited what she was doing, because he said, "That's not necessary. I come in peace."

Then Annabeth saw it: the faint, almost transparent outline of wings just over his shoulder. She sucked in a breath, astonished. An electric shiver ran from her head to her knees. An angel, here, in their pawnshop! She stared, awed and amazed to be this near to one.

Theodora must have seen his wings at the same time, but she had a different reaction. "Fuck. No." The bat made a distinct metallic zing as she pulled it. It was to her shoulder and ready to swing faster than Annabeth could blink. Theodora's face was a mask of rage. Her eyes burned.

The angel stepped back, hands up in the universal expression of placation. Even knowing he wasn't human, Annabeth still couldn't help seeing him first and foremost as a frail old man with loose, wrinkled skin. Instinct made her want to protect him, even though he would have no problem protecting himself.

"Theodora, no!" she hissed, horrified.

"It's an angel." Theodora said. She looked like an all-star batter about to swing for the fences. "In our shop."

The angel dropped his eyes submissively, trying to appease some of her wrath. "Please, I'm not here for trouble. I've come seeking your help."

Annabeth couldn't believe what was happening. An angel in their shop. An angel *seeking their help*. But what could an angel possibly need from them? She couldn't imagine.

Theodora snorted. "Yeah, right. And I'm Jesus." She didn't lower the bat an inch. It remained poised, ready for action. But if she did swing it, they all knew she would never be able to connect with the angel. The demons called them untouchable for a reason. Even Theodora wasn't foolish enough to think she could actually hit one.

Harriet looked him up and down. The slant of her eyebrows showed she was curious and suspicious at the same time—not as impressed as Annabeth, but not as skeptical as Theodora. As ever, she was in between their two poles. "Help with what?"

The angel's eyes skimmed the small shop, as though he were nervous someone might overhear, an impossibility given how small it was and the existence of only the one door. Then he leaned forward conspiratorially and dropped his voice. "Someone has opened the first seal." He said the words as though declaring that someone had shot the president, as though there could be no graver crime.

He waited, obviously expecting the women to react with some powerful emotion, but they only stared at him blankly. After an embarrassingly long beat, Annabeth asked, "The what?"

"The *seal*," he repeated urgently.

Annabeth had assumed that angels, as immaculate, immortal beings, didn't feel fear, but when he looked around the pawnshop a second time, his alarm was both tangible and contagious. It made the hair at the back of her neck stand up. His voice dropped to a whisper and he stared at her in particular, entreating her to understand. "*Pestilence* has been released."

Finally, she understood.

"The seven seals of the Apocalypse," she breathed. She was half-astonished, half-awed.

At the end of the first century *anno Domini*, John of Patmos, also called John the Revelator, had a prophetic vision of the end of the world. In it, he was shown a scroll upon which were seven seals. He was told that when the first seal was opened, it would unleash Pestilence, the first of the four Horsemen of the Apocalypse, into the human world. If the first seal had been opened, that meant…

"Are you saying the Apocalypse has begun?" she asked.

Theodora looked between her and the angel. The bat drooped in her hands. Some of the fury left her face, replaced by disbelief. "You've got to be shitting me."

"Is it really…*time*…for the Apocalypse?" Annabeth asked. For more than two thousand years, humans had believed they were living in the end times, but she had never imagined *she* would be.

"No! That's the problem!" The angel's eyes seemed to fill his glasses lenses. His voice was an excited hiss. "*Someone opened the seal who wasn't supposed to.*"

Silence followed this astonishing declaration. Annabeth had no idea what to make of it. She could hardly comprehend that the first seal of the Apocalypse had been opened, much less that it had been done…*illicitly.*

Finally, Harriet spoke. "How's that possible? Who?"

The angel's shoulders fell, dejected. He looked like nothing more than a small, fragile human, not the radiant celestial he was. "I don't know."

"What do you mean you don't know?" Theodora's voice was sharp and accusatory. It stabbed through the air like a knife. Her expression was equally fierce, but the angel didn't so much as flinch.

He shrugged, helpless. "The location of the seals is one of the most closely held secrets of the angelic host. I don't know how someone found it. And I certainly don't know by whom."

Annabeth frowned and shook her head, remembering, if somewhat vaguely, Revelation 5:4. "But the seals are on a scroll in Heaven. Are you saying someone broke into Heaven *and* opened the first seal?" That seemed like a lot.

The angel looked at her for a moment, confused. Then his eyebrows jumped as he realized what she meant. "Oh! I see. No, the seals are gates. And they are on Earth."

Annabeth's mind reeled, struggling to take it all in. Seals that weren't seals. Gates on Earth. Pestilence unleashed.

"Are you saying some unknown person somehow found and opened the first seal and you have absolutely no idea how?" Harriet asked. There was an edge to her voice.

"Yes, that is exactly what I'm saying. And what's more, if they find and open the other six seals, they'll bring about the end of days." Annabeth wasn't imagining the alarm and fear in his voice. It made her blood run cold. Something that scared even an angel was certainly bad news. But there was an obvious question that had to be asked.

"Why don't you stop them? You're angels. Can't you just…fix it?"

The angels, as servants of God, were all-knowing. Or at least close to it. It should be easy for them to identify the culprit and stop whoever it was. Furthermore, if they were worried about more seals being opened, surely they could move them. Stick them in Ft. Knox or inside a volcano or something, where no one could reach them. The angels were almost omnipotent. So why was one here, asking for help? And to do what?

The angel dropped his eyes. His scarecrow-like body seemed to shrink even more into itself, reminding her of the shriveled leaves of the last plant she'd attempted—and failed—to nurture. He said, "I've tried informing Uriel, but I've received no response. I've been having trouble reaching *any* of the leadership of the host, in fact…"

As he trailed off miserably, Theodora unleashed a cackle of laughter. She was so amused, in fact, that she finally set the baseball bat down. She crossed her arms and grinned. "So the big bosses won't take a call from a peon." Annabeth was mortified by her irreverent tone.

"They have many important matters to attend to…" he mumbled, still not meeting their eyes.

Harriet raised her eyebrows. Now she, too, was picking up some of Theodora's skepticism. "More important than stopping someone from triggering the Apocalypse?"

He took a breath and looked up, his thin lips twitching into a weak, optimistic smile. "In any case, that's why I came here."

Although she knew all but nothing about the angels (and even worked for their mortal enemy, the Daemonium), Annabeth had a deep-seated respect for them. They were the messengers of God, the guardians of humankind. They were the light to the demons' dark. But… She couldn't help staring at the angel. Why *had* he come?

She must not have been the only baffled one, because after scanning the women's faces, he cleared his throat and offered a clarification. "I need your help. To stop whoever has opened the first seal from opening the second."

Annabeth blinked rapidly, trying to process this bizarre request, but it was impossible. He wasn't asking for some salt or a ride to the airport. He was asking them to save the world. Shocked silence followed his words. Finally, she said the first thing that came to mind. "But we don't know where it is."

He lit up. "*I* do."

"But why *us*?" Harriet asked.

Of all the possible or potential allies he could have approached, they were an unexpected choice at best. And while it didn't necessarily surprise her to discover that angels knew about their existence, surely there were *much* better options. They were half-*demon*, to name just one problem.

"The seal is located in the office of the Daemonium. You are best positioned of anyone to protect it," the angel replied.

Annabeth and Harriet exchanged dumbfounded glances. The situation had gone from strange to outright absurd. Surely he couldn't be saying...

"The second seal is literally under the demons' noses?" Harriet asked, incredulous.

"Why would something so..." Annabeth looked for the right word, then settled on "*important* be located inside a building filled with demons?" It was beyond incredible. If it hadn't been an angel telling them, she would never have believed it. Even now she wasn't entirely sure she did.

The angel shook his head. "The demons don't know it's there. They can't see it. Demons can't see angelic seals."

"Bullshit." Theodora's cold, hard expletive exploded in the air like a blast from her shotgun. She glared at the angel over her crossed arms. "You said the location of the seals was a closely guarded secret, so how do *you* know where it is? What's your real play here? What are the angels up to?"

The angel drew himself up with quiet dignity. "I know the location of the seal because I, Arakiel, am its guardian. Only my blood will open it." He paused, and as he did, his eyes filled with unexpected sadness. "Now that Soraph, guardian of the first seal, is dead, I may be next."

Annabeth gasped automatically. Her hand flew to her mouth. "Someone killed an angel?"

Not only was the idea that someone had murdered an angel viscerally abhorrent, she couldn't believe it was physically possible. Angels were *angels*. Even the demons couldn't do it, and they had certainly tried.

Theodora raised a single black eyebrow. Her expression was flat and impassive. Annabeth couldn't believe how unaffected she was by the news. "So you're afraid of getting virgin-sacrificed like your friend Soraph and you need *us* to protect the seal because you got ghosted by everyone else and you know we can get into the building."

Annabeth wanted to protest the characterization as being unduly rude, but the assessment was technically accurate, so she kept her mouth shut.

Theodora leaned forward with a sneer, eyes drilling through the angel. "Why should we help you?"

Arakiel removed his glasses, carefully folding them and placing them in the front pocket of his jacket. Annabeth hadn't considered until that moment that they were unnecessary. They were merely a show, like the deep wrinkles on his face and the paper-thin skin of his hands. Everything about his corporeal body was an illusion, designed to enable him to blend in on Earth. In his true form, he was magnificent. Or so she'd read.

When he looked back to Theodora, his eyes were older than Earth itself, older than time. They were eyes that had looked upon the universe when all that existed was God and His angels. He said quietly, "When the second seal is opened, War will be released. With the third seal, Famine. The fourth seal will unleash Death. And these will be but a shadow of the horrors yet to be inflicted upon the world. The sun will turn black, the moon red. The stars will plummet to the Earth."

Annabeth flinched, her flexed cheeks drawing her lips into a grimace as she began to remember the horrors promised by the Book of Revelation. Arakiel continued, "Hail and fire will rain down on the Earth. The sea will turn to blood. Rivers will be filled with poison. Then will come the floods and fires that will consume the Earth…"

She clutched the edge of the counter, queasy and slightly dizzy. The Apocalypse was a terrible thing for humanity. And if Arakiel was right—and she had no reason to believe he was wrong—it had been set in motion.

"Right. Got it. We don't want any more seals to be opened," Harriet said. Her face was noticeably paler than it had been a minute ago. "So what do we do to stop that?"

"We must find out who opened the first seal and apprehend them before they come for the second." The angel answered with certainty, but Annabeth knew it was much easier said than done. If it was that simple, Arakiel would have done it himself already.

"Okay, how do we do that?" Harriet asked.

"We go to the site of the first seal and look for clues. I'm sure there will be something there to give away the killer's identity. No crime is committed without evidence."

Arakiel's determined confidence was met with a grunt from Theodora. "We're not fucking detectives."

Annabeth nodded. Looking for clues was a job for the police, who were trained for that kind of thing. She couldn't imagine what the four of them might find that could help them identify the culprit. Hunting down rebellious demons was very different from locating someone clever or powerful enough to open a seal of the Apocalypse.

"You're an angel. Why can't you just…tell?" Harriet asked.

Arakiel sighed deeply, somehow managing to look penitent, as though he were personally at fault for the current situation. "Angels aren't omniscient; only God is."

Oh. This new knowledge hit Annabeth harder than she anticipated. The angels weren't perfect after all. They had blind spots.

"So where was the seal?" Harriet asked.

"At St. Peter's Cathedral. The cardinal has temporarily closed the church while repairs are being made. Come with me now. We'll be alone and undisturbed."

Caught up in the mystery of the illicitly opened seal, Annabeth was willing to go without further question, but Theodora raised her hands in firm refusal. Her body was rooted immovably to the floor. "We're not going anywhere with you."

"Why not?" He looked from Harriet to Annabeth, lost.

"For all we know, we could be running into some kind of an ambush."

She put her hands on her hips. Whereas his mortal body looked weak and frail, she was a tower of strength and vigor. Dressed in all black, she looked like a thundercloud, and her eyes flashed with bottled lightning. She stared him down, using her height to full effect. "You've told us someone killed an angel and opened one of the seven motherfucking seals of the Apocalypse. I can't even imagine how fucking powerful that person must be. You say you don't know who did it, but there's no way you don't have an idea. So who is it? Who could be waiting for us at that church?"

"The danger has passed," Arakiel protested, his voice a few notes higher than before. "There is no fear of ambush."

She didn't budge.

He resisted for a moment, looking to the other women for support. But Theodora had a point. At last, he relented. He pulled his eyebrows together into a mournful pout and spread his hands. "Who else could it be but Samyaza? Who but the high lord of the Daemonium could find the first seal and kill its guardian?"

Despite herself, Annabeth sighed. She had guessed that would be the answer, but she had hoped it wouldn't. Inevitably, things in this city always seemed to come back to her father.

CHAPTER FOUR

The cab ride to the cathedral was tight and uncomfortable. Which was exactly how Theodora intended it to be. She wasn't a cruel person. Had Arakiel been a human, she would have treated him with all the respect due to someone of his age. But he was an angel, and as far as she was concerned, they were all murderers, every one of them. So she pressed hard against him, pinning his thin body against the door with her larger hips and shoulders. He winced, discomfort or pain on his narrow face, but he didn't say anything.

"If this is a setup, there aren't enough angels in this city to find all the pieces I'll cut you into," she growled to him under her breath, low enough that Annabeth, sitting next to her, couldn't hear.

Arakiel turned his head to look at her with wide, startled eyes. "I would never!" To his credit, he sounded genuinely horrified. But there was no rule Theodora knew of that said angels couldn't be good actors. He may have convinced Annabeth that he was sincere, but actions spoke louder than words, and so far he hadn't done anything trustworthy. The only reason she'd even gotten into the taxi at all was because the other two women had. If nothing else, she had to go to protect them.

She grunted. "We'll see about that."

She couldn't carry her shotgun in a taxi in the bright light of morning, so she had brought a Desert Eagle instead. The heavy handgun was holstered under her left armpit, concealed by her leather jacket. She fingered the grip with the fingers of her right hand, reassuring herself she could pull it at any time. Unless Arakiel could teleport, he wouldn't be able to dodge a bullet, not this close.

"Why would I bring you to harm?" the angel protested. "I need you to help protect the second seal."

"So you say. *I* think it all sounds fishy."

She didn't yet know what was happening, but she found it more than a little suspicious that an angel had suddenly turned up on their doorstep. The day after Harriet had seen another angel, no less. Even if his story hadn't been more than a little questionable, of all the people in the city to ask for help, they were the last he should have come to. It wasn't only that they worked for the Daemonium. It was the controversial issue of their parentage.

The only reason she hadn't tried to kill Arakiel on the spot at the pawnshop was to get information out of him. Where were the other angels? How could she get to them? She didn't care about Arakiel or his panic over the seals. Harriet and Annabeth might be alarmed that someone was trying to start the Apocalypse, but she knew the angels would never let it get anywhere. *If* someone really had opened the first seal, of course. What she wanted was tactical intelligence.

"I'm not the enemy, Theodora. We're on the same side. In fact, you three—"

She sucked in a sharp breath as all the muscles in her body clenched. Rage flared in her chest—thick, churning magma that burned through her veins to every part of her body. He might as well have ripped open the gaping wound just below the surface of her skin and poured a sea of salt in. Through gritted teeth, she growled, "Tell that to my father."

On the same side? The two of them? Not even close. He was her sworn enemy. He and every other angel, on Earth or in Heaven. They were all treacherous bastards.

Arakiel's eyes dimmed behind his glasses. He looked down at his hands, which were covered by pale brown liver spots. She wasn't fooled. They were decoration, a mere costume. He took a breath. "I knew your father. Long before the moon and stars were created, I knew him."

If she'd listened closely, she would have heard the grief and regret in his voice. The loss. But she wasn't listening. She was a bonfire of rage, her body humming with the intoxicating rush of unbridled emotion. "Were you one of the ones who murdered him?"

It took everything she had not to scream the question. To grab his gizzard neck and shake it until he cried out and begged her to let go. If he said yes, she would kill him. The first seal guardian, Soraph, had been killed, and that meant angels weren't invincible. If Arakiel had played a part in her father's death, she would end him just as he had ended her father. If he hadn't, she would force him to tell her who had.

"No." He said it with enough sincerity that she believed him.

"But you know who did."

He shifted uncomfortably and turned his attention to the beige headrest in front of him, addressing it rather than her. It was easier, even for an angel, to avoid meeting her eyes, a fact that gave her no small amount of satisfaction. "Kasdeja knew the consequences of his choices. Once fallen, an angel cannot seek to interfere with Heaven's plans."

"What the fuck is that supposed to mean?"

Theodora knew all but nothing about her father's death. All she knew was that angels had killed him, and that was only because Andromalius had told her. If not for him, she would have had nothing. And even he knew nothing else about where or why. The day her father had disappeared was a black hole in her memory. All she had to fill that gap was speculation and a deep sense of loss that forever hovered at the edge of her consciousness.

Arakiel answered quietly. "He and Samyaza were searching for the seals."

"What—"

Before she could ask what he meant, Annabeth placed a gentle hand on her thigh to attract her attention. "We're here."

In a world in which angels and demons had fought an invisible war of influence for millennia, the women assumed the angels had ceded this particular city long ago to their foes. Why else would it be such a total shithole? Why else did the filth of the Earth not only go unchallenged here but even thrive? There was a reason the women were the Daemonium's only revokers. Demons only seemed to go crazy here, or at least as far as Theodora could tell.

But St. Peter's Cathedral was proof the demons didn't control *everything* in the city. Its two tall, neo-Gothic spires, made of white marble like the rest of the church, pierced the sky as though they could reach all the way to Heaven. Bold and imposing, the cathedral pushed back the darkness trying to encroach around it. Or at least, it *had*. Now it was apparently a crime scene for a dead angel.

Arakiel led the way inside, pushing open one of the heavy bronze doors with no more difficulty than if it had been made of cardboard. Theodora walked close behind him, right hand still resting high on the backstrap of her pistol. Until they knew what was inside, she wasn't taking any chances.

As they walked down the central aisle, she swiveled her head in every direction, looking for any sign of danger. But the cathedral was as still and empty as a photo.

"Well? Where's the seal?" she asked gruffly. She didn't know what she had expected, but it wasn't an empty, serene church.

Arakiel said nothing, only pushed farther into the church. She made eye contact with Harriet, whose hands were resting lightly on her waist, consciously or unconsciously touching the knives Theodora knew she had tucked inside the waistband of her pants. To Theodora's unasked question, she shook her head and shrugged. She didn't know what to think either. Theodora tried to catch Annabeth's eye, but the other woman was distracted, peering around the church with intense concentration. At least someone was taking their Sherlock Holmes duty seriously.

Theodora was reminded of what Annabeth had whispered in her ear as they left the shop. "If the angels wanted to kill us, they could have done it at any time. I think we should trust Arakiel." Theodora hated to admit it, but she had a point. She released her grip on the pistol and let her arms hang.

It wasn't until they reached the transept that Theodora finally saw what Arakiel had meant when he said the cardinal had closed the cathedral for repairs. She stopped dead in her tracks.

"Whoa."

The altar platform looked as though a giant fist had smashed into it. The high altar had been shattered into large chunks of marble strewn on the platform like a fallen Jenga tower. Deep cracks radiated through the altar steps. The altar crucifix and six enormous, gilded candlesticks lay scattered on the sanctuary floor.

"Ooooh," Annabeth said, the sound a sort of moan of shock, as they moved closer.

Harriet, next to her, whistled. "Wow."

Arakiel knelt at the ruined altar and touched the marble platform with gentle fingertips, his face a mask of deep loss. At his back, his wings shivered, creating rainbow flashes in the air. From a distance, Theodora had only been able to see that the altar had been destroyed. Up close, she saw that where it had been was a giant hole five feet in diameter. The hole was almost perfectly round except for a small piece of marble that hadn't completely broken free.

"The seal was hidden beneath the high altar." Annabeth's low words were framed as a statement, not a question. Theodora understood why. There was no doubt they were looking at the broken seal.

The sight was unnerving, even for Theodora. The angels had hidden the seal in the single most sacred place in the entire city and it had still been broken. The idea was...unsettling. If the demonic high lord Samyaza had been able to get to it here, perhaps he really could get to all of the seals.

If it had been Samyaza. Theodora's mouth quirked into a tight frown. They didn't know it was him. But if not him, then who? Who else was clever enough to find the seal and then strong enough to open it?

"When was it opened?" Harriet asked.

Arakiel shook his head. His morose expression didn't change. If anything, his face became even longer. "I don't know. Sometime last night."

"So Soraph was kidnapped, dragged here, and then..." Harriet didn't bother finishing the sentence.

"When his blood touched the seal, it opened." Arakiel shuddered. "He was drained completely."

Theodora imagined the scene: a struggling, bound angel thrown onto the altar. His throat slit, thick red blood running down the smooth stone onto the floor below. The ground trembling as the seal absorbed the offering. The marble exploding in a geyser of rock as the seal opened. If it hadn't gone exactly like that, it must have been close.

She indicated the destruction with her chin. "What does the cardinal think happened here?" Whoever had been first on the scene would have encountered a grisly scene. It must have been pretty traumatic to someone not used to the sight of blood everywhere. Not to mention for whoever had to clean it all up.

"An explosion caused by an underground gas leak."

"A gas leak?" Harriet repeated, incredulous. "Are there even gas lines around here? Who the hell would believe this"—she pointed at the debris—"was caused by an accident?"

"It's easier to believe the unlikely than the impossible."

Theodora couldn't argue with that. It was basically the premise of their entire existence.

"What about Soraph?" she asked. "How do you explain away a dead angel?"

Arakiel cleared his throat, uncomfortable. He had known this angel. They might even have been friends. "The humans believe Soraph was a homeless man who had, unfortunately, taken refuge for the night near the altar. They believe it was…bad luck."

For a moment, Theodora was confused. How could anyone have mistaken an angel for a human? Then she remembered the humans wouldn't have been able to see his wings, just as they couldn't see the yellow eyes of demons. The humans had no reason to believe Soraph was anything but human. They had no more idea that an angel had been slaughtered in the church than that the first seal of the Apocalypse had been buried beneath the altar. Armageddon had been set in motion right in front of them, and they didn't have the slightest inkling. Nor would she, if Arakiel hadn't walked into their pawnshop half an hour ago. Now…it was impossible to deny that what she was looking at sure looked like what he said it was.

Harriet glanced around, surveying the church with keen eyes used to picking out demons on the lam. "There has to be CCTV footage for both the inside and the outside of the cathedral, right? We might be able to see exactly what happened."

Arakiel shook his head. "The cameras recorded nothing. They stopped working at midnight. Even now, they are not functioning."

Soraph's killer wanted privacy. And anonymity.

"Why?" Theodora motioned at the shattered altar, suddenly remembering what Arakiel had told her in the car. "Why would my father and Samyaza *want* to cause the Apocalypse?" Although she didn't look at Annabeth as she said the high lord's name, she knew Annabeth winced. She always did when her father's name was spoken. "It doesn't end well for the demons."

Her memory of the exact details of the Book of Revelation may have been a little hazy, but she was certain the final war between Heaven and Hell ended with Lucifer and his demons getting absolutely bitch-slapped by Jesus. The whole point of the Apocalypse was to remake Heaven and Earth, and part of that meant driving the demons back to Hell permanently. It seemed like the kind of thing Samyaza would want to delay or prevent, not usher in.

Arakiel stood. Behind him, his gossamer wings partially unfurled, dyed blue and yellow from the stained glass windows above. He looked skyward, as though he could see through the roof to Heaven above. Perhaps he could. "What you know of the Apocalypse, shown to John of Patmos, is only one possible future. The demons have always sought to drive the world toward a different outcome."

Wait, what?

"Are you saying the demons could actually *change* the future?" Annabeth asked.

The angel nodded. "The future is not a single road, but rather the branches of a tree. Humans, demons, and angels alike will decide which branch to follow."

Theodora took a deep breath and blew it out gustily. This was some shit. If Lucifer played his cards right, *he* might be the one doing the bitch-slapping.

Arakiel continued, "The future can't be fully predestined; that would preclude any possibility of free choice among God's creations. All living creatures would be mere wind-up toys. Puppets."

"But doesn't God know the future?" Annabeth asked.

"Perhaps. Or perhaps not."

Theodora scratched the corner of her right eyebrow. She could consider what the fuck that meant some other time. "So you think Samyaza decided to get the jump on the Apocalypse and try to somehow use it in the demons' favor." She had to admit, it sounded exactly like something the Daemonium would do.

"Who else? No human could find the seal, much less open it."

"I don't know, you got any other enemies?" As far as the women knew, the world had only angels, humans, and demons. But there was so much they didn't know, even about the demons, and they had spent years at the periphery of the Daemonium. For all she knew, the damn seal had been opened by Thor. Or the Spaghetti Monster.

"Samyaza spent years looking for the seals. He would have known exactly how to capture Soraph. What other evidence do you need?" Arakiel's wings fluttered unhappily. Perhaps he was thinking about Soraph's death, or perhaps he was imagining facing Samyaza himself, now a very real prospect.

"What happens now that the first seal's been opened? Will the city experience some sort of a plague?" Annabeth asked.

Distracted as she'd been by everything else, Theodora had completely forgotten about what the first seal's opening meant. Annabeth obviously hadn't.

"Whoever opens the seals controls what lies within. That includes the Horsemen," Arakiel replied.

"Metaphorical representations of calamities, you mean," Annabeth said. She sounded—and looked—like a graduate student asking a professor for clarification.

Arakiel blinked, surprised. "Not at all. The Horsemen are incarnate beings. Pestilence is as real as you and I, with the power to spread sickness around him."

"So Samyaza's got his own walking bioweapon," Harriet summarized flatly. Her face was pulled into a tight scowl.

Another kind of celestial. Great.

Annabeth adjusted her glasses thoughtfully. "Is there anyone Samyaza would use Pestilence against?"

Who wouldn't he use it against might be the better question. None of the women had ever met Samyaza, but his reputation preceded him. Even Andromalius was scared of him, although he would never admit it. If the high lord had taken control of the first Horseman of the Apocalypse, it didn't bode well for anyone.

Arakiel's mouth pulled tight with concern. "I don't know. We angels are immune to disease. But he could attack the clergy..."

Kill the angels' human allies. Of course. It was a logical play. In the eternal celestial chess game, it was a literal taking of the other side's bishops. Frustration became a heavy, expanding ball in Theodora's chest. This was getting out of hand. Protect the second seal. Stop Samyaza. Worry about Pestilence. Prevent the Apocalypse. Why couldn't the angels do this shit themselves? Arakiel's answer had been pretty damn vague about that.

And so she didn't believe it. She shook her head, causing her long, thick braid to bounce heavily against her shoulders. "Nope. Fuck this. We're out." She motioned to her companions in the universal gesture of departure. "Let's go."

Annabeth's head jerked in surprise. "But what about—"

Theodora felt the door inside her closing. It gave her peace. "Not our circus, not our fucking monkeys. This is angels versus demons shit. If Samyaza found the first seal, you think he's not going to notice the second one *in his office?*"

If the angels were so worried, they could fix it. This was all much ado about nothing. Arakiel was barking up the wrong tree.

The angel drew himself up, or at least as much as his small old body could. "Whether you want it or not, this *is* your circus. You carry in your veins the blood of angels. By birthright, you're—"

Theodora had pulled her gun before she was even aware she'd done it. She crossed the distance to him in two strides and grabbed his collar with her left hand, twisting her fist so the gray wool tightened around his throat and he couldn't back away. She shoved the muzzle under his chin, grinding it into his skin mercilessly, her finger on the trigger. If she accidentally pulled, she wouldn't mind. "Listen, you fuck, I don't have *shit* angelic in me. My father was turned into a demon for choosing to love my mother, so you know damn well my blood is *demonic*. That goes for all of us. We don't owe you angels jack shit."

Arakiel made no effort to fight. His thin body was limp in Theodora's hand, although a spark of what might have been defiance twinkled in his eyes. He wheezed, "Yes, the fallen were turned to demons, but even so, their children are half-angel. The sins of their fathers are not theirs to bear. The nephilim still have God's grace."

Not half-demon, but half-angel. That was his new play? She shook him angrily, enough to make his head bobble a little. "Bullshit."

Arakiel's voice was soft yet firm. "If you were half-demon, I would never have come to you. But you have angelic blood. And the fifth seal—"

She dropped him before he could finish. Because he hadn't anticipated the sudden release of her hold, he collapsed to his hands and knees. She kept her gun leveled at his head. At any moment, she would happily pull the trigger. She was tired of his efforts to manipulate them. If he thought they were stupid, he thought wrong. "You're lying. We have demonic talents."

That was all she needed to prove he was full of shit. The three half-humans may not have had the distinctive yellow eyes of demons, but they each had an ability that could only be explained by their demon genetics.

His lips twitched into an unexpected smile. She had to stop herself from trying to kick it off his face. "Your talents are *angelic*, a gift from God. We angels, too, have abilities."

"No." She shook her head too forcefully. He was still trying to play them, and she wasn't having it. "The Daemonium would never work with angels." The demons hated nothing on Earth more than angels. If they were half-angel, the demons would have killed them on sight years ago.

"The Daemonium doesn't know. Like you, they believe you to be half-demon." Arakiel's smile broadened into something beatific. "Rejoice. You are one of us."

Nope. Her feet turned and began to march back the way they'd come, carrying her with them. All conscious thought stopped. The cathedral around her was blurry and out of focus.

"Theodora!" She barely heard Annabeth's shout or her footfalls as the other woman chased after her. She didn't hear anything at all but the now-roar in her head.

What had first brought the three women together was a shared, unique experience: being half-demon in a world full of clueless humans. They had never belonged fully in either the mortal or celestial worlds. It had been an isolating and lonely experience as children, but as adults, working together, they had carved out their own place. Shitty as it was to be genetically half-evil, they had found a purpose revoking demons who overstepped their limits on Earth. Now this.

If Arakiel was right, then almost everything about the lives they had built for themselves had been a lie. Rather than reaching out to help them when they were young and vulnerable, accepting them as one of their own, the angels had ignored and abandoned them. And if the Daemonium found out this new secret, not only would it stop contracting with them for revocations, destroying their sense of purpose, it would have them exterminated. The women were good fighters, but they couldn't fight against an entire city full of demons out to kill them. Arakiel had handed them a death sentence. They were dead women walking.

Annabeth's hand wrapped around her elbow and pulled, trying to drag her to a stop. "Theodora, wait. We need to talk."

Theodora shook her arm, trying to throw the hand off. "Fuck this. We're not helping them." Not the people who murdered her father. It didn't matter if she was…possibly or definitely genetically one of them. She had nothing in common with them. And they had no right to ask for her help.

"I understand." The soft tone in Annabeth's voice said she really did. "But the seals. What if more are opened? And what about Pestilence?"

Theodora didn't care. She couldn't imagine caring right now. "Fuck the seals. If the angels can't protect them, then maybe they deserve to get the shit kicked out of them by the demons." The tips of her ears were burning. Anger and pain and hurt shot through her like zaps of electricity. It made her want to start running and not stop until her legs couldn't move any more.

"It's a lot to take in. Let's just give it a minute. Why don't we sit down?" She indicated the heavy wooden pew beside them.

If any of the women were half-angel, it was without a doubt Annabeth. Annabeth, daughter of the high lord of the Daemonium, was a goddamn Mother Teresa. Of course she would want to help the angels even though she didn't know anything about them. Of course she would forgive them for waiting until the last possible second to tell the women they were half-angels, and then only because they needed their help. But Theodora was not like her.

"If you care that much, *you* help. But you know you won't last a week if the Daemonium finds out you turned against it."

They both knew she wouldn't last even a day. Theodora didn't bother reminding her that her father wouldn't protect her.

Samyaza didn't give two shits for anyone but himself. Demons were incapable of love. Not that he'd been much better when he'd been an angel. There was a reason he'd fallen. That much, at least, they knew about him.

Annabeth, all hundred and fifteen pounds of her, stood her ground. "You know an Earth ruled by the demons would be literal Hell. You don't want that. None of us do. We can't let Samyaza open any more seals. We have to at least try to help."

The two stood facing each other in the middle of the aisle: Theodora in all black, Annabeth in a green bolero and ballet flats. They were different in almost every way, and yet after all these years they might as well have been sisters. Theodora ground her teeth in frustration. She didn't want to admit aloud that Annabeth was right, but of course she was. A future in which demons reshaped the world into their own image was too terrible to imagine. She was happy to work for the Daemonium, but that didn't mean she liked the demons. They didn't even like each other.

Still, it's not like they could go charging into a fight with the most powerful demon on Earth. The idea alone was a joke. Her eyes flickered past Annabeth to the shattered altar. The high lord of the Daemonium could do a hell of a lot more damage to their fragile flesh and bones than he could to a piece of stone that weighed more than a car. They healed quickly, but they weren't immortal. Even Annabeth had to admit he could destroy them with a flick of his wrist. And what the hell could they do to stop him from opening the second seal anyway?

But... She stared into Annabeth's pleading face. You couldn't say no to family. "I'll think about it."

CHAPTER FIVE

Harriet stared out the fingerprint-smudged window of the taxi, watching the city roll past in a blur of gray and white. She saw it all without seeing any of it, lost in her own thoughts. After Theodora's abrupt departure from the cathedral, she and Annabeth had tried to search for clues around the broken seal, but there were none to be found. She wasn't surprised. It wasn't as though Samyaza was going to leave a detailed description of how he'd found the first seal and whether he knew the location of the second. Still, it would have been nice to have at least *something* to go on.

She tapped her finger unconsciously on the white plastic bag in her lap, causing it to crinkle quietly. Theodora was right: the three of them weren't responsible for the future of the world. But Samyaza had unleashed Pestilence and might be on the verge of releasing War as well. She didn't know what the angels were doing, but she knew Samyaza furthering the Apocalypse was the last thing the world needed.

She slipped her phone out of her pocket and scrolled through the news, half looking for anything about the accident at St. Peter's. There was nothing. Either it hadn't hit the news yet or someone—

who? An angel?—had already managed to get a cover-up in place. Or maybe it was just that no one cared about a dead homeless man and a gas leak, not when there were so many other bad news stories to tell in a day. It was just one more tragedy in a tragic city.

She lowered her phone to her lap and resumed staring out the window. There was so much to unpack in what Arakiel had told them. Their first-ever contact with an angel had been more dramatic than she ever could have imagined. But for now, she compartmentalized her thoughts about his revelations. She needed to focus on her task at hand.

The taxi came to a smooth stop and she paid the driver before stepping out in front of a tall brick building. She checked her phone again, the action automatic, as a doctor approached from another direction. He wore pale blue scrubs and a white coat, and he turned his head to look at her as he passed. Familiar yellow irises stood out starkly in his youthful, handsome face. She flinched. She was used to seeing demons throughout the city, but she hadn't expected to see one here, at the hospital.

He kept walking, entering the building without hesitation. Her chest tightened with dread. She knew what would happen next. In a few minutes, a premature baby would inexplicably flatline. A cancer patient in remission would be discovered to have aggressive, metastatic stage IV cancer. She called his kind of demonic ability "bad luck," because someone was about to have it.

She jammed her hands into the pockets of her chinos, angry. Angry he was there, angry there was nothing she could do, angry that this was how life worked. By now she was used to running into demons in places she wished they had no business—nursing homes, for example, or schools—but she never got over the sting of it. It felt like the city was imbalanced—all evil, no good.

Her phone chimed as a text arrived, redirecting her attention. She smiled, relieved, as she read the message. It wasn't enough to release all the tension in her chest, but it did raise her spirits. She walked to the wall and leaned her shoulders against it, settling in for a short wait. The wail of an ambulance siren filled the air around her, high and piercing. Moments later, the vehicle pulled up next to her and two paramedics jumped out of the back. They dashed past her, pushing a gurney into the building. She looked away, feeling sick and a little guilty for being healthy when someone else was in distress. But there was nothing she could do for them, just as she couldn't stop the demon who might be waiting for them inside.

After a few minutes more, the doors to St. Luke's Medical Center opened to reveal Summer in teal scrubs, her chunky white tennis shoes, and a ponytail. Harriet pushed off the wall, putting her phone back in her pocket, and smiled. "Thanks for coming down."

Summer said nothing. She crossed her arms, watching Harriet warily. Summer the nurse-in-training looked different from Summer the waitress. She was sharper, more tense. Gone was any hint of the flirtation she'd shown at three that morning. She was all business. And accusation.

Harriet held up the plastic bag she was carrying. Inside was a small cardboard box that she had carefully protected until now. "I brought you a cupcake. I hope you like cupcakes."

It was the perfect opportunity for Summer to make a joke about pie, but she didn't take the bait. Her eyes darted hungrily to the peace offering, then came back to Harriet just as fast, still full of suspicion. "What happened last night?"

Harriet dropped her chin, wincing at Summer's sharp tone. To get the other woman to agree to see her again, she had promised to explain, and now that excuse was already due. So much for pleasantries first. She took a breath and delivered the justification she had prepared. "Two men were following us. I didn't see them until right when we got to your apartment. They stayed pretty well in the shadows."

As Harriet had predicted, Summer's face pulled together into a wrinkle of shock and confusion. "What? I didn't see anyone. The street was deserted. No one is awake at that hour."

"Yeah. They...looked dangerous. They probably wanted to mug us."

Harriet was a terrible liar. Even having planned out what she was going to say, she still couldn't manage to sound completely sincere. Still, Summer didn't seem to be picking up on it. "Then why didn't you come inside with me? Why did you push me in and then run away?"

Harriet stared at her black loafers. "I didn't want them to follow all the way to your door and know which apartment was yours. I thought if I stayed outside, they would follow me instead."

Summer's eyes widened, reminding Harriet just how much they resembled the sky. "That was so dangerous! They could have hurt you! If you'd come inside with me, we could have locked the door and called the police."

"Then they still would have known where you lived." Harriet shrugged, trying to dismiss the significance of the event. "I lost them pretty quickly, so it turned out all right." She paused for a beat, then added, "I don't think the police would have come anyway."

Not to that part of the city. If Summer didn't know that yet, Harriet hoped she would never find out the hard way. There were some places it was too dangerous for the police to go and some places the police didn't care enough to go. Summer lived in the overlapping Venn diagram of the two.

The nurse sighed heavily and rubbed her bare face with her palms. The skin under her eyes was puffy and dark. The makeup she wore in the diner had partially masked the effort it took to work an overnight job while also being a full-time nursing student, but it couldn't mitigate the physical effects. Harriet wondered whether she'd slept at all in the last twenty-four hours.

"The terrible thing is, as much as I don't want to believe you, it doesn't surprise me, you know? That neighborhood—it's why I carry mace. And why I hate walking home alone, no matter what time of day it is. It's awful, but what can I do? It's all I can afford right now."

Harriet nodded. She understood Summer's dilemma intimately. The neighborhood in which she had been raised hadn't been much better. There had been armed robberies every month, and at least once a week someone was shot or stabbed or beaten half to death in an alley. But their one-bedroom apartment over a small bodega had been all her mother had been able to afford. Harriet had moved to a better apartment when she'd started making money as a revoker, but she never totally got over the habit of checking over her shoulder every time she walked. It was too deeply ingrained in her not to.

Summer's eyebrows furrowed as she shook her head, returning to the issue at hand. "Still, you really shouldn't have done what you did. Those guys could have hurt you." Her eyes scanned up and down Harriet's slight frame, making an understandable yet incorrect assumption about how easy it would be for two human men to attack her.

Harriet shifted her weight uncomfortably. "All's well that ends well, I guess." She couldn't think of anything else to say. There was only so much one could talk about fictional bad guys.

She held up the cupcake again, trying to redirect the conversation to something more lighthearted. "It's chocolate and peanut butter. Please don't say no."

Summer stepped forward and took the bag, her face breaking into a grateful smile. It was exactly the reaction Harriet had hoped for. "Thanks. That's really sweet of you."

She pulled out the box and opened it, revealing the beautiful black cupcake inside. There was only one good bakery in the city, and Harriet had chosen the cupcake she thought would be the most delicious. If Summer had refused to meet her, she would have eaten it herself, but she was glad Summer had come. She could always get herself another cupcake, but she might not have gotten a second chance to talk to Summer.

Summer didn't stop to admire the artistry that had gone into the cupcake—the perfect piping of the frosting or the casual yet meticulous dusting of peanut on top. Nor did she comment on its large size or rich flavor. Instead, she tore into it like a lioness, devouring it hungrily, careless of the crumb-flecked tan frosting that smeared the corners of her mouth. The cupcake—the size of Harriet's fist with an almost equally large spiral of frosting—was gone in four bites. She wiped the frosting off her lips with her thumb and forefinger and then licked them clean.

Some of Harriet's surprise at how quickly and indelicately she'd inhaled the treat must have shown in her face, because Summer blushed when she saw it. "Sorry. I haven't eaten since last night and I'm starving. Today's been brutal. I've been here for five hours and it's been nonstop. I'm supposed to be off in an hour, but the ER is so flooded right now that at this rate I'll be lucky if I make it home for dinner."

Harriet cocked her head, confused. "Isn't that…normal?" She didn't know anything about nursing or hospitals, but she assumed emergency rooms were always a maelstrom of shouting doctors, bleeding patients, and beeping heart monitors.

Summer scrunched her face together. "No. That's the thing. I mean, I haven't been in my acute nursing rotation long, but it's never been like this before. Even the other nurses and doctors say it's crazy today."

"What's happening? A lot of people with injuries or something?"

Summer shook her head. "No, it's all kinds of diseases. Pneumonia, staph infections, shingles, a baby with whooping cough...Two of our patients have typhoid. In the city! Can you imagine? I have no idea how they got it, and they swear they don't either."

She scratched her forehead, bewildered. A few strands of blond hair had pulled free from her ponytail, and she pushed them back behind her ear. "We have a minor meningococcal meningitis outbreak too. I feel like someone opened an infectious disease textbook and started throwing darts at it." She sighed. "At least I'm learning a lot."

At the word "disease," Harriet's stomach dropped. *Pestilence.*

"Who's been coming in sick? Is it mostly a bunch of priests?" Her mind raced. If the angels didn't stop him, Samyaza could decimate the city's clerics in a matter of days, if not hours.

Summer frowned at her, confused. "Priests? No. It's been all sorts of people, from babies to grandmothers. In a city this size, it's normal to see—"

Harriet didn't hear her brief exposition on the average incidence of infectious disease per capita in a large city. She was too busy thinking. Why had Samyaza gone after regular humans? What did he get out of it? Did he have some grudge against humans? She had to tell Theodora and Annabeth. Perhaps one of them would have an idea what the high lord was up to.

Summer's voice, which had faded to a wordless drone as Harriet's thoughts raced, sharpened back into focus, reclaiming her attention. "Anyway, I shouldn't complain about aching feet. The paramedics are the ones who have been run totally ragged. The second they drop one patient off, there's already a call for another. And they work twenty-four-hour shifts. It's grueling."

Suddenly, Harriet had the unmistakable feeling she was being watched. It was a primal, subconscious sensation. Somewhere, eyes had fastened upon her. She knew it.

The hair on the back of her neck stood up, responding to the unknown voyeur. Trying not to be obvious, she scanned the hospital's tall windows, looking for the source. She half expected to encounter eyes staring out at her, but the glass was too reflective to see through. Her hand slipped to her switchblade, fingers closing around it. No one would try to attack them here in the open, surrounded by people. She knew that. Even so, she couldn't help the feeling of uneasiness that washed over her. Something was wrong.

"Is everything okay? You look distracted," Summer said.

Harriet turned her focus back to the nurse, hastily trying to smooth the alarm from her face. "Yeah. I was just thinking how awful it must be to see all that suffering. I don't know how you do it. I don't think I could."

Summer shrugged. "I guess it's because I know I'm helping people. I'm taking some of that pain and suffering away."

Harriet nodded, trying her best to appear engaged and sympathetic, but her attention was still split. Maybe it was her imagination. There was no way she was being watched twice within only a few hours. Perhaps she was unduly jumpy after what she'd seen at the cathedral.

Summer cast a look over her shoulder as though she could see through the door into the bustling emergency room inside. "I guess I should get back." There was wistful reluctance in her voice. She tilted her head down and looked up at Harriet from under her long black eyelashes, the same way she had as they'd walked to her apartment. "I'm off all tomorrow. I'll be half-dead for most of the day recovering from all this, but"—she raised her eyebrows—"maybe not all of it. I could text you. If you think you'll be free sometime?"

Harriet nodded enthusiastically. "Definitely."

Summer smiled. The expression momentarily chased the fatigue from her face, bringing out the sparkle of her eyes. "Deal." With a playful wink, she turned and made her way back into the hospital, taking the empty cupcake box and bag with her.

Harriet waited in case she turned back one last time, fighting the urge to get away from the hospital immediately. What would Summer think if she looked back and Harriet was hoofing it as fast as she could? But Summer never turned back, and when the door closed with precise finality, Harriet set off at last, pulling the lapels of her heather-blue coat up around her neck and tucking her chin.

As she walked through the neighborhood around the hospital, she took a series of turns. What may have seemed like a random, directionless route was purposeful: to keep from losing her, any surveillant would have to stay close. And close meant identifiable. Each time Harriet crossed the street to make a turn, she took a long, hard look down the sidewalk behind her, trying to catch sight of anyone who seemed to be mirroring her movements. But as many times as she looked, pretending to check for oncoming traffic, the result was always the same. Nothing. She was on her own.

She breathed a little heavier, unnerved. It was unlike her to be paranoid. But she trusted her instincts, and she couldn't shake the feeling that she *had* been followed. She could still feel eyes watching her, burning into her skin like lasers. The question was: whose eyes were they? All she knew for sure was that it couldn't be a human. No human was that good at hiding.

It was as she checked over her shoulder before crossing yet another intersection that she finally saw it. A figure was standing midway down the block, watching her with intense focus, as though they were the only two people on the street. He was tall and muscular, wearing what looked like white tights, a white breastplate, and a white cape. His eyes, too, were white as milk, with no pupil. The whiteness of his outfit made the blackness of his skin seem even darker, like the keys of a piano.

Unconsciously, Harriet froze. Under any other circumstance, she would have assumed he was in costume for some event—a birthday party or a fan convention, for example. She could easily imagine a character that looked like him in a comic book. But she knew with absolute, electrifying certainty that this was no costume. She could feel the unearthliness in him as though he were a vibrating tuning fork. It found resonance in the unearthliness in her. But unlike her, he didn't belong in this world. His presence felt like a sickness.

Upon closer scrutiny, what she had first thought was a white ring around his hairless black head was actually a small, spiked crown. And over his shoulder, she recognized the unmistakable shape of a bow.

"Oh shit."

Pestilence. Still watching her with his blank, penetrating eyes, he reached around his back to pull free his bow. The movement was enough to break the spell she was under.

"*Oh shit.*"

She whirled and began to run, arms pumping. Could she outstrip a Horseman of the Apocalypse? She didn't know, but she had a feeling she was about to find out.

CHAPTER SIX

"Wait, Harriet, slow down. What?" Annabeth held the phone away from her ear. The other woman's words had come through the speaker as a loud, indistinguishable jumble. She hadn't understood any of them.

"Pestilence. I just ran into him. Or he found me. I don't know." From the way she was panting, Annabeth could tell Harriet was running.

"What?" A thrill of shock and disbelief ran down her chest. "Where are you? Are you okay?"

"Near St. Luke's. I don't know if I lost him. Annabeth, he can *glamour*. And he's got a bow."

She took a sharp breath, reacting to the emotion in Harriet's voice. Her stomach balled into a knot. "Come back to the shop if you can. I'll call Theodora." Whatever was happening, whatever reason Pestilence had to chase Harriet, at least there was safety in numbers. Not to mention the arsenal of weapons in the back room. But Harriet had to make it there first.

"Okay."

"Be careful." The words were automatic. Harriet wasn't reckless, but that didn't mean she couldn't make a mistake. Any of them could.

The line went dead. Annabeth took a deep breath to steady herself, staring at the blank screen. Only a few hours ago they had learned about Pestilence. Now he was apparently stalking Harriet. Why?

Biting her lower lip so hard it almost tore the skin, she began to type. She knew Theodora wouldn't answer a phone call right now, not as emotional as she was, but she would read a text. Trying to be as concise as possible, Annabeth wrote, *Pestilence chasing Harriet. Come to shop.* No matter what Theodora thought about the angels and the seven seals, she would never ignore a message about Harriet being in danger.

She hit send, then set the black phone down on the countertop and stared at it absently. Each of the women had been hurt thousands of times before. In the early days, when they were still learning to fight, their wounds had sometimes been near fatal. More than once, they had shed premature tears of loss and agony. But they had always been there to bandage wounds and help each other limp to safety.

She didn't like that Harriet was on her own and in the crosshairs of a dangerous new celestial. This was uncharted territory. What if Pestilence got close enough to— She shook her head, fighting against her fears. There was no use worrying about something that might not happen. Better to wait and see.

Her thoughts shifted to Pestilence's master. To her father. Once upon a time, the high lord of the Daemonium had been a seraph. Of all the angelic orders, Samyaza had been part of the highest, the closest to God Himself. But by some defect in his composition, he hadn't been content to dutifully serve. He was ambitious. He wanted *more.*

According to what Annabeth had gathered over the years, Samyaza had left Heaven planning to reign over the Earth like a god. But he miscalculated. As a fallen angel turned demon, he could only influence human events indirectly. He had never come close to ruling the world. Instead, he became the head of the demonic bureaucracy, Lucifer's key representative on Earth. He was powerful, but he was contained, at least somewhat.

Now her father had opened the first seal of the Apocalypse. She rose and started the electric kettle, wrapping her arms around herself as she leaned against the counter and waited for the water to boil. The last thing the world needed was an empowered, vengeful high lord bent on taking on Heaven itself. But what could *she* do to stop him?

* * *

Ten minutes later, Theodora blew into the shop, her presence filling the room like a summer storm. Harriet arrived five minutes later.

"What the fuck happened?" Theodora shouted the second she stepped inside.

Harriet was disheveled. Her short hair was matted, and sweat had soaked through her coat in dark rings under her arms. She blew out a breath and shook her head. "I don't know."

"Annabeth?" Theodora gave her a severe look. "Go check."

Nodding, Annabeth strode past Harriet and cracked the door open, just enough to stick her head out and scan the neighborhood. She clutched her heavy morning star tightly, prepared to use it if necessary. Her angelic affinity was the ability to see celestial presence—blessings on objects, for example, or the fingerprints of demonic influence. It also meant she could see through glamours. If Pestilence had followed Harriet across the city all the way here, she would spot him immediately.

But everything outside the shop was quiet and perfectly mortal. Exhaling the breath she hadn't realized she'd been holding, she ducked back inside. Returning to her seat at the counter, she set the morning star down and looked to Harriet expectantly. "So what happened?"

Harriet took off her coat and threw it onto one of the stools. Her white dress shirt was soaked, revealing her white sports bra beneath. Annabeth wondered how far she'd had to run to get away from the Horseman. Quickly, with no embellishment, she recounted her encounter with Pestilence and subsequent dash through the streets.

Theodora frowned. "So it was coincidence? Pestilence just happened to be at the hospital?"

Harriet shrugged. With the black cloth she pulled from her pocket, she delicately wiped the sweat off her forehead. Annabeth nodded, thinking. She could see how the situation might have unfolded. Pestilence, wreaking invisible havoc at the hospital, had sensed another celestial presence and followed it out of curiosity or malice. Samyaza hadn't sent him after Harriet specifically. It was a case of wrong place, wrong time.

"I'm glad you're all right," she told Harriet.

Harriet ran her hands through her hair, trying unsuccessfully to tame it back into some semblance of order. Her face twisted into an unhappy grimace, making her mouth a small pout. "Pestilence was on the street, out in the open. Where are the angels?"

Arakiel had said the angels weren't omniscient, but nevertheless, they had to know by now that the first seal had been opened. So why hadn't they taken action yet? Annabeth put her hands on her hips. They needed more information, and there was only one place they could get it. "We need to talk to Father Domenico."

Since the New Testament, the world's angelic population had gone almost completely silent. No more passing messages from God, no more guiding prophets. Even the clergy, who ostensibly served as cogs in the greater machine of God's plan, knew nothing of the angels' activities on Earth. Except Father Domenico. For reasons the women had never been able to wheedle out of him and he had never disclosed, the priest had an in with the host—or at least, at one point he'd *had* one. If anyone knew what the angels were doing right now, it would be him.

Annabeth grabbed her morning star and slipped it into the special holster on her belt that both hid its sharp head and protected her from being accidentally poked. Now that she knew Pestilence was out on the street, she felt better with the weapon close at hand. Theodora eyed her unhappily, and for a moment, Annabeth thought she might refuse to go. Theodora had hated Father Domenico since the day they'd met. She had hoped he would have answers about her father. But the priest been unable to tell her anything. Her animosity had only become worse over time. She picked fights with the priest or made snide comments. Her refusal to forgive him for what wasn't even his fault was why when Annabeth brought him their boxes of ammunition to bless, she went alone or with Harriet.

"Come on, Theodora," she coaxed. "We won't be there for long."

"We need to know what he knows," Harriet added.

Theodora glared at them. Then relented. "Fine. But only because I want to know what the fuck is going on."

Turning, she threw open the door to the armory behind them. Bright light spilled out of the room, staining the floor a fluorescent yellow. She stepped inside, eyes moving over the racks of spotless black and silver weapons. After a moment, she grabbed a kusarigama and hooked it to her belt on the right side. Originally a Japanese farming scythe, in time the kusarigama had been transformed into a deadly weapon with a weight and chain attached to the handle for added functionality. Theodora liked the weapon's versatility. And she could carry it without anyone noticing, unlike her shotgun. Beside her, Harriet grabbed her katana, settling the sheath over her shoulder with practiced ease. If she shifted the sheath down just a little and put her coat on, it was hard to tell she was even wearing it.

"Okay, let's see what Father Douchebag has to say," Theodora said.

Annabeth opened her mouth to protest, then closed it. They were going. That was what mattered.

* * *

St. Peter's Cathedral was the largest church in the city, but St. Francis Church was by far the oldest, predating the former by a hundred years or more. It looked as though it had been plucked out of medieval Europe and airdropped into the city, landing neatly between two low, red brick buildings in a quiet part of town. Father Domenico's office was an addition on the back side, built half a century ago out of the same brick that had been used for its neighbors and accessible from a door facing the alley behind it.

The priest looked up from his desk when the women walked in after a quick knock. "Ah, what an unexpected visit." He smiled broadly and stood to greet them, then motioned to the two chairs in front of his desk. "Please, sit."

He spoke with a thick accent. Based on his name, Annabeth had always assumed he was Italian, but she didn't know from where in

Italy he had come, or when. Like everything else about him, his past was a mystery. Over the years, any time she asked, he had somehow managed to deflect the question, and it was only later she realized what he had done. Finally, she had stopped asking. It was a battle she wasn't going to win.

Annabeth and Harriet took the chairs while Theodora remained standing behind them. Father Domenico settled himself back in his seat, the old black leather creaking beneath his weight. He was thinner than when Annabeth had last seen him. She hoped he wasn't having health issues. If he was, he likely wouldn't tell her. He wasn't the kind to complain.

"What can I do for you? A blessing, perhaps?" he asked solicitously, looking back and forth between them.

"No, Father, we're here about something else," Annabeth answered quickly, before Theodora could respond with some snark or another.

His eyebrows rose as he redirected his attention to her. "Oh?"

His thinning gray hair and brown-tinted, oblong glasses gave him a dignified, fatherly appearance. Annabeth could no longer remember exactly how many years ago she had met him. She had been a very young child, dragged around ceaselessly by her unraveling mother on an increasingly paranoid quest to find protection and salvation from the invisible demons that persecuted her, begging all the *santos* and *santas* for help. Like the doctors, psychiatrists, and charlatans before him, the priest had been unable to hold together the irreparably fragmenting shards of her mother's sanity, but he had held out a hand when Annabeth most needed it. He had even found a nice family to adopt her, and for that she would always be grateful.

And he had done something else for her, too. When she reached puberty, he had told her about her father, Samyaza. If not for him, she would never have known anything about her celestial heritage. Her life would have turned out very differently. Father Domenico was older now, but the kindness in his eyes had never dimmed. He was a good person. And he would know what was happening. She was sure of it.

She leaned forward, eager to hear what he would say about their news. "Last night someone opened the first seal of the Apocalypse."

He frowned. "I don't understand." He looked at Harriet. "Who told you this?"

"An angel," Annabeth replied. "He came to us for help. And then Harriet saw Pestilence in the city an hour ago. He's already begun infecting the city's humans."

Father Domenico shook his head slowly, troubled. "I cannot believe this."

"We saw the opened seal ourselves, Father. It was hidden beneath the altar at St. Peter's. The angel who guarded it was killed."

"But this is impossible. A seal, opened?"

"Surprise, bitch," Theodora whispered under her breath.

Annabeth pressed on urgently. "Father, we need to know what the angels are doing about this. If Samyaza opens more seals—"

He looked at her sharply. "Samyaza is behind it? The angel has told you this?"

"Yes. He thinks Samyaza is trying to start the Apocalypse."

The priest sat back. Concern lines creased his face like parched earth. "This is a very serious thing. Very serious indeed."

"Yes, that's why we're here. We need you to find out—"

He held up a hand, stopping her. His expression turned pained. "My child, I cannot help you."

She blinked rapidly, taken aback. Of all the possible reactions he could have had, she hadn't expected this one. "What do you mean you can't help us?"

He took off his glasses and set them gently on the desk, then rubbed his temples, sighing heavily. On the mahogany paneled wall behind him, the dark oil paintings of the church's previous priests stared down gravely at the women, the unbroken lineage of St. Francis's clerics. It was as though they were all listening…but equally unable to help. He started, "It is true that for many years, I assisted the angels to do God's work on Earth. In that time, I was shown and told many things." He looked at Annabeth significantly. "Some of these things I have even told you."

His gaze drifted to an invisible horizon and he sighed a second time. "And so you must understand that I wish I could help you now. But it is impossible. I cannot tell you what the angels may be doing because, my child, there are no angels here now. They have left the city."

"What do you mean they've left?" Harriet asked, alarmed. Annabeth could almost swear her hair was standing on end.

"It happened many, many years ago."

Theodora snorted. "Bullshit. We saw one this morning. And Harriet saw one last night. They haven't left the city. Guess they're just not talking to *you*."

Annabeth cringed. Perhaps she should have asked Theodora to wait outside. Now was not the time for her to mouth off. Father Domenico returned his glasses to their rightful place perched on his nose and looked at Theodora levelly, undisturbed by her disrespect. He nodded, as if accepting the argument's validity. "A few angels have not yet left, but I tell you, the rest have gone."

Annabeth felt a tiny thrill of satisfaction. So they'd been right. The angels *had* abandoned the city to rot. It was nice to finally receive a confirmation of what they had long sensed, even if it was simultaneously very bad news.

"Father, why did they leave?" she asked.

He shrugged. "They were recalled to Heaven, perhaps, or sent elsewhere in the world. I was not told. All I know is that the city has lost her angels. Uriel, the cherubim, the malakim, they are all gone."

Arakiel's words came back to Annabeth. *I've been having trouble reaching any of the leadership of the host.* Now they knew why. Or at least some of the why. The phone was ringing but no one was home.

"So what happens now?" Harriet asked, bringing the conversation back to the issue at hand. "If he hasn't already, Samyaza could open the second seal any minute. Will the angels come back to stop him?"

Annabeth winced. Once her father opened the seal, he would have *two* Horsemen at his disposal. And he would be that much closer to bringing on the full Apocalypse. But surely the angels wouldn't allow it. Whatever their original reason for leaving, they would return…

"It is clear what must happen now," Father Domenico replied.

A beat passed.

"You must try to stop him."

"Us?" Annabeth squawked, startled. That…was not at all what she had expected him to say.

"But of course. You stand with one foot in the human world, one foot in the celestial world. Who better to challenge Samyaza?"

"We can't fight Samyaza!" Harriet protested.

They were three half-humans. He was a fallen seraph with the entire Daemonium behind him. It wasn't David and Goliath. It was three ants against a tank.

Father Domenico sat back in his chair. His eyes traveled over his guests. "If not you, then who, my child? The city cannot defend herself. You know this. With the angels gone, only you are left."

Only you.

"Excuse me." Annabeth rose abruptly. The room was pulsing around her like a beating heart, each contraction pulling the walls in closer. She needed air. She staggered outside, closing the door behind her with shaking hands. She stood on the steps, her back to the church, and took a deep breath, trying to calm herself. If she closed her eyes, she could pretend the city was no different than it had been yesterday, before the first seal had been opened and her own father had set in motion the end of the world. But he had, and now she was being asked to try to stop him. As if that was even possible.

Her phone vibrated in the pocket of her black cigarette pants. She pulled it out and scanned the incoming text. *The kids asked for funfetti pancakes for dinner. Hope Theodora doesn't mind. Bon appetit!* She stared at the text for a moment, immobilized by the cognitive dissonance of her husband going about his life normally and her newfound knowledge that unless she, Harriet, and Theodora could find a way to stop Samyaza, that life was about to be destroyed. This must have been how the first citizen of Pompeii felt when they noticed Mount Vesuvius erupting.

The door opened behind her with a soft metallic squeal. Theodora stepped out. She looked at Annabeth, peered down the alley as though searching for something, then said out of the side of her mouth, "You know when I said you needed more excitement in your life?"

Annabeth nodded.

"I take it back."

Annabeth snorted. "I don't think it works like that."

Theodora smiled faintly. "Worth a try."

The corners of Annabeth's lips tugged down. Her chest felt tight. "The angels will come back, right?" She hadn't felt this much like a child since she'd actually been a child. All she wanted was an adult to come fix things. And maybe a cookie.

"Pfft. Of course they will. Arakiel's probably gotten in touch with them already."

At that moment, Theodora's phone chirped. Frowning, she pulled it from her jacket pocket and scanned the screen. Immediately, her face filled with concern.

"What?" Annabeth asked, dread trickling into her stomach like a water leak.

Theodora pressed her lips together briefly as if to hold the words in. "It's Andromalius. He's ordering us to come in."

Annabeth's heart dropped to her stomach. Her hands moved unconsciously to cover it, as if she could defend it from the bad news. "Come in? To the office?"

They rarely visited Andromalius's office. He preferred to conduct his business by text. That was just fine for Annabeth. She hated visiting the Daemonium's office. Theodora nodded.

Annabeth swallowed hard. "Do you think he knows?" Her question lacked specificity. What could he know, given they themselves knew all but nothing? But he had a knack for finding out about things, at least eventually.

Theodora put her phone back into her pocket, face grim. "I don't know. But if he somehow found out we met Arakiel, we're fucked."

CHAPTER SEVEN

Fuck. Fuck, fuck, fuck, fuck. The words were a rhythmic drum beat in Theodora's head. They made her ears ring, as though she had tinnitus. She rubbed the head of the kusarigama at her waist hard, until the smooth metal made her thumb throb. Andromalius was a fucking bloodhound. They'd always known that. He could sniff out trouble a mile away. But how the *fuck* had he smelled *them* out so soon?

A demon must have seen them at St. Peter's with Arakiel. But what was Andromalius planning to do about it? He wasn't known for his sympathy and understanding. He was a shoot first, ask questions never kind of demon. But he might also be curious what the angel was up to. If they were lucky. Maybe there was an opening there.

"When we get there, let me do the talking," she said. Her voice was tight with the same tension that filled the cab like static electricity, thick enough that even the driver must have felt it. It was a long shot, but there was a chance she could talk just fast enough to keep Andromalius from doing something rash the moment they walked through the door. After all, despite whatever he'd been told, they weren't helping the angels. No one could prove that. And she would educate him on that point if he gave her the time to say it before trying to extract her spine from her body.

"It could just be a coincidence and he wants us to do a revocation," Annabeth suggested hopefully from the back seat.

Theodora didn't bother answering. They all knew this had nothing to do with a revocation. If it had, Andromalius wouldn't have called them in to the Daemonium's office. No, he knew something. The question was what.

"Maybe we shouldn't go." Harriet's mouth was pulled down at the corners into a tight frown. Her body was tense, her shoulders hunched. Her hand moved in her pocket, playing with something there. "There's still time."

Still time. Time to ask the taxi driver to turn the fuck around and drive as far and as fast as he could out of town. Time to come up with a plan for what to say to Andromalius that might keep them alive. Samyaza's second in command had informants, but he wasn't psychic. He wouldn't know they'd skipped town for at least an hour, especially if she texted excuses about traffic or some other delay. If they left now, they would have a head start, even if it was a small one. But no.

"Andromalius would come after us. We don't need every goddamn demon in the world looking for us," Theodora growled. Running might buy them time, but only a few days, if not hours. And then when the agents of the Daemonium caught up, the three of them would be in *really* big fucking trouble. Andromalius had had many human lifetimes to learn some creative torture methods, and he loved a good opportunity to use them. She licked her lips. Her mouth was dry.

"I'll talk to him," she repeated, more insistently this time. But she didn't know whether she was trying to convince them or herself.

She avoided catching Annabeth's reflection in the rearview mirror. A few dozen blocks away, two boys were sitting at their desks at school. If Theodora wasn't clever enough, they wouldn't have a mother to come home to today, and Jonathan would be a widower. She shifted her hand to run her thumb along the sharp edge of the kusarigama, almost hard enough to break the skin but not quite. She respected Annabeth's choice to fall in love and have a family. It had made Annabeth happy. But it had been risky. There was always the possibility that the unthinkable would happen. Now, after all these years, her luck may have finally run out.

At least there would be no one waiting for Theodora or Harriet if they didn't come home. No strings meant no broken hearts. No mourners at a funeral. Theodora didn't even have so much as a goldfish or a houseplant. If she didn't make it back, nothing would die because of her. It was better that way. For everyone.

"I hope he doesn't throw us out the window," Harriet muttered darkly.

It wasn't an imaginary scenario—they had seen it happen a few years ago. The demon whom Andromalius had defenestrated in a pique of rage had flown like a lead balloon nineteen stories to the ground, where he had done his best, one-time-only impression of a bug against a windshield. Theodora winced, remembering the bright red blood splattering against the pale concrete right in front of them and onto their shoes. She had no desire to personally reenact the scene in the starring role. She shrugged, feeling the pistol rub against the inside of her arm. "We'll fight our way out if we have to."

She meant it. She would never go down without a fight, not to Andromalius or anyone else. But in truth, it wouldn't matter. If she couldn't talk their way out of whatever he knew or thought he knew, it was all over. The Daemonium's office building was like a beehive, filled with hundreds of demons who would come swarming out of every door and crevice to stop them if they tried to escape. They could fight, but they wouldn't last five minutes.

Theodora risked glancing at the back seat. Annabeth was playing with her phone, turning it over and over in her hands. Theodora could read her mind. Should she contact Jonathan? Should she give him a heads-up that she might not be coming home? Theodora knew the decision she would make. No. She wouldn't.

The Daemonium's office was a twenty-story building at the exact geographic heart of the city. It was an unremarkable, almost bland building, a blue-tinted glass rectangle surrounded by similar but slightly taller neighbors. It was, Theodora thought every time she saw it, exactly the banal, boring shit that would appeal to the sadistic yet obsessive-compulsive fucks in charge of all the demons on Earth. Sleek, shiny, and modern, no human would know from looking at it that inside could be found the machinery powering all demonic activity on Earth. Although to be fair, that wasn't so different from all the other office buildings in the city. The Devil came in many forms, most of them obscenely bureaucratic and soul-sucking.

Theodora didn't like going to the building. Not because it was the greatest source of evil in the world, but because she hated the demons themselves. In her experience, they were all assclowns. She worked for them, but that didn't mean she respected them. Nor, for the most part, were they as big and bad as they pretended to be. With very rare exceptions, a demon could only influence someone who was already predisposed to doing bad acts. So really, all they were doing was nudging someone to be worse than they already were and taking credit for the whole shebang.

She felt a twist in her gut looking at the reflective glass. If she had to die, she'd rather not die in *there*, surrounded by a bunch of yellow-eyed fucknuggets in suits whose cousins she'd spent years sending back to Hell. She'd rather choke on a tater tot.

"We should have some sort of a strategy," Annabeth suggested, subconsciously fingering the morning star at her waist. She stared up at the building as though she could see through it all the way to Andromalius's office.

"Our strategy is to not die," Theodora deadpanned.

"Theodora! I mean about how to handle Andromalius."

"Same thing."

"I could try to touch him," Harriet said quietly. "Maybe I could find out what he knows."

Technically, Harriet's visions of the future were a form of psychometry—she only received them after touching someone's skin. It's why she hadn't foreseen the opening of the first seal or running into Pestilence outside of the hospital. Ordinarily, she was careful to never touch demons, especially during a revocation. She had seen Hell itself more than once, and other things she refused to describe. Her offer to touch Andromalius was therefore a big sacrifice. There was no telling what awful things she might see.

Theodora shook her head. "No."

First of all, short of tackling Andromalius and pinning him to the floor, there was no chance Harriet would even get close to him. He was an arrogant fuck who liked to either sit behind his desk or pace in front of the window. He kept far away from his minions, and that included the three of them. Second of all, even if she did manage to make contact and see a glimpse of his future—something that wasn't a given, since her affinity was sporadic and unpredictable—there was no way she could communicate what she'd seen to the other women, not while they were standing in front of him. But it was a moot point anyway. They didn't need a vision to know their future. Andromalius would either twist their heads off like bottle caps the moment they stepped into his office, or they would live. With Andromalius, there wasn't a gray area.

Harriet nodded, accepting the decision without protest. She took a breath, her expression serious. "Well, I just want you guys to know I appreciate—"

"Oh, stop it. We're not dead yet," Theodora snapped. "I told you, we're not giving up. And if Andromalius tries to kill us, we're lopping that smug fuckweasel's dick off first."

She raised her chin defiantly, a show of courage meant to stiffen her companion's backbones. But as she struck out toward the building's front door, she cast one last surreptitious look at Annabeth. Fuck. She should never have had those goddamn adorable kids.

Theodora was always simultaneously impressed and repulsed by Andromalius's office. The dark, moody room was almost as large as her entire apartment and crafted with exactly the type of interior design one would expect of an immortal, demonic mob boss. Near the door, a larger-than-life fifteenth-century oil painting of goat-headed Bahomet reached floor to ceiling. A long aisle of black marble, inlaid with a gold pentacle at the middle—Annabeth said that when she looked at it, it burned white-hot with demonic fire—led to a massive ebony desk, the only piece of furniture in the room. The walls on the left and at the far end were glass, tinted darkly. Because illumination was provided by electric sconces set along the wood-paneled wall like torches, walking into the room always felt like stepping into a wine cellar where someone was about to be ritually sacrificed.

Andromalius's back was to them when they entered. He was looking out the window behind his desk, surveying the city. He turned when he heard them and motioned sharply to the demon that had escorted them. "Go." There was a vicious, angry snap to the word. It didn't bode well.

The redhaired demon bowed and retreated from the room, closing the door behind her. Her departure gave Theodora a grim shot of optimism. Without backup, it was three against one if Andromalius tried to yeet them out the window. He might still succeed, but it would be a lot harder than if he'd kept backup. This suggested he had other plans for them. Perhaps Annabeth was right and he didn't know anything about Arakiel. Or he felt like a bit of a workout.

Andromalius took several steps toward his guests, yellow eyes sweeping over them impatiently. If he hadn't been a demon lord, Andromalius would have fit in seamlessly as the unscrupulous, sociopathic CEO of a tobacco or diamond company. He had the look down pat, from his slicked-back hair to his egregiously expensive black suit. But he was a demon, and not just any demon, either. He was a monster of legend, a scourge upon generations of humans spanning centuries and continents. He was one of the bogeymen of mankind, a shadowy figure who had ridden with the likes of Genghis Khan and Attila the Hun. He had put his heel on the throat of entire civilizations and pressed until they had drawn their last gasp of air. Immortal unless the Daemonium ordered his revocation, he would continue to plague and torment the Earth until the end of time. Which was annoying as fuck given what an absolute dick he was.

"Took you long enough," he growled.

The head of a dark-gray snake was tattooed on the back of his left hand, almost completely covering it. The snake's body, hidden by his suit, wound up the rest of his arm all the way to his shoulders. As he got closer, Theodora realized with a stab of shock that the tattoo was moving. The black mamba—a real snake, not just a tattoo—raised its head and opened its mouth in a silent hiss, exposing a pitch-black mouth. She took an automatic step back. She had seen Andromalius's demonic affinity only a few times. The snake was an extension of the demon himself, like a sixth finger, but with long, venomous fangs.

Shit. Her mind panicked. So this was how he was going to kill them. Bite them and watch as they went into cardiac arrest. Her fingers, stiffening with fear, felt for her kusarigama. She might not be able to hit the fast-moving snake once Andromalius released it off his arm, but she could definitely reach him before the venom started to shut her body down. She would still die, but it would be better than nothing. Beside her, Harriet shifted, and she knew the other woman must be regretting that she couldn't unobtrusively reach for her weapon.

But the snake didn't launch itself to the ground and come slithering at them with terrifying, inescapable speed. Instead, Andromalius absently stroked it on the head with the index finger of his right hand in a light, self-soothing caress. It took a moment for Theodora to realize he wasn't going to kill them. And that the demon in front of them was not the Andromalius they knew. His face was devoid of its usual cocksureness, replaced by an emotion Theodora belatedly recognized as fear. When he was a few yards away, she saw he was actually sweating. In an instant, her fear was gone, replaced by curiosity. Something had happened, and whatever it was had been sufficiently dramatic to scare even him.

"Come," he barked.

He swept past them, the snake staring at them with tiny, black, emotionless eyes like onyx, and threw open the door to the hallway. He didn't so much as pause to confirm that his guests would follow him out. No one disobeyed a direct order by Andromalius.

Annabeth looked at her companions, concerned, as they fell in line behind him. Theodora was about to shrug, indicating her own confusion about the situation, when she saw the demon press the elevator call button. But not just any button. Her breath immediately caught in her chest. The first whispers of panic tickled her skin, freezing pinpricks that made the hair stand up. She had been scared before. Now a new feeling that transcended mere fear swept through her.

Although the building had twenty stories, in the many years the women had worked for the Daemonium, they had never gone above the nineteenth, where Andromalius's office was located. The twentieth held Samyaza's office, accessible only by a special key in the elevator. And Andromalius had hit the up button.

Theodora's legs turned to spaghetti. The Daemonium had found out everything. Samyaza was going to do to them things that made Vlad the Impaler and Ivan the Terrible look like cuddly teddy bears playing with puppies at a children's tea party. Even the merciless, bloodthirsty Andromalius was scared of what Samyaza was about to do to them. They were beyond fucked. One day, people would tell stories about just how fucked they were. They were fuckity-fuck fucked.

The elevator door opened and Andromalius stepped inside. He turned to face them with a closed expression. As if by tacit agreement, the three women balked, refusing to follow. It was better to die here, on this floor, than up there. Andromalius's face twisted into a sour scowl. "Get in the fucking elevator, you dipshits."

The words were like a magic spell. The women automatically obeyed, folding themselves into the small space obediently. It might as well have been a coffin. The elevator gave a slight jerk and then started to rise. Andromalius's eyes were fixed straight ahead, giving away nothing.

Then he spoke. His words were low and measured. "What you're about to see doesn't leave here, do you understand me?"

Theodora bit her lip. She might be about to watch her own head be literally shoved into her anus. Clearly, there was no risk she would be telling someone about the experience. The elevator shuddered to a halt. The doors whooshed open soundlessly.

And all hell broke loose.

Samyaza's office looked as though a bomb had gone off inside it. Chunks of red plaster ripped from the wall littered the floor, whose black marble tiles were cracked and ground into dust. A massive golden chandelier with what must have been hundreds of glass crystals had fallen to the floor and shattered, spreading sharp shards everywhere. The room was so chaotic and overwhelming that Theodora didn't know where to look. Her eyes glanced off all the destruction, unable to comprehend it. What the fuck had happened here?

Her eyes found the left wall, the apparent origin of the turmoil. A section had been blown apart, leaving a gigantic, ragged hole in the drywall. Through it, the building's innards were exposed, wires and rebar like the veins and arteries of a living creature. Not many things could have caused this kind of damage—an actual bomb, for example, or perhaps some sort of structural defect. Then—

Arakiel had sought out the women to ask their help protecting the second seal. He had foreseen Samyaza would come for it and knew he couldn't defend it alone. But he hadn't said anything about protecting himself, even knowing it could only be opened with his blood. Now he was dead. And the seal was open.

But Arakiel hadn't simply been killed. He had been butchered. His crumpled form lay in a puddle of blood that seemed far too voluminous to have ever all fit in his body. His wings—translucent and multicolored in life, turned to white feathers like a swan in death—had been hacked off and trod on. His eyes, open and staring behind skewed glasses, looked surprised, as though he couldn't believe he had met his end. Theodora couldn't believe it either. Only a few hours ago he had been alive, talking to them. Now this.

Even though she'd threatened to kill him herself, Theodora nevertheless felt a mixture of horror and pity for the angel. This was brutal, the work of a monster. Beside her, Annabeth dry heaved. They'd seen plenty of carnage in their time as revokers, but even Theodora felt a little queasy looking at the macabre scene.

"Shit," Harriet said softly beside her.

Theodora tried to remember which of the Horsemen the second seal contained. In the shock of the discovery, her mind had gone blank. What had Samyaza let loose in the world? And more importantly, what the fuck were they going to do now? Two Horsemen were free and one of the last remaining angels in the city was dead. Things had gone from bad to really fucking worse.

But... She frowned. Something was wrong about what she was seeing. Why was Arakiel's mortal husk still lying there? She would have expected the body to have been carried out and disposed of by the Daemonium's minions immediately, the blood mopped up and some sort of tarp put up over the wall until repairs could be made. The fact that everything still looked as though a tornado had touched down inside it was...weird. And why show the three women the room at all? The seal was opened, its Horseman dispatched to fulfill whatever task Samyaza had set him to. Unless Andromalius was about to hand them brooms, why had he brought them here?

The high lord's office was grandiose and imposing, as befitted the highest-ranked demon on Earth. It looked more like a reception hall than a room, with walls that reached almost thirty feet high. Samyaza's desk was located at the far end. It was so far away, in fact, that Theodora hadn't particularly noticed it when they'd stepped off the elevator. Now she did. And she immediately understood why Andromalius was behaving strangely.

The desk sat in front of a wall with windows inset as two stylish columns overlooking the western side of the city. There was a hole in each of the columns, as though a giant had punched through them with raging fists. And between them, hung upside down from the wall in an inverted crucifixion, was the high lord of the Daemonium himself.

Samyaza was dead.

CHAPTER EIGHT

When the Lamb opened the second seal, I heard the second living creature say, "Come!" Then another horse came out, a fiery red one. Its rider was given power to take peace from the Earth and to make men slay each other. To him was given a large sword.

Annabeth's mind refused to accept what she was seeing as reality. It couldn't be. It simply wasn't possible that Arakiel was dead and the high lord of the Daemonium with him. Andromalius had brought them onto the set of a movie, or he and Samyaza had set the scene up using red dye and corn syrup in some sort of twisted, demonic practical joke. Any second, someone wearing a headset and carrying a clapperboard would materialize to announce a scene cut. Arakiel would then stand up and reveal that his wings were actually tucked behind his back and the wings on the ground beside him were cheap props. Samyaza would lift his head and flex his arms, shaking out the heavy, swollen feeling in them.

That was what should have happened. But it didn't.

There was no movie, and the demons would never stage a practical joke. They were, as a species, humorless. What she was seeing was real. Something had gone terribly, egregiously wrong in Samyaza's office, something not even the high lord had seen coming.

She stared at her father's body, recognizing it only by context. Although it was far away, she could see that blood had run from his slit neck over his face and into his black hair, dying both a gruesome red as though someone had thrown paint on him. The sight made her shiver—but from horror at the violence, not out of sympathy for him or sadness at the loss. He was her progenitor, but that was all. Their genetic bond was the only thing that linked the two of them. In all the years of her life and in all the times she'd come to the office of the Daemonium, they'd never met. He was a stranger.

Whoever had killed Samyaza had stripped him down to his white underwear before fastening him somehow (Annabeth couldn't yet see how) to the wall. The meaning was clear. His body had been staged as a perverse imitation of Christ on the cross, a mockery of Christianity's most iconic symbol. She swallowed down the bile that filled her mouth, determined not to retch again. The violence in the room was nauseating, even to someone who routinely had to wash arterial spray off her clothing. But she couldn't show more weakness to Andromalius. Nothing was more dangerous than showing weakness around a demon.

"*Fuck.*" Theodora managed to imbue the word with awe, surprise, and amazement. It was an entire paragraph distilled into a single syllable. "Who the fuck kills the high lord of the Daemonium?"

Who indeed? There was no demon on Earth more powerful than Samyaza, and even in Hell the list was impressively short, or so they'd heard. Samyaza had been stripped of much of his power when he fell, but a fallen seraph was still formidable. That whoever killed him was even more powerful was a thrilling—and chilling— idea. Annabeth's mind quickly cycled through possible culprits. Could it have been the Horseman he'd just released? Arakiel had said that whoever opened a seal controlled what lay inside it, but what if he had been wrong? The angel clearly hadn't known everything, or he wouldn't have ended up here, dead. The newly freed Horseman could have turned on Samyaza and—

"But he's not *dead* dead, right?" Harriet's question interrupted Annabeth's train of thought. The other woman was staring at the high lord's body skeptically, as though at any moment the gaping wound at his neck might seamlessly close and his eyes pop open.

And that was...perfectly possible. Likely, even. Andromalius's reaction indicated that the high lord hadn't been condemned by the Daemonium, and that meant although he had been killed, he hadn't been revoked. Since he wasn't prohibited from returning to Earth, he could spring back to life at any moment. She shifted uneasily, crossing her arms to unconsciously create a barrier between herself and his body. She didn't want to be around when he resurrected. He wouldn't exactly be in a good mood.

Andromalius's answer was terse and unhappy. "He's gone. Toast." The snake had slithered out from his sleeve and wound itself around his neck, its head rising to lick the air at his shoulder. Annabeth realized then how much she didn't like snakes.

"Revoked?" Harriet followed up.

"No. But gone. He won't be coming back to Earth."

"Who—"

He interrupted before Annabeth could finish her question. "You know who did it." He pointed an agitated, well-manicured finger at the dead high lord. Fury and hate burned in his yellow eyes, making them glow. At his shoulder, the snake hissed, a surprisingly loud and throaty sound. Annabeth jumped. She hadn't known it could make sounds. "Those bastards flew in here and killed him. Uriel or Michael must have done it, those fuckers."

Annabeth was shocked by the accusation. And yet, for the windows on the twentieth story to be broken, someone (or someones, she supposed) must have flown through them. That meant the killer had wings. And not only could an archangel probably have overpowered the fallen seraph, they could have revoked him as well. Andromalius's was a more than logical conclusion.

In an already unbelievable day, this was an unexpected twist. But possibly an optimistic one. Could it be the angels had come back to the city? Given Samyaza had already opened two seals, they were a bit late, but at least they were here now. She observed Andromalius, now the acting head of the Daemonium, more closely. Although his face was twisted with anger and loathing, underneath it was the same nervous fear he'd exhibited in his office. If the angels could kill Samyaza that easily, they could kill any demon. He must have been wondering if he was next.

In that moment, she realized he had good reason to worry. Samyaza wouldn't have acted alone in opening the seals. Surely all the Daemonium's leaders had participated, including Andromalius. The angels could be planning to take all of them out as punishment. There was every chance he would be next.

"What happens now?" Harriet asked.

It was a great question.

"This means war," Andromalius fumed. His fists and jaw clenched, muscles bulging under skin. "For thousands of years, we've kept our side of the bargain. We've never touched a hair on the head of an angel, not a damn hair."

Not for lack of trying, Annabeth suspected.

He continued, "This, this is an act of treachery. The angels will pay for what they've done. I've informed the leadership Downstairs—"

War. The word hit her like the jolt of an electric current, reminding her of the missing element in the room. She blurted out, "Where *is* War? Did the angels take him?"

Andromalius's face went blank. His rant was derailed. He blinked. "What?"

The second seal was open. That meant the second Horseman had been released. Since he wasn't in the office, he must have gone somewhere. But where? There were two possibilities: either Samyaza had deployed War to fulfill some task before he was killed, meaning that both War and Pestilence might be currently roaming the city, masterless, or War had been present when the angels arrived.

"The Horseman, War," she repeated. There was a significant risk he wouldn't appreciate the intrusive question, but it seemed imperative to discover what, exactly, became of the celestials once their master was dead. She could only hope they returned to wherever they came from. If that was the case, the women might as well celebrate Samyaza's death for another reason. The end of the world had been averted.

He scowled, irritated. "What the fuck are you talking about?"

It was too late for him to play dumb now. She tilted her head to indicate the jagged hole in the wall. "We know about the seals."

The women might as well admit they knew what had happened in the high lord's office before the angel's arrival. The jig was up for the Daemonium. Samyaza was dead and there was no way the angels would allow another demon anywhere close to the third seal. The Daemonium's scheme had been effectively stopped in its tracks.

But rather than finally admitting it, Andromalius only frowned harder, his thick dark eyebrows furrowing into a single line. "Seals? What seals? What are you talking about?" His eyes skipped to the other two women, looking for an answer from them.

A beat passed as his questions sank in. Then another. Annabeth realized his bewildered expression was genuine. He really didn't know.

"The seven seals of the Apocalypse," Annabeth tried, less certainly this time.

"What about them?" The words hadn't sparked even a flicker of recognition in Andromalius's face.

She sucked in a sharp breath. Andromalius was no accomplished actor. That meant he had no idea what Samyaza had been up to. *And* it meant he didn't know who Arakiel was or why there was a gaping hole in the wall. Samyaza hadn't told his own lieutenant what he had been doing. He had been moonlighting.

Harriet's eyes flickered to Annabeth. Her question was clear. Should they tell him? Annabeth nodded. They might as well.

Harriet explained, "Samyaza was opening them."

Andromalius narrowed his eyes, nostrils flaring. "I don't know what's going on or what the fuck you think you know, but whatever it is, you don't. Fucking seals of the Apocalypse? A demon can't open those seals. They're in Heaven. No one can get to them."

The snake slithered to his left shoulder, stretching out to get closer to Harriet. It opened its mouth, baring its long fangs. In response, Harriet put her left hand in her pocket, where Annabeth knew a knife would be.

Annabeth closed her eyes, trying to make sense of what she was hearing. So Samyaza hadn't told the Daemonium what he was doing. Why not? For how long had he expected his activities to go unnoticed by the other demons? He was starting the Apocalypse. He had to know it would prompt angelic intervention. So why didn't he give the other demons at least some kind of a heads-up that he was poking the angelic beehive?

Theodora spoke up for the first time. "Turns out you're wrong about that. Samyaza opened the first seal less than twelve hours ago at St. Peter's. Then this one." She indicated the hole in the wall.

Andromalius's head jerked. His bright eyes fastened on her, boring into her in a way only a demon's could. "Twelve hours ago? Samyaza wasn't even in the city. His plane landed at noon. He came straight here."

"What? Are you sure?" Harriet asked, startled.

He nodded impatiently. "Of course I'm sure. I sent the car myself. He called me on the way in."

The women exchanged surprised, confused looks. This was...a wrinkle.

"He had an accomplice?" Annabeth suggested.

If Andromalius was right, and there was no reason he wouldn't be, it was the only way Samyaza could have had the first seal opened in his absence. And yet, what other demon was powerful enough to have found Soraph, dragged him to St. Peter's, and killed him? Moreover, why would the high lord have delegated such an important task to someone else?

Andromalius waved a dismissive hand as the snake returned to his neck, disappearing into his collar with a sinuousness that made Annabeth's skin crawl. "Whoever you've been talking to is fucking you around. The angels attacked Samyaza, he killed one, then another one finished him off. End of story."

Annabeth gaped. He didn't believe them. But what did he think had blown a hole through the wall?

Andromalius played with his cuff links as the snake tattoo reappeared on the back of his hand. "In five minutes, a cleaning crew is going to come in and mop up. Until I hear back from Downstairs, I'm keeping *this*"—he motioned at the dead body at the other end of the room—"quiet. No one finds out what happened here, you got it?"

"Okay, but...what do you want *us* to do?" Theodora asked.

He had shown them the body for a reason, and it wasn't because Samyaza was Annabeth's father and he wanted her to have the chance to say goodbye.

The demon's jaw twitched. "I want you to find the motherfucker who murdered Samyaza and kill him. An eye for an eye. One of them for one of ours."

Theodora's mouth made a small, perfect circle of surprise and dismay. "Oh."

He glared at Arakiel's body with murderous eyes. "You have two days. If you can't eradicate that fucking bastard by then, it's war. We'll murder every priest in this city and burn down all the churches. The angels don't get away with killing the high lord. They'll pay for what they did."

"Assassinate an archangel or else the demons launch a pogrom against humans?" Harriet asked, eyes as wide as they could go.

Andromalius's nostrils flared. "Samyaza deserves justice."

The world spun around Annabeth. At any moment, she would either be flung to the ground or into space. Both were equally likely. Through the haze, a question found its way out of her mouth. "Why *us*?"

Of all the demons Andromalius could have called, why had he chosen three half-humans? They were hardly an elite paramilitary unit. Surely there was someone better qualified...

He checked his watch, heavy, gold, and chunky. "Four minutes." He looked up, his eyes sliding over the women with cold indifference. Then he explained. "A demon can't get within a hundred feet of an archangel. You half-breeds"—Annabeth winced at the insult—"might."

"How the fuck do you expect us to kill an archangel?" Theodora's expression vacillated between dismay, confusion, and disbelief. Annabeth realized the kusarigama at her hip, which was brutally effective against wayward demons, would be about as useful against an archangel as a pool noodle. Nor would her pistol, Annabeth's morning star, or Harriet's katana do any better. Every weapon on Earth, from a stick to a nuclear warhead, was equally useless.

Andromalius snorted. "Use a ballpoint pen for all I care. You figure it out." His expression turned dark. "But make it hurt. Make that fucker bleed for what he did to Samyaza."

Andromalius was used to being obeyed, but this was one order Annabeth was certain they couldn't fulfill. Without waiting for an answer, the demon spun away, heading for the elevator with sharp, determined steps. He didn't spare a final look at the destruction around him. He had already dismissed it from his mind, just as he had dismissed the half-humans. He had the Daemonium to run now. And a war to plan.

"Call me when it's done," he called over his shoulder as the elevator door opened soundlessly before him. Then he was gone.

The women stared at each other.

"What the fuck just happened?" Theodora asked. "What the *fuck* just happened?"

A dead angel. An opened seal. The assassinated high lord. Andromalius's total ignorance of Samyaza's secret hunt for the seals. The command to kill an archangel. The women had come to the building worried Andromalius intended to kill them. They had walked into a maelstrom.

"What do we do?" Annabeth asked. She genuinely didn't know.

"What do you mean what do we do?" Theodora replied.

"We can't kill an archangel, obviously!"

Harriet scowled. "This is so fucked up."

Theodora tugged at the edges of her leather jacket uncomfortably and glanced unwillingly at Arakiel's body. "Let the angels figure it out. This is their problem." Her bright red lips pressed together momentarily, then she added with a flash of anger, "They shouldn't have let it get this far. They should have stopped Samyaza before he opened the first seal."

"Then we'd have the same problem with Andromalius," Harriet pointed out. "We have to do something. Otherwise, innocent people will die. Andromalius wasn't bluffing about going after priests and churches."

Annabeth took a step back, horrified. "You're not suggesting we try to kill an archangel."

The idea was impossible for a variety of reasons, including, but not limited to, the fact that they had no idea how to find one, especially since there weren't supposed to be any in the city at all, and that even if they did, they had no idea which one was the *right* one.

"No, of course not." Harriet ran her hand through her hair, frustrated. Her face filled with anguish. "I don't know! I don't know what to do!"

"Fuck!" Theodora yelled, slamming her palms against her black jeans. "Why the fuck didn't we skip town when he called? We could have been halfway to another state by now."

Annabeth wished it was that easy.

"He'd have just found someone else," she reminded Theodora. "And then we wouldn't have found out about Arakiel and the second seal."

"Then what do we do? Pretend to look and hope the angels do something in the meantime?" Harriet asked.

"If they kill Andromalius, that solves our problem," Theodora said.

Annabeth looked around the room. They had probably three minutes left before the cleaning crew came. Three minutes until Samyaza's body would be bundled away like so much trash, dumped…wherever demons ditched the remains of earthly bodies. She walked forward, half-numb. This was the first and only time she would look upon her father's face in person. She didn't care about him and was glad he was dead, but nevertheless, something in her pushed her to see before the opportunity was lost forever.

She stepped over chunks of drywall, the rubber soles of her flats crunching against the shattered crystal. The air was heavy and still. While she was used to creating violent tableaux in the course of a revocation, she had never before walked into the aftermath of someone else's. It was unsettling. Almost dreamlike. She pushed through the feeling, focusing on putting one foot in front of the other.

The air that blew through the broken windows was unexpectedly chilly. It snatched at the strands of long black hair curled around her ears and made them dance. She hugged herself even tighter, although less because she was cold than as a defense against what she was seeing. Samyaza's desk sat on a dais, a modern throne for a modern bureaucrat. Over it, hung high in grim, brutal mockery, was his body. Playing with the wedding ring on her finger, she stared into the demon's blank yellow eyes, made more stark by the red around them. She didn't know what she was looking for, but covered as his face was with blood, if there were any commonalities between herself and him, she couldn't see them. If they had similar eyebrows or cheekbones, if their lips had the same shape, these shared features were lost in the distracting, matte red.

She wasn't sure if it surprised or pleased her that there was nothing familiar about the demon in front of her. She had never wanted a single thing in common with him. Since the day Father Domenico had told her about Samyaza and how he had purposely set out to destroy her mother using his ability to project terrifying visions into the minds of humans, she had wanted to be as opposite him as possible. Seeing him dead now, she didn't know what to feel, but she felt one thing for certain: relief. Samyaza had been an awful, terrible monster, and the world was better off now that he had been returned permanently to Hell.

"Come on, let's go." Harriet touched her elbow lightly. Her voice was soft and sympathetic.

Annabeth startled. Had she stared longer than she'd thought, sucked into the quicksand of memory and regret? She turned away quickly, troubled by the emotions welling up inside her. She neither needed nor wanted to see any more of Samyaza. He wasn't her father. Her adoptive father, Jerry, had filled that role. Samyaza was just one more dead demon, one more fiend who could never return to Earth to plague humanity. If she could have revoked him herself, she would have. But she had never had the chance, and now it was too late.

As she looked down to pick her way back to the elevator, her eyes caught the sparkle of glass on the dais, like hundreds of shattered icicles. She looked to the window nearest her, marveling at the size of the hole in it, and automatically began to reconstruct what must have happened. The black leather chair behind the desk had been pushed to the side, but otherwise there was no sign of struggle. Samyaza had likely been sitting at his desk when the archangel had flown through the window. Caught off guard, perhaps he had stood suddenly, thrusting the chair back. But the angel had dispatched him quickly, before he could defend himself, slitting his throat with the smooth cut of a blade.

It had been a clean kill, and when Samyaza's killer had hung his body (Annabeth refused to examine how, exactly), the demon had finished exsanguinating. The blood had pooled into such a large dark puddle beneath him that the angel had gotten it on his shoes, which he had tracked back into the office when he walked— Wait. She frowned and shook her head. No. Something was wrong.

With growing alarm, she followed the large, bloody footprints from the dais back to the seal and Arakiel. The footprints had marched with certainty, never deviating from their course. Then they were everywhere around the hole in the wall, mixing the high lord's dark blood with the angel's blood. A shiver ran through her body. She looked to her companions. "Samyaza didn't open the second seal."

Theodora's brows pulled together sharply. "What do you mean?"

She pointed at the telltale footprints. "His killer opened it."

CHAPTER NINE

The short hair on the back of Harriet's neck stood on end. "Are you sure?" She didn't doubt Annabeth, but the question was an instinctive response, a way to buy time as she absorbed the assertion.

Annabeth nodded and pointed to the pool of blood around Arakiel's body. "The footprints—they lead *to* the seal. Samyaza was already dead when it was opened."

Harriet took a step closer. Yes, Annabeth was right. Bloody tracks made their way toward Arakiel, then disappeared, covered by his blood. She rubbed the back of her neck, unconsciously trying to force the hair back down. Someone had killed the high lord and then, while his body was still warm, opened the seal.

No. That was an insufficient description. It didn't capture the full violence of what had occurred. Someone had brazenly breached the walls of the Daemonium, crashing through the window like a special forces operation, slaughtered the most powerful demon on Earth, then blown open the gate to let War into the world.

But just because it was clear *what* had happened didn't mean she understood *why*. She looked to the hole in the wall where the seal had been, trying to cobble together some sort of idea. "So Andromalius was right? Samyaza didn't open the first seal?"

Annabeth shook her head. "I don't see how he could have."

"And he definitely didn't open the second one."

"We know an archangel wouldn't have opened the seals," Annabeth offered. "But that means..."

"Someone really fucking scary did," Theodora finished for her, joining them. "Someone who sliced and diced the high lord like it was nothing."

"But who?" The list of beings that fit that description was incredibly short. Harriet rubbed her forehead. This was making her head hurt.

"Fuck if I know."

"What if it was Pestilence?" Annabeth suggested. "Maybe he killed Samyaza and opened the second seal himself."

"You think he went rogue?" Harriet asked. It was certainly an interesting idea.

"Maybe."

"Hmm. But he doesn't have wings," she pointed out. She was confident she would have noticed if he had. "He couldn't have flown through that window. And he carries a bow, not a sword, remember? Besides, why go rogue?"

"I don't know."

"And it doesn't answer who opened the first seal..."

"Okay, so it wasn't Pestilence!" Annabeth pouted, unhappy.

"Could there be something that's not an angel or a demon out there that we don't know about? Vishnu riding in on Garuda or some shit?" Theodora asked.

"Garuda?" Harriet repeated. She knew Vishnu, but the other name was new to her.

"Garuda's a bird...Never mind." Theodora waved her hand, dismissing the idea.

"I think we would have heard about other celestials before now," Annabeth said.

It was a conversation they'd often had at the beginning of their friendship. If there were angels and demons, were there other celestials too, like djinn? But they had decided the answer was no. At least, they had never seen or heard of anything else, not in their city.

An idea struck Harriet. "Could it be a demon? What if one of the demons from Hell incarnated here?"

The top ten big bad demons were exiled to Hell, barred by divine command from ever leaving it. If one of them had somehow found a way to make it to Earth, they definitely could have wrought this kind of damage. But discovering that Beelzebub, Leviathan, or Asmodeus was running around on Earth would be very, very bad news indeed. If there hadn't been enough evidence the end times were upon them, that would be the nail in the coffin.

Annabeth shook her head, making her chunky black earrings dance. "No. There's no way God would allow one of the archdemons to incarnate on Earth."

Theodora snorted. "Allow? God's already *allowed* two seals to be opened and the angels guarding them to be slaughtered. Are you sure He's paying attention to what's happening on Earth? Or *cares?*"

This was a reference to another long-standing debate: the extent to which God watched or cared about His creations. The existence of God was indisputable. But His emotional attachment to humans was more questionable, or at least when it came to those who lived in this particular city. And in a city already overrun by demons, what was one more demonic incarnation?

Annabeth frowned but didn't contest the point. "Even if one managed to incarnate, why kill Samyaza? They're on the same side."

Theodora shrugged. "Power struggle? Asmodeus shows up, demands Samyaza's swanky penthouse office, Samyaza refuses, and the archdemon guts him. Demons are assholes. One could have killed your dad just to be a dick." She nodded to Harriet. "It's not a bad theory."

Behind them, the elevator door slid open, revealing two old-looking, almost comically small cleaning ladies on either side of a rickety cleaning cart. A dirty mop tilted out of an equally filthy brown bucket. The demons pushed the cart out, one wheel squealing as it refused to turn in the right direction. They would have their work cut out for them cleaning up the blood of two celestials and sweeping away the broken plaster and tile. And what about the two bodies? There was no way they would fit on the cart. Harriet realized with a frisson of discomfort that they might be the kind of demon that could eat a body whole. She had no interest in seeing that in person.

"Come on, time's up," Theodora grunted.

As she marched toward the elevator, Harriet and Annabeth fell in behind her. The demons' yellow eyes observed them with dull disinterest as they exchanged places. If the demons wondered what had happened in the high lord's office, they didn't show it. They were the Daemonium's janitorial staff, and this was just one more mess to be cleaned up.

"Should we tell Andromalius Samyaza may have been killed by someone from Downstairs?" Annabeth whispered as the elevator began to descend.

"Why?" Theodora asked. "If we're right, he'll find out soon enough."

Harriet stared at her blurred reflection in the door. Like a Russian nesting doll, each issue they'd encountered so far today had harbored others inside. She ran her teeth over her bottom lip. "There's another problem. We still have no idea whether the angels know the seals have been opened, which means they may not know to protect the third seal. It only took whichever demon is opening the seals half a day to go from the first to the second. At this rate, all seven will be open in a few days."

"Jesus," Theodora cursed.

"Maybe the third seal guardian isn't on Earth," Annabeth suggested hopefully. "Maybe they left with all the other angels decades ago. Then the seal couldn't be opened."

It was an easy, perfect solution to the problem. But...

Harriet shook her head, troubled. "I don't think so."

"Why not?"

"I think the guardians have to stay with their seals." Harriet's forehead wrinkled with concentration as she expressed the problem she'd been pondering since she first saw Arakiel's body. "Arakiel knew he was in danger and that he would be hunted next. Couldn't he have gone somewhere safe? Then he would still be alive and the seal wouldn't have been opened." She paused, letting the idea sink in. "I think he didn't because he couldn't. If that's true, the next guardian may be a sitting duck, just like Arakiel was." She played with the switchblade in her pocket as she drew her assessment out to its logical conclusion. "And that means if we can't figure out which demon is opening the seals and stop them, we don't have long before the stars start falling out of the sky and we all die."

Ironically, perhaps, it was exactly what Father Domenico had already asked them to do. Only then they had thought the culprit was Samyaza. Now it was someone worse.

Theodora stared at her, horrified. "How the fuck are we supposed to do that?"

"If there's an archdemon in our world, you know who would know about it," Annabeth said. There was a thoughtful expression on her face. Predictably, she was already mapping out solutions.

"Oh, fuck no. We're not going there," Theodora snarled.

Harriet smiled, quietly amused by her reaction. Theodora wasn't wrong, but they didn't have a choice.

"Five minutes," she said. "We'll just be there for five minutes."

Any longer and someone would probably try to kill them anyway.

* * *

The Faithless Monk was not a dive bar. It didn't even aspire to one day better itself into becoming a dive bar. Instead, it relished being a cesspool of filth and stank. Even cockroaches had better taste than to patronize the nauseatingly grubby bar tucked in the alley of a neighborhood that had never, not once in all its existence, seen better days. It was, therefore, the perfect place for the seedy underbelly of the demonic world to fester and ferment. The Daemonium represented evil tamed by bureaucracy and harnessed for a strategic—if nefarious—purpose. The Faithless Monk, on the other hand, represented the unbridled, anarchic evil of the demons who lived on the margins of that system. Or as Theodora would have said, it was a bunch of stupid-ass dickweasels whom even the Daemonium hated but didn't quite care enough to have revoked.

The memory of their last visit hit Harriet at the same time as the smell of the rotting garbage piled against the wall beside the entrance. Two broken fingers, a knife lodged in her thigh, and one demon revoked with a pool cue later, it was more than clear they would not be welcome back. Oh well. This was the only way to find Cimaris. And, unfortunately for them, they needed her.

Harriet yanked the rusting door open and stopped dead for a moment as the combined musk of sweating demons, sour beer, urine, and vomit wheezed into her face like car exhaust. Behind her, Annabeth gagged. Composing herself as best she could, Harriet pushed through the stench, trying to inhale as little as possible. If a record had been playing, it would have scratched and fallen silent. Scores of yellow eyes turned to spotlight the women, full of burning, angry suspicion.

As the Daemonium's revokers, they weren't exactly anonymous. Their unpopular reputation often preceded them, especially in a place like this. Every demon in the bar knew who they were, and they assumed that if the women were there, likely one of them was about to be revoked. Since they didn't know who, they *all* became defensive. Hands moved to pockets and boots, palms finding weapons both real and makeshift. Harriet walked slowly, cautiously watching the movement around them. They couldn't afford for a brawl to break out. Even if they were able to fight their way to the exit, they'd lose their chance to collect information. Then there'd be no one else to talk to about which archdemon might have incarnated from Hell and was trying to destroy the world.

"Oh God, I think I just stepped in gum," Annabeth squeaked behind her. "I hope that's gum. Please let that be gum."

Two rough-looking demons in black leather jackets stood and moved around the side of the room in an unmistakable flanking maneuver. Spikes started to grow out of the arms of one of the demons, puncturing the leather. Harriet fought the instinct to put her hands on the set of knives tucked along the inside edge of her pants. It would only make the situation worse. She kept her hands out and visible, trying to telegraph that they came in peace.

A demon twice her size with a face that looked like it had been hit with a shovel grabbed a pool cue off the wall and clutched it in both hands, glowering at her from across the room. Trying to ignore him, she kept moving forward resolutely, angling toward the bar. The demons that had been sitting there sidled away as she reached it, oil separating from water. Cimaris, who had been watching their entrance with a sour face, set down the pint glass she'd been cleaning. She tossed her long, straight brown hair over her shoulder and crossed her arms. Elaborate gray tattoos reached in full sleeves from her fingertips all the way up her neck, stopping only at her chin. She looked as though she were being eaten by the art on her skin.

"You're bad for business," she grunted.

"We're not here to revoke anyone," Harriet said.

Cimaris looked back at her expressionlessly. "Do I look like I care? Fuck off. You're upsetting my clientele."

"That's a big word to describe a bunch of blobfish with hands," Theodora snapped.

The door behind them opened and then closed as some of the bar's patrons exited. At the same time, a demon who had been sitting at the far end of the bar edged closer to the women, a hungry expression on his face. Harriet gave him a hard look, encouraging him to back away. Sleaze was sleaze, whether it was a human or a demon. He licked the air with a black, forked tongue, and returned to his previous seat, still watching.

Annabeth dropped her voice, trying to evade the listening ears of the demons still in the bar. "We don't want any trouble. We just have some questions for you."

The Faithless Monk, that sweaty, rancid armpit of the world, was the epicenter of the demonic underground in the city. Almost all shady, unsanctioned demonic activities were either born here or passed through it in some way, and that meant Cimaris saw it all. No one knew more about what was happening in the demonic world than she did. Annoyed, the demon breathed out a dense puff of gray smoke. It curled around her mouth and under her nose before dissolving. The display was a warning: she was a fire-breather, and she wouldn't hesitate to roast them if she felt like it. Harriet had no desire for that to happen. She hated the awful feeling of her skin regenerating.

"Questions? What are you, the police? Does Andromalius have you half-breeds snooping around for him now?"

Ignoring the insult, Harriet gingerly placed her forearms on the bar, hoping she wasn't putting them into something sticky. "Did you hear about what happened at St. Peter's this morning?" Already, it felt like a lifetime ago.

The demon's yellow eyes narrowed and darted cagily between the women in front of her. She uncrossed her arms and picked up a dirty rag that hadn't been white in years. "Maybe." Her demeanor indicated the answer was yes.

Harriet sighed to herself, hoping that getting answers from her wouldn't be like pulling teeth. "We're here on official Daemonium business. We need to know what you've heard about it." She really *did* sound like the police. And it was mostly true. Andromalius *had* tasked them to identify who had killed Samyaza. But calling it official Daemonium business was a bit of a stretch.

Cimaris rolled her eyes and held up a rude finger inches from Harriet's face that had equally rude writing tattooed on it. "Fuck the Daemonium." She would never say that to an actual member of the Daemonium, but obviously she felt safe saying it to three half-human contractors.

Harriet ignored the provocation and waited. Under demonic law, Cimaris was required to help the Daemonium whether she wanted to or not. If she didn't, she risked punishment that could include being revoked. Harriet knew she wouldn't risk that. It was too big of a bluff to call, even for Cimaris.

Cimaris glared at her, testing her resolve, then after a moment, shrugged, relinquishing the fight. "A dead angel. Very hush-hush."

Of course the lower demons already knew. The city had all but no secrets when it came to them. But like any bureaucracy, that news was a bit slower to filter its way to the upper ranks of the Daemonium, which was why Andromalius was still in the dark about it. He had spies, but spy networks worked much more slowly than gossip networks.

"What else do you know?" Theodora asked.

Cimaris glanced around the bar, evaluating the mood. The other demons had relaxed slightly, but they were still watching the exchange intently. She glowered at them, reminding them to mind their own business, then returned her attention to the women. She shrugged. "No one can remember an angel ever having died before. We didn't know it was possible." She grinned, revealing teeth that had been filed into terrifying points. "Maybe someone's finally taking the angels down a peg."

"He was guarding the first seal of the Apocalypse," Harriet said. "Did you know that?"

There was no use hiding it. If Cimaris didn't know yet, she would soon.

Cimaris's expression turned guarded. "No." Unlike Andromalius, however, she didn't immediately reject the idea that the seal was located on Earth. She continued after a moment's pause, "But I may have heard of some strange happenings in the city this morning. Celestials that aren't angels or demons tend to stand out in this world." She looked Harriet up and down and then sneered. "Including half-breeds. Especially when they're on our turf."

Harriet ignored the jibe. She was used to it. Instead, she focused on what Cimaris had implied. Andromalius may not have known about the Horsemen, but some of the lower demons had evidently seen Pestilence. Possibly, some had even seen War already. Even if they hadn't known exactly what the Horsemen were, they had recognized them as anomalies that didn't belong in the human world. And word of them had gotten around in the parts of the community Andromalius considered himself too good to visit.

"So you knew a seal had been opened?" Harriet pressed.

Cimaris bared her teeth in a creepy facsimile of a smile. "Call it an educated guess. A celestial in white wearing a crown and carrying a bow is pretty...unique."

"Do you know who's opening the seals?" Annabeth asked.

The demon cast her a look of such searing disdain it could have melted plastic. "Is that what Andromalius sent you to find out? To see if a lower demon has been fucking around against orders? Well, he's a bigger dumbass than I thought if he thinks that. If it were that easy to kill angels and open seals, we would have done it already, wouldn't we?"

She had a point.

"Could someone from Downstairs have made it through to Earth and done it?" Harriet asked.

Cimaris narrowed her eyes and opened her mouth, undoubtedly planning to snark her. But then her eyes went wide and she sucked in a deep breath. Her fingers gripped the edge of the bar, her black nails like talons. "You think it's the fulfillment of the Psellus Prophecy."

Harriet stared at her blankly. "The what?"

Cimaris's standoffishness vanished in an instant, replaced by excited energy that crackled palpably in the air. "A thousand years ago, a monk in Turkey, Psellus, had a vision. In it, he saw Lucifer ascending to Earth and ruling over the humans for eternity." Her eyes sparkled, enthralled by the prospect. Needless to say, Harriet didn't share the emotion.

"But the Book of Revelation says—" Annabeth protested.

Cimaris's attention snapped to her. "Fuck the Book of Revelation. You think John of Patmos was the only one to see the end of the world? No. His version is just the most famous. There are at least five prophecies about the Apocalypse, two of which are included in the *Liber Rerum Occultarum*." She flashed that terrible imitation of a smile again. "When it comes to the future of this shitty world, it's almost fifty-fifty odds for us demons."

"What's the *Liber Rerum Occultarum*?" Annabeth asked. She looked like a librarian hearing about a fascinating tome for the first time.

Cimaris rolled her eyes, sneering. "Half-human mutts. You don't know shit about anything, do you? Think of it as the demonic Bible. Humans have theirs, we have ours."

Harriet was surprised. A demonic Bible? How had they never heard of it before? But then, who was going to tell them? They'd been raised in the human world by human mothers. Everything they knew about the demons they'd had to stitch together over time through experience, tidbits of information from Father Domenico, and clues from Andromalius and other demons. They knew far more than they used to, but even so, it still felt like they were constantly ten steps behind, never closing the gap. The women may have worked for the Daemonium, but that didn't mean they were let into the demons' secrets. At the end of the day, they were still half-human outsiders. And, it turned out, not even half-demon.

Although Harriet was curious what else was in the demonic Bible—she knew Annabeth would be absolutely dying to know—they didn't have time to go off on that tangent. Redirecting the conversation, she asked, "Okay so…what, Lucifer incarnates on Earth and opens the seals? Then what?"

The smile Cimaris turned on her made Harriet's skin crawl. It wasn't just inhuman. It was malevolent. "The Lamb of God comes. Opening all seven seals is the only way to get Him to incarnate again on Earth. Then Lucifer kills Him. Game over for the angels."

Harriet felt like someone had just thrown a bucket of ice water on her. What Cimaris had proposed was too awful, too horrific to even imagine. It wasn't just sacrilege—it was evil.

When she spoke, she tried to keep her voice level. The demons already didn't trust them. Showing any sympathy for humans now would only confirm the demons' doubts about their loyalty. "How would we know if that's what was happening?"

Cimaris continued to grin. "Humans will start to die." She turned her attention to Annabeth. "And dear old dad too. I hear Lucifer doesn't like competition."

She hadn't heard about Samyaza yet. Harriet wondered how long it would be until she did.

"Sounds interesting," Theodora said. "Do you have a copy of the book we can borrow?"

Harriet was amazed at how casual Theodora sounded, as though the execution of the Son of God and a mass genocide of the world's human population was inconsequential to her. Which…was not entirely incorrect. Theodora had strong anarchic traits and limited sympathy for strangers. If the world was going to burn, she would be there with the ingredients for s'mores.

Cimaris looked at Theodora with a belittling mixture of condescension and contempt. "Of the *Liber Rerum Occultarum*? No one has a copy. There are only two on Earth. They're written in the blood of a martyr and bound with human skin."

"Oh."

Of course it was. Leave it to the demons to eschew regular paper and ink.

Cimaris sighed and rolled her eyes again. For a demon who had walked the Earth for thousands of years, she sometimes looked and behaved remarkably like an immature teenage girl. "There's one in the public library. The rare books collection."

"There's a copy *here*, in the city?" Harriet asked. It was a hell of a coincidence.

Cimaris raised a thin, meticulously plucked eyebrow. "There are a lot of things in this city, haven't you noticed?"

Theodora rapped on the countertop, indicating closure. "Thanks for the information. We'll be heading out now." She caught Annabeth's elbow and started to guide her away.

As Harriet turned to accompany them, Cimaris shot out a hand and grabbed her by the wrist. Her fingers tightened with inhuman strength, holding her fast. "You may have Andromalius fooled, but not me. You're not—"

Harriet didn't hear whatever she said next because at that moment, time skipped forward. The floor turned upside down, dumping her into the alley outside the bar. For a moment, she was too dazed to think. Her knees hurt. Her palms were scraped. A pounding in her head suggested she had likely taken a blow. She blinked and waited for the world to come into focus. Although it was dark around her—night, she realized—there was just enough light to see the tattoos on her hands and arms, including gray plate armor that went from her left wrist to her shoulder. She coughed. Pale gray smoke came out of her nose as though she were a hoarse dragon.

The rest of her senses returned all at once. The smell of burning wood filled her nostrils, sharp and hot. Raising her head, she saw that the Faithless Monk was on fire, black smoke billowing out from every crack and crevice. Orange-red flames licked into the air from under the closed door. Screams and shouts filled the air around her, alerting her for the first time to the fact that she wasn't alone. Two demons lay face down in a glistening pool of blood on the concrete to her left. One of them was groaning. The other was motionless.

A demon engulfed in fire staggered out of the bar howling, and sprinted down the alley, his footsteps echoing behind him. Before he reached the end, he fell, smoldering. She struggled uselessly against the weight pinning her down, fighting to either help her fellow demons or escape, but it was useless. She was trapped.

Her head was yanked up violently by her hair. Her scalp screamed in pain. A face moved in front of hers until she was staring into a pair of bright, unnaturally blue eyes.

"In nomine Patris et Filii et Spiritus Sancti," the cruel mouth below them intoned.

Harriet's mouth moved, but it wasn't her voice that came out. "Fuck you."

There was a sharp stab of pain at the front of her neck, then the world went black.

Harriet fell back into the present with a sickening jolt. Cimaris was still speaking, but Harriet didn't hear a word she said. Horrified, she yanked her hand away from the demon, not even feeling when Cimaris's long, sharp nails left red scratches across her wrist. The demon's plate-armor-covered arm fell to the counter. Without a word, Harriet fled, the echo of beating wings still in her ears and the taste of smoke on her tongue.

CHAPTER TEN

"Shit. Did you get a sense of *when* Cimaris will be killed?" Theodora asked. They were far enough from the bar that any malingering patrons wouldn't hear, but still within eyesight of it as they walked back toward the street.

Harriet, whose mouth had carved itself into a tight, pained line after she relayed the details of her vision, shook her head, eyes on the pavement. "No. All I know is that it will be at night."

She reached up and rubbed the back of her neck. Then her fingers subconsciously slipped to the front, where Theodora knew the angel's sword must have cut Cimaris in Harriet's vision. Theodora felt a twinge of sympathy. It must have been terrible to vicariously experience the demon's death. But she didn't regret that it was Cimaris who was getting whacked. She'd yet to meet a demon whose death she regretted.

Annabeth looked back and forth between her companions. Her face was filled with bright optimism. "This is good news! It means the angels come back and start fighting. I knew they would. How could they not?"

Harriet shrugged, still looking uncomfortable. "I guess."

"Did you recognize the angel? Was it Uriel?"

None of them had ever seen the archangel Uriel. The closest they had come was an oil painting that hung beside Father Domenico's desk. It depicted the city's patron angel with long, wheat-colored hair and fire-red wings. Theodora suspected the portrayal was more idealistic than realistic, but given it was all they had, it was better than nothing.

Harriet crossed her arms, using her palms to press her elbows tight against her body. It was amazing how small she could make herself, even in her wool coat. That was her Thai heritage. She was thin as a rice noodle. Theodora, despite her Indian roots, was much bigger boned. Harriet shook her head. "No. It was a female angel."

"It's kind of weird, isn't it?" Theodora said.

"What? A female angel?" Annabeth asked, cocking her head quizzically.

"No, of course not. I mean why would the angels bother razing that shithole?" She glanced back at the bar over her shoulder. It might as well have been held together with used gum and some duct tape. "What's it got to do with all this? If Lucifer has incarnated on Earth, shouldn't they be concentrating on stopping him?"

Annabeth frowned and pawed at her pocket. Pulling her phone out, she read the incoming message quickly, then looked blankly at Theodora. "Jonathan wants to know what time for dinner."

Theodora threw up her hands a little. "I don't know, six?" She had bigger things to worry about than what time she might eat dinner. At this rate, they might not eat dinner at all anyway.

"Maybe we should make it five," Annabeth mused, half to herself. Her eyes had taken on a faraway look. "The boys could have schoolwork…"

Theodora shrugged. "Fine, whatever."

As Annabeth texted back furiously, Harriet returned to their previous line of conversation. "Maybe the angels are going to take a scorched-earth approach to the demons. They've found out Lucifer has incarnated on Earth and they retaliate by eradicating all of the demons' lairs."

"Do you think it *is* Lucifer?" Theodora asked.

"The fact that there's a prophecy about him opening the seals and now some impossibly powerful demon is opening seals seems like an awfully big coincidence." She buttoned her lips together and shook her head. "Then again, if it *was* him, you'd think every angel would be out here right now trying to stop him. And wouldn't the Daemonium have known?"

Right. Lucifer tiptoeing back to Earth through the back door and then keeping mum seemed out of character, at least based on the old stories about him. Then again, if he *was* on Earth, he'd been here fewer than twenty-four hours. It was hard to draw any firm conclusions about his behavior from that.

"We need to see this *Liber Rerum Occultarum*," Annabeth said with a firm nod, returning her phone to her pocket. She pawed at her bangs, pushing them away from her glasses. "Maybe that will help us."

Suddenly, she stopped dead. "Oh no."

The tone in her voice made her companions stop dead in their tracks. Theodora's skin immediately prickled. Her hand fell to her kusarigama. "What? What is it?" She followed Annabeth's worried gaze down the alley, but saw nothing—only blue sky, dirty white concrete, and stained green dumpsters.

"It's War." Annabeth's low voice hummed with alarm.

Theodora looked around with renewed vigor, still seeing nothing. "Where?"

She had forgotten Pestilence had used a glamour near Harriet. It looked like War had that particular ability too.

"He's about fifty yards in front of us."

Fifty yards was much closer than Theodora wanted him to be, especially given she couldn't see him. She drew her kusarigama as Harriet unsheathed the katana at her back. Harriet raised the sword above her shoulder into a ready position. "Does he look like he's going to attack?"

Annabeth pulled free her morning star, eyes fixed on a spot ahead of them. "Yes."

Theodora didn't know how they were going to fight an invisible opponent, but the question of standing and fighting or running back to the Faithless Monk immediately became moot as the Horseman dropped his glamour. One moment the alley was empty, the next it was filled by a giant wearing heavy red armor and wielding a massive broadsword. Theodora didn't even have time to absorb what she was seeing before he charged toward them with the mass and force of a locomotive. She was so stupefied by the sight of the towering celestial that she didn't move until she was almost in range of his swinging blade. Coming back to herself with a start, she dodged left, hearing the *whoop* of the metal as it sliced through the air close to where she'd been standing. A second or two longer and he wouldn't have missed.

"Holy shit!" she yelled. "How is he this big?"

If he was under seven feet tall, it wasn't by much. Harriet lunged toward him from the right, the tip of her katana slicing at his neck. If he had been a regular demon, the blow might have landed. But he was not. Moving with speed that belied his size, he spun and confronted her head-on, blocking her sword with his. The two weapons clanged as they made contact, one sharp and delicate as a boning knife, the other ponderous as a meat cleaver. Before Harriet even realized what was happening, he landed a fist the size of a head of cauliflower in her stomach, sending her flying backward into the rough concrete wall.

She hit hard and slid to the ground, so dazed her sword fell from her hands and to the ground beside her. Theodora winced, but she couldn't check on her. She couldn't let her attention drift from War for more than a second, lest he see her inattention and take advantage of it.

Jumping into action, Annabeth swung her morning star at War's half-turned back. He saw her coming, though, and easily parried her short weapon. The morning star slid down his blade all the way to the guard. As she struggled to disengage it, he raised his massive foot and brought it down hard on the inside of her left knee. She collapsed to the ground with a scream of pain. He raised his foot again, preparing to crush her beneath a boot the size of a cement block.

Before he could stomp down, however, Theodora swung the metal chain of the kusarigama like a lasso at his leg. It whipped up his calf, wrapping tight. She pulled with all her might, grunting with the effort. For a moment, she thought it wouldn't work. He was too heavy; it was like pulling a car. Then the Horseman crashed to the ground, landing heavily on his side.

He immediately rolled to his back and began kicking his leg to free himself. Harriet staggered to stand, her hand on her stomach, wincing. Theodora expected she'd cracked a few ribs, but at least that was all. It would have been worse if he'd hit her in the head. Or if he'd run her through with his sword.

"Get out of here," Theodora growled to her. The longer they stayed and fought, the more likely it was that one of them would be killed. They might have been good at revoking demons, but War was a foot taller and a hundred or more pounds heavier than any demon, not to mention heavily armored from head to toe. It was like fighting a bear in a suit of armor. There was no winning against him, only making it out alive.

Harriet tried to straighten and failed. "I can—"

"Go!" she roared. "We can't stand around punching this fucking tank. We have to get out of here. Go and we'll be right behind you."

It didn't matter that Harriet was their best fighter. She was hurt. And if she tried to keep fighting, she would only get hurt worse. Besides, they weren't fighting. They were surviving. Harriet looked uncertainly from Theodora to War to Annabeth, who was still on the ground but trying to crawl farther away from the celestial. Theodora knew what she was thinking.

"I'll make sure she makes it out," Theodora said.

That was what Harriet needed to hear. Nodding, she took off down the alley as fast as she could. It was little more than a doubled-over hobble, but it was enough. War wasn't going to stop her.

A moment later, the celestial clambered back to his feet. Theodora placed herself between him and Annabeth and braced herself. Pulling back the chain he'd kicked off, she prepared for his next attack. It came quickly. With an animal-like snarl, he rushed forward. He swung his sword up and then brought it down like an axe, trying to crush her skull. She jumped backward, unleashing the chain so that this time it wrapped around his hand. As the blade continued to fall, the chain twirled around it, binding the sword so he couldn't use its edge.

Springing forward, she slashed the hooked blade of the kama toward his neck, aiming for the exposed flesh there between his helmet and breastplate. But he was too fast for her. Before the blade could reach him, he jerked his body backward, dragging her with him so that she was almost pulled off her feet. He slammed his left fist down on her hand where it was holding the kama. Pain screamed up her arm as the small bones cracked like ice over a lake. Her fingers opened, no longer under her control, relinquishing the kama. It clattered to the ground. Cradling her hand, she backed up, out of his range, and glanced over her shoulder.

"Can you walk?" she asked Annabeth through gritted teeth. It took a significant effort not to put her broken hand between her knees and yell through the pain.

Annabeth had pulled herself to a standing position, leaning against the wall to keep weight off her left leg. She was in no condition to keep fighting, but could she make it out of the alley unassisted? Theodora didn't know how she could both fight War *and* support Annabeth. Annabeth met her eyes and nodded. She was breathing heavily, her jaw clamped tight. Theodora had seen that look of determination plenty of times. If Annabeth said she could do it, she could.

Theodora looked back at the Horseman, calculating. There was only one way out of the alley and he was blocking it. He planted his feet and raised his sword, as though reading Theodora's mind. With her left hand, she pulled aside the front of her jacket and drew her Desert Eagle. Celestials didn't just die like humans when shot. They often kept fighting after an injury that would have dropped a mortal. But desperate times called for desperate measures.

War's helmet reminded her of an ancient Corinthian helmet, with two eye holes and an opening for his mouth. It was an efficient, effective design, providing protection against a variety of weapons. But it wasn't invincible. And fast as War was, he wasn't fast enough to dodge a bullet. Holding her breath, Theodora aimed and fired.

The recoil was so strong the gun almost flew out of her hand. She had to fight to keep control of the bucking barrel, a struggle made worse by the fact that it was her nondominant hand holding it. Nevertheless, the shot went through the helmet's right eye hole, right on target. The Horseman's head was thrown back sharply, carried backward by the momentum of the bullet. For a human, the shot would have been fatal. But for a Horseman? He staggered backward, his free hand going to his face. He was hurt, but not dead.

Theodora reholstered the gun. They didn't have much time. She ran to Annabeth and threw the other woman's arm over her shoulder, taking as much of her weight as Annabeth would give her. "Let's go."

War took up most of the alley, but there was just enough space for them to slip past if they pressed themselves against the wall. And if War didn't recover enough to notice them. Theodora walked with quick steps, Annabeth hopping beside her. The Horseman howled, thrashing around with blood dripping from beneath his helmet.

"Are we just going to leave him?" Annabeth asked with concern as they cautiously passed him. He was too distracted to try to stop them.

"Yup," Theodora said. The angels could send his ass back to wherever he came from. Not her circus, not her monkeys.

* * *

"Why would War come after *us*?" Annabeth asked as the taxi carried them through busy streets. Her bangs were wild, contributing to how flustered she looked. She was gingerly trying to massage her left knee. "First Pestilence, now this. Why try to kill us? We're nobody!"

Theodora, in the middle of texting Harriet their destination with her left hand, looked up. "Fuck if I know." She scowled. "Why is any of this shit happening?"

The idea of taking the first flight out of town was fast gaining appeal. Let the angels deal with everything while she drank piña coladas on the beach. She'd never really taken a vacation. Maybe it was finally time.

"Do you suppose it's"—Annabeth dropped her voice so the taxi driver wouldn't hear her. As if he cared. He probably didn't even speak English—"because of who we are?"

Theodora looked at her sharply. "What do you mean?"

"Maybe the Horsemen have been ordered to destroy anything angelic." She didn't have to say aloud that as that as half-angels, that would include them.

Theodora drummed her fingers against her knee, thinking. Annabeth might be happy to believe they were half-angel, but she still wasn't convinced. Among other things, Arakiel's explanation that the Daemonium simply "hadn't noticed" its revokers' angelic nature was patently bullshit. Andromalius was a shithead, but he wasn't a stupid, oblivious shithead. Theodora found it equally or more likely that the angel had lied in an effort to secure their help. But whatever the truth, it didn't give her any more ideas for why War had attacked them.

She shook her head. "I don't know, but I don't like it."

Annabeth put her hand over Theodora's, just for a moment, her palm warm. "We'll figure it out. Maybe the *Liber Rerum Occultarum* will have some answers."

Theodora nodded automatically. Maybe they would figure it out. Or maybe they were pawns in a really fucking big chess game they didn't want to be in. That seemed more likely. And everyone knew that pawns were the most disposable pieces in chess.

Ten minutes later, the taxi pulled up in front of the library. Harriet was already there, waiting anxiously. She held the door open for Annabeth, either mostly recovered from the hit she'd taken in the alley or hiding it well. Annabeth, on the other hand, was still barely at the point of walking unassisted. She stepped delicately out of the car, limping painfully on the left side. Theodora flexed her fingers gingerly. The screaming pain from the fractured bones had mellowed a little, but she wouldn't be using that hand to punch anyone any time soon.

She grumbled, "We look like we just got our asses beat."

"We did," Harriet said. "At least Pestilence wasn't there."

Two Horsemen in that small alley and they definitely would have been toast. Theodora didn't want to think about that.

The library had been modeled in much smaller scale on the Stephen A. Schwarzman Building in New York. Its Beaux-Arts style and white marble were supposed to look elegant and Greek, but to Theodora, the architecture looked out of place, as much an anachronism as St. Francis Church. The future wasn't Corinthian columns and yellowing paper, it was slick glass and bytes of data. If the world managed not to end in the next few days, twenty years from now the building would be as outdated as eight-track players and pet rocks.

Giving Annabeth her arm to lean on, Theodora led the way in. The main hall of the library was reminiscent of the nave of a church—a long central aisle divided two rows of wooden desks, around which were row upon row of shelves. Pendant lights made to look like candle-lit chandeliers provided soft yellow illumination.

"The rare books section is this way," Annabeth said, pointing to the left.

Leave it to her to know its location. Theodora hadn't even known there was a rare books section. Although in her defense, she hadn't been in the library since she was ten years old, if not younger.

In a church, the room that held the books would have been called a side chapel. This secular version was not remarkably different. It was small and dimly lit. Since windows would let in harmful UV rays from the sun, it was windowless, and the only sound was the hum of a dehumidifier that ran softly in the background. Seeing the hundreds—thousands?—of books lined neatly on row upon row of shelves ten feet tall, Theodora adjusted her shoulders uncomfortably. "How do we find it?" It was like looking for a needle in a haystack.

Annabeth's eyes narrowed in concentration. She regarded the room with keen focus. "I'll find it."

Of course. Theodora should have realized Annabeth's affinity would be helpful here. Maybe it wouldn't be a needle at all.

Annabeth's head moved like a spectator at Wimbledon as her eyes traced the seemingly infinite lines of book spines. Since what Annabeth was searching for would be invisible to anyone but her, Harriet and Theodora stood idly, waiting. After a minute, Annabeth pointed. "There." Her voice was full of certainty.

She had indicated a large glass case, inside of which a book was opened to its midway point. Theodora led her to it, and all three women peered at it. The book was old, with discolored, unevenly cut pages and a fraying leather cover. The words were written in an unusual dark-brown ink. Theodora remembered too late what Cimaris had said about it—not ink but blood. She wrinkled her nose. Ew. Gross.

"How do we read it?" Harriet asked, examining the clear case. It was sealed on all sides, with no evident means of accessing the book inside.

Before either of her companions could answer, a round, balding man appeared seemingly out of nowhere. He leaned over their shoulders and into their personal space to have a look at the book. "The *Liber Rerum Occultarum*—The Book of the Occult. It's one of only nineteen confirmed anthropodermic books in the entire world."

"Anthropo...?" Harriet repeated, confused.

"Anthropodermic. It means made of human skin. And the practice of binding books in human skin is called anthropodermic bibliopegy. We're very, *very* lucky to have this piece. Most of the others in the world are held by medical or university libraries. The Historical Medical Library of the College of Physicians of Philadelphia owns five alone." The man—Theodora realized he must be a librarian—made a small, dismissive sound. "Well, of course France and the UK claim to have plenty of their own anthropodermic books, but no peptide mass fingerprinting has been performed on them and so they can't be confirmed. They're"—he sniffed, and the sanctimony rolled off him in waves—"probably bovine."

"Oh."

The librarian wasn't finished. "Before the discovery of this book, the oldest confirmed anthropodermic book was a copy of Vesalius's *De humani corporis fabrica*, held by the John Hay Library at Brown University. It was bound in 1867 in Brussels for the Paris International Exposition. *This* book, however, is significantly older. Some people believe it goes as far back as the eleventh century, although as you can imagine, there's fierce debate about that. If true, it would be one of the oldest books in the world, roughly contemporaneous with the Celtic Psalter now on exhibition at the University of Edinburgh."

He gazed fondly at the book. "Of course, most people who walk into this room have no idea they're looking at human skin. Anthropodermic book covers look just like every other kind of leather. To those patrons, it's one more old book."

Theodora didn't care about the Paris International Exhibition or whatever the fuck the Celtic Psalter was. They'd come to find out what the book said about Lucifer incarnating on Earth and the seals of the Apocalypse. She asked impatiently, "Can we read it?"

She might as well have suggested they eat a baby on live TV. The librarian looked at her with horror spawned from the very depths of his soul.

"Ma'am," he gasped. "Those are human remains. They must be treated with care, respect, and dignity by only the most carefully trained professionals. One doesn't simply *read* a book like that." He raised his chin and somehow managed to look down his nose at the women even though Theodora was taller than him. He looked like a puffed-up crow. "Besides, this book is priceless. It can't be handled by people uneducated in the care of rare and fragile books. It could be damaged."

Anger flushed through her body. Sanctimonious bastard. If anyone had a right to read the demonic Bible, it was a bunch of half-demons. Or half-angels. Whichever the fuck they were.

Beside her, Annabeth, who had been bent over examining the open pages, straightened. She sighed loudly, adjusting her glasses and blinking. "I suppose it doesn't matter anyway. What language is it written in?"

"Byzantine Greek, for the most part," the librarian answered promptly. "It was the language of the Eastern Roman Empire until the fall of Constantinople to the Turks in 1453."

Great. The book was unreadable. Somewhere, Cimaris was laughing her fucking ass off at them.

CHAPTER ELEVEN

"Do you want to know what I think?" the librarian asked.

"No," Theodora replied flatly.

Simultaneously, Harriet said, "Not really."

Pretending not to hear them, he continued anyway. "Some scholars of the text think it was created by a heretical sect of monks located in Asia Minor around the first millennium. These monks—if they really existed, because really there isn't much evidence for it—believed in the literal presence of angels and demons on Earth. There are even alternate versions of major events in Judeo-Christian history."

He rocked back on his heels and let his gaze travel over the wall of books in front of them with a sort of self-satisfied possessiveness, as though history and knowledge were tangible things that could be owned and these books represented his own, personal treasury. As if he were a dragon and this was his horde. "*I* think it's all junk." He pointed at the tome. "This book is more like the Voynich manuscript." He raised his eyebrows significantly, as though his listeners should recognize the allusion.

They did not.

His face falling a little, he explained, "I mean that it's a hoax. A clever and very detailed fabrication meant to enrage and mock the beliefs of the Byzantine clergy."

Harriet crossed her arms, feeling her coat stretch a little tighter across the katana at her back. They were getting nowhere. The *Liber Rerum Occultarum* was a dead end. *Everything* so far had been a dead end in terms of learning what was happening. They might as well go home.

Annabeth eyed the librarian with a combination of hope and defeat. "Is there anything in the book about the Apocalypse? Maybe the seven seals in particular?"

He shrugged. "I have no idea. I've never read it. You can find the full translation online if you're that interested. It's linked from the library website. Although I don't know why you would—"

Harriet had heard enough. It was clear they wouldn't be learning anything else useful, at least not from him. And she was hungry. It was dinnertime, and what with running around the city all day, she'd missed lunch. She was bordering dangerously close to hanger. She grabbed Annabeth's hand.

"Thank you. We'll be sure to look that up," she said.

He sputtered, "I could show you—"

"Nope, we're good."

And that was that. As they headed to the main door, Theodora looked sourly over her shoulder. "Well, that was a fucking waste of time."

"Not entirely," Annabeth said. "Now we know the book has been digitized and translated. Also, there might be an index or a word search capability. We can easily find what we're looking for. It'll actually be easier than if we'd had to manually flip through the pages."

There was something discomfiting about being able to control the demonic Bible, but Harriet had other things on her mind. "Are we going to tell Andromalius about all this?"

He had tasked them to find the high lord's killer. If it was Lucifer, they might as well tell him so he would stop expecting them to bring him the head of an archangel on a platter.

Annabeth's expression turned pensive. She wrapped a long, loose curl of black hair around her finger, eyes unfocused. "If Lucifer is here, why doesn't the Daemonium already know?"

"Last time he was on Earth was before the invention of bureaucracy," Theodora suggested. "Maybe he doesn't know he needs to fill out his world domination form in triplicate."

Harriet checked her watch. It was clear they had reached the end of any productive conversation. At this point, all they were doing was going round in circles. Speculating wouldn't get them any closer to the truth; it would only send them down more rabbit holes. And besides, hadn't they agreed that the angels were going to fix everything soon?

"Let's call it a night," she said. "We're getting nowhere. And besides, by tomorrow this could all be irrelevant."

The unwelcome memory of the bright blue eyes of Cimaris's killer intruded into her mind. She shuddered. The angel hadn't been the kind, merciful, compassionate celestial of popular culture. She hadn't been gentle and harmless like Arakiel. And while she had been beautiful, there had been a vicious, cold twist to her thin lips, and her eyes had burned with malicious delight. She hadn't killed Cimaris. She had exterminated her. And she had enjoyed it.

Annabeth may have been optimistic about the prospect of an angelic housecleaning that put the demons in their place and rolled back the Apocalypse, but Harriet was quietly worried. The three women lived in a dangerously gray area. They worked for the Daemonium. They might be half-angel, but in an angelic purge of the demonic presence on Earth, they might share Cimaris's fate. After all, even though he blessed their weapons, Father Domenico had never given them a straight answer regarding how the angelic host would interpret their activities as revokers.

Annabeth glanced at her phone, and even from a few feet away Harriet could see the numerous missed texts. She pouted. "We're going to be late for dinner."

She was still on the verge of being unable to walk. Whatever ligaments War had torn would take quite a bit longer to heal. Clever as she was, however, she would find a way to explain it all away. Harriet had always been impressed by Annabeth's ability to separate the two lives she lived. In over a decade as a revoker, she had never once slipped up enough for Jonathan to notice. He had no idea about her real occupation.

Theodora always said he was either gullible or stupid, but Harriet thought he was trusting. Maybe they were the same thing.

She'd never been in a relationship long enough to find out. And now, as they stood on the brink of Armageddon, Annabeth was worried about being late to dinner. At least she knew her priorities.

Harriet disentangled herself from Annabeth and stepped to the curb. A short line of cabs was parked near the library, awaiting passengers. Seeing her signal, the nearest pulled forward to meet her.

"Stay safe," she warned her friends as she opened the back door. Shit was hitting the fan, and they seemed to be standing directly under it. There was no telling what might happen next.

* * *

Harriet leaned over the white bowl and used her chopsticks to shovel a wad of thin yellow noodles and strips of pale pork into her mouth. In front of her, the cook worked with almost superhuman speed, boiling noodles, frying meat, and stirring broth with deft skill. Steam rose in shimmering puffs from stainless-steel pots while vegetables in black woks sizzled. The murmur of voices behind her, the scraping of metal on porcelain, and the clatter of silverware and dishes produced a soothing, familiar soundtrack. After leaving the library, she had only stopped at her apartment long enough to stow away her katana and change into a new white dress shirt. The benefit of always wearing the same thing was that she never had to spend time deciding what to wear.

Apart from sleeping, she spent little time in her apartment. It was more like a one-star hotel room than a home. She had never put any effort into adding personal touches. The coffee table in front of the battered brown couch had seen its prime in the 1970s. The walls were bare. In the kitchen were three forks, two spoons, and a knife. Since no one ever came over, she'd never made an effort to make it inviting. Annabeth had offered to help decorate, but there was no point—who would see it?

Besides, it reminded her of her roots. Her mother had raised her to value people, not things. The former were transient. The latter were forever. She picked up her phone and began to scroll through the news, chewing on a piece of shrimp spiced with curry. With two Horsemen loose in the city, she knew she would find something about them. As bad as the city was, there were always ways for things to get worse.

Her search didn't take long. A cholera outbreak had resulted in dozens of people being hospitalized. Three subway stops had been indefinitely closed after authorities had detected hantavirus in them, likely linked to persistent rat infestations. A preschool had shut down due to a child contracting and spreading pertussis. But while the effects of Pestilence in the city were obvious, those of War were more subtle. A turf war between two gangs had resulted in three deaths and a half dozen gunshot injuries. Two people had been stabbed to death outside a pharmacy in a drug deal gone wrong. The deaths might have been related to War, but maybe not. Those stories weren't particularly unique or noteworthy in the city; they happened every day.

Unexpectedly, a text message flashed across her screen. *Couldn't sleep. Too wound up. How was your day?*

She blinked. She hadn't expected to hear from Summer until tomorrow. Her thumbs hovered over the screen as she considered how to respond. After a moment, she typed back: *Full of surprises.* It was both an understatement and the truth. She hit send and set the phone down, waiting for Summer's response.

Too late, she realized her answer didn't invite further conversation. Scrambling, she hastily added, *What are you doing now?*

Three dots appeared on the screen. Harriet waited impatiently for the words to follow.

Netflix. To the message, Summer had attached a photo of her socked feet propped up on an espresso-colored coffee table, next to an opened beer can. The socks looked fuzzy and warm. Behind them, in the background, was a large flatscreen TV. Three more dots appeared. *I can't promise I won't burn it, but I do have popcorn if you're interested. I'll even let you pick the movie.* Below the words was a GIF of a house engulfed in a giant, blazing fire.

Harriet smiled, both at the GIF and the invitation. She hadn't expected an offer like this. It was enough to make her temporarily forget about the chaos igniting all over the city. Yes, the Apocalypse had literally started and two seals had been opened, but... The world was always on the verge of melting down. There was nothing she could do about it. All she could do was live in the moment.

She stared at her phone for what felt like minutes, trying to think of a clever response. In this modern courtship ritual, she knew funny GIFs could make or break a flirtation, but her mind was blank, exhausted by her long day. She knew Summer must be even more drained. Finally, she wrote, *How did you know burned popcorn is my favorite?* It took her a moment, but she found the GIF of Michael Jackson eating popcorn in the music video for "Thriller" and sent it. Too late, she remembered that Jackson was a controversial figure. Oh well, there was no way to recall the message now.

She was rewarded with a winking emoji. *Do you remember my address? I'm in apartment four.*

That was all the encouragement Harriet needed. Abandoning the little that remained of her noodles, she tossed a twenty onto the counter and threw on her coat, adjusting the collar of her shirt so that it lay smoothly. Almost as an afterthought, she grabbed the fortune cookie that had come with her meal. As she swept out of the small noodle shop, nodding to the thin young receptionist, she snapped it in half and read the message inside. *Life is a dashing and bold adventure.*

* * *

Summer answered the door in an oversized pink plaid button-down and white terrycloth shorts so short that for a moment Harriet wasn't sure she was wearing pants at all. Her blond hair fell in enchanting waves halfway down her chest. Although exhaustion had pulled some of the liveliness from her face, she still brightened when she recognized Harriet. "Hi!"

Harriet stared at her for a moment before she caught herself, sucked into her casual beauty and the way her eyes seemed to sparkle like light through a gemstone. She blinked quickly and tried to cover by scrounging in the plastic bag in her hand. She pulled out the pint of dark chocolate coconut ice cream she'd brought. "Hi. I brought this."

Summer reached for it with a luminous smile. "Someone knows the way to a woman's heart. Come on in!"

She turned and carried the ice cream back into the apartment, leaving Harriet to follow. As she disappeared into the galley kitchen, Harriet peered around the small one-bedroom apartment curiously. It was modestly decorated, with walls a nameless shade of blue and a mass-produced painting of a rainbow-colored elephant hung over the two-person dining table. Above the couch was a white stencil of a half-moon and a vine, beside which were the words "What if I fall? Oh but darling, what if you fly?"

Gingerly, not knowing what else to do, she sat on the brown suede couch, next to a dark-blue pillow upon which the word "Home" was written in looping white cursive. She pulled off her coat and laid it on the back of the couch as the sound of popping corn kernels filled the air. A minute later, it was followed by the smell of popcorn. She relaxed a little and leaned back against the cushions. She had to admit, this couch was much more comfortable than hers. She could easily fall asleep on it if she wasn't careful.

She recognized the coffee table in front of her from the picture Summer had sent. A white candle in a jar that said "Storms don't last forever" burned near the left edge, unleashing a mellow, sandalwood odor.

"So, tell me about those surprises," Summer called over the rattling sounds she was making in the kitchen. "Did someone bring in something cool to the shop today?"

"The shop?" Harriet repeated, confused.

"The pawnshop."

"Oh. I guess you could say that." She wrinkled her nose. There was an unsettling cognitive dissonance in pretending she hadn't discovered that the end of the world had been set in motion and that instead, the biggest problem she had faced today was related to some sort of small commercial transaction. If only that had been the case! But all lies carry with them the seed of truth, so she replied, "A family heirloom." Family, but not a human family.

"I bet you get a lot of those. Was it valuable?"

She considered the *Liber Rerum Occultarum*, sitting in its case at the library, and the two broken seals. "Priceless."

"So did you take it?"

Before Harriet could come up with an answer, Summer reappeared, the ice cream and two spoons grasped in her left hand, a red bowl of popcorn in her right. She set the bowl down on the coffee table and offered Harriet a spoon. When Harriet took it, she settled down on the couch next to her, knees pulled to her chest, and picked up the remote control. Harriet fought to not let her eyes sweep over the exposed skin of her thighs. Surely, Summer was aware of the effect of such short shorts. She could have changed into something less exposing.

"So, murder documentary or baking show?" Summer asked lightly, tossing some popcorn into her mouth.

"Uh." Harriet didn't have any opinion either way. "Whatever you feel like."

Summer grinned, a glint in her eyes, and wriggled further into the pillows. "Zombie bank heist it is. I've been dying to see it."

Harriet was baffled. "Zombie...bank heist? The zombies are going to rob a bank?" Suddenly, she felt every one of the ten or so years between them. This seemed one of those almost insurmountable generational differences, like the latest social media trends or popular slang. She could feel gray hairs breaking out all over her scalp.

Summer expertly navigated the menu. "No, no, not like that. The robbers are robbing a bank while *surrounded* by zombies."

"Oh," Harriet said, as though that made more sense to her. It didn't.

"You can do zombie anything these days," Summer explained breezily, reaching for another handful of popcorn. "Zombie Christmas musical, zombie rom-com, zombie Western, zombie Nazis, zombies in space..." She frowned. "Probably zombies in space. I'm not sure, actually." She cocked her head, eyes narrowing thoughtfully. "Zombies are this blank canvas on which we can paint whatever we want. Zombies as the mindless consumption of capitalism. Zombies as vessels for existential humor. Zombies as the nameless, faceless dread of looming mortality. Zombies are like...symbols of the things that scare us the most, you know? That's why they're so adaptable to multiple genres."

Harriet was impressed. "I never knew it was such a deep topic."

The movie started. Not wanting the ice cream to melt, Harriet stuck a spoon in. Suddenly, Summer bolted upright, almost startling her into dropping it. "Wait! I have a blanket."

"A bl—"

Before Harriet could finish, Summer rocketed off the couch and disappeared into the bedroom. She reemerged a moment later with a pale-blue, hand-knit blanket. She sat back down and spread it over the two of them, making sure it covered Harriet's lap completely even though Harriet wasn't cold. As she worked, she explained, "Growing up, we always watched movies under a blanket. That way, if something got too scary, we could cover our eyes."

Harriet found the idea of a young Summer hiding behind a fraying old blanket adorable, and the fact that she had kept it with her even when she struck out from home oddly charming. She asked, "Do you think this will be a scary movie?"

Summer eyed the ice cream curiously and shrugged. "It could be. I get scared easily."

It was not a scary movie, but somehow, within ten minutes and without Harriet noticing how she had done it, Summer had snuggled in tight against her, laying her head against her shoulder. As smoothly as she could, Harriet snaked her arm around Summer's opposite shoulder, settling it comfortably. It had been a long time since she'd been this close to someone else. Summer smelled like magnolias and antibacterial soap, a lingering reminder of her long day working in the emergency room.

In the dim light cast by the TV, Harriet could just make out a splash of brown freckles across her chest, exposed by the open collar of her shirt. Harriet was keenly aware of the feel of Summer's body against hers. It made her heart beat faster and her skin tingle. It was hard to concentrate on the movie when there was something even more interesting sitting beside her, especially someone as vivacious and warm as the young nurse. Summer's hand found hers beneath the blanket and pulled it into her lap.

"Would you go into a zombie-infested city to steal from a bank casino?" Summer had a serious expression on her face, even as she kept staring forward at the screen.

Harriet shook her head. "Why bother? At that point, would money even matter? It seems like by then everything would be so screwed up it would be useless."

"It wouldn't be useless," Summer argued. "The zombies are contained in one place, you know? Everything else is normal. Millions of dollars, just waiting to be used. Would you try for it?"

Harriet shrugged. She needed money to put a roof over her head and food on the table, but that's as far as she cared about it. What would she do with millions?

"I'd rather not get eaten by another human being," she replied. "It sounds...painful."

She'd been bitten enough times by angry demons with fangs. She didn't need to become a meal for smaller, duller human teeth.

Summer pulled their hands out from under the blanket and nibbled on Harriet's fingers playfully. "Not even a little taste? A little bite?"

Harriet's face went slack. She was mesmerized by the shift in Summer's demeanor from serious to flirtatious. Her body reacted accordingly.

"What if the zombie was cute?" Summer persisted. She shifted, turning her body toward Harriet, and leaned in to brush her teeth against Harriet's neck.

A thrill ran down Harriet's body, awakening nerves everywhere. Summer nipped her earlobe. Harriet's breath hitched, reminding her of her mending ribs. When she regained her breath, she managed to say, "Oh. Well, I guess if the zombie was *you...*"

The blanket was cast to the floor with impressive fluidity and then Summer was sliding into Harriet's lap. Her knees came to rest past Harriet's hips. Harriet tilted her head back to meet Summer's gaze as her hands settled on the crest of Summer's hips. This was a pleasant development, and much more interesting than a zombie heist movie. Summer brushed Harriet's hair away from her eyebrows and examined her face closely. Then, slowly, her hands on Harriet's cheeks, she leaned in to kiss her.

Harriet enjoyed the feeling of Summer's body pressing into hers, her weight sinking onto the tops of her thighs, the soft cushion of her lips. She loved the feeling of Summer's hands, the warmth of her breath as it whispered over her skin. Summer dropped her head, kissing a spot below her earlobe and then tracing a line down to her collar. Harriet huffed sharply, heart beating faster. She licked her lips. She felt electrified, every sensation heightened.

Abruptly, Summer stopped and leaned back. Her face was stern. "There's no one waiting for you at home, right? No partner who thinks you're working late?"

Harriet had been surprised—and disappointed—for a moment by the unexpected break in contact, but she quickly recovered. "No." She shook her head. "Definitely not."

"And you swear you're not a serial killer? Or some weird pervert?"

"Yes. No. I mean I'm not a...either of those."

"Good."

Summer went back to kissing her, fingers wrapping around the back of her neck and thumbs pressed against her cheeks. Harriet was achingly aware of every place she touched. Her fingers were as warm as the candle on the coffee table; they left gently burning impressions to mark where they'd been. Summer pressed forward hungrily, unapologetically, belying her long day at the hospital. Harriet ran her hands up her sides beneath her shirt, feeling her gentle skin and soft curves. She didn't know how far this might go, but she wasn't going to waste the opportunity. She kissed Summer's collar and the other woman bucked into her, muffling a soft groan. It set Harriet on fire.

Several long minutes later, Summer's fingers found a new home at the top button of Harriet's shirt. She paused, eyes searching Harriet's for permission. In response, Harriet quickly undid the buttons of Summer's own shirt, pushing it off her shoulders and watching as she shrugged it the rest of the way. What remained was a white push-up bra decorated with a gentle lace at approximately Harriet's eye level. Summer tossed her long hair over her shoulders with a proud, satisfied grin. She had a beautiful body and she knew it. She wasn't shy about Harriet knowing too.

She leaned forward and kissed Harriet again, fingers playing down the front of Harriet's shirt with the agile skill of a guitarist. Harriet knew when the last of the buttons were undone because of the tickle of cooler air against her skin. The feeling was followed by the warmth of Summer's palm against it, running lightly from her belt to the center of her chest. She shivered, exhilarated by the sensation. Her breath caught as she waited to see where the hand would go next. She was helpless, and Summer in full control.

Summer's right hand buried itself firmly in the hair at the base of Harriet's neck. She rolled her hips hard into Harriet's, grinning. Harriet wrapped her arms around Summer's back and pulled her forward until her forehead almost met Summer's chest. She brought her lips to the smooth skin there. Summer arched, helping her unhook the bra clasp. Tiny fireworks exploded throughout Harriet's body as the fabric fell away, lighting her up from the inside. She kissed anywhere she could reach, hungry for more, letting the way Summer's breath caught and wavered guide her.

Summer's hips shifted and twitched as she responded to Harriet's hands and lips. Her breath turned into a rasp. But after a minute more, she pressed her palm to Harriet's chest and pushed her body back, breaking the contact between them. Harriet stopped, concerned she'd done something wrong. Summer watched her with slightly unfocused eyes. Her shoulders hiccupped with quick breaths that pushed her chest forward and back.

"You know what you do if a zombie bites you?" she asked.

Harriet frowned, bemused by both the question and its timing. Zombies again? Was this going to be—

Summer leaned close, pressing her mouth against Harriet's ear and her chest against Harriet's so that Harriet struggled to focus on what she said next. "You bite back."

Oh. Harriet didn't need to be told twice. With strength that was more celestial than human, she held Summer to her as she stood. Summer wrapped her legs around Harriet's waist and rested her arms loosely around her neck, making a muffled giggle. Harriet ignored the ache of her healing ribs—the pain would pass. As she carried Summer to the bedroom, she noticed for the first time that the nurse had chosen the movie from her "Recently Watched" queue. She had been set up.

CHAPTER TWELVE

The only time Annabeth could be alone and undisturbed in her small apartment was at one in the morning, when Jonathan and the kids were happily asleep in their beds. Then she could sit at the narrow desk shoved into the corner of the messy living room and finish whatever work she couldn't do with the boys falling all over her. It was lucky she could get by on only a few hours of sleep, because it seemed something was always popping up that needed her attention—bills to be paid or parent-teacher association emails to be answered. It was rare that she could go to bed at eleven and stay there until six, like Jonathan, but at least she was able to keep her head above water on all the things that needed doing.

Her eyes scanned the small black words on the computer screen, the soft white glare reflecting on her face and glasses as she read the paragraph in front of her a second time. The librarian hadn't been completely wrong about the *Liber Rerum Occultarum* coming off like a hoax. It often read as though the author had eaten tainted mushrooms and then written down what they'd seen while hallucinating. But no matter how bizarre and confusing, she knew the book must contain more than a few grains of truth. Cimaris hadn't called it the demonic Bible for nothing. Just as the actual Bible contained history and directives for humans, this book must, in some way, do the same for demons. It was just a matter of untangling it.

She took off her glasses and rubbed her eyes, then stared blankly at the pages of notes she'd taken. The Psellus Prophecy wasn't as clear-cut as Cimaris had made it seem. Lucifer's return to Earth didn't immediately lead to a full demonic conquest, for one thing. There was a lot of fighting and monsters and terrifying meteorological events before that—just like in the Book of Revelation. The difference was, in the *Liber Rerum Occultarum* there was no hope of an angelic rally once Lucifer killed Jesus.

She doodled aimlessly on the paper, drawing arrows with so much force the tip of the pen started to tear through it. There was *something* in the book that could help them. She was sure of it. Michael Psellus may have been a pessimist with a penchant for the dramatic, but he seemed to have been right about at least some things that John the Revelator hadn't been: for example, where the seven seals had been hidden. Regarding the first, he had written, "And I saw the first seal, which held within it the vessel of disease and his bow, and lo, the priests bowed to it without knowing because it was located in the holiest of churches." And regarding the second, "And then I saw the second seal, which held within it the usher of war and his sword, and lo, it was masked by sin because it was located in the unholiest of places."

She understood why no one had been able to guess the seals' location until now based on those vague and cryptic references. The holiest of holy churches, for example, was usually considered to be the Church of the Holy Sepulchre in Jerusalem. Who would have thought to look here, far from the Holy Land? Meanwhile, there were limitless "unholy" places. The second seal could have been absolutely anywhere.

But she didn't know what to make of the description of the third seal: "And then I saw the third seal, which held within it the immoral man and his balance, and it was protected because it was located in the temple of desire." The third Horseman was Famine, but what was the "temple of desire"? The only place she could think of was a strip club, and she couldn't imagine that's what Psellus meant. Or at least, she hoped that wasn't where the seal was.

She tapped her bare foot impatiently against the chair leg. She had so many unanswered questions about the seals. The first two had been in the city—were the rest here too? If so, why? The world was such a large place. The angels could have hidden them anywhere; finding them would have been like finding a specific grain of sand at the bottom of the ocean. Lucifer and his demons could have spent eternity looking for them and never found even one. Or better yet, the seals could have been kept in God's throne room, like John had seen in his vision. Then Lucifer could never have reached them. Not to second-guess the angelic host, but putting them on Earth, possibly all in the same city, seemed like an egregious oversight on its part.

That wasn't the only thing bothering her. How could the second seal, which presumably had been made sometime shortly after the creation of the Earth, be located in a building built in the last thirty years? The seal must have been somewhere else before then. So were the seals occasionally moved? How often and by whom?

Cimaris had said, "There are a lot of things in this city, haven't you noticed?" At the time, Annabeth hadn't thought much of the snide comment. Now the demon's words took on a deeper meaning. The city was the seat of the Daemonium, but was there more to it? If so, what?

A hand landed heavily on her shoulder. A moment later, lips brushed against the top of her head. "What are you doing up so late?" Annabeth's husband leaned over her shoulder a little to inspect her screen, his bare chest pressing into her shoulders.

"Reading. Did you know the so-called 'demonic Bible' is located right here in our library? It's written in human blood. The only other book in history known to have been written in blood is a Qur'an commissioned by Saddam Hussein."

Jonathan leaned back, letting go of her. "Okay, creepy. Why are you reading about it at this time of night? It's not really bedtime reading."

She turned to face him, wrapping her white cotton shawl tighter over her shoulders. "Long story. If you read something was located in the 'temple of desire,' where do you think it would be?"

He raised his eyebrows, so light yellow they were almost invisible against his skin. "I'm guessing this isn't a reference to a sex club, right?"

She shook her head, secretly glad she hadn't been the only one to think something like that.

"Then I guess it would depend on what I wanted." He waggled his eyebrows. "If I were hungry, it would be an all-you-can-eat buffet."

She sighed, not at him but at the situation. That was the problem: Psellus's description was as vague as a Nostradamus prediction. It could mean anything. She pulled the tie from her hair, shaking her long dark locks out around her and smoothing them with her hand. "All right, let me ask a different way. If you had to hide something in the city, something you didn't want anyone to find, where would you hide it?"

He looked thoughtful for a moment. Annabeth adored the way his deep blue eyes narrowed in concentration, the small wrinkle that appeared between his eyebrows. She had to keep herself from reaching out and smoothing it. One day, it would be permanent, like his father's. By then, he would look dignified, with the well-coifed silver hair of a politician. She, on the other hand...would look like a wrinkled potato.

At last, he said, "There's a big vault in the basement of the First City Bank, one of those old ones from the 1920s. It's got a round steel door three-and-a-half-feet thick, the kind you see in movies. I bet it hasn't been used in decades." He nodded to himself. "I would hide something there."

She cocked her head, curious. "Why don't they use it anymore?"

"It's a dinosaur compared to the newer one they have upstairs. It looks imposing, but you could cut through it with a blowtorch. The technology used in modern vaults is light-years ahead. Since it's too massive and heavy to move, the old one just sits there. It's definitely not a place anyone would go looking for anything."

She frowned at him. "How do *you* know it's there?" How did he know anything at all about it, in fact?

"Last year there was a podcast that mentioned it, something about the hidden history of the city. I wish they'd done more episodes. I thought it was fun. There was one about bootlegging too."

She sat back in her swivel chair, thinking. *If* the third seal was in the city, and there was no guarantee it was, could it be in the old bank vault? Maybe. It was as good a guess as anywhere else. But it was just that: a guess. She needed more than that.

Jonathan crouched a little and put his strong arms around her neck, cuddling her in a loose hug with his chin resting on the top of her head. He smelled faintly of bergamot, the persistent scent of the soap she'd bought him for his birthday. "Are we going to hide a body or are we going to rob a bank? I need to know to plan my outfit accordingly. And get a babysitter."

It would have been cute if she hadn't been distracted by the endless parade of questions without answers. "Neither. I was just thinking about something."

"I see that. Okay." He released her and gave her a comically exaggerated wink. "Just remember, teeth and fingerprints are what make a body identifiable. Everything else is just circumstantial evidence."

"Very funny."

She put on her glasses again and his features sharpened into focus—high cheekbones, a cleft chin, and a dimple on the right side. As Theodora teased, she couldn't have chosen someone more Captain America. He pointed to her knee. "Do you need ice for that?"

Instinctively, her hands went to her knee. It was healing, but slowly. She would still be limping tomorrow. Still, it was nothing compared to how it would have felt if she was a full human. There was no doubt it would have required surgery.

She smiled at him, appreciating his solicitousness. "No, thank you. It feels better already. Just a tweak."

"I'm glad Theodora was there to take you to the urgent care to get it checked out."

Officially, Annabeth had hurt her knee tripping over the curb coming into the pawnshop. That was the only story he needed to know. He covered his mouth with his hand as he yawned, then checked his watch. "Come back to bed. Your blood book and whatever crime you're secretly planning will be there in the morning. *Wait.*" He stood stock-still, as though struck by an idea. "Are you planning to kill someone, use *their* blood to write a book, then hide the body in the bank?"

She shook her head, chuckling. "No. Of course not!"

He held up his hands in mock surrender. "Say no more. I'll tell the cops I had no idea about any of it. I was totally in the dark. Asleep, in fact. I didn't know what you were planning." He winked, then walked backward out of the room, eyes still on her.

She watched him go fondly, part of her wishing she could just abandon her research and join him. Every day, she was amazed he was part of her life. He was kind, caring, handsome, smart, and funny. He was everything she could have dreamed of. And he was in danger. If Psellus was right—and so far he seemed to be more right than John—they were all in danger. Not just her family, but the whole world. She couldn't go to sleep now, not with the Apocalypse looming over them.

She closed her eyes and tilted her head back. Arakiel. Pestilence. Her father's shocking murder. War. The demonic Bible. Everything was happening so quickly that there was no time to fully process any of it. Theodora had told her in the cab home to let it all go, to let the angels handle it, but what if they couldn't? What if Lucifer really had figured out a way to beat them?

She glanced at her notes, then at the screen, restless. Without knowing what she was looking for, she Googled Revelation 6:5-6. *When the Lamb opened the third seal, I heard the third living creature say, "Come!" I looked, and there before me was a black horse! Its rider was holding a pair of scales in his hand. Then I heard what sounded like a voice among the four living creatures, saying, "A quart of wheat for a day's wages, and three quarts of barley for a day's wages, and do not damage the oil and the wine!"* What did any of it mean?

* * *

"Annabeth? What's going on? Is something happening?" Theodora's voice came through the line sharp and full of concern. If she had been sleeping, there was no sign of it.

Before Annabeth could reply, she heard a groggy male voice ask in the background, "Who the fuck calls this early in the morning?" Theodora's voice, muffled, shushed him.

Annabeth ignored the exchange. "I need you to come meet me."

"Right now?" Theodora sounded uncertain.

"Yes."

A pause. "What's this about? Is this about...yesterday?"

Annabeth licked her lips, excited but nervous. "I think I know where the third seal is."

The pause this time was longer. And then... "And?"

"And?" Annabeth was disconcerted by Theodora's unenthusiastic response. "What do you mean, *and?*"

"What do you want me to say?"

Annabeth stared at her notes, feeling slightly deflated. "Don't you want to go see it?"

"No. Why would I? In fact, if you know where it is, we should stay as far the fuck away from it as we can. We don't want to be anywhere near it."

The air went out of her like she'd been punched. "But—"

Theodora softened her tone. "Annabeth, think about it. This isn't some dumbfuck demon trying to summon a hellhound in his bathtub. This could be Lucifer himself. If by some chance he hasn't opened the seal already, do you really want to risk being there when he shows up? He killed his own fucking high lord. You think he wouldn't crush our skulls like pomegranate seeds and use our blood as bodywash if he found us there?"

Annabeth winced at the vivid description, feeling it down to her bones. She wasn't stupid. She knew the risks of being anywhere near the seals right now. But... She wanted to see if she was right. She knew that with her affinity, she would be able to recognize the seal instantly.

"Besides, if it is there, what are we going to do about it?"

Theodora was right, of course. They could neither move the seal nor defend it. All they could do was confirm whether it had been opened or not. Her eyes strayed to the bacon she'd laid out for Jonathan and the boys, the eggs and bread ready to be placed in the frying pan and toaster. If she closed her eyes, she could pretend it was a day just like any other. In half an hour, her family could be eating breakfast together, laughing over some silly joke and discussing the boys' homework like they always did. But it wasn't a normal day. It was day two of the Apocalypse.

She stood straighter, pulling the sleeves of her pink cardigan down to her wrists. Theodora had once said she looked like the last person who would show up to blow a demon away, but appearances could be deceiving. She was a wife and a mother, but she was also the daughter of Samyaza, fallen seraph and former high lord of the Daemonium. And she was a fighter. She grabbed her house keys and shoved them into her pocket. "I want to see the seal. You can come with me or not, but I'm going."

"Jesus, Annabeth." A brief pause. "Fuck. You're not going alone. Hold on."

Annabeth heard rustling on the other end. Her voice muffled, Theodora said to whomever was with her, "Get your shit and go." When the man started to argue, she repeated the command more forcefully. After a few more seconds of rustling, she returned to the line. "Okay, where are we going?"

Annabeth released a small breath of relief at the commitment in Theodora's voice. She would have gone without her, but she was happier not to. She tapped her pen against the address on her notepad. "First City Bank. The one on 8th street. It opens at eight. I'll call Harriet and let her know too."

"Okay. And Annabeth?"

"Yes?"

"If I die because you wanted to see this damn seal, I'm going to fucking haunt the shit out of you."

* * *

"Why do you think the third seal is here?" Harriet asked, pulling the lapels of her brown trench coat tighter against her chin. It was a futile gesture. A cold snap had hit the city overnight, and the bitter wind it produced easily sliced through fabric. Although she'd gotten out of the taxi only a minute ago, already her cheeks were flushed a pale pink.

Annabeth, shivering, looked up at the bank. Like the library, it had been designed in the Beaux-Arts style. Tall, white, and imposing, it was both a monument to the city's wealth and a fortress to protect it. She was more certain than ever the seal was here. All the pieces fit.

She gestured toward it. "I think the locations of the seals are tied to the ideas they represent. It came to me when I looked up the history of St. Peter's. It was built in 1901, but do you know what was there before?"

As she expected, her question was met with blank stares. She answered her own question triumphantly. "A hospital."

Harriet's forehead puckered as she considered Annabeth's claim. The wind swirled her hair into cowlicks. If Annabeth didn't know better, she would have sworn she saw a hickey peeking out beneath the collar of the other woman's shirt. Slowly, Harriet said, "You're saying the seal containing Pestilence was originally hidden in a hospital."

Annabeth nodded. "I think so. At least, I'm betting that's where it was at the end of the 1800s. Who knows where it was before that? But it stayed in that location when the hospital was replaced by the cathedral."

Harriet's eyebrows pulled even lower. "So was the church built over it on purpose?"

Annabeth shrugged, wishing she'd worn a coat. She'd been distracted, and regretted it now. "I don't know. Obviously, the humans wouldn't have known about the seal, but if the angels influenced them..."

"What about the second seal?"

Annabeth's mind flashed back to the city's historical records website. "Until 1912, there was an armory where the office of the Daemonium is now. It served the National Guard unit stationed in the city."

"And then somehow the angels got the seal into Samyaza's office?" Harriet was impressed.

Annabeth shrugged a second time. "I guess so."

She had no idea how, exactly, they'd done it. A big wooden horse had worked for the Greeks. Maybe the angels had used the same trick against the demons. Perhaps they'd secretly gifted Samyaza a big painting that he'd unwittingly hung on the wall. Since she didn't know what a seal looked like, she could only guess.

Theodora motioned toward the building in front of them. Although she was wearing her usual tank top and leather jacket, she didn't seem affected by the temperature. "Okay, I buy your argument about the seals being linked to symbolic places, but why the bank? What's that got to do with Famine?"

Annabeth resettled her glasses on her nose, preparing to deliver her theory. This is what it had taken her half the night to figure out. Correctly identifying the location of the third seal hinged on her hypothesis being right. "We know the third Horseman is Famine. But in the *Liber Rerum Occultarum*, Psellus calls him 'the immoral man' and says his seal is in the 'temple of desire.' That got me thinking. In the Book of Revelation, the voice John hears calls for the price of wheat and barley to go up but not oil and wine. I think it's a clue. The rich get their wine, the poor struggle to pay for bread."

"Nope, you lost me," Theodora said.

Harriet nodded slowly. "I get it. Famine is an economic problem. Let them eat cake, right?"

"Exactly!" Annabeth was relieved Harriet had seen what she had. It suggested her theory wasn't as wild as it seemed. "What if the *bank* is the temple of desire? The rich hoard wealth, making the poor starve."

Theodora grunted. "I guess it makes as much sense as a grocery store." She scrutinized the building. "So we go in and sniff around for something that looks old and biblical?"

Annabeth was relieved to notice that whatever Theodora was armed with, it wasn't her Desert Eagle. If they walked through the doors with that, the only exploring they'd be doing was the inside of a jail cell. She subtly fingered the sheath strapped to her forearm. The metal throwing spikes wouldn't do much good against the massive, armored War and even less against Lucifer, but it was better than nothing. She explained, "There's an old vault in the basement. I think if the seal is here, that's where it will be."

Before leaving her apartment, Annabeth had pieced together the bank's floorplan using Google images. The teller counter ran most of the length of the lobby's north wall, but on the west end was a corridor that led to offices and the new vault. She knew the stairs to the old vault had to be somewhere in that corridor. What she didn't know was whether access to the corridor was restricted. There would be nothing they could do if so.

"So how do we explain what we're doing?" Harriet asked. "Do people normally just walk in and ask to look at a bank vault?"

Annabeth had prepared for this. "If anyone asks, we're looking for the vault to discuss it on our podcast. We're doing an episode about the evolution of anti-theft measures used in bank vaults over the last hundred years."

She was proud of her cover story. If they couldn't get to the vault on their own, they might be able to convince someone to take them to it. And it wasn't a bad topic, either. She would listen to a podcast about it.

Theodora gave Annabeth a skeptical look. "Do people who look like us make podcasts about this kind of stuff?"

Annabeth grimaced. Coconut. That's what Theodora called her sometimes. Brown on the outside, white on the inside. It wasn't her fault her adoptive parents were white and she'd been raised in their culture. But Theodora was no different. She'd spent her life doing everything she could to minimize her South Asian heritage and fit in with everyone else. And Theodora was wrong. Times were changing.

"Of course they do," Annabeth said. "Now come on, let's go."

Marching forward as well as she could despite her pronounced limp, she pushed the bank's heavy door open. Once inside, she scanned the lobby, assessing. The two tellers at the counter were both busy serving customers. She didn't see any security guards. The coast was as clear as it could be. Casually but with purpose, she strolled toward the corridor. The key to pulling this off was to look as though she knew what she was doing.

As she walked, she repeated her cover story to herself. They were here for a podcast about vault mechanics. They were not here to rob the bank. They were not acting suspicious. There was no reason for anyone to look twice at them. If someone did approach them, there was no reason to panic.

The closer she got to the edge of the teller counter, the faster her heart beat. The bank was calm, sleepy even. That meant the seal beneath their feet, if indeed it was there, must be intact. If not, the bank would have been in chaos. Possibly even in ruins.

She reached the corner and ducked around it a little too quickly. She was immediately confronted by a plain wooden door on the right side of the corridor. She stopped in front of it and laid her palm against its smooth surface. She'd seen enough bank blueprints while researching that morning to know that vaults were almost always located immediately next to teller counters. That meant this was very likely the door she was looking for. She gripped the knob and turned it. Her heart fell.

"It's locked."

Harriet looked at it over her shoulder. "Oh, it's just a regular doorknob lock. Hold on."

Digging into her coat pocket, she retrieved a battered black leather wallet. Flipping it open, she selected a credit card from one of the sleeves and pulled it out. She gently pushed Annabeth aside, then slipped it into the thin line between the door and the frame.

Annabeth would have sworn there hadn't been space for it to fit, and yet somehow there was even enough for Harriet to wiggle it a little. A moment later, as if by magic, the door popped open.

Harriet slipped the card back into her wallet and pushed the door open. "If security saw that, they'll be on us fast. We better hurry."

Annabeth was pleased to see she'd been right about the location of the old vault. On the other side of the door was a staircase. Harriet found the light switch on the wall to their right and hit it, illuminating the space.

Theodora whistled. "Damn."

Below them was a small basement consisting of a narrow antechamber and the vault. The women went down the stairs. The vault was a behemoth. Its round door was at least seven feet tall, with so many bolts visible on the inside that it looked like the machinery of a watch. Two massive hinges allowed the door to close into a steel frame that looked like it might have been able to withstand a nuclear blast. Annabeth couldn't imagine anyone being able to break into it, and yet successful robberies had been so common in the 1920s that this safe type had been completely revamped.

Harriet walked into the vault but returned a moment later. "Well, where's the seal? There's nothing in there."

But she was wrong. Annabeth stepped forward, arm outstretched. Her tawny fingers traced over the glowing sapphire of the seal, the light rippling and shining over her skin. She had never seen anything so beautiful in her life. Filaments of silver shot through from the edge to the center, which pulsed its own shade of lapis. Words in an alphabet she'd never seen, more runes than letters, were written in beautiful calligraphy across the seal's surface. The language of the angels?

It took several beats until she was able to speak. When she did, her voice was full of awe. "The seal is here. It's in the door. And it's intact."

CHAPTER THIRTEEN

Theodora didn't see anything when she looked at the vault door—just thick-ass steel, huge bolts, and some sort of complicated, intimidating locking mechanism. But from the way Annabeth's face went slack as her fingers caressed the lines of the bolts, as though she were touching the finest jewelry in the world, she knew the other woman was seeing something else entirely. Theodora looked around anxiously, her fidgeting fingers closing around the push dagger in her jacket pocket for comfort. She didn't like closed spaces. If trouble showed up, there was no way to run. The only way in and out was that staircase. And trouble seemed to have found them a lot in the last day.

"Okay, you've seen it, so let's go," she said.

Now that Annabeth had confirmed the seal was both in the bank and intact, there was nothing else they could do with it. They couldn't sit on it like a hen. If the angels hadn't unleashed holy fury overnight, it was still game on for Lucifer to show up and open the third seal of Apocalyptic whoop-ass. If and when that happened, they wanted to be halfway across the city, if not halfway across the state.

Annabeth tore her eyes away from the door with effort. "I wish you could see what I see. It's so beautiful." There was a breathless, awed quality to her voice.

Theodora appreciated that, but she also appreciated being alive, and that seal was a homing beacon for bad shit. She looked to Harriet for support, hoping their third member saw things the way she did.

"Theodora's right. We should get out of here," Harriet said nervously.

"We could open it ourselves."

Annabeth's suggestion, delivered in fast, feverish words, was so unexpected that all Theodora could do was gape at her. "What do you mean we can open it ourselves?"

Annabeth's eyes shone behind the lenses of her glasses. "The Horsemen are controlled by whoever opens their seal. If we open this one before Lucifer, *we'll* have control over Famine, not him."

Harriet tilted her head. "Yeah, but then the third seal would be open. That's not exactly the direction we want to go in."

Theodora added energetically, "And what the fuck do you think we're going to do with a damn Horseman?"

This wasn't a dog they were considering adopting from an animal shelter. This was a class of celestial whose superpower was really fucking bad juju. They didn't need that, even if Famine was supposed to follow their orders. And what if he didn't? What if only a full celestial could control him?

"We could use him to stop the other Horsemen!" Annabeth argued.

Horseman versus Horsemen. Theodora put her hands on her hips. Whatever had come over Annabeth, her ideas were getting wilder by the second. And she'd forgotten the single biggest hurdle anyway.

"Even if we did want to open the seal, you do remember we'd have to find its guardian, right? Do you really think we can find an angel in this huge-ass city—much less the *right* one—and then drag him here before Lucifer does? And then *kill* him?" She didn't have any qualms about taking an angel out, but she knew Annabeth would.

Annabeth's face fell. "I forgot about that. I just—"

"*Excuse me.*" A woman was standing at the top of the stairs, looking down at them. Based on her precise red skirt suit and the authority with which she carried herself, Theodora guessed she was a bank employee. Shit. "What are you doing down there?"

A moment of silence followed as the women stared at each other dumbly. Theodora tried to remember what Annabeth had told them to say. Something about a podcast. And locks. Vaults?

Annabeth snapped out of it first. "Oh, hello there." Theodora was amazed at how friendly and nonchalant she managed to sound. As if they hadn't been caught poking around somewhere they shouldn't be by someone who could get them into *significant* trouble with the police. "We're just looking at this old vault."

The woman crossed her arms and narrowed her eyes. There wasn't a hair out of place or a single wrinkle in her clothing. It was fucking unnatural. "This is a restricted area. How did you get in here?"

It was Harriet who answered this time. "The door was unlocked."

"We're doing a podcast," Annabeth supplied, although she hadn't been asked. "It's about anti-theft measures in old bank vaults. This is the last of the old-style vaults in the city, so we wanted to see it in person, maybe take a picture for the episode thumbnail."

The woman's eyes narrowed even farther, dark slits of suspicion that hadn't been allayed in the least by Annabeth's words. Theodora knew they were in trouble. They might as well have been wearing balaclavas and carrying canvas sacks, as far as the bank employee was concerned. In a clipped voice, she said, "I doubt that very much. Why are you really here?"

Before they had time to answer, she started down the stairs, legs pumping like pistons. When she reached the bottom of the stairs, she glared at them, her eyes sharp. She wasn't a beautiful woman. Her lips were too large; they pulled her mouth into a wavy, uneven line. And there was a subliminal, animal ferocity to her that turned into hard angles what should have been soft curves.

Theodora took a step back, repelled from her like a magnet of equal polarity. As her back brushed against the wall, her hand subconsciously clenched the push dagger, flesh pressing into the hard plastic handle even though she wouldn't dare reveal she was armed. It was bad enough that they'd been discovered. It would be far worse if the woman knew they were armed.

"I said, why are you really here?"

Harriet replied, "We told you, we have a podcast—"

The woman's head whipped in her direction like a striking snake. "A lie." The word crackled in the air, sharp and accusatory. She wasn't guessing. She knew.

Panic began to bubble in the pit of Theodora's stomach. The walls were closing in, trapping them. She reminded herself the woman was just one human and they were revokers. If they had to, they could easily overpower her and run. But still the room crowded closer.

"You're an angel."

Theodora heard the awe in Annabeth's voice before she registered the meaning of the words. It was only then, cued by Annabeth's realization, that she saw the faint but unmistakable glimmer of wings over the woman's shoulder. Theodora hadn't seen them before because the angel had been partially backlit at the top of the stairs.

"You must be the seal guardian!" Annabeth exclaimed.

The angel cocked her head. If possible, her expression turned even fiercer. Her gaze was an acetylene torch cutting through them in search of the truth. "Who are you?"

They had prepared a cover story. They had not prepared the truth. But the truth might not help them anyway. Arakiel had believed they were half-angel, but this angel might not, and Theodora didn't think she would take kindly to the Daemonium's revokers standing so close to her seal. She had neither the means nor the time to share this concern with Annabeth, however, who pushed forward with honest earnestness.

"You're in danger. The first two seals have been opened."

The urgency in Annabeth's voice was a plea to not only be heard but to be understood. The look the angel turned on her could have frozen mercury. It was a merciless, scathing combination of derision and condescension, as though Annabeth were a bug she'd marred her shoe by stepping on. "I know."

Annabeth recoiled, surprised. "You do? But then why are you here? You should be as far away as you can get." She paused, then asked hopefully, "Unless the angels are back?"

The seal guardian took another step into the small room. Her heels clicked loudly on the concrete. The hair on Theodora's arms stood on end. This was not a kindly, benign angel like Arakiel had been. A whisper of violence surrounded her, an intangible suggestion of barely suppressed feral impulses. Theodora recognized it because she was the same way. Like knew like.

The angel's penetrating gaze seemed to judge Annabeth down to her soul. "I am the steward of this seal. It is my great honor and duty. I would not abandon it even if I could." Score one for Harriet.

Her scrutiny shifted to Theodora, stripping her as bare as she had Annabeth. "What are you? You're not human. How do you know the location of the seal?"

Theodora didn't like the look at all. It was a challenge, and Theodora never backed down from challenges. Still, she was smart enough to know that this was one fight it was better to avoid. She raised her hands in the universal sign of coming the fuck in peace. "We're on your side." Sort of. "Before he died, Arakiel asked us to help protect the seals."

The angel tilted her head, considering the three half-humans before her, then reached behind her neck and tapped her dark chignon as though to adjust it. "Hmm." The sound was noncommittal. It indicated she neither believed them nor disbelieved them. She was keeping her options open. "Well, this one is safely in my care. Your assistance is unnecessary. Now, I have work to do, and I can't have you running around in a restricted area."

Her lips twitched into a momentary imitation of a smile, a flicker of feigned, insincere politeness, then it was gone. She stepped to the side of the stairs and indicated them with her upraised palm. It wasn't an invitation. It was an order.

Theodora obeyed without hesitation. She rushed past the angel and took the stairs two at a time, eager to get back onto the main level, where there were wide-open spaces and multiple exits. She had done what Annabeth had asked: confirmed the location of the seal. Now that they'd done that, she was more than happy to leave it to the care of its icy guardian. Whatever happened to it next was out of their hands. She took no responsibility.

Once they were out, the angel locked the door to the seal as Annabeth watched wistfully, then she ushered them back into the lobby like a sheepdog managing a flock of wayward sheep. The lobby was empty now. Even the tellers had stepped away. The angel caught Theodora's arm, delaying them a few paces. Wordlessly, she studied Theodora's face, her own face revealing nothing.

Theodora shook her off angrily. "Let me go."

The angel's face twisted in disgust. "I knew there was something familiar about you. I recognize your face now. You have Kasdeja's eyes." Her gaze flickered to the other women. "They're daughters of the fallen, too, aren't they? Samyaza and Gader'el?"

Theodora automatically stiffened at the mention of her father, adrenaline flushing her body in preparation to fight, even if only through words. Her hands balled into unconscious fists.

"I see now why Arakiel came to you. Although…it would have been better had he not." The guardian paused, then sneered. "Your father was a fool to give up Heaven for a human. And a still greater one to try to open a seal out of time. You are no angel. Your blood is tainted."

Theodora ground her teeth together. Fucking sanctimonious piece of shit. How dare she judge her father? For all the angel's holier-than-thou attitude, what had she done on Earth but hang around and babysit a seal for thousands of years? She had done nothing to make this shitty city any better. She hadn't even helped the other seal guardians when they were being picked off one by one. It would serve her right for Lucifer to show up right now and—

Ahead of them, one of the doors opened. Theodora didn't register the fact that no one had actually come through it until Annabeth suddenly halted in front of her. It was the type of complete motionlessness that signaled the unmistakable presence of danger. Theodora didn't have time to ask what was wrong before two beings materialized out of thin air right in front of them. One of them was War. Theodora didn't have to guess who the other was.

"Fuck. Me," she whispered.

The two Horsemen looked like supervillains who had come to rob the bank to finance their dastardly plans for world destruction. Which was weirdly close to the truth, only the Horsemen were no fictional characters and there was no superhero about to fly in and trounce them.

"They're here for the seal," Annabeth all but shouted, panicked.

"No shit," Theodora hissed back. If they were here, Lucifer could show up at any time. The three women needed to get out of the bank immediately. She glanced over her shoulder, searching for an escape route.

"We have to stop them! We can't let them open it," Annabeth cried.

Theodora didn't have time to waste arguing with her. She was too busy calculating angles and distances. The Horsemen were here for the angel and the seal. That meant the three of them were mere collateral. If the celestials charged for the angel, she, Harriet, and Annabeth could slip around them by hugging the teller counter and then running out the door. It wasn't a great plan, but with luck it could work.

In front of her, Harriet reached behind her back with both hands. Her coat twitched as she felt for something at her waist. A moment later, she pulled out two kamas like rabbits from a magician's top hat. Theodora was amazed. It had been a hell of a risk for her to bring long, sharp blades like that into a bank. But she was grateful Harriet had. Those kamas were the best weapons they had right now. Pestilence drew his bow from behind his back and then reached for an arrow.

"Give me one of your weapons!" she called to Harriet. If it came to it, there was no way she was going to take on a Horseman of the Apocalypse using the three-inch blade of her push dagger. She might as well start jabbing at him with a toothpick.

With a smooth motion, Harriet half turned and tossed her the kama from her right hand. The sickle blade made a gentle arc in the air before Theodora caught the shaft. It was a good thing her hand was almost totally healed from the day before; the kama was heavier than it looked.

"If you have any angel superpower shit to bring to the fight, now's the time," she muttered out of the side of her mouth to the seal guardian. She didn't care about the angel herself, but she wasn't thrilled by the prospect of Lucifer opening yet another seal.

Her prompt was met with silence. Annoyed, she glanced to her left. The angel was gone.

The weapon in her hand drooped a few inches, forgotten, as she scanned the room. The angel was nowhere to be seen. She let loose an angry growl. "How about that? That bitch left us alone with these chucklefucks."

"Good." Annabeth had a throwing spike in her hand, its sharp black tip sticking a few inches past her fingers, ready to throw. She was gripping two more in her other fist. Not that they'd do much against either of the celestials. At this range and against armor, they were as deadly as unsharpened pencils. Annabeth finished, "If she's gone, Lucifer can't open the seal."

"Tell *them* that."

Whether the Horsemen realized they had lost their prey or not, they continued to fan out over the lobby with slow, deliberate steps. Theodora's initial plan was ruined. The only way to get out of the bank now was to run between them in a deadly gauntlet. She kept her eyes on Pestilence. He was the more dangerous of the two. She could dodge a sword, but she couldn't dodge an arrow.

Pestilence stalked forward like a big cat, watching the women unblinkingly. Although he had nocked an arrow, he hadn't pulled the string back yet. That, at least, was hopeful. Theodora knew their best chance of getting out relatively unscathed was to make sure he never got to that point.

"Harriet, do you think you can distract Pestilence while I hold off War?" she asked.

"Maybe." It was a surprisingly pessimistic admission from their strongest member.

"Whatever you do, don't let him get that arrow up." A long-range weapon like his beat a short-range weapon like their kamas every time. Things could get ugly fast, and Theodora didn't feel like becoming a human pincushion.

Harriet nodded, her face an impenetrable mask that concealed whatever she was feeling about the prospect of facing not one Horseman but two. "Got it."

"What about me? Which one do you want me to attack?" Annabeth asked, earnestly brandishing her throwing spike as though it were something other than a pokey metal chopstick.

"Neither. While we distract these asswipes, I want you to run as fast as you can to the door and get out of here." It was a replay of what they'd done in the alley when they'd last encountered War, only this time, Annabeth and Harriet's roles were reversed. Theodora glanced down at Annabeth's yellow suede ballet flats, then up at her silk blouse and cardigan. The other woman hadn't dressed for a hundred-meter dash, but it would do.

Annabeth opened her mouth to protest, but Theodora cut her off. "Just go."

By now, the Horsemen had them almost completely flanked. The moment for action had come.

"Ready?" she asked. The question was addressed to both of her companions, but mostly to Harriet.

Harriet switched her kama to her right hand, then reached into the inside pocket of her coat with her left, producing a thin, razor-edged circle the size of a saucer. Before Theodora had time to think about the fact that she had smuggled yet another weapon into the bank, Harriet threw it. Her aim and strength would have made a minor league baseball pitcher jealous. As though drawn there by a magnet, the throwing star buried itself in the side of Pestilence's exposed neck. Bow and arrow dropped to the ground as he reflexively grabbed for the shuriken, roaring like a wounded sea serpent.

The guttural, inhuman sound was a siren that galvanized the other women into action. Annabeth took off toward the door, her black bun bouncing and shedding strands with every limping step. Theodora followed, walking backward with the kama held in front of her, keeping herself between War and her fleeing companion. To her left, Harriet, too, started to fall back.

War tilted his goliath head, assessing. One mortal fleeing, the other two guarding her as they retreated, and his partner ripping out pieces of his own flesh as he wrestled the steel disc from his neck. The celestial turned his attention back to Theodora. He strode confidently toward her, sword hefted over his shoulder like a baseball bat. Theodora didn't allow herself to feel fear that her only defense was a seven-inch knife on a footlong stick. Instead, she let rage fill her like helium in a mylar balloon.

Fuck Arakiel for getting them into this mess. Fuck the angels for not giving a shit about what was happening in this city. And double fuck these two cartoon characters for showing up at the worst time. She didn't deserve any of this shit, and nor did her friends. She was not going to die, not this way, and they weren't either.

War was so close she could hear his heavy, muffled breathing under his helmet. She braced herself, glaring at him, hating every inch of him. His massive broadsword was daunting, but it didn't make him invincible. If she could get past its reach, the playing field would be more level. She hadn't been a revoker for all these years without learning a trick or two or ten. War was bigger than the demons she hunted, but he might be just as stupid.

The lobby around her, Harriet and Pestilence included, disappeared. Only War existed. He was a mountain of steel and muscle, but she was blazing, fluid lava. As he stopped in front of her, swinging his sword down at her head as though he could cleave her in half, she dropped to her knee. Bringing the kama up the inside of his right leg, she slashed recklessly at what she hoped would be an unprotected area. He bellowed, hurt, and staggered away from her sharp blade.

"That's right, you dingleberry!" she hollered, pleased with herself.

Her knee grumbled about the excessive contact it had made against the marble floor and how she wasn't as young as she used to be, but she ignored it. Returning to her feet with a huff of exertion, she dropped into a tense crouch beyond the reach of his sword, close enough to dart in if he gave her an opening but far enough away that if he lunged, she would be able to evade him. Blood streamed down his leg, leaving a slick trail on the beige marble floor. Her small victory, satisfying as it was, wouldn't last long. He would heal quickly. Besides, she couldn't kill him through a thousand paper cuts.

She risked a glance over her shoulder. Annabeth was almost at the door. A few more steps and she would be through it. Then she would only have to worry about Harriet. And herself.

War lunged, thrusting his sword at her chest, trying to skewer rather than slice her this time. She caught the blade with the hook of the kama, redirecting it away from her body. When it was clear, she retreated. She tried to count seconds in her head. At four, Annabeth would be safe. At twenty, Harriet might be too. All she had to do was buy them time, then figure out how to get away from War and make sure he couldn't immediately follow.

She'd only made it to three when War charged. Even hobbling, he was formidable. He windmilled his sword as he advanced, trying to evade the kama's wicked hook. She fell back a few more steps, watching warily. Although none of the demons they'd revoked had ever fought back with a sword, the principles were the same as fighting an angry demon with a baseball bat: don't get hit by the long, ouchie weapon.

War pulled his arm a little too far back, winding up for a heavy blow, and she darted forward, trying to slice his unprotected wrist or fingers and force him to drop the weapon. It might have worked... had she not made a mistake. To reach his arm, even the end of it, she had come into his range. Focused as she was on evading his sword, she hadn't seen his free hand moving. She didn't realize her error until his thick fingers wrapped around her throat, squeezing with a strength that could crush bone.

Roaring in triumph, the celestial lifted her off the ground until her toes dangled inches from the floor. She could neither breathe nor swallow. The pressure against her windpipe was terrifying, but it was the tingling in her toes, signifying a sudden lack of blood flow, that really worried her. Panic made her wild. She began to thrash, hammering at his arm with her fist, slashing with her kama, and kicking him anywhere her boots could reach.

She knew she had limited time before he would strangle her into unconsciousness, but those precious seconds ticked by as her blows rained uselessly on him. She couldn't loosen his grip in the least. Dark shadows formed at the edge of her field of vision. The tingling ran up her legs.

This wasn't how things were supposed to end. This wasn't how she was supposed to die. And yet... The kama fell out of her hand. Then the world went black.

CHAPTER FOURTEEN

By habit, Harriet had wanted to go on the offensive against Pestilence the moment her shuriken struck him. The best defense was a good offense, and he would never be more vulnerable than he was at that moment. Had he been a demon, it would have been easy to slice the blade of her kama across his neck from ear to ear and pronounce the words of revocation that would banish him from the Earth forever. But he wasn't a demon, and the words of revocation would likely do nothing to him. In fact, she didn't know whether it was even possible to kill the Horsemen. It wasn't like there was a handbook they could consult about this kind of thing.

But all this was moot anyway. She wasn't supposed to fight. The priority was getting out of the bank before the Horsemen's master arrived. Before Lucifer arrived. So against her impulse, she began to retreat instead of advance, taking slow steps backward, her kama held ready at her side.

From the corner of her eye, she saw War charge Theodora, but as the two started to spar, her attention was quickly recaptured by Pestilence. In what felt like mere seconds, he had already recovered enough to reach for his bow. She watched him with intense focus, evaluating. He was healing much faster than a demon would have. If she ran now, she was confident she could make it to the door before he nocked the arrow and sighted her. But it was a small window that was quickly closing.

She was about to call to Theodora, telling her to disengage from War and run, when she became aware of silence to her right where she should have been hearing the sounds of fighting. Concerned, she looked over her shoulder. And then did a double take. War was holding Theodora off the ground like a life-size doll, his colossal hand wrapped completely around her neck. His opponent had stopped fighting. Her body was limp, and her kama was on the floor beneath her feet.

She was in trouble.

Without a moment's hesitation, Harriet took off toward her. If she didn't make the Horseman let go of Theodora, he would kill her. At the same time, she had to be careful of his broadsword. If he managed to land even a glancing blow, both women would be in jeopardy.

Seeing her coming, War roared, shaking his prize defiantly. Harriet ignored his bluster, focused on the kama on the floor. Two kamas weren't just better than one—they would be essential to surviving.

The smooth lobby floor was polished to a high shine. With a lunge, she dropped onto it and slid like a batter into home plate. Her momentum carried her right in front of War and then past him. On the way, she grabbed the second kama. Regaining her feet, she brandished her two weapons. Now the odds were better. He was heavy and powerful, but she was nimble. It might just be enough.

The Horseman turned slowly to confront her, huffing like an angry bear. Realizing he couldn't continue to carry Theodora with his left hand *and* effectively swing his sword to fight Harriet with only his right, he cast the unconscious woman to the ground. She landed bonelessly. Her eyes remained closed. Harriet could only hope she was okay.

Harriet evaluated the celestial before her, thinking fast. She needed to find a way to neutralize him before Pestilence could pile on, but armored as he was, he had few weak points. There was only one place she was relatively sure was both vulnerable and within reach. She jumped at him, feinting with a high slice intended to direct his attention to his upper torso. He parried easily, swinging the kama out of the way. She was ready for it. With a quick flip of her wrist that disengaged her blade, she dropped into a crouch and immediately raked both kama blades against the unprotected backs of his knees.

Steel sliced mercilessly through thick tendons, so sharp she felt only a little resistance from the tissue before the blades were free. She straightened and slammed her foot into War's left knee with every ounce of strength she had, a brutal stomping kick that was payback for what he'd done to Annabeth. The knee buckled as tendons and ligaments stretched past their breaking point and snapped. As she sprang out of the way, War toppled to the ground, bellowing his rage and pain like a foghorn. Blood pooled around him as he thrashed and wailed, unable to move his legs.

For a human, hamstringing could be deadly. It was possible to exsanguinate from the injury. For a celestial like War, however, the best Harriet could hope for was that she had a few minutes before he would be on his feet again. She raced to Theodora, crouching to feel her pulse. There. It was, faint but she could feel it. Theodora may have been unresponsive, but at least her heart was beating.

Harriet didn't have time to do anything else before she had to turn her attention back to Pestilence. His arrow was up, and as she watched, he pulled back the string. There was no time to think. She sprinted toward the teller counter, the only cover in the entire lobby.

The arrow sliced across her left shoulder, carving a channel through skin, muscle, and fabric. She clamped her mouth shut against the sudden blast of pain. The scored line burned like it had been touched by a white-hot poker. But she was lucky—it could have gone straight through her heart. Or her head.

As Pestilence reloaded, she reached the counter and, summoning all her agility—she couldn't help thinking how she had been so much more athletic even ten years ago—vaulted over it and took cover on the other side. Her legs weak, she sank down on the floor. She leaned her head back against an old metal filing cabinet and took three deep, sucking breaths. Stress made everything harder, even breathing.

The lobby echoed with War's agonized roars. At least it was a helpful cue—when his cries stopped, she would know he had healed and become a threat once more. She put her hand to her shoulder and pressed down on the fabric of her coat, trying to staunch the bleeding and think. The situation wasn't looking good. So long as Pestilence had his bow and arrows, he had an almost insurmountable advantage.

Not to mention she had to not only keep herself safe, but protect the defenseless Theodora as well. And there was no use worrying about what would happen if they were still in the bank when Lucifer arrived. She got to her knees. She needed to keep Pestilence's attention on her. She popped her head above the edge of the counter to see what the Horseman was doing.

Immediately, an arrow grazed her right ear. She ducked back down, biting back a gargle of pain. It felt like a razor had been taken to her ear and then alcohol poured on the wound. But it was better than the alternative. A few inches to the right and she would be dead.

Trying to ignore the pain, she set off in a bent-over creep, keeping her body concealed below the line of the countertop. Warm blood that quickly turned cold dripped down her chest and back, leaving red blotches on her white shirt. When she estimated she was parallel to Pestilence, she stopped and cautiously raised her head above the counter a second time—far enough to survey the room, but without exposing anything below her eyes. The celestial had been waiting for her to reappear. When he saw her, he immediately tried to sight her with his arrow, but before he could shoot, she dropped down again.

What to do, what to do? Not only was she pinned down behind the counter, but Pestilence would soon realize he could walk forward and shoot down the line, turning her into the only fish in a woefully small barrel. And then once she was taken care of, he could turn his attention to Theodora. She had to somehow close the distance between them and take away the advantage his bow gave him. There was only one way to do that. She needed a distraction.

She inventoried the things around her: a coffee mug full of white pens branded with the bank's red logo, a large gray landline phone, a black swivel chair, a metal filing cabinet, and a family photo in a cheap plastic frame. She stared at the photo for a moment—a smiling family of four on vacation somewhere sunny and tropical. Wait. Where were the tellers? The reminder that the bank shouldn't be this empty struck her like a slap to the face. How long had it been since the Horsemen had entered the building? Three minutes? Two? The missing tellers must have hidden in the offices down the corridor. Surely, one of them had called the police. How quickly could they come?

But also, what would happen when they did? A brazen assault like this, especially if it resulted in a police standoff, would be front and center news. Even if the celestials ran at the sound of police sirens, there was no way to explain away the CCTV footage of them materializing from thin air. The city's human population was about to discover there were nonhumans walking the streets. There was no going back from that.

She set her kamas down and grabbed the mug, dumping the pens out in a messy pile in front of her. She needed to get Theodora out of the bank immediately. Surviving the Horsemen aside, they couldn't afford to still be there when the police arrived. If they were detained, it would be impossible to explain why they'd brought weapons into a bank without sounding crazy, much less that they'd gotten into a fight with two beings from the Book of Revelation. At the very least, they'd be put into detention while the police tried to sort things out, and in the meantime, the police might dig up evidence of what would look from the outside like their involvement in a decade-and-a-half-long murder spree.

Grasping the mug like a baseball, she threw it as hard as she could at the opposite end of the counter, grimacing against the pain that blazed in her shoulder in response. The mug exploded into a dozen ceramic shards as it hit the floor. Immediately, she grabbed the chair next to her and shoved it after the mug. The chair rolled roughly over the thin red carpet, bouncing as it hit wrinkles in the fabric. This was a Hail Mary pass. She needed Pestilence to be distracted by the sounds long enough for her to clear the counter and charge him. But her window of opportunity would be a second or two at best. At worst, he wouldn't fall for the diversion at all.

She moved with fluid grace, in a single motion collecting the kamas and vaulting over the counter. As she had hoped, Pestilence's head was turned away from her, his attention attracted by her decoy sounds. Time slowed to a crawl as she flung herself at him, legs churning. She was a teenager again, chasing her first demon, her first revocation, not knowing who would end up with the upper hand. One step, two steps. The distance didn't seem to change between them. She had inadvertently trained half her life for this moment, but was it enough?

His head turned back toward her, his white eyes locking on her. The bow followed in a delayed reaction, the arrow not yet pointing at her but on its way. A thrill of fear exploded in her chest. She was too far away. She wouldn't reach him in time to stop him from shooting her.

The kama was not designed to be thrown. As a farming implement, it had harvested rice. As a weapon, it was meant for close combat—hooking, stabbing, or slashing. But that didn't mean it *couldn't* be thrown. Realizing that if she didn't do something she would be dead in a few heartbeats, Harriet raised the kama in her left hand and threw it. All her hopes were pinned on the blade landing properly and not glancing off the Horseman's armor.

The kama's tip found a home at the base of Pestilence's neck just above his armor, now stained a messy, ugly red from the shuriken hit. Harriet couldn't tell how far the blade had penetrated. All she could see was that it had lodged there, the handle sticking out like a scene from a horror movie. The celestial staggered two steps backward, eyes dropping to the weapon. It was the opening she needed.

Harriet's priority was neutralizing the Horseman's weapon. So long as he had it, she and Theodora were in trouble. Distracted by the kama embedded in his body, the celestial had lowered his bow. Now, Harriet swung her remaining kama at the string. When the blade touched it, the thin line severed easily, the two ends silently snapping away from each other as the tension was released.

She didn't stick around to see what he would do now that his weapon had been broken. Spinning on the balls of her feet, she ran back to Theodora. The other woman had rolled onto her hands and knees and was coughing weakly. War writhed several feet away from her, a wide trail of bright red blood around him. The way his legs were starting to move indicated that although he was still down, he was recovering fast.

"Let's go!" Harriet bellowed.

Her ears buzzed. Her body hummed with adrenaline. For the first time, she felt certain they could get out safely. Unbelievably, the odds had turned in their favor. Theodora staggered to her feet, her face a paler shade of brown than usual, as Harriet glanced over her shoulder. Good. Pestilence hadn't followed her. He was standing exactly where she had left him, watching, his broken bow held limply in his hand.

"Come on." She half pulled, half dragged Theodora toward the door.

The distinctive wail of sirens in the distance pierced the air. Finally, the police were coming. Perhaps the Horsemen would drag themselves away, licking their wounds and planning a future return at which time they could successfully snare the seal guardian. Or maybe they would glamour, hiding in plain sight as the police swarmed over a bloody, empty crime scene. Harriet didn't care what happened, so long as she and Theodora were well on their way by then.

They were almost to the door, Harriet's hand reaching for the burnished metal handle, when Theodora screamed. The sound tore through Harriet. She felt it to her bones. She half turned to see what was wrong. An arrow was sticking most of the way out of Theodora's chest.

Theodora stumbled a little, and Harriet grabbed her to keep her from falling. Her fingers grabbed for the arrow's shaft, but there was nothing she could do now. The damage was done. Harriet looked back at Pestilence, disbelieving. He was already nocking another arrow, staring them down from across the lobby. Stupid. It was a stupid mistake for her to have made. She should have known his magic bow would repair itself, just as War's tendons and ligaments were currently mending. Why wouldn't it? It wasn't like it was a normal, human-made weapon.

"It's all right. You're all right," she murmured to Theodora. "We're almost there."

In truth, she didn't know for certain if the situation would be all right. The arrow was lodged high in Theodora's chest. It had definitely punctured her right lung, but the lung hadn't collapsed yet. It would be a race between the onset of a possible tension pneumothorax and Theodora's body healing itself. Harriet hoped her nonmortal side would win out, but if it didn't, they would have to go straight to the ER. At least it wasn't fatal. Yet.

Theodora began to pant, making a strangled, high-pitched sound. Harriet recognized that shock was rapidly setting in. She pushed aside her worry about the injury, saving it for later. In their years as revokers, they had endured many kinds of injuries. Being shot by an arrow was new, but the solution was the same: keep moving. Get out of danger.

Before Pestilence could release his second shot, she grabbed the heavy door and pulled. Then she seized Theodora's hand, ignoring the other woman's yowl of pain, and yanked her through. The two women stumbled onto the sidewalk outside…and found Annabeth waiting for them with a taxi. Harriet had never been so relieved to see one of the city's grimy cabs in her life.

"I. Told you. To go," Theodora wheezed as Harriet manhandled her toward it.

Theodora may have sounded annoyed to see Annabeth, but she was lucky their third member had ignored her orders. She and Harriet couldn't have stood around waiting to hail a cab of their own, not with the Horsemen inside and the police on their way. Nor could they have limped off down the street with an arrow still in Theodora's chest and her lung on the verge of collapse. Annabeth helpfully opened the back door. She looked as concerned as Harriet felt.

"You know how hard it is to get a taxi in this part of town at this hour," she said by explanation.

Harriet slid into the taxi as quickly as she could. At any moment, Pestilence could come charging out after them. They needed to get away, and fast. She caught the driver's attention and looked him dead in the eye. "I'll give you a thousand dollars to drive faster than you ever have."

CHAPTER FIFTEEN

"What happened?" Annabeth couldn't stop staring at the arrow sticking out of Theodora's chest. It was a good two-and-a-half-feet long, and the other woman had to sit diagonally in the back seat so that neither end touched anything. Annabeth had once taken a knitting needle to the stomach, delivered by a feisty demon with an evident passion for knitting and an aversion to returning to Hell, but she'd never seen anything quite like this. If she hadn't known about Pestilence and his bow, she would have assumed it was a gag prop.

Theodora's jaw clenched. "I got fucking shot with an arrow is what happened."

Her bright red fingernails scraped against her thighs as she gripped her black jeans, fighting against the pain. She must have been bleeding, but either the blood hadn't soaked through her jacket yet or the black leather hid the stain. Or perhaps, Annabeth thought with concern, the arrow was acting like a plug, holding the blood in.

"I cut Pestilence's bowstring, but..." Harriet grabbed the hair on the top of her head and pulled, frustrated. "Fuck! What are we supposed to do against these guys? They heal faster than demons, and that bow…" She trailed off, overwhelmed.

Annabeth understood Harriet's despair. She felt guilty for not having been there with them. Even though there was nothing she could have done, she couldn't shake the illogical feeling that maybe she could somehow have helped. If she had been there, perhaps Theodora wouldn't have been hurt.

The driver took a turn going forty-five miles per hour on a twenty-five miles-per-hour road, causing Harriet to list into her hard. Annabeth could have sworn two of the car's tires had fully left the pavement, leaving the vehicle balancing precariously on the remaining two. The taxi was simultaneously in control and out of control, Schrödinger's car. She grabbed the door handle for dear life. The driver had taken Harriet's offer too seriously. It wouldn't do them any good to escape the Horsemen only to die in a car crash. Not to mention that fleeing from a bank in a speeding car looked more than a little suspicious. She didn't want anyone thinking they'd just robbed it.

"Slow down!" she commanded the driver, using her best mom voice.

The taxi stabilized on a straightaway, now moving a few miles per hour slower, and she relaxed a fraction of an inch.

"We're going to have to get that arrow out so you can heal," Harriet told Theodora.

Moving carefully in the tight space, she shucked her coat off and handed it to Theodora. Annabeth saw for the first time that Harriet's shoulder was stained bright red with blood. The blood had run in streaks down both the front and back of her shirt, leaving fuzzy blotches. But whatever the injury and however bad it was—Annabeth couldn't tell—Harriet didn't complain. Annabeth made a note to ask her about it once they had figured out how to help Theodora. Harriet could be just as stubborn as Theodora. Just because she wasn't outwardly hurting didn't mean she wasn't in pain.

Theodora stared at the coat as though she had been handed dirty laundry. "What's this for?"

"To bite down on."

"You want to do it here? Now?"

Annabeth sucked in a breath. If the injury was bad enough that they couldn't wait until they made it back to the pawnshop to tend to it, perhaps they should tell the driver to take them to the closest hospital instead. She glanced at him, checking to see if he'd overheard them. That he had let them into the car with Theodora looking as she did was incredible and suggested he may not have been paying attention. But he probably drew the line at Theodora bleeding all over his back seat. Luckily, at that moment he was focused on the road in front of him.

Harriet rolled her sleeves up to the elbows like a doctor preparing for surgery. It was a good thing she'd had some emergency medical training years ago. It had reaped dividends over time. She nodded curtly. "We have to. We need to know if that lung is going to collapse or not."

Annabeth winced at the word "collapse." Theodora wasn't happy about it either, but her skin was starting to turn ashy. She wasn't looking good. With deep misgiving in her eyes, she obediently put the coat sleeve in her mouth, having folded it over on itself so it would be thicker. She clenched her hands together in anticipation of what was about to happen, and Annabeth unconsciously mirrored the movement.

"Annabeth, start singing as loud as you can," Harriet commanded. Her face was grim.

"What?"

Harriet tilted her head toward the driver, partitioned from them by a thick plastic pane. Her implication was clear. He may not have overheard them discussing pulling the arrow out, but he would definitely hear the act itself. Annabeth hesitated. She was no Aretha Franklin. She couldn't even consistently stay on key. But this wasn't a singing competition, and it wasn't for an audience. It was for Theodora. She opened her mouth and began to warble, shakily at first but then with a little more gusto.

Harriet reached for the arrow sticking out of Theodora's chest, bracing her legs against the floor for leverage. Theodora watched with silent trepidation. Loud enough for Theodora to hear but not the driver, Harriet said, "On the count of three, I'm going to pull the arrow just a little more forward."

Theodora nodded, her face strained. Annabeth's own chest clenched in sympathy. She sang louder, like a drunk college student coming home from a football game. The driver must have thought she was crazy.

"One, two—"

Harriet pulled a beat early, catching the other women off guard. The arrow moved a few inches farther out of Theodora's chest, gliding with an ease that made Annabeth squeamish. The shaft glimmered, covered with fresh blood. Theodora screamed into the coat, eyes squeezed shut. As Harriet let go of the arrow, she rocked back and forth, growling like a wounded animal. Annabeth's heart ached, wishing she could take away some of the pain for her.

After a few seconds, Theodora stilled. She looked at Harriet, shoulders quivering, and nodded. Strong as she was, trepidation nibbled at the corners of her eyes. This was going to hurt.

Harriet didn't bother counting a second time. She grasped the arrow with both hands and bent it until the wood snapped. Theodora bit down so hard on the coat her face turned almost purple. She stomped her foot and tugged at the coat in her lap as if trying to tear it apart. Harriet threw the broken end of the arrow onto the floor, then, without pausing to allow Theodora to recover, reached around and ripped the other half of the arrow out of her back.

Theodora spit the sleeve out of her mouth. "*Fuck.* Fuck, fuck, fuck, fuck." She hunched over, groaning through gritted teeth. "God *damn* it."

Although her outburst overpowered Annabeth's singing, the driver never looked in the rearview mirror. Whether by some miracle he hadn't heard, didn't care, or knew better in this city than to want to know, Annabeth couldn't tell. After one last verse, she tapered off, letting her voice die away. Theodora was breathing heavily, her cheeks flexed, but she was valiantly holding in any further whimpers.

"Will she be all right?" Annabeth asked Harriet anxiously. She was still thinking about that terrible word "collapse" and what it would mean for Theodora if it happened.

Theodora answered for herself. "I'm always all right. It's just a scratch. I'll walk it off." But her voice was weak, and her eyes were filled with hurting.

Harriet took her coat from Theodora and pressed it against Theodora's shoulder to absorb the blood, which had now started to flow in earnest. "We need to seal the wound so air doesn't get in and cause pneumothorax. We need—*There!*" Harriet stabbed her finger at the window, pointing animatedly at something outside. Then she started banging wildly on the plastic partition. "Pull over! We need to get something."

With a speed and agility that didn't shock Annabeth at all, the driver maneuvered the taxi to the side of the road only a few dozen yards from where Harriet had pointed, barely avoiding sideswiping two cars in the process. The building Harriet had indicated was a small, unassuming drugstore with a flickering sign and a smattering of graffiti on the walls. Harriet turned to Annabeth. "Get anything you can find that will act as a sealant. Not gauze or a Band-Aid—something like a Ziploc bag or Saran Wrap. And duct tape."

Annabeth didn't know how those items could possibly have a medical application, but she nodded, trusting Harriet. "Okay."

The store was empty but for a single employee, who sat at the register reading a magazine. Annabeth stalked past with hasty determination. Finding a small clothing section at the end of the first aisle, she grabbed two shirts at random and slung them over her forearm, not pausing to check the sizes. Her friends needed clothing that wasn't covered in their own blood, and beggars couldn't be choosers. From the kitchen supplies in the next aisle, she snatched a box of sandwich-sized plastic bags. The duct tape was in the cleaning section. Her list complete, she half ran to the front of the store, her knee protesting that it wasn't fully healed yet, and dumped her items on the counter. The employee, a teenager with thick, bright blue eyeshadow, heavy mascara, and piercings in her nose, lip, and cheek, slowly began to scan the items.

Annabeth tapped her foot impatiently, biting the inside of her cheek to keep herself from urging the girl to work faster. Her eyes fell on a newspaper next to the register. A headline announced a bout of skirmishing on the Kashmiri border between India and Pakistan. Below it, there was an article on a polio outbreak in Africa. Her stomach lurched. The shockwaves from the start of the Apocalypse were already starting to spread, and it was only day two.

"Are you a rewards member?" the girl asked, derailing her train of thought. Annabeth could see the blue gum in her mouth.

"What? Yes. No." Annabeth was too distracted to answer properly.

"Would you like to be? It's free—"

"No." Annabeth didn't mean to be rude, but she didn't have time to hear about the wonderful benefits of owning a rewards card for that particular chain of drugstores. She had a friend with a hole in her chest and the end of the world to worry about. She swiped her credit card through the card reader and began to stuff her purchases into a plastic bag.

Racing back to the cab, she tossed the bag to Harriet and then flung herself in after it. Harriet looked inside and gave her a funny look. "What is this?" She held up a piece of fabric.

"Shirts." Annabeth reached into the bag and extracted the plastic bags and duct tape, handing them to Harriet. "Here. Will this work?"

"Yeah." Harriet moved her coat to uncover the wound on Theodora's chest. The round hole oozed pink foam, blood mixed with oxygen. Ripping open the box of plastic bags, she took one and held it to the wound. She indicated the tape to Annabeth with her chin. "Tear that into strips for me."

Annabeth did as she was told, handing each piece of tape to Harriet as soon as she had torn it. Harriet taped three of the four sides of the plastic bag tight to Theodora's chest, leaving the last side free. When she was finished, she evaluated her work with a critical expression. She said, "That should work well enough as an occlusive dressing." She motioned to Theodora. "Take your jacket off. We need to get the entry wound, too."

Theodora looked at her balefully.

"Don't be a baby," Harriet told her, heartless.

Theodora scowled at her, but moving gingerly with her teeth clenched, she slowly eased her left arm out of the jacket. Harriet pulled the jacket off the rest of the way, exposing an identical hole in Theodora's back when she leaned forward. Annabeth hissed silently. The puncture looked large enough she could have put a finger through.

Harriet repeated the same procedure for the entry wound. When she finished, she asked Theodora, "How are you feeling?"

"Like shit," Theodora complained. "I can hear whistling through my own chest every time I breathe."

"Maybe you can get some of that hot air out, then," Harriet deadpanned.

"Fuck you," Theodora wheezed.

Good. If she had the energy to curse, she must be feeling at least a little better. Annabeth pulled one of the shirts from the bag and held it out to Harriet. "Here, put this on."

Harriet took the pale green shirt and held it up. Her face immediately twisted into a combination of confusion and horror. And accusation.

"What? What is it?" Annabeth asked.

"A Hawaiian shirt with prints of Jesus holding a baby dinosaur? Is that a joke?"

Annabeth had learned a lot from being a mother. How to touch someone else's vomit without instantly retching, for example, or how to watch the same movie six times in a row. One of the most lasting takeaways, however, was that it didn't matter what a shirt looked like. If you needed one, you wore whatever was available. She gave Harriet a stern look, brooking no argument. "Put it on. You can't go around wearing your bloody shirt. We don't need to draw any more attention to ourselves than we already have." She reached for the other shirt. "And Theodora—"

"Can't change shirts yet," Harriet intervened firmly. "We need to limit her motion for now." She rapped on the plastic to get the driver's attention. "We're good to go now. Thanks for stopping."

As the taxi lurched into motion, one of the halves of the broken arrow rolled into Annabeth's foot. She stared at it. Although it looked like the type of arrow that might have been used in some medieval battle, the wood came from no tree any human had ever seen, and the arrowhead glowed white with what she called "celestial light." Objectively, this arrow was priceless—a celestial object used by the first Horseman of the Apocalypse. It was proof of the existence of angels and demons, Heaven and Hell. But on the other hand, it had very nearly killed Theodora. She intended to chuck it into the next available trash can.

* * *

The pawnshop was on the opposite side of the city, and traffic was bad even on the best day. As they sat in yet another standstill, Annabeth pulled her phone out to see if there was any news yet about what had happened at the bank. For all she knew, it could be hours before the first article appeared, depending on what had happened after the women left. As she pulled up the news home page, however, she saw it, the scrolling red headline reading, "Breaking news: failed robbery attempt at First City Bank."

Heart beating faster, she clicked the link. She didn't know what she would do if there was CCTV footage of them. There was no easy way to explain her presence there to Jonathan, much less to strangers who might recognize her on the street. Nor did she know how it would be to see Pestilence and War captured in a grainy, gray image or video. Luckily, the short article was pictureless. It read:

Breaking: Police are reporting a chaotic scene this morning at First City Bank after robbers attempted to blast into the bank's vault. No customers appear to have been inside the bank at the time and no money was taken. Police have closed the building for investigation, but so far reports indicate one person, a bank employee, was killed. More details to follow on this developing story.

Horrified, she read the words a second time. And then a third. She set the phone down in her lap, numb. It couldn't be. It wasn't possible. The angel had left. Theodora had said so. Lucifer couldn't have killed her and opened the seal.

And yet there it was, right in front of her. The third seal had been opened. Famine was free.

In her mind, she saw the third seal guardian lying broken on the floor, her dark eyes staring blankly at the ceiling, her lower legs akimbo and her arm outstretched in one final effort to touch the seal she had spent untold years guarding. Around her, shards of metal and concrete that had been blown from the wall scattered everywhere like confetti. The vault door itself bent and twisted, mangled by the fantastically powerful force that appeared to be unleashed when seals were opened. And the beautiful seal to which Annabeth had pressed her hand so recently shattered, its blue radiance gone.

Had the angel died with surprise on her face? Regret? What had she thought as she faced the Prince of Darkness?

"Annabeth?"

She came back to herself with a start. Harriet was peering curiously at her, sensing something was wrong. She blinked, her eyes dry, and licked her lips. Even though the words describing what had happened were simple, her mouth refused to form them.

Cars moved slowly past them outside the window. Their drivers cursed the traffic or thought about their kids or sang along to the radio, unaware their world was this much closer to catastrophe. But she knew. Lucifer was almost halfway to the Apocalypse now.

"Annabeth?" Harriet repeated, more urgently this time.

She took a breath, trying to bring feeling back to her body. Trying to push through the feeling of helplessness. She murmured, "The third seal was opened."

"What the fuck?" Theodora barked. She immediately clenched her teeth, swallowing hard against the pain that her outburst had caused. Her eyelids fluttered.

Harriet drew her eyebrows together into a dark line, her expression instantly stern. The effect was mitigated, however, by the ridiculous, photoshopped pattern on her shirt. Harriet had been right; as dire as the situation was, it was difficult to take her seriously when looking at the Lamb cradling a baby velociraptor. "What do you mean the third seal was opened?"

Annabeth held up her phone. "It's in the news."

She had found the seal. She had been there, seen it, touched it. But she hadn't been able to save it. Nor had the angels. Where *were* they? When were they going to step in and stop Lucifer?

Theodora's face wrinkled in confusion. "The news reported the seal was opened? How the fuck do they know about the seal?"

"No," Annabeth said weakly. She was sinking beneath the waves, drowning. "The news said robbers tried to open the vault and a bank employee was killed."

As far as the reporters knew, what happened at the bank was nothing more than a crime gone wrong in a city full of crime. The police were on the scene and everything was safe and sound now. The danger had passed. As it had always done, the human world tottered on, oblivious to the activities of the celestials tiptoeing through it. But it couldn't remain oblivious for much longer, not at this rate.

"So now Famine's been released." Theodora's voice was flat.

Annabeth flinched. Her friends were probably thinking how useless their foray to the bank had been. Theodora could have been killed and Lucifer would still have succeeded. Everything had been for nothing. They might as well have stayed home.

Harriet rubbed her forehead. It was only because she'd wiped her hands on her coat—now ruined—before putting the ridiculous shirt on that she didn't leave a smear of Theodora's blood across it. She sighed. "Three Horsemen in the city. That's not good. Especially now that we know they work together."

"What the fuck weapon does Famine have? A flamethrower?" Theodora grouched.

It was unclear whether her question was rhetorical or not, but it made Annabeth think. She frowned and adjusted her glasses, pushing them back up her nose. "I don't know. He's only described in the Bible as carrying scales."

Psellus's "immoral man" wasn't like the first two Horsemen. He wasn't described as a conqueror or a warlord. But whether that made him any less dangerous than the other two, she didn't know. Probably not. With their luck, he was the worst yet.

"Jesus fucking Christ," Theodora muttered, tilting her head back against the seat and squeezing her eyes shut. Her chest moved in short, light breaths.

"How did Lucifer catch the seal guardian?" Harriet wondered.

Theodora shook her head without opening her eyes. "Who cares? It's Lucifer. He probably can do any damn thing he wants to on Earth."

"How long do you think until he opens the fourth seal?"

What Harriet was really asking was how quickly was the sand draining out of the hourglass?

"Don't know, don't care. We saw the seal, we got our asses kicked, we're done. Finished. No more running into those big-ass bastards. We're tapping out."

Annabeth stared at her lap miserably. She couldn't disagree with that. They were in over their heads. The Apocalypse, Lucifer, this was all way bigger than them. But... "What if by the time the angels finally come they're too late? Arakiel said the angels don't know everything. What if they don't know about the seals yet?"

Theodora snorted. "Lucifer didn't just Great Escape out of Hell without anyone noticing, then put on some glasses and a Groucho Marx moustache to creep around on Earth incognito, opening up the seals to the *Apocalypse*." She stressed the last word hard. "They know."

Annabeth pressed her lips together and fell silent. They were going around in circles, asking the same questions to each other over and over again without finding any answers. Abruptly,

Theodora's phone rang. The cab fell silent as the three women simultaneously recognized the ringtone. Andromalius.

As one, they stared at Theodora's pocket. Two days. Andromalius had given them only two days to hunt down her father's killer. He would be expecting some kind of an update from them.

"Shit." Theodora eased the phone out of her pocket and stared at it as though it were a bomb whose timer had counted down to thirty seconds. "Do we answer it?"

"He must know about Lucifer and is calling us off," Harriet said. But she didn't sound convinced.

Annabeth shivered. "If the Daemonium knows Lucifer's on Earth, Andromalius will be even more eager to start his war." The angels so far hadn't been able to stop Lucifer from opening seals. She didn't see how they could simultaneously stop him *and* control a city full of rebelling demons.

"Only one way to find out," Theodora said. She held the phone to her ear. "Hello?"

CHAPTER SIXTEEN

"Where the fuck are you?"

Andromalius's voice exploded from the phone like the chattering fire of an anti-aircraft gun. Theodora winced. Although he sounded angry, she knew it wasn't necessarily at them. Annabeth had once theorized that he woke up every day and growled into the mirror while brushing his teeth, preparing to hate the day and everything in it. Theodora didn't disagree. If he had been human, that simmering rage would probably have given him a heart attack in his early fifties. Since he was a demon, however, no such luck. And to be fair, he was under more than a little stress right now, what with leading the next demonic uprising against Heaven.

She put the phone on speaker, even though her companions could hear him well enough without it, and put it in her lap. "We're in a cab." She didn't offer any more explanation. It was none of his business what they were doing, and besides, she wasn't interested in a long-winded recounting of the sequence of events that had led them to this point. Every time she spoke, there was an uncomfortable whistling feeling in her chest as air rushed out of her body through places it shouldn't. The holes punched into her by Pestilence's arrow were starting to heal, but it would be hours more until they were completely re-covered by skin, and even longer until the tissue fully restored itself.

Luckily, the demon had no interest in learning why his revokers were in a taxi. True to his nature, all he cared about was himself. He quipped, "Did you hear about last night?"

The way he asked the question immediately caught Theodora's attention. It was obviously something big. She looked to her companions for their reactions. Under the circumstances, there was absolutely no telling what he was talking about. For all she knew, the Horsemen could have put on a burlesque show at city hall while she was sleeping. Which...she might just have paid to see.

Taking her silence as a no, he answered his own question. "Those fuckers burned down the Faithless Monk. They fucking burned it to the ground."

He might as well have reached through the phone and punched her in the face. She stared at the phone, reeling. "What?"

"We're going in hard and fast against them. They want a war? We'll give it to them."

His words sizzled with emotion. She could imagine him at his desk, eyes burning and fist pounding against his desk as he snarled into the phone. Maybe the snake was hissing too, like an angry little black worm. Her eyes met Harriet's as she tried to make sense of what he was saying. The *angels* had started the war? Hardly. Not with Lucifer going around opening seals.

But more importantly, what the fuck were the angels thinking? They had destroyed the seedy, grubby demon bar but hadn't even tried to prevent what happened in the bank? Were they going to wait until the fourth seal? The fifth? What kind of shitty-ass plan was that?

Andromalius wasn't done. "Those fucking angels should never have come back to our city. They should never have come back! Now they're gonna pay for it." He paused, then his tone shifted, a train switching tracks. "I need you to get something for me."

"Okay..." Theodora had no idea where this was going to go, but she suspected it wasn't going to be good.

"It's what we need to win this war—the only thing that will kill an archangel. I'm texting you the information now. Bring it back to me immediately. I don't care what you have to do to get it."

Without waiting for them to agree, he hung up. Andromalius, acting high lord of the Daemonium, assumed the women were on his side, because as far as he knew, his three half-demon employees were. Theodora was hardly going to call back and tell him they weren't on anyone's side. She wanted no fucking part in an end-of-the-world shootout between Heaven and Hell.

A second later, he sent a text containing a link. Curious despite herself about what on earth Andromalius thought could kill an archangel, she clicked it. The link sent her to a news article about a long-standing but rather dull exhibit at the city's history museum chronicling the Roman colonization of the Middle East. At the top of the article was a picture of an old yet well-preserved spear in a long glass case. Huh? What did he want them to do? Brush up on their history?

A second text message arrived. All it said was, "Lance of Longinus."

"What is it?" Harriet asked. She was tense, her dark eyes full of concern.

"What the fuck is the lance of Longinus?" Theodora asked, helplessly confused.

Annabeth gasped. "Oh my God, it's the spear. The spear that was used to stab Jesus!" She reached across Harriet to pluck the phone out of Theodora's limp hands. As she scrolled animatedly, she explained, "According to the Gospel of John, after Jesus was crucified, a centurion named Longinus stabbed him in the side to make sure he was dead. Water and blood came out."

"Okay, that's weird," Theodora muttered. Blood she understood, but water?

Harriet tilted her head. "Aren't there a bunch of so-called Holy Lances floating around Europe? Besides, even if it were real, why would it be *here*?"

Annabeth shrugged, reading intently. "Artifacts have been lost all the time throughout history. Just think of the Ark of the Covenant. It's not impossible that someone could have brought the real Holy Lance here, thinking it was just a regular old first-century Roman spear."

"That's a heck of a coincidence," Harriet said.

Theodora briefly shut her eyes. Everything that had happened in the last two days felt like a giant acid trip. The only way she knew any of it had really happened was the two holes in her chest that felt like being stabbed over and over again by an icepick and the occasional ache in her hand. She sighed. "Okay, let me get this straight. Andromalius is ordering us to steal a spear that stabbed Jesus and bring it to him so he can use it to kill angels."

"Obviously we're not going to do that," Harriet said.

But to Theodora's surprise, Annabeth didn't immediately agree. Instead, when she did speak, there was an unexpectedly thoughtful, excited tone in her voice. "If the Holy Lance can kill archangels, do you think it can kill *any* celestial?"

Theodora narrowed her eyes suspiciously. She could almost see the wheels turning in Annabeth's head, and she already didn't like whatever the other woman was thinking. "Have anyone in particular in mind?"

"Do you think it could kill Lucifer?"

"Oh, fuck no." Theodora moved too much again. Pain set her chest on fire and she had to stop for a moment to catch her breath before continuing, "I know you're not suggesting we steal it for ourselves and try to use it against him. Did you hit your head somewhere?"

Annabeth licked her lips and pulled at the sleeves of her cardigan anxiously. "Not us. Of course not. But maybe we could give it to someone…an angel. We can't let it fall into Andromalius's hands, not knowing what he intends to do with it."

Theodora was hurting. All she wanted was to go home and pull the covers over her head until the world went back to normal. The last thing she wanted to do was head off on yet another harebrained scheme that could get them killed. They had come close enough already today. She picked at the hole in her jacket, once her favorite, now ruined forever, and brought up the first obvious flaw in Andromalius's stupid-ass plan. "Andromalius won't even be able to find an archangel to use it against. Seen one around lately?"

"Annabeth has a point."

Theodora gaped at Harriet. What? They were normally on the same page. Why would she agree with Annabeth now?

Harriet looked pale and disheveled. Her gimmicky joke shirt may have hidden the hit she'd taken to her shoulder, but her ear was still caked with dried blood, which had run down her neck and below her collar. The three women weren't human, but they weren't superhuman either. Their batteries were running low.

They needed to recharge. If this was a sports game, they needed a substitution.

With a look of apology to Theodora, Harriet continued, "The Daemonium is going to war. If we don't take the Holy Lance, Andromalius will just keep sending his minions until he finally gets it. At least if *we* have it, he won't. It's not a lot, but it's something."

Theodora wanted to argue that if the lance was that dangerous, the angels should have known better than to leave it lying around, but Harriet didn't give her the chance. She put her hand on Theodora's thigh. "You don't have to come with us."

Theodora frowned unhappily. She didn't particularly care if the angels and demons started sniping each other in the street, but she cared about her friends. If they were bound and determined to keep doing stupid things, she couldn't let them go alone. Someone had to show some common sense. She pushed Harriet's hand off. "How are we going to steal a museum exhibit and make it out without being caught? I don't think they'll give it to us if we say please."

Annabeth smiled. "I have an idea."

* * *

Theodora waited impatiently outside the museum, leaning against the wall beneath one of the tall windows and trying to look both inconspicuous and casual despite the kama tucked in the back of her pants. In front of her, the taxi waited with its hazard lights on, illegally parked on the busy street. The driver hadn't asked any questions when they'd requested he add a stop to their route that took them a quarter of the way around the city, and the women hadn't offered him any information other than to ask him to wait for five minutes while they ran an errand. But now it had been closer to ten and Theodora was starting to worry that something had gone wrong. Stuck outside with no way of knowing what was happening inside, all she could do was wait. And hope for the best.

They didn't have a great plan. In fact, what Annabeth had come up with had every hallmark of being a really fucking bad one. The women were basically demon bounty hunters, not international jewel thieves. Since there was no way they were going to be able to finesse open the spear case without triggering an alarm, then sneak out of the building with the six-foot-long weapon hidden inside Harriet's Jesus shirt, that had left only one solution: the old smash and grab. Unlike most other modern museums, this one hadn't installed metal detectors yet. Using one of her kamas like a fireman's axe, the plan was for Harriet to break the glass case holding the spear, then she and Annabeth would snatch the Holy Lance, run to the window where Theodora was standing, break it, and jump through.

Of course, in the meantime, alarms would be going off and security guards would be scrambling to stop them. In the best-case scenario, they would pull off an unsophisticated, hugely amateur burglary of an artifact probably no one outside the museum staff cared about. In the worst-case scenario, however, the case would be made out of laminated glass rather than tempered glass, which would mean no matter how hard Harriet hit it, they wouldn't be able to get to the spear. In that case, since there was no other way to get the lance, they'd have to abandon it. Harriet and Annabeth wouldn't know which type of glass it was until the first or second blow.

A father and daughter walked past, catching Theodora's attention. The girl, who must have been six or seven years old, was clutching the thin red ribbon of a helium-filled balloon that said "Birthday Girl" in rainbow letters. Her other hand was held tightly by her father. The scene triggered a memory Theodora had long forgotten. In a flash, she was standing on this same street approximately thirty-seven years before. It was late spring, and she wore an oversized T-shirt with bold geometric prints that hung down almost to the knees of her black leggings.

"Don't tell *amma* about this," her father said, handing her a fast-melting vanilla ice cream cone. His warm brown eyes twinkled. "It's our little secret today."

Her hand briefly touched his as she took the wafer-thin cone from him. Those large, capable hands could do anything. *He* could do anything. She smiled at him, feeling like the most special girl in the world. "I won't, Daddy."

He winked. "Good, that's my girl."

He led her to the museum steps and they sat down to eat in the bright, warm sunlight. He had explained to her once why there were seasons, but she had been too young to understand. All she knew was that there were four of them, and this was her favorite. This was the time when they walked home together from school and got ice cream or shaved ice. When it was warm without being unbearably hot.

After she finished her cone, licking away the ice cream that had dripped onto her hand, he had carried her on his shoulders through the museum, telling her everything he knew about each exhibit. She didn't understand then just how much he knew. Her father had been present at the creation of the Earth. What was history to most people was fond memories to him. But she wouldn't realize that until it was far too late to ask him about it.

When they went home, they had pretended not to have eaten ice cream so they wouldn't spoil their dinner, although now Theodora understood her father must have told her mother in advance, and her mother too had played her part in that charade. Father Domenico had told Annabeth many times that demons were incapable of love. Stripped of God's grace, they were soulless, selfish, abhorrent creatures that lived only to sow suffering and hatred in the human world. Theodora had seen this firsthand, from vile, corporate snakes like Andromalius to filthy, degenerate toads like Merihem. But the priest was wrong about her father.

She knew without a shadow of a doubt that her father loved both her and her mother. He had taught her to jump rope and to write her name with crayons. He had watched as she played on the playground to make sure she didn't get hurt and made chapatis with her. Her father hadn't had an unkind bone in his body. And then one day not long after their visit to the museum, he was gone, killed by his own people. If he had known what was going to happen and told her, if he had let slip some sign that he was in danger, she couldn't remember now. Everything from those days was gone, irretrievably lost in the fog of time.

The window above her shattered, pulling her back into the present. Bits of glass rained down like clear hail onto the oversized black T-shirt Annabeth had gotten her from the drugstore. Theodora let out a yelp and danced away, shaking her head to dislodge any shards that had gotten caught in her hair. The wail of an alarm escaped from the broken window like smoke from a fire.

Annabeth leaned out the window, pushing a thin spear at Theodora butt-first. "Take it!"

Springing into action, Theodora pulled the lance through. Once it was out of the way, Annabeth followed, then Harriet. Their faces were flushed from the sprint from the case to the window and the fear of being caught.

"Go, go, go!" Harriet yelled.

They were running—well, kind of—away from the museum carrying a six-foot-long, two-thousand-year-old artifact, chased by screaming alarms. But the city's unofficial motto was "mind your own damn business," and the cab driver seemed to have taken that to heart. As they finished piling into the back seat, opening the passenger-side window so the sharp metal head of the Holy Lance could poke out, he turned into traffic with astounding calm. Theodora could only imagine he was either going to drive them directly to the nearest police station and hand them over, or this wasn't his first robbery getaway. Both hypotheses were equally plausible.

"So what do we do with this?" Theodora asked.

Although she would never admit it, she felt uncomfortable in the lance's presence. It was one thing to know about angels and demons and be genetically linked to the celestial world. It was another to be in the presence of something that had been used to stab the Lamb of God.

"We need to make contact with the angels and tell them what we have," Annabeth announced. She drew her phone. "I'm going to call Father Domenico. Maybe now that the angels have returned, he can reach them."

Theodora said nothing. Father Domenico hadn't been any help the first time; she didn't expect he'd be much better now. But it was the only angelic connection they had.

As the phone rang, Harriet ran her finger along the shaft of the spear curiously. Theodora knew she was wondering how anyone—angel or demon—could even use it in a fight. The answer to that was: awkwardly, and only in wide-open spaces. There was a reason no one fought with spears anymore, not the least because there was absolutely no element of surprise to it. No one was sneaking a spear into a fight. And, also, the whole guns thing. In her opinion, if the lance really was as powerful as Andromalius thought, his best bet would have been to melt it down and turn it into bullets. Hopefully he wouldn't have the chance now.

After a minute of monotonous, irritating ringing that Theodora could hear even though the phone wasn't on speaker, Annabeth hung up with a pout. A beat later, her disappointment turned to frantic concern. "You don't think the demons got to him, do you?"

Theodora bit back a snarky response. He may have blessed their ammunition for years to make it more effective against demons, but that didn't mean he was their ally, and it *definitely* didn't make him their friend. For all his knowledge about celestials, there was a lot he hadn't told them, things that could have been immensely helpful as they were first navigating the demonic underworld. And she never could shake the belief that he knew more about what had happened to her father than he told them. Even if she didn't know his true motives, she had always felt he was running some kind of game. She just didn't know to what end.

"I'm sure he's fine," Harriet said, trying to comfort Annabeth. "He probably just stepped away from the phone."

"What if he needs help? We need to make sure he's all right!" Panic raised the pitch of Annabeth's voice until it was a shrill squeak.

Theodora rested her head on the back of the seat, absorbing the rumble of the car. "Not me. I'm out." She knew what Father Domenico meant to Annabeth and wouldn't try to dissuade her from going to find him, but she was done running around the city for the day. She wasn't a young woman anymore. She needed a fucking nap and some ibuprofen.

Annabeth's eyes fell to the place where, beneath the T-shirt she'd bought at the drugstore, a plastic bag was duct-taped to Theodora's chest. She looked suitably contrite. "You're right. You need to rest. I'll go alone."

Theodora indicated the lance with her chin. "Take this damn spear with you. And if he refuses to tell you what the angels are up to, shove it up his—"

The driver honked as another car swerved in front of them, drowning her out. Annabeth got the message anyway.

CHAPTER SEVENTEEN

Harriet watched as Annabeth worried at a hangnail on her left index finger. Then, likely to keep herself from causing further damage, she shoved the hand between her thigh and the seat, trapping it. Immediately, her other leg began to bounce restlessly. Harriet frowned, wishing there was something she could do to make her friend feel better.

"I'm sure Father Domenico is fine," she said.

It was the same thing she'd said before they dropped Theodora off at her apartment, and she would keep repeating it for as long as she had to. Of course, she had no idea if he actually was, but at least it was better than admitting the alternative, which was that at Andromalius's order, a pack of demons had swarmed like locusts over the brown roof of St. Francis and through every window and door, ripping the church apart nail by nail and reducing it to splinters and shards of stained glass. This was war, and even in the best of times demons were awful. Fueled by excitement over Lucifer's appearance and anger over Samyaza's death and the destruction of the Faithless Monk—not to mention the promise of vengeance against the angelic host after thousands of years of festering resentment—there was no telling what atrocities they might commit against the city's clergy. The streets would run red with blood, and not metaphorically.

"I should have warned him," Annabeth moaned. "I should have called him after our meeting with Andromalius and told him what the Daemonium was planning. He could have told the other priests. They could have gotten out of the city."

She checked her phone again, then put it down, her face full of anguished defeat. Harriet put her hand on Annabeth's thigh and pressed firmly, stilling it. "It'll be all right. We don't know that anything has happened. You could be worrying for nothing."

Annabeth drew in a deep breath, trying to pull herself together. "I hope so," she replied. But her hands were still trembling.

"Look at me."

Annabeth obeyed without protest. Harriet took in the long, stray hairs that had escaped her bun, one or two of which were white, the thick, black-rimmed glasses perched on her nose, and her large, worried eyes. The three of them had experienced so much together over the years. It was easy, in fact, to forget just how much time exactly had passed. How many years had flown by when they weren't looking. Then she noticed the fine lines forming at the corners of Annabeth's eyes or the pull of gravity on Theodora's cheeks, and she remembered they were no longer young women. But while they may have been older, they were wiser. They no longer charged into danger as though they were invincible. They had learned from their mistakes.

"The angels are back," Harriet reminded her. "They wouldn't let him be hurt."

Suddenly, her phone chimed loudly. Both women startled, then stared at her pocket, Annabeth with trepidation, Harriet with confusion. What now? Harriet pulled the phone out and read the incoming text. A small, happy smile traced its way across her mouth.

Hope your day is going well! Summer had put a smiley face at the end of her message, her usual mixture of cheerful and flirty.

"What is it?" Annabeth asked.

It was amazing how even in the middle of a storm, sometimes a ray of light still managed to burst through. Harriet's smile lingered as she tapped a quick response. *Needs more pie.* When she slipped the phone back into her pocket and looked back at Annabeth, however, her expression was more carefully guarded. "Nothing."

"Oh."

She hesitated. Was it really necessary to conceal Summer's existence from Annabeth? After a moment, she added uncomfortably, "I...met someone."

Excitement filled Annabeth's face. "That's great!"

Harriet shrugged, looking down at the kama resting in her lap. "It's too soon to tell anything."

A night together, a cupcake... It was far too early to see where any of it was going. Right now they were having fun. But she'd been here a few times before and it had never gone anywhere beyond that. Things always fell apart eventually. Personalities didn't match or they wanted different things... Perhaps she was meant to be alone. She and Theodora both, in their own ways.

"But you like her?" Annabeth nudged, undeterred.

Harriet thought of Summer's long blond hair, which had tickled against her nose last night when she tried to sleep, and the unexpected tattoos on her right arm that the sleeve of her white cardigan had hidden at the diner. She thought of the way Summer had groaned and tried to keep her in bed when Annabeth had called that morning, and how her eyes had twinkled when she'd told Harriet she'd see her later. The corners of Harriet's mouth twitched up, the ghost of a smile she wouldn't allow escape. "Yes, I do."

Annabeth nodded. "I hope it works out then."

She did too. But first, the angels had to stop Armageddon.

* * *

"Is that...Jesus? Holding a dinosaur?" Summer's eyes searched Harriet's for an explanation. "I didn't peg you for that type of person." Her voice carried an overtone of dismay.

Harriet looked down automatically. She had all but forgotten she was wearing the slightly too-big shirt Annabeth had brought her from the drugstore. It was the opposite of what she normally wore. She preferred modern and understated. This was...a joke. She touched the fabric, which was thin and slightly rough. "It's a long story."

"There's blood on your ear." Surprised, Summer reached toward it. "What did you do? Here, come inside." She stepped back, inviting Harriet to follow.

Harriet brought her hand to her ear. She had forgotten about the arrow that had grazed her there; the pain had stopped before they'd even made it to the museum. She should have wiped it off. Now she had a problem: although the dried blood remained, there wouldn't be so much as a scrape there anymore. How could she explain that? There was only one possible excuse. "It's...not mine."

Summer tilted her head, confused. She didn't need to verbalize the question. If it wasn't Harriet's blood, whose was it? Harriet suddenly found the paint on the wall extremely interesting. Perhaps she should have gone with Annabeth to St. Francis after all. She wasn't prepared to make up excuses on the spot. At least she wasn't still wearing her bloody shirt and coat, both of which she had shoved into the nearest trash can upon leaving the taxi. Saturated as they were with the blood of not one but two people, she would have been even harder pressed to explain why it looked like she'd been involved in a murder.

Summer made for the kitchen, and Harriet trailed after her. She must have been stewing about something, because when she reached it, she whirled, hands on her hips. Anger rippled across her face. There was no sparkle in her eyes now.

"What is it?" she demanded. "Are you part of the mob? In a gang?"

Harriet took a step back, her hands automatically rising into a sign of protest and defense. "No! Of course not."

It felt like Summer had punched her in the stomach.

"Did you kill someone?"

"No!"

"Then why do you have someone else's blood on you?"

Harriet grimaced, but an answer came to her quickly. Conveniently, it was mostly the truth. "My friend got hurt."

The anger in Summer's face dissipated immediately. "Oh, I'm so sorry. What happened?"

Harriet ducked her head and ran her hand through her hair, buying time to think of a suitable answer. Lying took so much effort. She couldn't imagine how Annabeth had done it to Jonathan for years. But then, Annabeth was more clever than she was, and she'd had more than enough time to practice.

"We were jumped," Harriet explained. That was technically accurate. "She…got shot in the chest." She left it to Summer to assume by what.

Summer's hands went to her mouth, stoppering the horror that wanted to spill out. "Is she okay?" There was genuine concern in her voice.

"She's fine. It wasn't bad…" Well, it had been bad, but Theodora would recover, which came out to the same thing.

Kneeling to access the cabinet beneath the sink, Summer pulled out a white dish towel. She held it under the tap for a moment, then brought it back to Harriet. "Hold still." Tilting Harriet's head to the side, she gently wiped the blood away, pressing just hard enough to scrub off the particularly stubborn spots.

Harriet was grateful Summer had used warm water. It felt nice against her skin. She closed her eyes and relaxed, leaning into Summer's touch. The nurse's hands were sure but gentle as they held Harriet's head, her left hand pressing against Harriet's cheek, her right hand holding the towel. Harriet wasn't used to such tenderness. Theodora was always rough when cleaning up after an injury, while Annabeth was quick and efficient. She wouldn't mind having Summer take care of her like this after revocations gone sideways.

Once the blood was gone, Summer ran her fingers lightly through Harriet's hair and over her head, checking automatically for any injury. She clucked disapprovingly. "First people following us, then you get jumped. This city is becoming more dangerous by the day. A friend of mine who's working in the ER today said they got some dog-bite victims too. Even the animals here are dangerous."

"Yeah," Harriet agreed. She took Summer's free hand in hers and gave her a serious, imploring look. "You should get away from here. Take a vacation, at least for the next few days. The city's not safe right now."

She was thinking of Father Domenico and the Faithless Monk. No matter what happened, war between the angels and demons was inevitable. Both sides had made that abundantly clear. That meant the entire city was going to be turned into the battlefield on which their contest would be fought. Summer's best chance to not get caught in the crossfire was to get away from it as fast as she could. Harriet would happily escort her herself.

Summer pulled her hand back, sighing. "I wish I could take a vacation. Believe me, I need it. But I can't do anything until I'm done with school. I'm stuck here."

Stepping back, she folded the now-bloody towel and set it next to the sink beside an empty coffee cup. Then she leaned against the counter and fixed Harriet with a serious look. Uh-oh. Harriet didn't need her angelic affinity to know what was coming next.

"What's really happening? Why did someone shoot your friend? And why are you wearing someone else's shirt?" Her voice wasn't accusatory, but it was clear she wasn't buying the excuse of a random act of violence either. "Are you caught up in something illegal? Drugs?"

"No!" Harriet replied, indignant. She wasn't some low-life thug…although she spent enough time around unsavory demons.

"What is it then?"

Harriet had never told anyone what she really did. None of the three women had, other than Father Domenico. Technically, the Daemonium had never told them they couldn't, but they had agreed it was wiser to keep this part of their lives a secret, not the least because the truth was so incredible no one would ever believe it. And it went without saying that no one would ever believe they were only half-human. Harriet unconsciously rubbed her shoulder, where Pestilence's second arrow had scored her, wishing she had Annabeth's quick wit. What would Annabeth have said? How would she have gotten out of this situation?

She sighed. "You wouldn't believe me if I told you." Truth was stranger than fiction, and she was fresh out of fictions.

Summer crossed her arms. "Try me."

The truth was, Harriet was…*lonely*. Although she never told Theodora or Annabeth, she was tired of bearing the burden of their heritage almost totally alone. She had lived her whole life stuck in limbo between the human and the demon worlds, not fitting into either. She had found it easier to keep other people at a distance, to compartmentalize her life the way Annabeth did, but it had come at a cost. She had never been able to build a real life for herself. But now maybe keeping her secret didn't matter anymore. It turned out she wasn't half-demon, and since the Apocalypse was in motion, tomorrow both she and Summer could be gone.

So what if she told the nurse the truth about the last few days? The worst that could happen was that Summer would reject her.

But perhaps...perhaps she wouldn't. Could it be worth a try? Harriet watched her cautiously. "Do you believe in Heaven and Hell?"

Summer narrowed her eyes, searching for the meaning behind the seemingly random question. "I was raised Baptist. Why?"

Harriet didn't miss that Summer's response wasn't a direct answer. Maybe she did believe in the celestial world, maybe not, but Harriet pushed on anyway, committed now. "Did you hear about what happened at the First City Bank this morning?"

"No..." Wariness danced across Summer's face.

"We were there. A fight broke out. That's how Theodora was hurt."

She stopped, struggling to find the words to explain what had happened and why without scaring Summer away. She shoved her hands in her pant pockets, finding the familiar pocketknife there. She clutched it like a lucky charm. Since she'd left Annabeth the two kamas, it was the only weapon she was carrying. It gave her some reassurance to touch it.

Summer recoiled, or as much as she could given she was already pressed against the sink. "Oh my God, did you try to rob a bank? Are you on the run from the cops?"

"No." Harriet hastened to intervene before Summer's imagination took her in the wrong direction. "What I'm trying to say is, two...ah, men...walked in with weapons. One had a sword and the other had a bow. But they weren't...humans."

She faltered a second time, feeling simultaneously absurd and uncredible. No matter that it was the truth, there was no way to make this part sound anything but crazy.

Summer crossed her arms tightly over her chest, stony faced. "Oh yeah? Then what were they?" There was an undercurrent of anger in her voice. She thought Harriet was jerking her around. Harriet didn't blame her.

"The first two Horsemen of the Apocalypse, War and Pestilence. They were there to help open the third seal of the Apocalypse. Which they did after we got out of there."

She couldn't look at Summer. She couldn't bear to see the horrified disbelief on her face.

"Okay, let's say you're not making this up." There was a spark of frustration woven into the anger in Summer's voice. This was what she got for trusting a stranger from the diner. "There should be evidence, right? Let's check the news. I'm pretty sure if what you say happened someone would have reported it."

She pulled her phone from her pocket and began to type furiously, fingers flying across the screen. A moment later, they stilled. A minute after that, her face went slack. Harriet knew what she was looking at because she'd already seen it herself: black-and-white CCTV footage of War and Pestilence, obtained from the security camera in the bank's lobby. And depending on whether it was a screenshot or a video clip, Harriet herself might be in the frame as well. If they survived the Apocalypse, she, Annabeth, and Theodora would have a hell of a lot of explaining to do to the police.

"Oh my God. They really are carrying a bow and sword. What the—" Summer raised her eyes and looked at Harriet, astonished. "What is going on? Who *are* you?"

Harriet nodded. "You're going to want to sit down."

CHAPTER EIGHTEEN

When the taxi pulled up in front of the church, Annabeth felt for the first time a whisper of hope tickle her chest. The building looked just as it always had—quiet and pristine, with a reference to 2 Corinthians 4:18 in white letters on the black marquee sign outside. If the demons had beaten her here, they hadn't ransacked the place or set fire to it. Or, she dared to believe, they hadn't come yet and Father Domenico was safe. It was better to have hope than to have nothing.

She eased her way out of the taxi, navigating the long spear clumsily, and scanned the neighborhood intently. The street was quiet and empty, a haven of peace in a city on fire. When she reached Father Domenico's office, she pressed her ear to the door, listening for trouble. The wood was cool against her flesh. The day had warmed a little, but traces of the cold snap still lingered. She heard nothing on the other side. That could be either good or bad news.

Gently, she turned touched the brass knob. Her heart beat faster as she worried once more about what she might find inside. If the priest had been killed... The knob turned easily—the door was unlocked. She swung it open, flinching in anticipation.

But her fears had been for nothing. Father Domenico was sitting at his desk, his black-robed body bent over a thin stack of papers. He looked up at the intrusion, surprised. "Annabeth!" His hand had jerked into the air, holding a pen.

She slipped into the office, holding the Holy Lance in front of her. Seeing the priest alive and well, the anchor of fear that had been weighing her down was cut loose. She felt as though she were shooting toward the surface, dizzy with relief.

"Thank God you're safe," she gasped. Her heart was beating just as hard with relief as it had with fear.

He frowned, confused. "Is something wrong?"

"I tried to call you but you didn't answer." It was half-explanation, half-accusation.

He glanced helplessly at the black phone on his desk, as though he'd never noticed it before. It was moot now why he hadn't heard it ring. Perhaps the ringer was broken or perhaps he hadn't been in the room every time she'd called. What mattered was that she had made it to the church before the demons' war had reached it. With luck, he would be long gone by the time it did.

Words tumbled out of her mouth breathlessly. "You have to leave the city. Immediately. Three seals have been opened now. Samyaza is dead and Andromalius has declared war on the angels and every priest and church in the city."

She felt like time was barreling past them, telescoping minutes into seconds. The window to leave was fast closing. But Father Domenico didn't seem to grasp the urgency of the situation. He set the pen down carefully. "This is troubling news."

Troubling news was a school bulletin announcing a lice outbreak among second-grade students. This was Lucifer triggering Armageddon and a war between Heaven and Hell. To her dismay, rather than jumping to his feet and rushing to the door, as he should have, he leaned back in his chair, settling in more comfortably. He pointed to the spear in her hand. "What is that?"

She followed his gaze, for a moment almost shocked to see the Holy Lance in her grasp. "Oh!" In her single-minded focus, the fact that she was toting around one of the most important artifacts in the world had completely slipped her mind. She held it out it toward him. "This is the Holy Lance." When he didn't respond, she added helpfully, "The one that stabbed Jesus."

The confusion on his face didn't abate.

"Andromalius ordered us to steal it. He thinks it can kill archangels, so we took it to keep it from him. And I thought maybe the angels could use it to kill Lucifer."

As soon as the words were out of her mouth, she felt sheepish. Surely the angels didn't need the fumbling help of three half-humans. She might as well have been making a few points about theology to the Pope. Still, whether the angels needed it or not, it was better the Holy Lance not fall into the Daemonium's hands.

The priest stood and reached for the spear. She passed it to him with relief. He would know what to do with it. He hefted the weapon, feeling its weight, and examined the metal tip, which was long and almost pyramidal. After a moment's review, he gave her a sharp look. "Andromalius has said he believes this is the Holy Lance?"

She nodded.

"And do you?"

The question pulled Annabeth up short. Andromalius was the acting head of the Daemonium. He had been on Earth at the same time as the Lamb Himself. She had assumed without question that he must be right about the spear. But the tone in the priest's voice stirred doubt in her mind. Now that she thought about it, the demons' track record hadn't been so great lately. Samyaza hadn't detected the second seal of the Apocalypse and it had been in his own office for decades. The demons clearly weren't infallible.

Confused, she replied, "I don't know."

"What do you see when you look at it?"

He was asking, she realized, about Christ's blood. If the tip hadn't been cleaned well—or perhaps even if it had—it might have a telltale glow from the celestial blood that stained it. She squinted at the spear, searching for even the smallest flicker of unearthly shine. But she saw nothing. It was just a dull metal tip on a wooden shaft.

She winced. "It looks like a normal spear."

Another monumental error on her part, one that could have gotten her friends arrested had the museum security guards been a little quicker on their toes. She crossed her arms, but the self-soothing motion brought her no comfort. "I guess it's not the Holy Lance after all."

Father Domenico made a noncommittal sound, still contemplating the spear in his hands. "Maybe it is. Maybe it is not."

"But you just—"

Without warning, he raised the spear and then snapped it in half over his knee. The wood splintered with a loud crack. Annabeth watched, shocked, as he dropped the two ends on the ground carelessly. "It does not matter what it is. It is a weapon of man. It cannot kill an archangel, just as it could not kill the Lamb."

Annabeth stared at the shattered weapon. Aside from the fact that they hadn't ruled out that it *could* be the Holy Lance—and the important detail that whether it was or wasn't, it was still stolen property—how had he managed to break it? It was thick enough she was certain she couldn't have snapped it if she'd tried, and Father Domenico was much older and weaker than she was. Had the wood hollowed out with age and it was much more brittle than it had seemed? Had termites gotten to it? And could she glue it back together and leave it somewhere for the police to find with an apology letter?

An indistinct sound somewhere outside pulled her back to the situation at hand, reminding her the clock was ticking. She shook her head, forcing herself to forget the spear. She urged, "We need to hurry. And let the other priests in the city know what's happening. Is there some sort of a messaging system, a phone tree or something we can activate?"

Father Domenico cocked his head. "A phone tree?" The concept was clearly alien to him.

She waved her hands impatiently, almost jabbing herself in the wrist with her throwing spikes in the process. "A list of contacts we can start calling from the cab on the way to the Amtrak station?" It would be fastest to take a train or bus out of town. Any direction would do.

"No."

Annabeth wasn't ready to give up. "There's got to be some way we can contact them."

They could find phone numbers on websites or social media pages. They could post a warning to social media. Her mind raced, thinking up all sorts of possibilities. The process would be slower than she would like to start, but it could quickly take on a life of its own as the priests they managed to contact began to reach out to others.

Father Domenico held up his hands in a placating gesture. "Annabeth, you must be calm. All will be well."

His voice was full of serene faith and acceptance. Annabeth needed him to have a little less confidence and a lot more panic. She cast a look toward the door, trying to avoid imagining a mob of demons gathering outside it. "Father, I don't mean to argue, but all *isn't* going well. In fact, it seems to be going terribly. We have to warn the priests or there's a very real chance many of them will die."

Unexpectedly, he sat back down. His body relaxed into the seat, filling it. "My child, everything is in the hands of God and His angels. Have faith that what is happening is part of God's plan. Go home to your family for now."

Annabeth's mouth opened and closed like a fish. She was speechless. Yesterday, he had urged them to fight to defend the city. Today, when the situation was much, much worse, he was telling her to walk away and let the chips fall where they may. And why hadn't he even acknowledged the need to inform anyone else of the danger? It was as if…

A shiver ran down her arms as though she'd been brushed by a frozen feather. "You're not Father Domenico. Who are you?"

She had known Father Domenico since almost before she could tie her own shoes. He had held her while she cried at her mother's funeral and quietly helped pay her college tuition. She had spent more hours than she could count in his office, first playing with dolls and then reading chapter books. He had been a safe space, a reliable shoulder, an available ear. The man in front of her may have looked identical to Father Domenico in every way, but it was not him.

As far as Annabeth knew, her angelic affinity enabled her to see anything celestial. That included the ability to see through glamours to the celestial beings hiding behind them. Now she discovered for the first time that her ability had limitations. Before her eyes, Father Domenico's figure reshaped itself, the nose shrinking and the hair sprouting and then lengthening. In the priest's place was someone she'd never seen before. Or rather, she had, in a way. Sitting before her, a vague likeness to the painting beside him, was the archangel Uriel.

She gasped. "Uriel."

The angel had an ageless face, with a square jaw and deep brown eyes topped by long, dark eyelashes. He wasn't breathtakingly beautiful, as his painter had assumed he would be, but nevertheless there was a striking quality to him. Divinity radiated from him like the light from a torch. It was at once magnetic and distinctly inhuman.

Annabeth stared at him, speechless. This was the first archangel she'd ever seen, a seraphim in his full power. She was awed... and yet she had questions. How had he disguised himself as Father Domenico without her noticing? And why? Why hadn't he revealed himself from the start? Why was he here, in Father Domenico's office, and not out trying to stop Lucifer? But perhaps most importantly, "Where is Father Domenico?"

"You do not need to worry about our faithful servant." Uriel's voice was deep and resonant, like the plucked string of a cello. He shifted, and his wings shimmered behind him. These weren't the pale, translucent wings of the seal guardians. Instead, their red and orange colors seemed to have been pulled from the flames of every campfire that had ever been lit. The way they reflected in the gleaming silver of his simple plate armor—discomfortingly anachronistic in an era of guns and jet planes—made it seem almost as though he, himself, were on fire.

Although he had ducked the question of Father Domenico's location, Annabeth didn't pursue the issue further. She had other questions to ask. "Why are you here? Why aren't you out there fighting the demons? Fighting Lucifer?"

"Fear not for God's children. The wheels of justice are in motion."

Was it another nonanswer, or was he telling her the angels were starting to get things back in hand? She couldn't tell. Uriel was dressed for war. She wanted to imagine that even now, the army of Heaven was charging into battle against the demons, beating them back and revoking them to Hell. She wanted to hope that finally the tide was turning and that in a minute, Uriel would use those wings to fly to the defense of the human world. But something still felt off. Something was wrong.

Uriel continued, "Nothing happens without God's will. Take comfort in that."

An alarm bell started ringing in her head, soft but insistent. If she had learned one thing over the years, it was to trust her instincts. Her heart started to beat a little faster. "Uriel, why didn't the angels stop Lucifer from opening the seals?"

"Go home, child. There is nothing to worry about."

The alarm became a scream, loud and clamoring like steam whistling out of a kettle. The angels knew the seals were being opened and yet they'd done nothing.

"Are you *allowing* Lucifer to open the seals?"

A look of profound contempt crossed Uriel's face. Finally, she had provoked a reaction. "Lucifer is bound in Hell."

"But he—" She stopped. The air in the room disappeared. The floor fell away. She was falling, falling.

She had been so terribly wrong. About everything. She had seen the clues but she had assembled them incorrectly. One set of footprints in her father's blood. A broken window twenty floors up. A permanently dead high lord. Three dead angels. The angelic host's deafening silence.

The person who had started the Apocalypse hadn't spent years hunting for the seals—they knew exactly where they were. They knew who the guardians were too and where to find them. They had not, she understood now, kidnapped them, but rather ordered them to come to their own deaths. If she hadn't been distracted by the Psellus Prophecy, she would have realized it sooner.

"It was you," she breathed. Even though she knew it was true, she still couldn't believe it. "*You*'ve been opening the seals. *You* killed Arakiel and Samyaza. It's been you all along."

Uriel shrugged, unfazed by the accusation. It was such a human gesture from someone who looked like he just stepped out of a Renaissance painting. "Not me personally. Michael."

Annabeth felt sick. "But why? Why would he *want* to start the Apocalypse?" Had he gone rogue? Had he lost his mind?

Uriel's expression was utterly blank as he looked at her. Her horror and disbelief didn't bother him in the least. "Want? This has nothing to do with wanting. For the new Heaven and Earth to be created, the Apocalypse must occur. The old world must be destroyed so that the new one can be built. Armageddon is greater than we angels. We are only its executors."

Annabeth struggled to catch her breath. She felt so weak. She stumbled to one of the chairs in front of Father Domenico's desk and collapsed into it. Almost panting, she gripped the hard wooden arms, squeezing them tightly to ground herself. She had wanted to stop the Apocalypse and save the world. Now she saw the end of the world was inevitable. The rivers would run red with blood. The stars would fall from the sky. And there was nothing she could do about it.

Uriel's expression never changed. He either didn't notice or didn't care that he had turned her world upside down. To him, this was one more event foretold by the prophets. Perhaps he even saw it as being analogous to the extinction of the dinosaurs. What did it matter to him if humans and their loved ones died? He had existed long before God created Adam. Unlike frail, fragile humans, he was all but immortal. How different the Apocalypse must seem to someone who had watched the birth and death of stars. But to her, a human...

"But it's so awful," she said, her voice barely louder than a whisper. She wished Theodora and Harriet were here with her. This was terrible knowledge to bear alone. It was too heavy for her to carry.

"Go home, Annabeth. Soon enough, it will be time for you to do your duty."

She stared at him. Duty? What duty? What could he possibly expect her to do? How could she be part of the horrific things that were to come? Because they would come. Regardless of whether the narrator was John the Revelator or Michael Psellus, the description of Armageddon was the same: death, suffering, and sorrow. Fire from the sky, poisoned waters, grotesque monsters, global war—the Horsemen were just the beginning. Before Earth could be remade into the new Heaven Uriel had claimed, first it had to be turned into Hell.

She could cry. Everything had gone wrong. "Why did Arakiel come to us? Why did Father Domenico tell us to fight?" Why had she believed that somehow, the Apocalypse could be rolled back?

A flicker of annoyance crossed the archangel's face and then was immediately smoothed away. "They acted in error. They did not yet know God's plan."

One set of footprints in her father's office, tracking his blood carelessly across the marble floor. Michael hadn't dragged Arakiel to his death. The guardian had been summoned to the second seal to lay down his life and he had done it. He had gone knowing the cost because he was an angel and it was his duty—or perhaps because to refuse would be to fall like Lucifer, a fate no good angel would ever consider. Yet for Arakiel's sacrifice, he had been brutally, mercilessly slaughtered. Even an angel wasn't safe from the violence of the Apocalypse.

"So many people will die," she said. She couldn't get over what was to come. Already, the city's death toll was climbing. It would take some time for the news to catch the trend, but it would eventually. And the ripple had spread beyond the city, too, even to other countries. And when Death was released, the effect would be catastrophic. "Millions of people…"

"Billions," Uriel corrected without blinking.

He might as well have clocked her on the chin. She had understood, at least at an intellectual level, the scale of the carnage, but the casualness with which Uriel spoke of it was beyond belief. How little he cared for those lives that would be lost! But she cared. Anguish ripped through her. "How can this be what God wants?"

What kind of God was that cruel? What kind of God was willing to destroy the majority of His creation in terrible, hurtful ways?

Uriel's face contorted angrily. "How dare you question Him! What would a mortal know about God's will?"

Unsteady as they were, she sprang to her feet. Her face was flushed. "That's not an answer!" She pointed a finger at him. "You're supposed to protect humans! Do *you* think billions of humans deserve to die?"

Abruptly, he stood to confront her. Behind him, his wings unfurled to fill the space around him like controlled fire. But if his intention was to intimidate her, it wasn't working. She refused to be cowed. His lips twitched angrily. "I think humans were a mistake. They have ruined everything they have ever touched. Should billions die? Yes. Without question. *All have turned away, all have become corrupt; there is no one who does good, not even one.*"

His words took the wind completely out of Annabeth's sail, leaving her dead on the water. Never would she have predicted that an angel could *hate* humanity, much less one who had a reputation as a protector of humankind. Theodora had always mistrusted the angels, questioning their commitment to helping humans. At least when it came to this one, she was right. How deep did the angelic dislike for humans run? Was Uriel the exception…or the rule?

Her legs itched to move. She needed to get out of there and tell Harriet and Theodora what she'd learned. She turned to leave, but as she did, she informed Uriel, "You're wrong about humans."

He sneered. "Believe what you will, but when the time comes, you will do your duty. All three of you halflings."

She paused midstep, then turned back to look at him with narrowed eyes. "What are you talking about?"

A cruel smile ghosted across his lips. "Your blood is necessary to open the next three seals."

"*What?*"

He was lying. Of course he was. This was one more angelic manipulation, another jerk of the puppet strings.

Uriel's wings folded behind him. "Before he fell, Samyaza was a seal guardian. As were Kasdeja and Gader'el."

She rocked back, feeling as though he'd slapped her. Samyaza, high lord of the Daemonium...had been a seal guardian? And not only hers, but Harriet and Theodora's fathers as well? She shook her head. "No."

Someone would have told the women...wouldn't they? Then again, who? She couldn't imagine Andromalius casually dropping that into a conversation. And it was entirely possible Father Domenico hadn't known. That left only the angels, who had proven they couldn't be relied upon to share information in a timely manner.

Uriel continued, ignoring her outburst, "The seals they guarded are irrevocably keyed to their blood. When they fell and were turned to demons, it broke their own connection to the seals, but that blood still runs in your veins. *You* are now those seals' guardians."

Annabeth shook her head, trying to dispel the fog that was gathering around it. She couldn't believe him...and yet she didn't entirely disbelieve him, either. He was a bigot, but she had no evidence he was lying.

"We're not even full angels. Why would *we* be seal guardians?" she asked.

"So long as their blood persisted, the guardianship could not be reassigned." He paused, then added unnecessarily, "Even if your blood is not pure."

Annabeth was at a loss. "Why…Why are you telling me this now?"

Why hadn't the angels told them earlier? Why had the women been left on their own for so many years? But the answer Uriel gave had nothing to do with that. "The Apocalypse has begun. All seven seals *must* be opened. Only then will the new Heaven be made." He stared her down with the eyes of a falcon. "When the time comes, you will do your duty. All of you."

Die, and through their sacrifice directly cause the death of billions of people and the destruction of the Earth. Annabeth didn't share his commitment to that plan. Maybe if she had been a full angel, she would have felt differently. But Annabeth had children. She had a husband. And even if she had none of these things, she didn't *want* to die. Uriel could talk about duty all he wanted, but she wasn't going to be part of the extermination of the vast majority of humanity. She might be half-angel, but she was half-human too.

"I won't do it," she told him. "And I'm sure Theodora and Harriet won't either."

His eyes hardened. His right cheek twitched as he briefly clenched his teeth. "Your blood will open the seals. With or without your consent."

CHAPTER NINETEEN

"Theo, dear, where are your needles?" On the small laptop screen, Edith's face was barely larger than Theodora's thumb. She was sitting too far back from her camera, and with her halo of thin white hair and her ivory muumuu, she looked like a friendly cotton ball in oversized glasses.

"No knitting for me today," Theodora replied, settling farther into her chair and pulling her plush pink bathrobe tighter around herself. "I hurt my shoulder this morning. I'm giving it a rest."

Already, a thin layer of new skin had grown over the holes in both sides of her body, but the area still hurt. Since knitting would only prolong the pain, she would have to attend this week's Knit and Sandwich session as a spectator only.

"Hurt yourself working too hard, I imagine," Mabel opined with unassailable certainty. "Haven't I told you that you got to learn to take it slow? Live longer that way."

"It's all right," Florence said in her creaky, wavering voice. She repositioned the red blanket she'd been knitting for the last two weeks. "We all go at different paces."

"Oh, Theo, I got your pattern," Edith announced, starting a new conversation over the other two women. She waved a piece of white paper that she'd picked up from somewhere off-screen. "My grandson printed it off for me. You know I'm no good with electronics. Anyway, I'm going to start this today."

"I can mail it next time," Theodora offered.

"No, no, that's not necessary. It gives me an excuse to see him. He's doing better now that he's off those nasty drugs. Much healthier looking."

Speaking to herself, Florence muttered, "Now where did I put my glasses?" Her small figure began to move around her square on the screen as she searched for the missing accessory.

"On top of your head, you old coot," Mabel cackled. "If it had been a snake, it would have bitten you."

"Oh!" Florence fumbled at the crown of her head. Retrieving her glasses, she placed them over her nose.

Theodora's phone vibrated in the pocket of her bath robe. She clenched her jaw and ignored it for a second. She wasn't in the mood to answer. Florence had promised to share her ambrosia salad recipe today after months of "will she or won't she," and Mabel hadn't yet given an update on the Mystery of the Nursing Home Ketchup Thief. But she knew she couldn't ignore the call. Annabeth or Harriet could be in trouble.

She muted her microphone so the Knit and 'wich ladies couldn't hear and pulled out the phone. The caller ID informed her it was Annabeth. She held the phone to her ear. "What's going on?"

"Meet at the pawnshop. Now." Annabeth's voice was terse. It raised the hackles on the back of Theodora's neck. Annabeth wasn't one for dramatics.

"Are you safe?"

Annabeth's response was ominous. "None of us are safe. I'll tell you more in person."

Theodora lowered the phone and looked at the small faces on her screen. The mysteries of the knitting club would have to remain unsolved. She unmuted her microphone. "Excuse me. I just got a work call. I'm going to have to go in."

"See?" Mabel said. "I told you that you work too hard."

"Tell them they owe you overtime," Florence suggested.

"Or a big bonus!" Mabel agreed.

"Be careful of your shoulder, sweetie!" Edith added.

Theodora thanked them, then left the chat and closed the screen. Putting her computer aside, she strode to her bedroom and found where she'd left her jeans in a pile on the floor. There was no use putting on a new pair. She dropped her bath robe off her shoulders, then slowly peeled the duct tape off her skin, growling as the adhesive clung to her skin. It was clear more trouble was brewing, and she wasn't going to face it with sandwich bags taped to her body.

She shrugged on a new tank top from the dresser, left arm first, then threw open her closet door to evaluate the arsenal she kept at home. With three Horsemen on the loose, there was no telling what was waiting outside her apartment. She grabbed a thick leather bandolier belt filled with shiny brass shells and cinched it tight around her waist. The weight settled heavily but reassuringly on her hips. Next, she clipped a nylon sheath to her right thigh, filling it with a straight-edge KA-BAR knife. Her backup kusarigama hung from a peg on the left wall, the chain looped neatly. She seized it, regretting the loss of the other one at the Faithless Monk, and dropped it through one of the cartridge loops.

Since her favorite black leather jacket was now ruined, she pulled a red one that matched the shade of her nail polish from its hanger, slipping it on gingerly. Finally, she grabbed her shotgun, settling the strap over her left shoulder so the weapon settled comfortably against her back. Whatever was about to happen, she was as ready as she could be.

* * *

"So," Theodora said, "the Scooby Doo fucker in the mask was the angels along."

Of course they were. Of course the self-proclaimed good guy in the story turned out to be the bad guy. Hadn't she always said not to trust the angels? She was furious and righteous at the same time, but now wasn't the time to rub it in. Michael opening the seals was bad fucking news. At least when they thought Lucifer was behind everything, they had hope the angels would intervene. But who could stop the angels? Not the Daemonium and its ragtag army of demons, that was for damn sure.

"This is bad," Harriet said. "Really bad."

Annabeth twisted her hands together anxiously, not meeting their eyes. "There's something else. It gets worse."

"How does it get worse than this?" Harriet grumbled.

Theodora crossed her arms, bracing for the impact. When it rained, it poured, and it hadn't stopped raining since Arakiel had walked through their door yesterday. If she could go back in time, she would lock that damn door and not let him in.

"We're...seal guardians."

A long, weird silence followed. Neither Theodora nor Harriet knew what to say. Then Theodora started to chuckle. The short, sharp hiccups made her chest throb, but she couldn't help it. It wasn't like Annabeth to make a joke like this. Deadpanning was Harriet's specialty. But why not lighten the mood a little? A little gallows humor to take the edge off.

Annabeth's mouth pulled into a tight, unhappy line. "Theodora, I'm serious."

If Annabeth wasn't the joker, then she was the butt of someone else's joke. Theodora smiled at her. "Uriel told you that? And you believed him?" Annabeth was naturally credulous, but this was too much, even for her.

Annabeth crossed her arms. "He said our fathers were seal guardians before they fell, and because we're their children we inherited the seals."

"Sure, and I've got a bridge to sell you," Theodora snorted.

"He didn't have a reason to lie."

"Did he have a reason to tell the truth?"

"They'll kill us." Annabeth's serious expression and voice stopped her cold. "The angels will kill us for our blood. That was the last thing Uriel said to me. I think that's why he was at St. Francis—to tell me we were guardians and let us know what would happen if we didn't come to our seals willingly."

"Jesus," Harriet muttered.

Theodora glanced at her, eyebrow raised. "You believe it?"

Harriet scowled and fiddled with the pocketknife in her hand. "I don't know what to believe. But..." She shook her head. "I don't see why he would lie about something like that."

Theodora rubbed her forehead. She didn't even care that the movement hurt her chest. "This is fucking insane."

"Murder by angelic host to further the Apocalypse" hadn't exactly been on her top ten list of ways she might die. Then again, she always suspected it wouldn't be a demon that finally did her in but an angel, just like her father. Even so, she wasn't going to just roll over and give up. "They can't kill us if they can't catch us. We get a car and head out of the city."

"Have you ever left the city?" Annabeth asked.

"No, but—"

"Have *you*?" she asked Harriet.

"No…"

"Who cares?" Theodora snapped, impatient. "We hop a bus if we have to. Hitchhike. Fuck, we carjack someone if we have to."

"We can't," Annabeth said. There was heavy, hopeless resignation in her voice and face. "If we really are seal guardians, we can't leave the city."

Theodora opened her mouth to argue that Annabeth was being ridiculous. Of course they could leave the city. There was no chain tethering them here. Just because none of them had tried to leave before didn't mean they physically couldn't. Before she could speak, however, Harriet shook her head. "Even if we could, they'd just come after us. Hide, fight, it's all the same outcome."

Three half-humans against the entire heavenly host. But what did that leave? Acceptance? Resignation? Abso-fucking-lutely not. If they wanted Theodora's blood, they'd have to come get it from her.

"Why didn't the angels tell us earlier?" Harriet wondered.

"Maybe they thought if we knew, we'd tell the Daemonium," Annabeth suggested.

"If we'd known we were fucking half-angels tied to the seals of the Apocalypse, we never would have worked for the Daemonium in the first place!" There was so much fucked-up about that, Theodora couldn't begin to even think about it.

"You know, we could go to Andromalius," Harriet said quietly. She looked from Annabeth to Theodora, gauging their reactions. "The demons would never turn us over to the angels, not now. I can't believe I'm saying this given an hour ago we thought Lucifer was trying to destroy the world, but the Daemonium is our best— our *only*—ally right now."

It really was a sign of the end days if they were seriously considering aligning themselves with the Daemonium against the angelic host, but Harriet was right. They were out of options. At least the demons weren't openly plotting to execute them as part of a sick plan to exterminate most of mankind. Not yet, at any rate. But there was one massive, glaring problem.

"Michael got to Samyaza in his own office," Theodora reminded her. "How could the Daemonium stop the angels from getting to us too?"

Harriet winced. "I don't know."

Theodora sat down next to her on the second stool behind the counter. There had to be something they could do. Go big or go home. "What if we find a way to stop the Apocalypse?"

"What?" Harriet said, startled by the suggestion.

"What do you mean?" Annabeth, too, was confused.

"Fuck up the angels' shit. Derail their plans before they can take us out."

Harriet squinted at her. "How...would we do that?"

Theodora thought of her father. What would he do in her shoes? Then, a different question occurred to her: what *had* he done? Assuming Uriel hadn't lied to Annabeth, Kasdeja had been a seal guardian. But even after falling, he had been interested in the seals. Both Arakiel and the third seal guardian had been in agreement about that. Why? What did he want from them?

She opened her mouth, thinking through the question aloud. "Samyaza and my father were looking for the seals when he was killed, right? Arakiel assumed they were trying to get back into Heaven and that's why the angels went after him. But that can't be right."

She jumped to her feet and started to pace, excitement building inside her. "He wouldn't have to look. My father had only been fallen for a few years when they killed him. He *knew* where the seals were. And both my father and Samyaza knew the other seal guardians; Arakiel said as much. So if they wanted to open all the seals, why didn't they? They could have started the Apocalypse decades ago."

Annabeth rubbed her chin thoughtfully. "Uriel said that when the seal guardians fell, they lost their connection to their seals. It would make sense their seals were moved as well, just in case. If that's true, there would be one seal whose location they didn't know: your father's. Could it be they needed to know where all seven were before they could start opening them?"

Theodora considered this theory. "Maybe, but my father wouldn't have done anything that would hurt the world. He wasn't a monster. He was a good person. The Bible says angels who fall are turned to demons, but maybe that's not always true. My father didn't fall centuries ago like Samyaza and Gader'el. He wasn't part of Samyaza's scheme to take over the mortal world. He fell for love—for my mother."

The pieces were trying to arrange themselves in her mind. She could feel them shifting and bumping against each other. She paused for a moment, giving them the opportunity to find their rightful places. "He wouldn't have been looking for the seal if it wasn't important in some way. I know him. And I know he wouldn't have been trying to get back to Heaven *or* let Lucifer into the world. He loved his life on Earth. He didn't regret falling."

She licked her lips. The next part was speculation, but it had the ring of truth to it. "He must have known I was the new seal guardian. But as a half-human, I was mortal. That meant the Apocalypse would have to happen in my lifetime. What if he was trying to find the seal to protect me? Or if not me exactly, then the Earth. He must have known something, some way to stop the Apocalypse, if only he could find his seal again."

She looked to Annabeth. Had she made any sense? Annabeth appraised her for a minute, processing her arguments. Finally, she asked, "If Kasdeja wasn't a demon, why would Samyaza help him?"

Demons didn't help humans. They didn't like humans. Their entire purpose was to subvert and corrupt them. Samyaza would sooner have killed Kasdeja than help him if he thought Kasdeja was one of them. So what would explain the unexpected relationship between Theodora's father and the high lord? Theodora thought hard. It wasn't friendship, of that she was certain. All she could offer was a guess.

"My father must have been manipulating him. Think about it: my father knew the second seal was in Samyaza's office, but he didn't tell him. Maybe he claimed *all* the seals were moved after he fell and so he didn't know where any of them were. He must have tricked Samyaza into believing they were going to take down Heaven by helping Lucifer incarnate on Earth and open all the seals."

Annabeth rocked back on her heels and bit her lower lip. "Maybe." She didn't sound convinced.

Two possible scenarios. In the first, two demons searched for the seals that would unleash the Apocalypse and set up the fall of

Heaven and the enslavement of mankind. In the second, a clever yet desperate fallen angel tricked the demonic high lord in an effort to protect the human world from annihilation. Which scenario was closer to the truth? Everything came down to Kasdeja—what he was and what, exactly, he was looking for.

"Did your father keep a diary? Some place he might have written down what he was doing?" Harriet asked.

"No."

Even if he had, it was long gone now. All she had left of her father was a shoebox of photos and his favorite shirt. He had always been a minimalist, and after his death her mother had thrown out almost everything of his. The memories were too painful.

"Is there anyone he might have talked to about it?"

"No." When he wasn't working long hours as a janitor, pushing a mop down the winding halls of the high school next to their apartment, her father had spent all of his time with his family. And whatever he'd told her mother, if he'd told her anything at all, she'd taken with her to the grave.

Harriet looked mildly frustrated. "And he didn't tell you *anything* about what he was doing right before he was killed?"

Theodora remembered many things about her father. She remembered how he always put his left shoe on first, never his right. How his hands were large as baseball mitts but with long, fine fingers. How he never got angry, not even when she tried to make him pancakes for breakfast and almost set the kitchen on fire instead. But if he had said something all those years ago that might help them now, it was gone.

She sighed. "I wish I could remember."

"Remember..." Annabeth repeated the word contemplatively. Suddenly, she jerked her head to look at Harriet. Her eyes were wide. "That's it! Harriet, is there any chance you could see *backward* in time?"

CHAPTER TWENTY

Annabeth might as well have asked Harriet if she liked having three legs.

"Backward?" she repeated, flummoxed.

Theodora was equally perplexed. Harriet's celestial affinity was precognition. How did Annabeth think she was going to be able to see into the past? That was going the wrong way down a one-way street.

Annabeth's hands flapped, animated by frenetic energy. "I know it's a long shot, but what if you could see a flashback? You could find what Kasdeja might have told her…If he told her anything."

Harriet shook her head slowly. "I don't think it works that way."

Annabeth persisted, undaunted. "Time is a continuum. Why shouldn't you be able to see in both directions? It's worth trying, isn't it? We have nothing else to go on." Her lips twitched at the corners in an unhappy grimace. "If this doesn't work, it's only a matter of time until Michael hunts us down. We might as well try."

It was more than a long shot, but if ever there was a time for a miracle…

"Try it," Theodora said. She offered her hands to Harriet. "It can't hurt, right?"

Harriet looked at them skittishly and refused to touch them. "I don't think…"

She snatched her pocketknife off the counter and moved to put it in her pocket. Before she could, Theodora grabbed her wrists, forcing their skin to make contact, rich brown against almost buff. She had no idea whether Annabeth's idea would work, but she knew it would definitely fail if Harriet didn't at least make an effort.

"Try." The word was a firm suggestion, but not a command. She wouldn't force Harriet to do anything she didn't want to.

"I can't!" Harriet protested unhappily. "I don't know how. You know the visions just come to me. I don't have any control over them. How do I make one come *and* have it be from the past?"

"You can do it," Annabeth said, trying to be supportive. She smiled encouragingly. "Believe in yourself."

"How would I even know *when* to go?" Harriet asked.

Theodora shrugged. "I don't know. Just…see where you land." It was all moot if she couldn't see backward in time anyway. They could try to fine-tune the *when* later. First steps first.

Harriet pressed her lips together. Her dark eyes were full of worry. Theodora could see she wanted to keep protesting, but she forced herself to concede. "Fine, I'll try. But don't be surprised when it doesn't work."

She closed her eyes. After a few seconds, her face went slack. Her shoulders rose and fell as she breathed deeply. Theodora waited. And waited. She started to wonder at what point they would have to admit Harriet was right, that she couldn't manipulate her affinity.

Then she fell through the floor.

* * *

The first thing Theodora notices is the perspective. Everything is at the wrong height. It's like she's looking through a funhouse mirror—although everything appears nearly the same, it's all ever so slightly off. The ground is far too close to her feet, the horizon too tall. Trees reach higher than they should, as though blown up by an invisible magnifying glass. Intrigued by this unexpected optical illusion, she's tempted to reach down and touch the grass, which seems to be only a few feet from her short, stubby fingers. Instead, she's distracted by her hand, which is small and puffy with rounded, unpainted nails.

She stares at them, confused. She can't remember a time when her nails weren't a bright, blood red. They're a representation of who she is: bold and unapologetic. But as she looks harder, she realizes she's staring at the hands of a child.

"Where are we?"

The voice isn't hers, but somehow it's in her head. Although she recognizes it, she can't immediately place it. Responding to the question, she pulls her attention away from the hands—her hands yet not her hands—and looks around. She's in a park. There's a small round pond to her left, and trees are in bloom all around her. It must be spring. Although she's wearing a jean jacket, she's not cold. The sun is bright, with fluffy white clouds in the sky. It's a nice day.

I don't know where we are, *she thinks. But she doesn't know who "we" are. Everything feels surreal, as though she's dreaming. She doesn't know to whom she's speaking or whose body she's in. She's never experienced anything like this before.*

It's only after a few more seconds of looking around that she notices the oblong stones sticking up from the grass. They're half as tall as she is, gray and weathered. They have words written on them. No, not words. Names. She immediately feels uncomfortable as she recognizes what they are. This isn't a park at all.

"Do you feel anything, Theo?" *This voice, unlike the first, she recognizes without question. It belongs to her father. She would know it anywhere. She looks up to see him beside her. He has a tender, solicitous expression on his face.*

Theodora the child, the one to whom he's speaking, replies, "What do you mean, Daddy?" *Her voice is high and immature. Theodora the adult, who is here inside the child's body, feels her jaw move, but she's not the one working it. She is a passenger.*

Theodora is overcome with emotion. She hasn't seen her father or heard his voice in thirty-seven years. The ecstasy of beholding him once more, of being in his presence, is indescribable. She wants to grab him and hug him and cry all at once. But this body isn't hers to control.

"That's your father, isn't it?" *the voice in her head asks again. The speaker is curious; excited, even.*

At the same time, Kasdeja asks the child in front of him, "Is there any place here you'd like to visit? Do you feel like we should look at anything?"

Theodora ignores the voice in her head, focused on what her father is saying instead. It's an odd question to ask a child in a cemetery. Why are they here at all? Thinking about it breaks the spell her father's presence and this weird, dreamlike feeling has cast over her. Suddenly, she understands where she is and what's happening. Somehow, Harriet has managed to access this moment in time and they're here together. Harriet is the voice in her head.

Yet she doesn't remember any of this. Where is this cemetery? When did her father take her here and why?

"I don't like it here." *Theodora feels her childhood self wrap her arms around her body, trapping her hands in her armpits.* "There are dead people here." *She whispers the words, looking around as though they can hear her.*

Her father nods. On his face is love and understanding. "There are. But that's all right. They don't want to hurt you. They're sleeping for now." *Looking away from her and at their surroundings, he murmurs,* "It must be here. This is the last one. It's here somewhere."

Theodora tugs on her father's sleeve. He's wearing a thin wool sweater. "Can we leave, Daddy? I want to go home."

"Just a little longer. We can walk, okay?" *His voice is still kind, but Theodora the adult hears the stress in his voice. It puts her on alert.*

He takes her hand, and her hand disappears into his.

"If you feel a pull, follow that pull, okay?" *he tells her.* "Let it lead you."

"Okay, Daddy." *Young Theodora wants to please him. She'll agree to anything he says, regardless of whether she understands what he's saying or not.*

They start down the cement path that goes past the pond. Theodora has to take two steps for every one of Kasdeja's long strides. Adult Theodora notices he's holding his daughter's hand too tightly. He's anxious. His head moves constantly, scanning. He's looking for trouble.

They've only gone a dozen yards or so when a man appears between two of the tall obelisk gravestones. Materializes may be a better word, because Theodora is certain he wasn't there a moment before—there wasn't space to hide, and anyway, they would have seen him approaching. Her father grabs her by the shoulder and shoves her roughly behind him, putting his body in between her and the stranger.

"Michael, what are you doing here?" *His voice ripples with alarm. Perhaps fear, even.*

Theodora the child pokes her head out next to his ribs curiously so she can see the stranger. He has dark, wavy black hair that reaches to his shoulders and a neatly trimmed beard. His pale green eyes are round and slightly too small for his face. His almond skin is lighter than her father's, which has almost ochre hues.

"I could ask you the same."

The stranger is wearing a white suit with a green shirt that matches his eyes. Theodora the child can't decide whether he looks nice or not, but Theodora the adult has been on guard since the moment her father named him. Dread fills the pit of her stomach like the stagnant water at the bottom of an ice-cold well. Nothing good can come of Michael being here. And while her younger self can't sense the tension, she can. The air between the archangel and the fallen angel is thick and charged with electricity. For the first time, she truly understands the expression about being able to cut tension with a knife.

"You know better than to come here," Michael says reprovingly.

He doesn't move. The two celestials are in a standoff, like cowboys about to draw their weapons in a shoot-out.

"So it is here." There's a note of triumph in her father's voice.

Michael's face hardens. It was the wrong thing to say. "Walk away now and don't return, Kasdeja. As a favor to you, I give you this warning. I will not ask twice."

Kasdeja shakes his head. "I can't do that. It's not fair to my daughter. And not just her. It's not right and you know it. It's cruelty to—"

"Oh, Kasdeja." Michael sighs loudly, dramatically. He curls his lip in a sneer, and Theodora the child decides she doesn't like him after all. He's not a good man. Theodora the adult, of course, has already hated him on sight. "You are such a disappointment. Questioning God's will? It is not for us to decide. Our job is only to obey and carry out God's plan."

"Our job is to help the humans. Yet what have we done for them? We have left them to walk alone. Now how can we punish them? Where is the justice in that?"

Michael's face is hard and angry. Tension fills his body and makes it stiff. "It is not for you to judge, Kasdeja. Not you, who have chosen to work with the demons. Did you think we wouldn't know?"

The mood shifts. Theodora can feel it like a cold gust of air. If she could, she would shiver.

Her father raises his hands slowly. "It doesn't have to be like this, Michael. There is still time to change things. Nothing is set in stone, you know that. The future can be better. We can make it better. Mercy triumphs over judgment."

From nowhere, Michael draws a sword. Theodora recognizes it as a gladius, a two foot-long weapon that no one has used since the Roman

Empire. It looks more like a wide, oversized dagger than a sword. Even though it's not a particularly intimidating weapon, the energy around them pivots a second time. Her father is unarmed, and Michael is not bluffing. Theodora realizes Michael intends to kill him.

Kasdeja knows it too. He holds out his hands, long fingers splayed in the universal sign of supplication. "Not in front of my daughter. Please."

He doesn't beg for his life. He doesn't even try to convince Michael to reconsider. This is all he asks.

Theodora the adult, a helpless spectator, begins to scream. She demands he resist. She urges him to fight and save himself. Why isn't he trying harder to convince Michael to spare him? Why is he letting this happen? Her heart pounds. She understands now what she's seeing and she feels sick. Harriet has brought her to her father's death.

Michael glances down at the child in front of him. His face is a mask of indifference. He might as well be looking at one of the tombstones. He nods curtly. "Fine. The priest will take her." His eyes skip back up to Kasdeja. "I do this as a mercy for you. Your last favor."

He whistles, a high, shrill note. As they wait for whomever he has called to come, Theodora's father crouches in front of her, blocking her view of the archangel. There's heartbreaking sadness in his eyes. Tears brim but don't fall. He takes her hands in his, holding them for the last time. "My beautiful baby girl, go with the priest, okay? I love you. Tell your mother…"

He pauses, searching for the right thing to say. "Tell her I ran into an old friend and I can't come home. Tell her I love her too, and I'm sorry. Tell her to be strong. It will all be all right."

"Daddy?" Theodora the child is scared. She knows the sword is dangerous and she senses something bad is happening, but she doesn't understand what or why. Why would this man want to hurt her father?

Theodora the adult, on the other hand, understands too well. She's shrieking, crying, but it makes no difference. She's not really here. This is the past. Her father is already dead.

Her father snatches her up into a bear hug, engulfing her with his larger body. She would hug him back, but he has caught her by surprise and her arms are pinned to her sides. He presses the back of her head with his palm and brings his mouth close to her ear. "Demons can be martyrs too, Theo. Remember that. Remember."

Theodora wants to stop this moment and live here forever. She wants him to keep holding her and never let go. She wants the two of them to run away where Michael can never find them. But ruthless hands pry them apart. Both Theodoras immediately feel the absence of Kasdeja's warmth. They reach for him, trying to hold on to him, recognizing this is the last time they'll have the chance.

A hand grabs Theodora's wrist before she can touch him again, wrapping around it with an iron grip. Someone begins to drag her away. She lets out a wail and yanks against her captor, fighting to get to her father, but she might as well be fighting against a mountain.

"Be quiet and do not look."

Wait. She knows this voice. It's the thick Italian accent. It's unmistakable.

"Tomorrow, you will not remember."

"Holy shit," *Harriet's disembodied voice says.* "It's Father Domenico."

Then the ground bucks like a wild horse, throwing Theodora off of it.

* * *

When she came to, she was looking into Harriet's dark, bleary eyes. She was so surprised to no longer be in the cemetery, fighting against the priest's unyielding grip, that all she could do was blink. Then, the spell broken, she stumbled off the stool, letting go of Harriet's wrists and bringing her trembling hands to her mouth. How could she be here now, in the present? A moment ago, her father had been standing right before her. It felt like if she just shut her eyes, she would see him again.

Across the counter, Annabeth sighed, disappointed. "Well, it was worth trying. I guess now we hope the Daemonium has an idea for how to stop the angels."

Theodora closed her eyes, but all she saw was darkness. The other world, the one in which her father was still alive and within arm's reach, didn't return. Panic and denial swept over her with the force of a tidal wave. It couldn't be over so soon. She had to get back there. She had to see her father again, had to find a way to save him. If only she could—

"It did work."

Harriet's voice was so low she almost didn't hear it. Or else the rushing in her ears made everything else seem dim and distant, as though spoken on the other end of a tunnel. She swayed, unsteady on her feet but needing to be standing. The animal, illogical part of her was ready to move Heaven and Earth to go back to the cemetery. Anything to see her father again. The logical part knew it was useless. All that waited there were ghosts.

She leaned her forearms on the counter, letting it carry some of the weight her body no longer could. She felt like glass that has shattered but hasn't yet collapsed. Loss, grief, misery—seeing her father once again meant losing him a second time and enduring all the emotions that went with it. All the joy she'd felt was utterly wiped away by the deep sorrow and powerful anguish that followed. It drained every ounce of her spirit and her strength.

"What do you mean? It was only a second between when she touched you and—"

"It worked. I don't know how, but I took us back to the last time she was with her father. We saw Michael and Kasdeja in a cemetery. He found the seal."

"Oh my God, he did? Wait, Michael was there?"

Michael hadn't just killed her father. He had murdered him in cold blood, not caring at all about the fallen angel or his family. He hadn't even pretended to look sad about it. He was a snake, a viper.

Theodora straightened, then slammed her fist down on the counter, making it shake. "That motherfucker! That goddamn fucking piece of shit!"

Loss was a complex, difficult emotion. But anger was easy. Easier to feel, easier to express. It didn't hurt quite the same way.

Hot tears pricked the corners of Theodora's eyes, burning like acid. For decades, she had wondered what had happened to her father. Why had he been killed? Now she knew. Her pain was an uncontrollable wildfire. It couldn't stay inside her. It needed release. If there had been an empty wall near her, she would have started punching it, ramming her knuckles into the drywall over and over again until the skin was split and bloody. Instead, she smashed her fist down on the counter again, wishing it was Michael's face.

"I'll kill him!" she screamed. "I'll tear his fucking arms off and watch him fucking bleed to death."

Again and again she pummeled the countertop, until her hand ached and her chest—still tender and vulnerable—screamed with blazing agony. She couldn't save her father. He was gone forever. She would never see him again. There was nothing she could do.

It was becoming hard to breathe. Grief was turning her lungs to stone. She bent over and put her hands on her knees, gasping loud, labored breaths. It felt like she was sucking air through a straw. Harriet stood and placed her hand lightly on Theodora's back.

"I know," she said gently. "I know."

Harriet was the first real friend Theodora had ever had. She'd been there during some of Theodora's wildest days and seen how pain and grief had expressed themselves as reckless, dangerous behavior. For that reason, Theodora didn't resist her sympathy, even if she couldn't entirely accept it.

"What now?" Annabeth asked. "Do you want to go after Michael? It may be hard to find him."

It was an understatement. Finding the archangel would be like finding a specific grain of rice from among all the rice paddies in her great grandparents' village. There was no way they'd be able to track him down on their own, especially not in the middle of the Apocalypse he was leading. Theodora pulled herself together and straightened. The fire within her burned white-hot, giving her strength. They weren't on their own. "Call Andromalius."

CHAPTER TWENTY-ONE

Harriet nodded. "Okay."

There was no question of disagreement. It didn't matter that they were in the middle of the Apocalypse and the world was actively crumbling around them. It didn't matter that the next seal contained Death and that today or tomorrow or next week half the world's population could be killed with the snap of Michael's fingers. It didn't even matter that the entire angelic host was about to come after them and try to kill them. If hunting Michael down was what Theodora needed, they would do it or die trying. Theodora would have done the same for them. This was what it meant to be family.

She put her hands in her pockets to hide their trembling. Although she didn't show it outwardly, she, too, had been shaken by their trip back in time. She had never had a father figure, but she had felt Theodora's loss by proxy and it was gut-wrenching. She could still hear the shrill fear in young Theodora's voice and feel the sudden loss of contact as Kasdeja was ripped away from her. She understood, even if it was only a brief glimpse, what it might have been like to have a father who loved her and then to have lost him. It was not a feeling she would wish on anyone.

Once they called Andromalius to invoke the demons' help to get to Michael, there was no going back. Arakiel had told them they still had God's grace, but this would certainly put an end to that. They were choosing demons over angels. Then again, it was hard to care about the consequences of siding with the Daemonium when they were dead women walking anyway. They might as well go out guns blazing if the ending would be the same either way.

She made eye contact with Annabeth, silently asking whether their third member was in. Was she willing to go on what would certainly be a suicide mission? Annabeth nodded without hesitation. They would find and take out Michael, come what may.

Harriet turned and threw open the door to the back room. By the time Annabeth got around the counter, she already had the cabinets open and was perusing their arsenal. Her eyes skimmed over dozens of cutting, stabbing, and slicing weapons. She wasn't sure what to take. They still hadn't established that a human-made object even could kill an angel. Only a few hours ago, they had confidently assumed that only the Holy Lance had that power. Now they were deep in uncharted territory. All they could do was wing it with what they had and hope for the best.

Falling back on what she knew, she decided to stick to her usual approach: she would carry a short-range, medium-range, and long-range weapon. The close- and mid-range weapons were the easiest choice. To the kama she had taken back from Annabeth, she added her katana, shrugging the scabbard on over her shoulder like an extension of her own body. Then she turned and contemplated the wall of firearms. Theodora had always accused her of having a snobbish distaste for modern weapons, but to Harriet, they were too unreliable. A gun could run out of ammunition or jam, but a blade was always ready to go. Unfortunately, to use that blade, she had to be close to her opponent, which carried its own risk, especially when that opponent was an archangel.

After a moment's indecision, she slipped a grenade in each of her pockets. The women had only ever gotten the two. Although the explosives had been surprisingly easy to acquire, over the years there had never been a use for them—setting off a grenade in the city merely to take down a recalcitrant demon would not only have been overkill, it would have brought far more attention than they wanted. After this morning, however, there was no use trying to keep a low profile. They were already on CCTV not only for the bank, but probably the museum as well. She might as well bring them. You never knew if they might come in handy.

Annabeth strapped a crossbow on her back and holstered her morning star at her hip. When she finished, Harriet locked the door for what she assumed—given the high probability they would be killed in the next few hours—would be the last time and put the key in its hiding place under the counter.

"Ready?" she asked.

The question was rhetorical. There was no such thing as being ready to hunt the archangel Michael. She retrieved her phone and unlocked the screen. Immediately, she saw a text from Summer. *Going in to the hospital. CEO called an all-hands. Talk later?*

Before she could type a message back, the phone rang in her hand. She blinked, surprised by the coincidence of reading Summer's text just at the moment she called. Based on the timing of the text, the nurse must have been calling from the hospital. Theodora and Annabeth watched her, waiting for her to do something. She hesitated, uncertain whether to decline the video call or give Summer a warning about what they were going to do. And the truth behind who was opening the seals.

Theodora raised an eyebrow as the phone continued to ring. "Going to get that?"

"Uh, yeah." She squirmed, uncomfortable. She hadn't yet mentioned to the others that she had confessed everything to Summer. She wasn't sure how they would respond to the discovery that a human now knew their secrets. And a stranger, at that.

She raised the phone. She would tell Summer that she would text her, then finish her message in the taxi. That would solve the problem. She wouldn't have to tell Annabeth and Theodora what she'd done. She hit answer.

But the face on the other end wasn't Summer's.

"Harriet, daughter of Gader'el."

Harriet froze, immobilized by shock and horror. She recognized the speaker all too well. She had seen his face only minutes ago.

"This is the Great Prince Michael, Supreme Commander of the Heavenly Hosts. I have something of yours."

The angel panned the phone's camera and her blood instantly ran cold. There were five figures behind him. Two she identified immediately: the massive, brutish War and the stout, muscular

Pestilence. A third figure, wearing a black robe and a cowl that covered its face, she guessed must be Famine. But it was the two figures between them who caught her attention and made her heart skip a beat.

"Shit. He has Jonathan," she said aloud for Annabeth's benefit.

And not just Jonathan. He had Summer too. The two humans were sitting on metal folding chairs, their hands bound behind their backs and their mouths gagged. Harriet didn't need a close-up of their faces to know they must be terrified. They'd been kidnapped by three Horsemen of the Apocalypse and the most powerful angel in Heaven. There was no way they weren't. She squinted, trying to see better. At least they didn't appear to be hurt. She didn't see any obvious blood on them. She would have gone willingly if War had shown up at her door too.

"Come immediately to the address I will give you and I will release them. If you are not here within an hour, I will kill them both."

Before Harriet could even breathe, much less react, the call disconnected, leaving her staring at her home screen. The entire call had lasted fewer than ten seconds. She felt like she'd been kicked in the stomach by a draft horse.

"What the fuck was that? What just happened?" Theodora asked.

"He has them. Oh God, he has them."

Harriet couldn't look away from her phone. Her entire body was numb. It was like she'd been put in a box that was turned upside down and shaken. The three women had assumed their biggest immediate problem was finding a way to track down Kasdeja's killer. They had been wrong. She swallowed, the feeling like sandpaper in her dry mouth. It would have been impossible enough to try to fight Michael on his own. They couldn't fight three Horsemen *and* the archangel.

"What do you mean he has Jonathan?" Annabeth demanded.

Only Harriet had been able to see what was on the phone's small screen. The others didn't yet know the full extent of their problem. She hated to be the one to tell them. "Michael kidnapped Jonathan and…" She faltered. She hadn't told Theodora about Summer. Now was not the time to go into details. "Someone else."

"Fuck. He's using them as bait," Theodora growled. "He knows we don't want to be part of his goddamn Apocalypse."

Uriel must have contacted him the second Annabeth left the church. Or maybe the plan had already been set in motion before then, insurance in case any of the women balked. But how did they know about Summer? Unless... She remembered the angel outside Summer's apartment. How long had the angels been watching them?

"The boys. What about the boys? Were they there too?" Annabeth grabbed for Harriet's arm. Her face was full of fear and panic. Her family was her whole life, her world.

Harriet rushed to reassure her before she had a heart attack. "No, just Jonathan."

"Okay, so we get them back?" Theodora said.

She said it as though it would be as easy as picking up groceries. She hadn't seen what awaited them other than Michael himself, and he was a big enough obstacle.

"We have to go," Annabeth agreed frantically. "We have to go to wherever they are. It's Jonathan."

Jonathan wasn't just anyone. He was her other half. And he would have been totally blindsided by the kidnapping. Summer too, although at least she'd had some warning about what was happening. Annabeth's decision not to let Jonathan into her other life was coming back to bite them at the worst possible time.

A heavy weight settled in Harriet's stomach. Resignation. Her lips twitched in a flash of an ironic smile. "At least we no longer have to go looking for Michael." It wasn't much of a silver lining.

Her phone vibrated in her hand, signaling an incoming text message. Dismay wrapped around her insides like the cold, wet tentacles of an octopus and began to squeeze. The address was familiar. Too familiar. She swallowed, then cleared her throat for good measure. "He wants us to meet him at St. Luke's Hospital."

"Why there?" Theodora asked.

Harriet was about to say it was because Summer worked there, but before she could, Annabeth gasped. "Oh my God, the catacombs!"

"What?" Theodora said.

"The hidden history of the city! St. Luke's Hospital was built in the 1970s. Before that, there was a church there, the original St. Luke's. When it burned down, they built over the catacombs."

"Why the *fuck* are there catacombs in this city? What is *wrong* with this place?" Theodora exclaimed angrily.

Annabeth bounced on the balls of her feet, agitated. "The fourth seal contains Death. I bet it's down in the catacombs somewhere. That's why Michael wants us there."

Harriet shivered, imagining dark, damp catacombs full of rats and spiders. She had no interest in creeping around a place like that. Then she remembered what she'd seen on the call. Michael definitely hadn't been below ground. When he'd panned the camera, she had seen what looked like a large conference room with bright, floor-to-ceiling windows. The archangel may have intended to eventually lure them into the catacombs, but at least for now his hostages were *above* ground.

She squared her shoulders, mentally preparing herself for what they were about to do. "Okay, so all we have to do is kill Michael, grab Jonathan and Summer, and get out of there before the Horsemen can stop us, right?" *Just* those things, nothing too difficult.

"Wait," Annabeth said suddenly. "We don't know whose seal is there. Whoever it is shouldn't go."

"Why does it have to be one of our seals?" Harriet asked, confused.

Annabeth gave her an impatient look. "Uriel said the next three seals were ours. And why else would Michael make us go there?"

"Oh. Yeah."

"And you said Death is next?" Theodora said.

Annabeth nodded.

"Shit."

That was an understatement. If Harriet had to pick, Death definitely sounded like the most undesirable of the four Horsemen, a celestial they absolutely didn't want released. Based on her flashback, Theodora's seal was in a cemetery. That meant the seal in the catacombs—assuming Annabeth was right and there was one there—belonged to either Annabeth or her. There was no way to know in advance who. Then again, it didn't matter whose seal it was. They all had to go. It would be hard enough to rescue Michael's hostages with the three of them. With only two, it would almost certainly be impossible.

"Let's just…be careful," she said.

She shouldn't have, but she hoped it wasn't her seal.

* * *

Annabeth worried some of her thumbnail off, leaving a ragged edge she had to stop herself from fixing with her teeth. To distract herself from causing further damage, she reached for her phone. Perhaps she'd intended to check the news, to see if there was any more information about what had happened at the bank or the museum. For all she knew, their faces might be on the front page of every news website by now. They might walk into the hospital and be immediately tackled to the ground by security guards who thought the women were in the middle of a madcap crime spree.

But without realizing it, she found herself staring at a photo of her family. It was from Jonathan's last birthday, when they had all dressed up as superheroes. Noah was wearing a nylon Hulk costume that he had begged her to buy even though it drooped off his shoulders when he moved and tripped him when he walked. Ethan, a very small but dramatic Batman, was almost unrecognizable under the mask he wore. She had felt uncomfortable in her formfitting Elastigirl outfit, but Jonathan, looking dashing as Hawkeye, had sworn she'd never been more desirable, and so she had kept it on just long enough for the photo before escaping to change into something more modest.

Smiling over the two-tiered cake Noah would later smash into Ethan's face, they were a happy family frozen in time. She stared at the photo, crushed by the overwhelming weight of nostalgia and sadness. She wanted to go back to that time and live there forever. She didn't want to be here, now, with Jonathan in mortal danger and the world hurtling toward total destruction. There would never again be another birthday party like the one in the picture. And, most likely, she would never see her family again after today.

She set the phone down on her lap and stared at the smiling cartoon face on its shiny black case. The various components of her identity fought each other, clamoring for action. The planner—strong, logical, and distanced from emotion—wanted to write down all the things Jonathan would need to do once she was gone. There was a permission slip Noah had brought home on Wednesday to sign, for example. The mother—terrified, desolate, and aching—wanted to tell the taxi driver to take her to the school so she could hold her boys in her arms and tell them she loved them. And the wife—guilty and yet full of love—wanted to apologize to Jonathan for not having told him what was happening. To tell him she loved him and kiss him one last time. She had hidden her dealings with the Daemonium from her family to protect it, but in the end, the celestial world had come crashing into the mortal one anyway. If all she could do now was save Jonathan, trading her life for his, she would do it happily.

The hospital was bustling when they arrived. Sirens wailed as ambulances rushed to the door, dropped patients, and screamed away. The emergency room was so inundated that patients spilled out the door, lining up against the red brick wall in huddled, miserable lumps with blankets and bandages wrapped around them. The women exchanged worried glances as they edged past on the way to the nonemergency entrance. The handiwork of War and Pestilence was unmistakable, and things would only get worse if Death was released too.

"Stay focused," Theodora growled.

Annabeth pressed her lips together and wished she could. It was impossible to see their suffering and not be affected. She thought of Uriel and his hatred for humans. The children cradled in their mothers' arms, too, were being punished. How could the sight of their pain not thaw his frozen heart?

Theodora led the way into the reception hall. It was only slightly less busy than the emergency room. Nurses sped past, pushing wheelchairs or clutching charts. Their preoccupation worked in the women's favor. If they had been any less harried, they would have noticed the weapons strapped to the women's backs. There was nothing subtle about a crossbow, katana, and shotgun (although the cab driver, too, had kept silent about it). As it was, however, the half-humans were just more obstacles to be dodged.

Annabeth's nose twitched as the scent of disinfectant hit it. The unmistakable hospital smell, with its overtones of death and misery, made her want to immediately walk back out the door. But she was here for Jonathan. That was all that mattered. Freeing him and making sure he got away safely so that he could take the boys somewhere far away from the city.

"What are we looking for?" Theodora asked.

"A big conference room," Harriet said. "On the west side, I think."

Without warning, Theodora froze. "Fuck."

Annabeth stopped immediately, on guard, and followed her gaze. Hanging on the wall beside them were a dozen bright photos of hospital administrators. "What?"

"You have got to be shitting me."

"*What?*" she demanded.

Theodora marched up to them and pointed at the topmost picture. The man staring back was clean cut, with green eyes and dark hair long enough that it tucked behind his ears. In his crisp black suit and bright red tie, he looked like any other administrator, if a little less...fair skinned than the others.

"Oh no." If it was possible, Harriet looked a little green.

Annabeth still didn't understand their reactions. "What's wrong?"

"Fucking Michael," Theodora spat.

"What?"

"*Michael,*" Theodora repeated, significantly.

Even so, it still took Annabeth a minute. Then it hit her. The archangel Michael, Supreme Commander of the Heavenly Hosts, first among angels, was also apparently CEO of St. Luke's Hospital. She had no idea what to say to that, so she just said, "Oh."

At that moment, a nurse in bubble-gum-pink scrubs was passing by. Annabeth grabbed her forearm, clutching it tightly to keep her from being swept away in the current of motion around them. She pointed to the photo. "Excuse me, does he have an office here?"

The nurse gaped at Annabeth, shocked at the impropriety of having been touched without permission. When Annabeth didn't take the hint and relinquish her, she grudgingly looked at the indicated photo. "Yes, on the top floor." She glanced over Annabeth skeptically. If she noticed the crossbow over her shoulder or the morning star at her waist, she didn't visibly react to it. "Do you have an appointment?"

"Yeah," Theodora replied. "We do."

Annabeth released the nurse, who marched off without further challenge. This was the Apocalypse. She was busy.

Looking across the atrium, Annabeth spotted the elevator bay. "There!"

Somehow, despite the turmoil around them, they managed to grab an empty car. Annabeth mashed the button for the top floor.

Slowly, the doors slid together, sealing their fate. The car rose, shaking slightly as steel cables fought against the pull of gravity to lift it. No one spoke. There was nothing to say.

Finally, the car rattled to a stop, then dinged, cheerfully announcing its arrival on the top floor. When the door opened, the women were prepared for a fight. Annabeth's crossbow was loaded and held at the ready. Theodora had seated the shotgun in her shoulder, sighting over the barrel with her finger on the trigger. Harriet brandished her katana in front of her, prepared to cut down anything that jumped in her path. But instead of three Horsemen and an archangel, they were met by emptiness and silence.

Exchanging wary looks, they crept off the elevator and into the hallway. Annabeth's nerves screamed. At any moment, Michael's trap would spring closed around them. The doors in the hallway around them would fly open and they would be ambushed.

"Where the fuck are they?" Theodora whispered. She swept the corridor with the barrel of her gun, but nothing moved.

The floor was so quiet they could have heard a mouse breathe. It was an eerie, uneasy silence that made the hair on Annabeth's arms stand up even beneath the sleeves of her cardigan. Celestials aside, there should have been hospital employees up here. Where were they? Had Michael and his Horsemen killed them all?

The door to the conference room was closed. They approached it on tiptoe, weapons pointed in case it suddenly blew open and the Horsemen came charging out. But even as they reached it, there was only stillness. Once more, they exchanged anxious, confused glances. What was Michael up to? When was the hammer going to fall?

Harriet put her hand on the metal handle, testing to see if it was locked. There were no windows looking in, no way to see what awaited them on the other side. It could be half the heavenly host, or it could be nothing.

"On the count of three," she whispered. "One...two...three!"

She threw the door open.

There was only one person there.

CHAPTER TWENTY-TWO

"Jonathan!"

Annabeth was not a careless woman. Everything about her was conscientious and measured. But the second her eyes landed on her husband, her heart overpowered her head, taking control of her body and sending it flying across the room. She ran toward him so fast her feet barely touched the floor.

It was a thoughtless reaction. There was no end to the danger that could have been lying in wait for them in the conference room. But in that moment, all she saw was her husband—that innocent, beautiful man, the father of her children—tied helplessly to a chair. He was the only thing that existed in the world, and she had to get to him.

He made muffled sounds as she approached, rocking the chair in a futile effort to wrestle free. Her heart was in her throat, pounding wildly. When she reached him, she wrapped him up in her arms, more to reassure herself than him. His body was firm and tangible against her. He was no mirage. It was really him.

"It's okay. It'll be okay. I'm here now." The words came out shaky. Her chest was so tight she could barely breathe. Although he didn't appear to be hurt, she couldn't stop thinking about what could have happened. How close she had come to losing him.

She set down her crossbow and began to work at the tight knot behind his head. Michael, or whoever had tied it, had not been kind. The gag was stretched taut, preventing Jonathan from articulating anything but grunts. Her fingers were clumsy, trembling with fear and adrenaline. She had to try multiple times before she was able to worry her short fingernails into the fabric. Theodora, with her long, press-on nails, would have done much better, but Jonathan was Annabeth's responsibility.

As she worked, he tried to talk through the gag, but she couldn't make out any of the words through the thick cloth that filled his mouth, and his movements only made it harder for her to tug at the fabric. Frustrated, she commanded, "Hold still!"

He did, and at last she got the ends loose. She pulled the cloth away and dropped it to the ground. Immediately, she knelt, sawing at the duct tape around his wrists with the only thing she was carrying with an edge: the key to their apartment.

"What are you doing here?" he demanded, watching her work. "You shouldn't be here. You have to get out before they come back!"

She pressed hard with the key, sawing through the obstinate tape with savage determination. She growled, "I'm getting you out of here."

She finished cutting through and ripped the tape off, undoubtedly pulling some of his arm hair with it. She moved to his feet as he shook his arms free.

"Is that a crossbow? Where did you even get it?"

She ignored the question. The beat of her heart filled her ears like the roar of ocean waves. Danger, danger, danger. There wasn't enough time to tell him everything he needed to know. Michael and the Horsemen could return any minute.

"You and the boys need to leave the city, okay? Go as far from here as you can."

The world was ending, and she wouldn't be around to protect her family from it. At least if they left the city they might somehow be spared the worst of it, at least at the beginning.

"What's happening? Annabeth, what's going on? Did something happen at the pawnshop? The people who took me—

are they trying to extort you? Why are they dressed like that? Are they in a gang?"

"A what?" She was so surprised by how wrong he was that for a moment she paused her sawing. She had to remind herself to continue.

She couldn't tell him the truth now. There wasn't time and he wouldn't believe her anyway. She finished sawing through the last of the duct tape. She tore it off his pants. "Just go. Don't bother taking anything other than food and some clothing. All that matters is getting out of the city."

For the first time, he noticed the other women. Theodora was stalking through the room, pointing the muzzle of her gun at every corner as though War might have folded himself up like an umbrella and was hiding there. Harriet, meanwhile, stood in the center of the room. She faced the door, katana held high in case something celestial and unwanted came through. It was only at that moment, when she could finally think about something other than Jonathan, that Annabeth realized how empty the conference room was. There was no long, heavy table, no chairs. The only thing in it was Jonathan. Which was lucky, given how reckless she'd been in charging into the room.

"Theodora? Harriet?" he asked. Annabeth understood that seeing his wife and what he knew as her pawnshop coworkers bursting through the door armed to the teeth must have been almost as surprising as being kidnapped by an archangel and his henchmen, but there was no time to explain that either.

"Where'd they go?" Theodora demanded. She lowered her gun and looked at him expectantly.

"I—I don't know."

"And the woman? The nurse?" Harriet queried sharply. Both women were on edge. There was no time to be polite.

"The man in the suit took her with him. I don't know where they went," he stammered.

Annabeth stood, all business now. "We need to get him out of here."

"What is going on?" Jonathan repeated. "And why does Harriet have a *sword*?"

Michael hadn't lured them to the hospital just to let them go. At some point, his trap would spring closed. Annabeth accepted it as inevitable, but she needed to make sure Jonathan wasn't in it when that happened. The archangel had promised to let his captives go, but if Uriel was anything to go by, the angels weren't particularly bothered by human collateral damage. She pulled her husband to his feet, trying to ignore the fact that this would likely be the last time she ever touched him. She needed to stay focused.

"Time to roll," Theodora announced gruffly, stalking toward the door.

"What about Summer?" Harriet asked.

"Who?"

"The other hostage," Harriet said, not meeting her eyes.

"Oh yeah, right." Theodora glanced at Annabeth, calculating. "You take him downstairs, we'll look for her on this floor."

"Okay," Annabeth agreed. She bent down to snatch up her crossbow, then grabbed Jonathan by the wrist, pulling him to his feet. She didn't like to leave the other women to potentially fight on their own, but her priority was getting her husband out of the hospital and far from danger. Harriet and Theodora could protect themselves. He couldn't.

She stepped forward, intending to lead him to the door, but he balked, digging his heels in and fighting her. She stopped and stared at him, confused. "What are you—"

He shook his wrist free and pointed toward the hallway with wide, haunted eyes. "We can't go out there. *They're* out there."

Annabeth winced. She hated how terrified he sounded. It broke her heart. This wasn't him. She touched his shoulder, pressing gently, trying to calm him down.

"We were just in the hallway. No one is there, sweetie," she soothed. If he lost his head, she wouldn't be able to throw him over her shoulder and forcibly carry him out, as much as she would like to. She was strong, but he was almost a foot taller than she was, and she needed her hands to hold her crossbow. "We'll take the elevator and get out of here. You'll never see them again." She hoped.

Jonathan's eyes were still wild. He clutched for her hands, forcing her to yank the crossbow away to keep him from accidentally setting it off or fouling the string. "No. We need to stay here. We'll find a way to barricade the door and call the police. You have your phone, right? They can send SWAT in. Those big guys, the ones with the weapons, were *huge*, like…football players."

"We don't have time for this shit," Theodora rumbled.

Time was running out. The longer they stayed in one place, the higher the likelihood something bad would happen there. With only one door in and out, the conference room was a kill box, and it would be too easy for Jonathan to be caught in the crossfire. She moved her hand to cup Jonathan's cheek, trying to bring his focus to her. "Sweetie, sweetie, listen to me. We need to go. We need to get out of this room. We can't stay here. It's not safe."

She turned back toward the door, ready to drag him behind her if necessary. And then Famine appeared. The Horseman drifted through the door like a black storm cloud. Or a ghost. She stiffened, horrorstruck.

War and Pestilence were physically powerful celestials—warriors from another world. One blow from them could, and had, easily cracked bone. But Famine was their opposite. The Horseman was less a corporeal being than the suggestion of one. He was a mound of what looked like black fabric, with neither a face nor even distinct limbs. What he lacked in brutish strength, however, he made up for with his unnerving aura. A floating Grim Reaper, he made Annabeth's skin crawl.

He may not have carried an obvious weapon, but that didn't mean he was harmless. All the Horsemen were deadly. And he wasn't alone. A moment later, the door flew open behind him, revealing War and Pestilence on the other side. The trap had sprung, and, fulfilling Annabeth's worst fear, Jonathan was still in it.

Theodora's gun was up in an instant, trained on the intruders. "Fuck!"

She started backing away from the door as Harriet, too, retreated a few steps. Annabeth raised her crossbow and centered her sights on Pestilence's forehead, trying to evaluate the situation. So long as the Horsemen were between them and the door, there was no way to get Jonathan out; they were trapped. Small and light though she was, she stepped in front of him, shielding him with her body and the weapons she carried.

"Oh God, they're back," Jonathan whimpered.

If only they could fly away like birds, Annabeth thought. That was the only way they could escape without having to fight their way out. Then a shock of realization ran all the way down to her toes, electric and powerful.

"Theodora, you have to get Jonathan out of here," she said urgently.

"Yeah, I know. But it's not that easy, not in this shitnado," Theodora replied between gritted teeth, tracking War with her sights as he lumbered into the room.

"No, I mean *you* have to get him out. You have to use your affinity. It's the only way."

They were in the most dangerous situation they'd ever faced, one in which even blinking could prove a deadly mistake, but even so, Theodora turned to face Annabeth. The shotgun in her hands drooped, the advancing celestials temporarily forgotten. "What?"

Annabeth was desperate. She had to be, to ask this favor. "Theodora, please. It's Jonathan. There's no other way. You know there's not. Only you can save him. Please."

Annabeth had never seen Theodora use her affinity. As far as she knew, Theodora had never used it more than once. She hated her gift and all of its associations. But Annabeth was out of options. They couldn't both fight the Horsemen and protect Jonathan. There was only one way to keep him safe, and that was Theodora. His life was in her hands.

Theodora looked genuinely pained. "I can't…" She shook her head, and for the first time, there was fear in her eyes.

Annabeth knew the problem wasn't whether Theodora could do it physically. It was an angelic gift—there was no question she could. The problem was whether she could summon the mental strength to accept that part of her. The part she had spent decades of her life suppressing. There wasn't time for her to examine her feelings and make peace with them. Their window of opportunity was seconds from slamming shut.

"You can do it," Annabeth said. "I know you can. Do it for Jonathan."

"Come on, Theo," Harriet urged. The stress in her voice was unmistakable.

"Please, Theodora," Annabeth tried, one final time.

Theodora looked from Jonathan to the Horsemen to Harriet to Annabeth, calculating. But the math would never work out in their favor, and she knew it. With a growl, she snapped her gun back up to her shoulder, turned a half-turn, and began shooting at the wall of windows. The rounds hit in a tight pattern. Cracks began to radiate out from the holes like spiderwebs. Then the glass cracked and shattered, falling in chunks to the floor.

The opening wasn't large, but it was enough. The integrity of the glass had been compromised. Throwing the shotgun to the ground in order to free her hands, she took off at a run, barreling into Jonathan like a linebacker. Annabeth felt his hand rip away from hers as his body was thrown backward by the impact. Theodora kept driving him forward as she wrapped her arms around his back.

They hit the window, crashing into the hole and then through it. Annabeth rushed to watch as they plummeted toward the ground ten stories below. For a moment, nothing happened. They plunged with terrifying speed, a single, conjoined mass.

She had a brief moment of doubt. Had she made a terrible, terrible mistake asking Theodora to use her gift? Had she inadvertently condemned both of them?

Then Theodora's wings opened. They were black as a raven's, twice as long as she was tall. As they extended, they caught the air, stopping her freefall as effectively as though she'd opened a parachute—and just as abruptly. Relief washed over Annabeth as the blur that was Theodora and Jonathan jerked, Theodora's wings catching an updraft.

She knew when Theodora dipped into a gentler glide that Jonathan would be safe. They had done it. They had saved him. She turned back to face the conference room and the Horsemen, galvanized.

"I'll take War, you take Pestilence," she told Harriet. She didn't have a plan for what to do about Famine. With Theodora gone, they were outnumbered. They would just have to try to avoid him.

"Okay."

Harriet dodged left, luring the white-clothed Horseman as far to the other side of the empty room as she could get. Meanwhile, Annabeth brought War into her sights. Her tactical repeating crossbow had seven bolts loaded. She had seven chances to debilitate him before she would have to take time to reload. She fired her first shot, hoping to strike him in the unprotected part of his throat above his breastplate. The arrow hit low, glancing off the right side of his chest. He roared defiantly, the sound like the crash of a waterfall against rocks, as she pumped the lever to recock the crossbow.

She immediately fired again, aiming for a new target. The bolt hit him in the leg right below his hip. He stopped, grabbing for the blue fletching protruding from his thigh. Taking advantage of his distraction, she attempted another shot at his neck, but missed again. The arrow dented the armor near his left shoulder without penetrating it. Snarling, he ripped the arrow out of his leg and lurched toward her, limping slightly. She pumped the lever and sent another shot at his thigh. He groaned as it landed inches from the last one.

She paused to assess. With only three arrows left, she had to be conservative. Although it slowed him down, she couldn't keep hitting him in the leg. But hitting a more vulnerable place likely meant getting closer to him, an uncomfortable position for her given he could smash her skull like a dry cracker with even a careless flick of his fist.

She glanced at Harriet, making sure she didn't need help. Relying on her speed and agility, the other woman was darting in and out of the range of Pestilence's arms, delivering slashing blows with her sword that he barely managed to parry with the frame of his bow. It was like watching a hornet fight a bear—Harriet wasn't inflicting debilitating damage, but at least she wasn't receiving any either. Not yet, at any rate. All it would take was one mistake for the tables to turn, and both the celestial and his half-human opponent knew it.

But where was Famine? Annabeth looked around the room but didn't see him anywhere. Then she felt him. Somehow, he'd managed to slip up beside her, just beyond her peripheral vision. The black cloth of his robe brushed against her, the touch whisper-light.

Instantly, every ounce of energy in her body was drained from her, as though she were an appliance whose power cord had come unplugged. She dropped to her knees, too weak to stand. It was a struggle even to hold her head up. Her mind screamed a panicked warning. She had to get away from him.

She tried to drag herself away on boneless hands and knees, fighting for every inch. As if the rest of the world was moving in slow motion too, she watched with despair as War straightened from his wounded, hunched position. Saw him notice her helpless on the floor and puff himself in anticipation of victory. Her arms shook violently, threatening to give out at any moment. It was over. There was nothing she could do to get away from him. She couldn't lift the crossbow an inch, much less aim it.

"Harriet." All she could do was whisper. The sound was barely loud enough to reach her own ears, much less all the way across the room.

War took a step forward. Then another. The space between them evaporated. She was going to die without being able to raise a finger to defend herself.

Harriet's kama sliced through the air, hurtling past her. Although Annabeth couldn't see what happened when it hit Famine, she knew it must have because her strength returned as immediately and unexpectedly as it had disappeared. Taking advantage of the reprieve Harriet's unexpected—but greatly appreciated—help had given her, she surged to her feet and sprinted away, trying to put as much distance between herself and Famine as she could. War stalked after her, sword raised.

She found a new location, one where Famine wouldn't be able to flank her, and waited, crossbow braced against her shoulder. She made herself wait until War was so close she couldn't possibly miss. Until she could hear the grating sound of his breathing and see the dark stain of blood around the bolt still lodged in his leg. Until he could almost reach her with his sword. Then she fired.

The bolt passed through the narrow opening of his helmet beneath his nose piece, a direct hit. His scream filled the room like a foghorn. The sound turned to a gurgle as his mouth filled with blood. Thick red drops fell from under his helmet onto his armor, streaking it like rain. Annabeth pumped the lever and fired again. This time, the bolt buried itself in his throat.

He fell silent as his windpipe suddenly sprang a leak. Then he collapsed, his legs crumbling beneath him. He writhed and choked as blood bubbled out of his throat and down his neck. It pooled around his shoulders, seeping into the brown carpet. She had one bolt left. She had to make it count. She sighted the crossbow for her final shot, hoping to hit the carotid artery in his neck.

At the last moment, right as her finger was preparing to pull the trigger, she realized Famine was moving again. He was drifting toward her, an ominous, airborne jellyfish. Her plan to shoot War was instantly upended. Redirecting the crossbow and aiming for what would be Famine's head, if he had one at all, she fired.

The bolt disappeared into the fabric of his cloak. Almost immediately, the celestial dissolved, fading away like smoke in the wind. One minute he was there, the next he was gone. Annabeth lowered her empty crossbow, surprised and worried. If he could vanish that easily, he could reappear just as effortlessly. And now she was out of bolts, with only her morning star left to fight with.

Before she had time to think about what to do when that happened, a dark shape surged through the broken window and into the room, sweeping low over the ground like a swift shadow. Annabeth's eyes finally recognized it as Theodora. Her companion landed with her feet straddling War's head. Black wings outstretched and eyes shining fiercely, she looked like a terrifying yet beautiful angel of vengeance. In her hands was her shotgun, which Annabeth realized she'd picked up from the ground on her way back in. She hefted the stock to her shoulder and pointed the barrel at the sputtering celestial's chest.

This was a familiar sight. How many times had Theodora broken down a door or confronted a demon in an alley, shoving that same shotgun into their face? She stared down at the celestial, sputtering weakly beneath her. "In the name of Theodora Wilson and these two fine-ass motherfucking women, your permission to dwell on Earth is officially revoked. Go the fuck back to wherever you came from."

She pulled the trigger. When the deafening boom of the gun subsided, War had a massive hole in his chest. His armor may have been strong enough to deflect arrows, but it worked as well as tissue paper against the explosive power of a shotgun. Blood welled sluggishly at the edges of the wound, no heart left to pump it through the severed veins and arteries.

"Theodora," Annabeth gasped. "Did you just revoke a Horseman?"

CHAPTER TWENTY-THREE

The roar of the shotgun tore through the air. Harriet jumped, startled, and instinctively turned toward the source. Theodora was standing above War, her wings outspread and the weapon in her hands. Annabeth, next to her, stared with her mouth agape at the celestial prone on the ground. Theodora racked the slide aggressively, ejecting the spent cartridge and seating a new round. Harriet didn't have to wonder what had just happened. One Horseman was now temporarily out of commission.

She scanned the room, looking for Famine. She hadn't been able to do anything other than throw her kama at him and hope it was enough to help Annabeth. She didn't know whether she had actually hurt him or not, or if the ghostly celestial even could be hurt. But the third Horseman was nowhere to be seen. She returned her attention to Pestilence, feeling a surge of optimism. With one Horseman incapacitated and the other missing, it was three against one.

Pestilence raised his bow, trying to find room to draw and fire, but she pressed closer, preventing him. He backed, maneuvering to keep clear of the razor-sharp edge of her katana as she took a swing toward his exposed hand. She kept on him, matching him step for step. The closer she stayed, the safer she was and the harder it was for him to fight.

She sensed rather than saw Theodora and Annabeth moving at the periphery of her vision. They were joining the fight, closing the net around him. Strong as he was, he couldn't fight them all.

The shotgun barked again. Pestilence jerked sideways, his shoulder thrown backward by the impact of the shot. Half a dozen small, black holes appeared in his white armor. As he turned his head to look at the shooter, redirecting his attention to this new threat, Harriet saw her opening. Lunging forward and swinging her sword high, she made a clean, horizontal slice above his shoulders.

Pestilence's head toppled forward, no longer anchored to his body by his neck. It fell straight down to the floor, where it landed heavily at her feet, white eyes staring at the ceiling. Half a second later, his body followed, crumpling in a heap.

Theodora strode forward. She had already retracted her wings, folding them back into her body or wherever they went when they weren't in use. She kicked the celestial's body, rolling it onto its back. Harriet had beheaded dozens of demons, but she never quite got over the disconcerting sight of a headless corpse. Some things were just too creepy to be normalized. Theodora hefted her gun. Shooting him again would be overkill, but Harriet didn't protest. The longer he was down, the more time it bought them. The shotgun roared a third time.

"By the power invested in us, your permission to dwell on Earth is officially revoked," Theodora intoned, speaking to the newly made hole in his chest.

Short of sawing his body into pieces and sprinkling them throughout the city, there was nothing else they could do to the Horseman.

"Are you trying to revoke him?" Harriet asked, surprised. The words of revocation only worked on demons when the Daemonium had ordered the revocation. She didn't see how they could self-initiate a revocation of a Horseman.

Theodora racked the slide and shrugged. "It's worth a try." She dug several bullets out of her bandolier and began to reload her gun.

She had a point.

Harriet nodded. "Right. Where's Famine?"

"I shot him and he...dissolved," Annabeth replied. She looked around uncomfortably. The room was so quiet it was almost unnerving. And between the broken window and the two bodies, it looked like yet another crime scene, albeit one with monsters.

"What does that mean?" Theodora asked sharply.

Annabeth shook her head. A bead of sweat ran down her cheek near her left ear. "I don't know. But I'm sure I didn't kill him."

"He sure didn't stick around to help his friends," Theodora scoffed.

"Maybe he went to tell Michael we're here," Harriet suggested.

"If he comes back, don't let him touch you," Annabeth warned. "He has some sort of...energy-sucking power." She shivered, remembering.

"Great. Of course he does," Theodora said. "Couldn't he make us just be really fucking hungry?"

The police sirens wailed softly outside. If they were audible even on the top floor of the hospital, Harriet realized, the police must be close. Her eyes went to the door. "We need to get out of here and find Michael and Summer."

Theodora had fired her shotgun three times in the conference room. It was a distinctive sound. There was no way someone, whether on this floor or the one below, hadn't called the police and reported an active shooter in the building, and that was if the nurse from the ground floor hadn't already called it in the moment she was away from them. In minutes, everything would be on lockdown. And who knew how quickly the two Horsemen would recover. Harriet didn't know whether Pestilence could reattach or regrow his head, but she didn't want to be here to find out.

Annabeth adjusted her grip on her crossbow. Her glasses were ever so slightly askew, and her hair starting to come out of its bun. "Where do we go? We have no idea where they went."

But Harriet did know. "They went to the seal." That was why Michael had lured them here, and that was where they would find him.

Theodora rolled her eyes. "Obviously, but we don't know where that is other than maybe in some catacombs we don't know how to get to."

"I can find it."

"How? By asking people if they've seen—"

"It's my seal."

Harriet had known from the moment they'd crossed the threshold into the hospital that she was the fourth seal guardian. It was odd: she hadn't felt it outside, but once inside, she felt the seal's call like a gravitational pull. It exerted its force upon her through concrete and metal, catching at her and trying to drag her to it. She knew without a shadow of a doubt that she could follow that pull back to wherever the seal was located.

"You sure?" The question was rhetorical and Theodora knew it. Harriet wouldn't have said it otherwise.

"Yeah."

"Shit." There was a grudging, unhappy quality to Theodora's expletive.

"We can go without you," Annabeth suggested. "You could go back to the shop. That way Michael can't—"

"I'm going."

Theodora grabbed her arm and stared into her eyes with naked honesty. "Don't be stupid. Let us handle Michael."

Harriet nodded, understanding what she really meant. Theodora was telling her she cared. And that she was worried. But Harriet had a responsibility to Summer. She had to go. She briefly pressed her hand against Theodora's. "It will be all right. Come on, let's go."

The elevator was empty when it arrived to the top floor, but they weren't lucky enough for it to travel to the bottom without stopping. To Harriet's chagrin, the doors opened three times to reveal nurses and their patients en route to other floors. The sight of Harriet's katana, Theodora's gun, and Annabeth's crossbow, which she had reloaded while they waited for the elevator, dissuaded them from stepping on, however. When they reached the basement, Harriet stepped off first. The call of the seal was like the deep vibration of a plucked bass string. It found resonance within her, making her rib cage shiver. It was both awful and wonderful at the same time, terrifying and pleasant. Half of her didn't want to go within five miles of the seal. The other half couldn't wait to find it.

"Where do we go now?" Annabeth asked, looking around.

The basement was clean and modern, with white walls and a polished beige floor that starkly reflected the bright industrial lighting. Surprisingly, given the chaos in the rest of the hospital, there was no one else around. No nurses running orders and test results, no gurneys being wheeled to other elevators, just silence. Perhaps the basement's residents had been the first to respond to an evacuation call. Harriet didn't dwell on the mystery. Instead, she let the seal's vibration guide her. Wordlessly, she set off to the right, the pull growing stronger with every step. When the vibration was so strong it felt like her teeth might start buzzing, she stopped.

The metal door in front of her was brown and nondescript. It had likely been overlooked by most everyone in the building, who must have thought it was a utility closet. She put her hand on the knob. "Here."

"We should make a plan," Annabeth declared. "What if Michael—"

The plan was to stay alive and rescue Summer. Everything else they would have to wing. Some things you couldn't plan for. Harriet pushed the door open, pleased that it was unlocked and they didn't have to kick it down.

"Fine, no plan it is," Annabeth muttered under her breath.

They crept down the cramped, narrow stairs on the other side. There were no lights, so they had to use the flashlight apps on their phones to see the tunnel-like corridor that awaited them at the bottom, waving the mobile devices to illuminate its bare walls.

"Oh, fuck this," Theodora whispered.

The concrete walls had once been white, but the dampness of the space was causing a dark mildew to grow up them, as though something dark and nefarious was consuming them. Every ten feet or so was a doorway. Although Harriet knew the doors must lead to crypts, they looked more like the doors to padded cells in a haunted insane asylum. Every cell in her body tingled in alarm. They were in a dark tunnel full of dark rooms. There was no telling what might pop out.

Theodora panned her shotgun around the empty hallway, the light of her phone struggling to illuminate the path in front of them. "This is some fucking bullshit."

"Shh," Harriet said, trying to listen for danger.

"Do you hear something?" Annabeth asked. She was pressed a little too close to Harriet. She didn't like this place any better than Harriet or Theodora did.

Harriet cocked her head. "It sounds like—" Then she was sprinting, running down the hallway, trying to reach whoever was calling for help through a gag.

She followed the muffled sound to one of the crypts. As she turned into it, she flashed the light from her phone around, looking for the source. The light raked over Summer, revealing she was tied to a metal chair in the middle of the small room. Her hair was messy and her eyes were large and terrified, her mascara smudged. She reacted explosively when she saw Harriet, shouting incomprehensibly into the gag.

Harriet didn't let herself think about what she was seeing or how it made her feel. This was not the time or place. She needed to focus. Emotions could come later.

She slipped around the chair and used her katana to cut the tape around Summer's wrists, taking care to keep the sharp blade away from the nurse's delicate skin. Then she returned to the front and dropped to her knees to do the same to the tape at Summer's feet. A few hours ago, she had been in Summer's kitchen, pouring out her life's secrets. Now she was cutting her free from a chair in a dank catacomb.

The moment Summer's ankles were free, she launched herself at Harriet. Her body smacked into Harriet's chest with enough force that Harriet rocked back. She wrapped her arms around Harriet's neck, clutching her. Harriet responded by setting down her sword and phone and hugging her back, trying to calm her. Summer smelled of disinfectant, sweat, and fear. The light from Theodora or Annabeth's phone swept over them as it illuminated the rest of the room, checking for danger.

"It's okay. It will be okay," Harriet said, trying to discreetly pull the gag down.

Summer started to cry, racking sobs of fear and relief that made her chest heave. Harriet caressed her hair, feeling sick to her stomach. She hadn't known Summer long, but she cared about her. The thought of what Michael had put her through just to get to Harriet…

"Shh, shh. You're safe now," she murmured.

"It was our CEO. Harriet, it was our CEO who took me," Summer gasped. "Why? Why would he do that?"

"Yeah, I know. Turns out he's…not human." There was no time to tell her that the man she knew as the head of the hospital was actually an archangel.

Summer pulled back a little and sniffed loudly. "Where's the other man, the one we left upstairs?"

"Jonathan is okay. We got him." She wiped away the tears from the soft skin under Summer's eyes. "I need you to go now and find somewhere safe to hide out. Someplace outside the city."

"You're coming too, right?" She felt Summer look at her, despite the darkness.

If only it was as easy as the four of them turning around and walking back out of the hospital. She felt for her phone and katana on the ground, gathering them back up. "I'll come in a few minutes. Don't wait for me." A lie to protect Summer from useless worrying.

Summer hesitated. Then, leaning forward, she kissed Harriet. She held the kiss for a second, then broke it. "Okay. But whatever you're doing, be safe."

If Harriet was going to die, at least she had that moment. At least she'd saved someone and gotten one last kiss. That had value to her.

Firmly but gently, she directed Summer to the door. On the other side, Annabeth and Theodora were flanking it like statues, illuminating the hallway as well as they could. The darkness seemed to swallow everything but the small area immediately around them.

"See anything?" Harriet asked.

"Not yet," Theodora grunted.

Harriet pointed her phone toward the stairs, illuminating the path Summer needed to take, then handed her the phone. "Run as fast as you can. Don't stop for anything…or anyone."

"We should go with her," Annabeth said as Summer took off down the hallway. "Michael isn't here. We could just walk away."

Harriet shook her head. "Then what? He'll just keep coming after us. This time it was Jonathan and Summer. Next time it might be your kids."

No matter what they did, Michael and the angels would always have the upper hand. They could hold the entire world hostage if they wanted; anything to force the three women to obey. Whether they wanted it or not, all roads led to the fourth seal.

"So we walk right into the next trap?" Theodora asked.

"We wanted to fight Michael anyway, right?"

Theodora said sourly, "This isn't exactly where I wanted to die, in this fucking rathole." She sighed. "But you're right. Okay, how do we find that archdouche? He could be anywhere down here."

No, not anywhere. "He'll be at the seal."

The women moved slowly through the catacombs; an ambush could come at any time from any of the vaults that opened onto the main corridor. It was like a terrible, sick jack-in-a-box. Exhausted by the stress of it, Harriet was starting to wonder if she had made the wrong decision to push forward after Michael. But there was no question of stopping now. Although she didn't mention it to her companions, the seal's pull on her had turned into an irresistible compulsion. Her steps were no longer voluntary—she couldn't have turned back if she'd tried. The seal had her, and she didn't know how to make it let go.

There was no need to announce when they reached their destination, and not only because they had hit a dead end. In front of them was a metal crypt door in the shape of angel wings folded together. Its vertical, thin bars suggested the outline of feathers, while at the top was the engraving of a book from which rays of figurative light emanated. Something was written on the door in what was likely Aramaic or Hebrew, although Harriet had no idea what it said.

"Obvious much?" Theodora grouched. But Harriet knew her irritation was only a more comfortable expression of her fear. They had reached the lion's den, and they knew for sure that the lion was at home.

Harriet's hands were clenched so tightly they were shaking. Her cheeks were rigid, her teeth gritted. The warmth she'd initially felt toward the seal was gone, replaced by that overwhelming sense of coercion. It didn't leave much room for any other feelings, which was probably for the best.

"Are you okay?" Annabeth asked, noticing her distress.

"It will be fine," Harriet replied. She forced her right hand to un-fist, then grabbed the door and pulled. It opened effortlessly, belying the century or more it must have been sealed shut. The metal didn't so much as squeak.

At first, she saw nothing, only a wall. She frowned. Was the seal behind it? If so, where was Michael? Then she realized the reason she was seeing a wall was because the crypt immediately turned to the left. A faint glow came from that direction, revealing the way.

She held up her hand. "Stay back. I don't want Michael to know you're here yet." She kept her voice low, in case he was nearby.

"What?" Annabeth squawked, startled.

"Don't come until I signal."

"Why the hell would you go in alone?" Theodora snapped. "We should all go in and blow this fucker away."

Harriet shook her head. "The only advantage we have right now is surprise. If Michael thinks I came alone, we might be able to ambush him. Maybe I can get his back to you." Of course it was a long shot, but all they were ever going to have was a long shot. If it were easy to kill angels, the demons would have done it millennia ago.

"You don't know who all is in there," Theodora argued. "It could be Michael and all his friends. We should all go in."

"Let me at least try to set up the ambush," Harriet begged. If any of the three could do it, it was her. She believed that.

Annabeth looked to Theodora, leaving the decision to her. Theodora scowled. "You have thirty seconds, max. After that we're coming in."

Harriet nodded. "Okay."

The crypt where Michael had left Summer had been of a mid- to late-1800s design, consistent with when the catacombs had been built. The unexpected room into which Harriet now cautiously inched, however, looked completely different. It had been designed to mimic the Gothic architecture of the Old World, with high, fake arches set into the walls and an ornate dome carved to resemble the roof of a basilica. In the center was a white sarcophagus, the final resting place of whoever's crypt this was.

Harriet shouldn't have been able to see *any* of it, however. With neither windows nor lights, the room should have been blacker than night. But set into the lid of the sarcophagus, producing the glow she had followed, was the fourth seal of the Apocalypse. Her father's seal. Her seal.

The seal's light illuminated the room like a disco ball lamp. The gate that would unleash Death pulsed orange, red, and yellow, fire transmuted into a two-dimensional mandala that spun slowly, almost hypnotically. Black words in some foreign alphabet swirled within it, a message from another world. The seal was beautiful beyond description. Harriet stepped into the room, mesmerized.

Michael chose that moment to reveal himself, emerging from the shadows behind the sarcophagus as if from thin air. Harriet pulled up short as the angel's wings spread behind him. They were magnificent. They pulled in the swirling colors beside him to create new hues that didn't exist on Earth. Beating them, Michael jumped into the air, landing gently on top of the seal with his legs planted widely in a posture of ownership and dominance. In a voice amplified by the acoustics of the crypt, he said, "Welcome, Harriet."

It was a cheap parlor trick, making himself sound scarier. It was beneath him. And yet it worked. He was undeniably, impossibly awe-inspiring. Michael, first among angels, was as similar to a human as a human was to a chimpanzee. Power radiated from him like light from a lightbulb.

"I can't exactly say I'm happy to be invited to my own death," Harriet said.

It took effort to speak. She hadn't expected to be so affected by his presence, but it felt like every cell in her body was quivering with fear. It was a new sensation, and she had to fight to keep her head and not give in to panic.

"You should be grateful," he admonished. "Although you are only half-angel, you have been blessed with the guardianship of this seal."

That broke a little of his spell. When she opened her mouth, a bit of Theodora's sass came out. "And now you want to murder me to open it."

His face twitched, a flicker of irritation. "As an angel, it is your duty to obey what has been set forth for you, without question and without protest."

"But I'm not an angel," she pointed out. "And I'm not going to let you kill me without a fight."

Anger turned Michael's face to stone. "You are angel enough. Do you think you can resist me? You will bow to your prince."

To her shock—and against her will—her body began to move. Bending stiffly, without her consent, her right knee dropped to the floor. Her hips followed, dragging her into a kneeling position. Her head bowed, neck taut. Her katana slipped from her fingers. There was nothing she could do to stop any of it. She couldn't so much as squeak in protest.

She stared at the ground, unable to lift her head. Her heart beat so wildly she wondered if she might pass out. What was happening? How was he doing this? When her neck finally relaxed and she was able to look up, Michael was grinning broadly.

The CEO of St. Luke's hospital had shed all imitation of human norms. Instead of the elegant, modern suit he'd been wearing in his photo, he was dressed in the vestments in which he was traditionally depicted in religious iconography: a bronze cuirass with a sort of dark brown leather skirt and sandals that laced up to his knees. He was ready for war, but against whom? The demons? Humans? In his hand was the sword with which he'd killed Kasdeja. And probably Samyaza too, she realized.

And if she didn't do something, her as well.

"How?" she croaked, still frozen but for her head. Was his affinity the ability to manipulate other beings like puppets? If so, how could she do anything but die?

"I am the Supreme Commander of the Heavenly Host. All things divine bow to my will," he preened.

It took Harriet several beats to understand what he was saying. He was a puppet master, yes, but only to some puppets—those with angelic blood. Her mind raced. If Annabeth and Theodora came now, he would control them as well. Then all three of them would be in trouble. She hoped they were listening and knew to stay hidden. In the meantime, what could she do?

Nothing. She was fully under Michael's control, and he knew it. There was no way out.

For a moment, despair washed over her. Everything they had done had been for nothing. He would kill her and open the fourth seal. Millions—no, billions—of people would die.

She tried to pull herself together, forcing herself to think of something, anything, else. "Where"—she had to stop and catch her breath, fighting for every word—"are the other seals?" How long would it take him to finish what he'd started?

Michael could have ignored the question. But instead, possibly because he sensed victory on the horizon, he chose to answer. "In the city, of course."

His words triggered a memory. *There are a lot of things in this city, haven't you noticed?* What was it about the city that drew all this celestial activity to it? What was Cimaris implying?

Her next question came more easily. "Why are they all here?"

Unexpectedly, the archangel started to laugh. It was a cruel, mocking laugh. "Don't you know this place, daughter of Adam? This is Eden."

CHAPTER TWENTY-FOUR

Harriet stared at him, so shocked that for a moment she forgot her fear. Eden? The Garden of Eden, Eden? How could her city be...*that*? The idea that humanity's original home, its paradise lost, was the very city in which she had been born and raised was almost beyond belief. Not to mention Eden—at least the Eden of legend—was sacred, and this city was anything but.

"No, it can't be." She wasn't necessarily doubting him—he would know, after all—but she couldn't believe him, either.

"It is."

"But..." She had so many questions. She asked the first one that came to mind. "If this is Eden, why did God allow the Daemonium to build its headquarters here?"

It felt sacrilegious, to say the least. The demons crawled over the city like ants at a picnic. How could God allow it? The least the angels could have done was push the Daemonium outside the city limits. Then again, the Serpent building his corporate headquarters on the site of his greatest victory and the angels watching it happen without lifting a finger to stop it was starting to feel very on-brand for both sides.

Michael shrugged off her shock. "The Garden was burned down to its roots when Adam and Eve were cast from it. This land is no longer sacred."

"Oh."

Although she'd never particularly cared about Eden before, Harriet couldn't help but feel sad. Adam and Eve's expulsion to a world of hardship and suffering was melancholy enough. Learning that the Garden had been razed and then co-opted by demons with no effort by the angels to protect it was demoralizing. Humans could never again return to that idyllic paradise. It was gone forever.

Her eyes went to her katana, lying on the floor inches from her foot. When Michael decided to finally kill her, it would do her no good. It might as well be miles away.

"Why do the seal guardians have to die for their seals to be opened?" she asked. It seemed unnecessarily brutal. Couldn't the guardians have just carried a key or used a handprint? Why was violence needed to beget violence?

Michael raised his eyebrows. "Die? Only humans die." His wings closed behind him and he took a casual step forward on the sarcophagus. Harriet wished he hadn't. It brought him that much closer to her. She swallowed. He continued, "A drop of the guardians' blood is enough to open the seals. I performed a mercy for my angels by destroying their human forms so they could return to Heaven and serve their Lord."

The only form Harriet had was her human form. Michael knew that. If he destroyed it, she would die. He looked down upon her with unveiled contempt. "This is how you will redeem yourself after having worked for the Prince of Darkness and his minions. Only by giving your blood can you expiate your sins and be welcomed into Heaven."

It took a moment for his words, his accusation, to sink in. She had been a teenager still when she had begun working for the Daemonium. The daughter of a single mother, living with her in a one-bedroom apartment in a rough neighborhood with no college degree or technical training, her options were that or Burger King or drug dealing. She never had the option to become a doctor or a lawyer. She had made the decision that had allowed her to help pay the rent and buy food. It was that simple. It had been the same for Annabeth and Theodora.

And it's not like the angels had offered an alternative. Not once had they come to provide guidance or support. No one had told her she was the half-angel guardian of the fourth seal of the Apocalypse. Maybe things would have been different if she'd known. Or maybe not. Survival was survival.

"Yeah, I spent years sending demons back to Hell," she growled, feeling the warm glow of anger spreading across her cheeks. "It's not like you angels were doing anything about it. And it's not like I had much of a choice."

Michael sneered. "There is always a choice."

Easy for him to say. He was an immortal being who was never tired, never hungry. If he got bored of Earth, he could nip back up to Heaven. Of course he assumed everyone had the luxury of choice. Choice was for people with privilege, people who had more than one option. She hadn't had any of that. Even now, her situation wasn't a choice. It had been forced upon her.

Then she realized. She was wrong. Seal guardianship *was* a choice. Gader'el, Samyaza, and Kasdeja had proven that. They had demonstrated, too, that angelic blood didn't mean Michael could control them unconditionally. She tried to flex her fingers into a fist, testing Michael's control. They didn't move an inch. Yet. But now she knew the way out.

"There's a lot I didn't choose," she told Michael. "I didn't choose for my father to rape my mother. I didn't choose for her to get cancer. But it happened anyway."

Between Michael's control and the pull of the seal, it felt like her body might rip apart, but she ignored it, focusing on her anger instead. Theodora would have been proud of her.

"The angelic host never did a single thing for us, not even when we desperately needed help."

Memories of those terrible times flooded back to her. Her mother crying herself to sleep. The two of them sharing a single cup of noodles because it's all they had. Holding her mother's hand one last time before she was wheeled away to the hospital morgue. Harriet would have done anything to go back in time and make her mother's life easier, but the world didn't work like that. She would never get that chance.

Michael would never understand any of that because he wasn't human. Being human meant experiencing loss. But there could be no loss without love. Father Domenico had accused the demons of being heartless and without compassion, but the angels, or at least some of them, had the same deficit. Empathy, it seemed, was a particularly human trait.

If there were official words of renunciation, of choosing her human side over her celestial side, Harriet didn't know them. So she said what was in her heart and hoped it would somehow be enough. "I'm not an angel. I never was. If you tell me everything is a choice, then I choose to be human. Fuck you and your Apocalypse. Find someone else to murder."

For a moment, nothing happened. She wondered if she'd been wrong and she couldn't simply renounce being half-angel. Perhaps only full angels could fall. Then a tingling filled her body, as though her limbs were waking up after having fallen asleep. It was mildly uncomfortable, but it didn't hurt. She didn't have to wonder what it meant. Immediately, Michael's control over her evaporated, and with it the pull of the seal. Her fingers twitched closed.

Repudiating Heaven undoubtedly carried consequences, but there was no time to think about what, exactly. She had to act before Michael realized she'd found a way to cut his puppet strings. Reaching into her pockets, she pulled out the two grenades. Once she pulled their pins and released the spoons, she would have three to four seconds to get clear of them. Provided they moved fast, she, Theodora, and Annabeth could be safely back in the corridor by then. With luck, Michael wouldn't be behind them. After that, they could regroup and decide what to do.

She ripped the pins free and lobbed the grenades in an underhand toss toward the archangel. As they hit the ground and rolled near the sarcophagus, she spun and ran. In her head, she counted off the fast seconds.

"*Run!*" she yelled as she barreled past her friends at the mouth of the crypt.

They had only made it a dozen yards or so when the first grenade exploded. It was followed immediately by the second. The explosions were loud but short, the sound muffled by the thick walls of the catacombs. Unlike in the movies, no dramatic tongue of flame licked out behind them from the crypt. Instead, the blast of air kicked up invisible dust and cobwebs, making the women cough.

"Did you just try to kill Michael with fucking grenades?" Theodora panted incredulously, a stride behind her.

"No. Of course not."

With a five-meter kill radius each, the grenades would almost certainly have killed any human in the tomb. But as she'd just learned, the only way to dispatch an angel was to all but dismember them. So for all she knew, the shrapnel might have bounced off Michael like party confetti.

"What happened in there?" Annabeth asked.

"Tell you later." The priority was getting out of the catacombs. The last thing they wanted was to face an angry archangel who could turn Theodora and Annabeth into puppets.

They were almost home free, the door leading back to the basement of St. Luke's a growing yellow rectangle in front of them, when something went wrong. One moment, Harriet's arms and legs were pumping, propelling her forward, the next she was collapsed in a heap, her body strewn over the ground like a shattered marble statue. It felt like someone had quadrupled Earth's gravity. Annabeth and Theodora barely managed to slide to a stop behind her, sensing danger.

"What the...?" Theodora said.

A swish of black fabric passed in front of Harriet's eyes, illuminated by the light from Annabeth's phone.

"It's Famine," Annabeth shouted to Theodora. "Stay back."

Harriet wished she could follow the command too, but she was no more able to move than she'd been able to resist Michael. She lay on the ground, helpless.

"Oh, hell no," Theodora growled. "We don't have time for this shit."

Theodora's gun roared. The sound was like cannon fire in the echoing hallway. The Horseman, already little more than a shadow, seemed to pale for a beat. Then he resolidified. Annabeth immediately fired two bolts from her crossbow into his chest. Famine was slower to fade this time, as though he couldn't keep up with the effort of dematerializing quickly enough.

"Keep shooting!" Harriet gasped. "It's working!"

Not needing any more encouragement, Theodora continued to fire, making Harriet's ears ring. With every bolt or bullet that struck the celestial, Harriet felt a little stronger. When Annabeth ran out of bolts, she threw down her crossbow and drew the morning star at her side. By now, Famine was no longer flickering. He was a solid black mass, as corporeal as Pestilence and War had been.

Harriet couldn't believe what she was seeing. Was it really that easy? The celestial hadn't even tried to attack. With one touch, he could easily have crippled all three of his antagonists, but instead, he had simply floated in front of them with no evident strategy. The demons they revoked had fought harder than that.

When Theodora stopped to reload, Annabeth lunged, swinging the morning star high and bringing it down on Famine's head. The metal made a dull thud as it connected with whatever lay underneath the Horseman's cowl. The celestial crumpled to the ground and lay there motionless, a heap of thick black fabric. A second of surprised silence passed, during which time Famine didn't stir. Then Theodora intoned automatically, "In the name of the Daemonium and the demonic hierarchy, your permission to dwell on Earth is officially revoked." Then she realized what she'd said. "Shit. Well, whatever, still counts."

Harriet got to her feet. "We need to keep going."

She stepped over the Horseman and started to jog down the hall. Theodora hastened to catch up with her. "Going where? What do we do now? Michael's going to keep coming after you."

They hadn't heard. They didn't know what Harriet had been forced to do to escape from the crypt. She shook her head. "Not me. You two."

"Why not you?" Theodora challenged. "The fourth seal—"

"Isn't mine anymore. I—" Harriet grappled with the next word, feeling uncomfortable using it to describe herself. "*Fell*. It was the only way to get away."

She grimaced, feeling an unexpected pang of shame. The phrase "fallen angel" carried a heavy stigma. And while until a few days ago she hadn't even been aware she had anything angelic in her, it felt strange to know she had officially repudiated that half of herself. But at least she was free. She no longer felt the seal's tug, trying to draw her to it. The thread that had tied her to it had been cut forever. For better or for worse.

"Shit," Theodora said, half-impressed, half-surprised. "So whose is it now?"

"I don't know."

If the seal was linked to Gader'el's bloodline, did she have a younger half-sibling somewhere in the world who had suddenly gained this unwanted position? She knew nothing about Gader'el— she could have hundreds of relatives in the world, or none. If she had a sibling, she hoped for their sake they were someplace safe, where the angels wouldn't be able to reach them.

"That's it! Harriet, you're a genius." Theodora slapped her on the back hard enough that it hurt. It was a sign Theodora's own back and chest must have already been feeling better.

"What?" Harriet asked, bemused.

"That's how we get out of this fucking shitshow. If we all fall, Michael won't come after us. We'll be safe. Fuck him and his kidnapping shit."

Theodora was right. If all three women fell, there would be no reason for the angels to care about them anymore. There would be no more encounters with Horsemen, no more standoffs with angels. But there was still one major, unavoidable problem. "It wouldn't stop the Apocalypse. Michael would just go after the next seal guardians. It might take a little longer, but we'd still die."

Theodora pulled up short. "Shit."

A beat passed as the women confronted the unavoidable truth. They could die for their seals or die during Armageddon, but right now, there wasn't a scenario in which they lived happily ever after. Then Annabeth spoke. "You said Theodora's seal is in a cemetery?"

"Yeah," Theodora replied. "Something with a pond."

"Then it must be the fifth seal, the seal of the martyrs."

"Huh? The seal of the martyrs? What does that mean?"

"The fifth seal is kind of an outlier," Annabeth explained. "It's the only seal that doesn't immediately lead to the death of a bunch of people. In the Book of Revelation, John says that when the fifth seal is opened, the souls of all the martyrs call out for God to avenge them, but they're told to wait a little longer, the time isn't right yet." She wrinkled her nose. Or at least Harriet thought she did. Even with two phone flashlights, it was still dark in the catacomb. "Think of it as the Apocalyptic intermission. After that, God starts tearing the world apart."

"Okay, but how do you know that's what Theodora's seal is?" Harriet asked.

"A cemetery seems like the most logical place for a seal with dead martyrs, don't you think?"

"Holy shit!" Theodora barked. "I know how to stop the Apocalypse."

CHAPTER TWENTY-FIVE

When he opened the fifth seal, I saw under the altar the souls of those who had been slain because of the word of God and the testimony they had maintained. They called out in a loud voice, "How long, Sovereign Lord, holy and true, until you judge the inhabitants of the Earth and avenge our blood?" Then each of them was given a white robe, and they were told to wait a little longer, until the number of their fellow servants and brothers who were to be killed as they had been was completed.

Annabeth was surprised to see Summer waiting for them at the end of the corridor. She would have expected the archangel's second hostage to be hightailing it as fast and as far away from the hospital as she could get. Had their roles been reversed, she would have been.

"What are you doing here?" Harriet demanded tersely when she realized it was Summer. The wail of a fire alarm filled the air around them, making it hard to hear her words. "I told you to go."

Summer was undaunted. "I did. But I came back when I realized you would need help."

"With what?"

"Getting out of the hospital. Everything is on lockdown. The police are looking for you."

"Get in line," Theodora muttered under her breath.

Annabeth bit her lip. This was a real problem. It was bad enough to be on the run from Michael. They couldn't afford to be actively dodging human law enforcement as well.

"We need to sneak you out." Summer pointed to Theodora's bandolier. "You're going to have to take that off. And leave the gun. You won't make it out of the building like that."

Theodora drew back, hands wrapping more firmly around the firearm. "Like hell I'm leaving them. The police can pry them from my—"

"Theodora," Annabeth snapped. The screaming of the fire alarm was like a nail being driven through her eardrum. They didn't have time to stand around and argue. "Leave it."

Her own crossbow was in the hallway somewhere far behind them, lost forever in the darkness where she threw it down, her bolts spent. She didn't like to lose a weapon any more than Theodora did, but their priority was getting out of the hospital. To do that, they needed to keep a low profile and pass undetected.

"Fine," Theodora grumbled. She set the gun against the wall and uncinched the belt from around her waist, letting it fall in a careless heap on the ground after removing her kusarigama. "Happy?"

"Now the rest of your weapons," Summer ordered.

With a huff, Theodora tucked her KA-BAR knife and kusarigama into her pants. Her efforts to hide the weapons weren't perfect, but so long as no one looked too closely, it would do.

"There's a side door on the first floor that leads to an alley," Summer said, moving on to the next issue. "The police might not be watching it."

Harriet gave her a worried look. "You shouldn't come with us. If we're caught…"

"You need me to show you where the door is. Now come on, before someone tells the police about it."

Turning, she led them up the stairs back to the basement, then to the left. After a few dozen yards, she stopped at a tan door topped by a red exit sign. She pulled it open to reveal a stairwell. Annabeth could hear the echo of footsteps above them as people rushed to evacuate the building. The emergency lights, triggered by the fire alarm, flashed a strobing white.

Annabeth's head was spinning. All she could do was keep moving as they climbed the stairs one story and exited onto the ground floor. One foot in front of the other, she told herself. Right foot. What had Theodora figured out about the seal of the martyrs? Left foot. Where was Jonathan now? Right foot. Would Michael go after the boys now? Left foot. Should she fall immediately to keep them safe? Right foot.

Doctors, nurses, and patients rushed past them, presumably headed for other exits. Annabeth's palm sweated as she unconsciously gripped the morning star's holster tighter. Their fear and panic was contagious, even though technically the three of them were the source.

"Here," Summer announced, stopping abruptly. She indicated the windowless door next to her. "This is a service entrance. A lot of the janitors like to hang out here and smoke. I'm going to go outside. If the coast is clear, I'll come back and let you know."

"Wait—"

Harriet reached out to stop her, but before she could, Summer disappeared through the door. Giving up, Harriet turned to Theodora. "So what's the plan?" She had to raise her voice a little to be heard over the endless wail of the alarm.

Annabeth leaned forward. This was important. She wanted to be sure she heard right the first time.

"We need to find my seal," Theodora said.

Annabeth had guessed as much, but with possibly dozens of cemeteries in the city, they had to find a way to narrow down the search. There was no time to visit all of them. She had an idea. She whipped her phone out of her pocket. "You said there was a pond, right? What else? Was there anything distinctive that you remember?"

Theodora thought for a beat, then shrugged. Annabeth could see she was frustrated. "Just grass. Lots of green grass. And some trees." She frowned, confused. "Where in the city is there even that much grass?"

Annabeth bit her lip. She had a point. It was a clue. "It's probably outside the city…"

Her thumbs tapped as she fell silent, quickly scrolling through pages and pages of images, looking for what she hoped would be the right one. Some cemeteries she could eliminate off the bat because they were inside the city, but more than one cemetery in the suburbs had a pond and grass. Then she saw it. With a surge of hope, she brandished her phone, waving it in front of Theodora's face to show her the photo on the screen. "Is this it? Is this the cemetery?"

Theodora took the phone from her and squinted, peering at the small screen. "The angle is different from what I remember. And this photo was taken in the winter, when the trees weren't in full bloom. But yeah, it's the right one." She pointed. "I recognize that small white building with the unpainted concrete dome next to the pond."

Annabeth took the phone back and read the description beneath the picture aloud. "Green Acres Cemetery was established in the mid-1900s in response to the city's blossoming population. Since then, hundreds of new graves have been added each year." She looked up at Theodora. "What do we do once we get there?"

This was the important question. How did they stop Michael from destroying the world?

Theodora nodded with confidence. "We open my seal."

"*What?*" Harriet and Annabeth said the word simultaneously, a joint chorus of alarm.

"Why would we do that?" Harriet demanded. Annabeth could have sworn her hair was standing on end even more than usual. "The whole idea is to *stop* more seals from being opened."

Theodora looked unfazed. In fact, she looked pleased with herself. Smug. "Whoever opens a seal controls its contents. So if *we* open my seal and not Michael..." She trailed off, waiting for them to realize what she had said.

Annabeth frowned so hard it made her face hurt. This was the exact same argument she'd made at the bank. At the time, they were discussing control over Famine. But now... "We control the martyrs? How does that stop the Apocalypse?"

Theodora grinned broadly. "Not the martyrs. *The timing of the Apocalypse.* You said it yourself: when the fifth seal is opened, the person opening it gets to tell the martyrs to sit down and shut the fuck up for a while longer. We can delay this bitch for at least another hundred years. Then, once we're dead the world can burn."

Annabeth shook her head slowly, skeptical. "I don't know."

They knew basically nothing about the seals. It might not work the way Theodora thought. But also, "You remember we would have to kill you to open it, right?"

As far as she was concerned, they needed to find another, better plan. This one was a nonstarter.

"Oh!" Harriet's eyebrows jumped and she blinked rapidly, remembering. "Michael said only a few drops of blood are enough to open a seal. We wouldn't have to kill Theodora." She paused, scrunching her face together. "Not that I necessarily agree with this idea."

Theodora put her hands on her hips, determination settling across her face. Annabeth knew that look. She had seen it often enough over the years. "My father knew something about the seal, and the angels killed him for it. I think it could be this. We're all fucked anyway if it doesn't work. We might as well try it, right? What if it works?"

Annabeth chewed the inside of her lip. It was true their only other plan was to beg the Daemonium for help. But if Theodora was wrong about what would happen once the seal was opened, they would be furthering the Apocalypse, bringing the world one step closer to its end. It was a hell of a gamble.

Before she had time to think about it any more, the door beside them opened and Summer squeezed back through. Her face was slightly flushed. "Okay, it's safe. Let's go."

She held the door open as Harriet, Annabeth, and Theodora slipped through. As Annabeth passed the threshold, she looked right, toward the hospital's main entrance. Through the thick crowd of people milling anxiously outside it, she could see the red-blue lights of police cars and a heavy black SWAT truck. She winced, hating the disruption they'd caused to the hospital's patients and their treatment. People might die, wheeled away from ventilators or other lifesaving machines.

Then again, she shouldn't take the blame for what was all on Michael. He was the one who had lured them here and then sent the Horsemen after them, forcing them to fight. Moreover, he was the one who had released Pestilence and War in the first place, overloading the hospital with new patients. And he was the one trying to destroy the world, not her. She was trying to save it.

"How are we going to get a cab?" Harriet asked, scanning the area around them. They were in what seemed to be a partially obstructed side alley, too narrow for a car to pass through.

"So, you agree about going to the cemetery?" Theodora asked.

Harriet shrugged. "Unless Annabeth has a better idea."

She didn't.

"That's a main street," Summer said, pointing at the intersection in the opposite direction of the police cars. "We can hail a taxi from there."

"Not 'we,'" Harriet corrected, but gently. "You're not coming with us."

"But—"

"Right now, we're a magnet for danger. You should go back to your apartment and stay there." She placed a quick hand on Summer's shoulder, soothing her.

Summer's face pulled into an unhappy, worried pout, but she nodded and set off toward the front of the hospital without further protest.

"So, who is she anyway?" Theodora asked once she was out of earshot.

"What?" Harriet frowned, confused.

Theodora motioned with her chin back over her shoulder. "The blonde."

"Oh. She...Her name is Summer." Harriet looked away uncomfortably.

Theodora raised her eyebrow. "And? She seems more than a little friendly. You been holding out on us?"

A soft rose started to creep up Harriet's neck. "It's new. It's not like we're...anything." She walked a little faster.

"Let it go," Annabeth cautioned Theodora. "She doesn't want to talk about it yet."

Theodora looked hurt. "You knew about this?"

"Can we not talk about this right now?" Harriet ran her fingers through her hair anxiously.

"I'm happy for you!" Theodora chirped, ignoring her request. "I thought you were turning into a nun. Come on, you have to give me something. I want to know my girl's being taken care of. She brings you breakfast in bed or whatever romantic shit you like."

Harriet gave her a baleful look. "Fine." She rubbed her neck just above the collar. "She's very nice and...if we make it through all this, I'd like to spend more time with her. Happy?"

By now, they had reached the main street. Annabeth was surprised how quiet it was. The police must have set up a barricade somewhere nearby, limiting the traffic in and out of the area. Only a few cars rolled past, the drivers rubbernecking at the chaos beyond the women. She was wondering how far they would have to walk to catch a taxi when a black sedan pulled up in front of them. It was the type used by professional chauffeur services, long and completely spotless. The back door swung open, revealing a luxurious black leather interior.

"Get in, shitheads."

Annabeth stared, unable to believe what she was seeing. How had Andromalius found them? Instinctively, her eyes went to Theodora and then Harriet, searching for their reactions. They looked just as astounded as she was.

"Today," Andromalius snarled impatiently.

She was so shocked by his appearance that it didn't even occur to Annabeth to refuse. She crawled into the car next to him. Theodora and Harriet followed, taking the seat across from them. The situation was surreal. Annabeth wasn't entirely sure she wasn't dreaming.

"Why are you here?" Theodora asked, giving voice to what they must all have been thinking.

"Someone saw an angel come busting out of a window on the top floor."

Annabeth's eyes widened. She had been so caught up thinking about Theodora's shotgun that she had completely forgotten there would be witnesses to her plunge through the window with Jonathan. A winged woman carrying a grown man was hard to miss, especially when there were so many people around. Perhaps that, not the shotgun, was why the hospital had been put under lockdown. She reflexively glanced at Theodora, but the other woman's poker face was flawless. If Andromalius didn't know it was her, Theodora clearly wasn't going to volunteer that information. Let him think it had been a full angel he had rushed to confront and not his half-angel revoker.

Andromalius added casually, "Plus I'm tracking your phones." Annabeth didn't have time to absorb his unexpected admission that he had been snooping on them before he pivoted to a question. "So, where's my fucking lance?"

Oh no. The lance. Annabeth hadn't thought about it since Father Domenico's office. There had been too much else going on, and besides, it was kindling now. Her mouth went dry. What could she tell him? He had tasked them to bring him an angel-killing relic, and here they were, empty-handed. But the answer came quickly. The truth.

"Uriel broke it. He snapped it in two. For what it's worth, he said it wasn't the lance of Longinus anyway."

"Uriel," Andromalius growled, yellow eyes glowing. Annabeth could hear the thousands of years of antagonism between the angels and the demons in his voice. "So that fucker is back."

He didn't ask how or where they had encountered the archangel, and for that she was grateful. She didn't know how she would have explained away the trip to St. Francis. Trying to sound helpful—and direct the conversation away from how Uriel had come to be holding the lance—she offered, "And Michael too. He's in the hospital right now. Well, in the catacombs beneath it, last we saw him."

She didn't know if he knew about Michael yet. Regardless, she was happy to tell him. They were woefully short of allies, and besides, the last thing they needed was for Andromalius to start suspecting they were in league with the angels—or that they were half-angel. They needed him to think they were still fully tools of the Daemonium, and offering him some information would help prove that. She continued, "He's been opening the seals of the Apocalypse—three so far."

Andromalius hadn't known about the seals the last time they saw him, but a day had passed. There was no way the Daemonium hadn't found out by now.

"Mmm." His face rippled with an unhappy scowl. He did know. And he wasn't pleased about it.

Theodora spoke up. "We have an idea."

Annabeth stared at her. What was she was doing?

The other woman leaned forward, her face intense. In order to sit down, she had been forced to remove the kama from her pants and lay it in her lap. Now she closed her right hand around its handle as though preparing to fight. "We know where the fifth seal is. If *we* open it, Michael can't. He won't be able to complete the Apocalypse and bring back the Lamb."

Annabeth took a breath, stunned. Theodora shouldn't have told him about the seal. If he found out she was its guardian...

Andromalius cocked his head and narrowed his eyes. The sharpness in his face could have cut glass. "How do you think you're going to open that seal? That is, if you're right about where it is."

Theodora managed to look amazingly nonchalant. Annabeth never knew she was such a good actress. She leaned back against the seat and let her expression relax. "We'll figure it out. There's got to be a way. Drop us and we'll grab a taxi."

"Where is the seal?" Andromalius demanded.

"Green Acres Cemetery, across the bridge."

"Driver!" he barked, making Annabeth jump. "You heard her. Take us to the cemetery. And step on it."

Out of the frying pan, into the fire.

CHAPTER TWENTY-SIX

Andromalius didn't speak to them for the rest of the drive, but that didn't mean he was silent. The acting high lord never set his phone down during the twenty-minute ride. He was too busy marshaling his forces against the invisible army of angels that he believed was finally in his reach, gruffly commanding his lieutenants to move resources and ragtag troops to locations around the city in a high-stakes game of celestial chess. Theodora didn't know how many demons were here, but it had to be a lot, based on his directions. But did any of his maneuvering matter? If no demon had ever been able to kill an angel before, how could they now?

She decided she didn't have the bandwidth to care. All his scheming was moot if Michael kept opening seals. Even if the demons managed to land a few blows initially, they would still be utterly wiped out in the end stages of the Apocalypse. The demons were just as screwed if not more than the humans when it came to the end of the world.

Realizing she was clutching her kusarigama, she forced herself to release her grip. Her chest ached, but she had compartmentalized the pain so that it was little more than a persistent throb. That

was one benefit of years of having been beaten up by demons—
she had learned to simply disregard pain. She looked out the
window and tried to ignore Andromalius's shouting. She needed
to think through what she was going to do once they found her
seal. How the fuck was she going to control the martyrs? She had
been bluffing. The truth was, she had no idea how all this seal stuff
worked.

A giant, Gothic archway came into view, marking the cemetery's
entrance, but Theodora would have known they had arrived even
with her eyes closed. The second they were on the cemetery
grounds, her heart started to race, her stomach squeezing tight. In
the memory Harriet had pulled her into, she hadn't felt the pull of
the seal. It must only have started after the first seal was opened,
the first domino down in the chain. She sure felt it now. The low
throbbing was both attractive and repellent. She leaned against the
door and fought to slow her breathing.

"You feel it, don't you? The call," Harriet whispered under her
breath so Andromalius couldn't hear.

Theodora swallowed, abhorring with every fiber of her being
the feeling of compulsion. "Yup." At least it would be easy to find
the seal. It seemed to sink hooks into her, trying to drag her toward
it. "It feels...wrong."

"I think it's because we're not full—" Harriet caught herself
and looked at Andromalius. "Because we're half-human."

Halflings. Half-breeds. They didn't fit into either world
correctly. And because of that, things hurt.

As they reached the red-brown arch, the demon lowered his
phone.

"Stop here," he ordered the driver. The car pulled to a stop.
Andromalius gestured to the women. "Get out."

"You're not coming?" Theodora asked. She had assumed he
would accompany them to the seal. Not that she wanted that. The
last thing she needed was him breathing down her neck and asking
how she was able to open a seal. But still. They were talking about
opening a seal of the Apocalypse. It seemed like something at
which he would want to be present.

"Michael's been spotted," Andromalius grunted. "He's headed
toward the office."

The office. So Michael was taking the fight to the Daemonium
a second time. And Andromalius had to go defend his turf. For all

the good that would do him. Theodora wasn't going to tell him not to go get his head shoved so far up his own ass he became a literal ass puppet. For one thing, demons were stubborn as shit, so he would just ignore her. For another, she didn't particularly care if he got revoked. So she just nodded.

Harriet got out first and she followed, looping the chain of her kusarigama around her fist as she readied herself for whatever awaited them past the cemetery gates. If Michael were smart, he'd send half the heavenly host to defend her seal. The door slammed behind Annabeth and the car burned rubber, peeling out of the cemetery with a piercing squeal.

"Good luck to us too," Theodora snarked at its retreating shape.

Annabeth unsheathed her morning star. Three half-humans against a platoon of angels would be about as successful as a pocketknife in a machine gun fight, but it was the best they could do.

"Come on, let's go," Theodora said, indicating the gate. "Time to fuck up some angel shit or die trying."

The seal's call led her down a black asphalt path, past hundreds of cenotaphs, grave markers, and tombstones. As they walked, she tried not to think about the last time she trod this same ground, small feet in bubble-gum-pink high-tops that she had begged her mother to buy. How close had she and her father come to reaching the seal before Michael had stopped them? How much hope had the archangel allowed her father to feel before he'd brutally ripped it away?

And then, another thought that pushed the air from her lungs. Did one of those graves belong to her father? What had Michael done with his body after killing him? Had he left it to be thrown into a potter's field, or had he given him a respectful burial? She had all but nothing left of her father. The least the angels could have done was tell her and her mother what had become of his remains. At least then they could have mourned him properly.

She pushed these thoughts aside with difficulty and focused on looking for the pond from her memory. She hated that all she had to guide her was a snapshot—a few seconds of what would have been a much longer day. What had they done before coming to the cemetery? Why couldn't she remember? She had been here on the most traumatic day of her life. Why had it taken Harriet diving back in her memories to resurface something she should never have forgotten? And why did none of this look familiar?

Confusion, loss, and anger whipped at her, raking her heart with their wicked, hurtful barbs. And she felt other emotions too. Every step she took deeper into the cemetery, the seal gripped her more tightly. Although she would never admit it to her companions, the compulsion to go to the seal was starting to overpower her. For the first time, she felt a whisper of fear. Perhaps this was a bad idea after all.

"The angels aren't much for imagination," she said, breaking the silence that was starting to become suffocating. "Just think, they could have put a seal in a glitter factory." Michael could still have been finding glitter in his hair a hundred years later.

"Are we close yet?" Harriet asked, ignoring Theodora's comment.

Theodora was miffed she hadn't acknowledged the cleverness of the idea, but she nodded anyway. "Close."

After a few hundred more feet, the seal's pull turned into an intense buzzing that ran through her body like electricity through a copper wire. She clenched her teeth, feeling as though the seal might pull her organs out of her body. She was gripping the handle of the kusarigama so tightly her knuckles turned tan.

Annabeth, who had been watching her closely, noticed the change. "Here?"

Theodora nodded again, nostrils flaring. Her chest felt like it was trapped in a vise. In this part of the cemetery, stubby gray and brown tombstones were spread haphazardly over the short-cropped green lawn. They were much less densely packed than the area near the gate, older, perhaps.

Annabeth looked around. "You think it's in—"

"Yeah." Theodora nodded at the mausoleum in front of them. "It's in there."

If the angels were going to hide a seal of the Apocalypse in a cemetery, this was an excellent location. A small building made of white marble discolored by time, the mausoleum looked like a miniature Gothic church, with a stone cross on the roof and two life-sized angel statues flanking a bronze door turned turquoise with age. The statues made Theodora's skin crawl. The algae that had grown on them over time made it look like the angels were weeping. If they came to life to defend the seal, that was it. Theodora was done. They could have it.

"All right, I'm going to—"

Before she could finish, the door swung open soundlessly, revealing a black void on the other side. Theodora fell silent. What now? Was Michael on the other side? A hit squad of angels?

But it was Father Domenico who stepped out.

"Theodora." His expression on his too-familiar face was stern. Gone was gentle benevolence with which he'd looked upon them earlier at St. Francis. "I am disappointed to see you here. But not surprised." His sanctimonious tone, the same one he used every time he spoke to her, was like nails against concrete.

Theodora's fury wasn't hot; it was like twenty shots of Red Bull and a line of Adderall. It made her forget the feeling of the seal sucking her soul from her body and the sharp ache of the healing holes in her chest and back. She raised the kusarigama, blade pointed at the priest. "Oh, hell no. I know you're not here in the very place you helped Michael kill my father."

Angry as she was, a tiny part of her was glad to see him. His presence blocking the door to the mausoleum meant she wouldn't have to hunt him down later. She could deal with him here and now. Two birds, one stone.

He took a stride forward onto the top step of the mausoleum, undaunted by the venom in her voice, and held up his hand. Wearing his priestly vestments, he looked like he was blessing a congregation. "Put away your weapon."

She curled her lip into a vicious snarl. "Fat chance." He had helped kill her father. Even the Bible agreed that an eye for an eye was the appropriate punishment.

He didn't so much as flinch, however. As though she hadn't spoken, he continued, "What is happening now is beyond you. It is beyond all of us. All we can do is submit to God's will and trust in His plan."

"Oh yeah?" She released the chain from her left hand, swinging the ball in a tight circle. Her head was buzzing from the adrenaline rush. A few feet closer and she could wrap the chain around his neck and drag him to her feet. She couldn't bring her father back, but she could make sure his killers paid for what they'd done. "It was God's plan for Michael to kill my father? Is that really the line you want to take right now?"

His face contracted in a familiar expression of censure, one she had seen too many times to count in the early days after she'd met him. Before Annabeth stopped bringing her to St. Francis. He chided, "Do not be foolish. This is not about him now. It is about the cleansing of the Earth to prepare it for the Lamb and His flock."

"Fuck you. It's about my father *to me*," she growled back, defiant.

Of course she cared about the Apocalypse. It was why they were here in the cemetery, after all. But right now, all she could see was red...and the memory of a younger Father Domenico telling her not to look as Michael murdered her father.

"Theodora." He crossed his arms over his chest. He looked like a frustrated schoolteacher confronting a wayward pupil. "All of that is in the past. The time for your stubbornness is over. God has given you a purpose. Rejoice in that."

The only reason Theodora didn't tackle him to the ground and smash his skull against the steps like a rotting pumpkin was because Annabeth put a hand on her shoulder and held her back. And because he had reminded her that her priority needed to be getting to the seal behind him. Save the world first, deal with him after.

"Step aside, Father," she ordered. "We're not letting Michael open that seal."

The heavenly host hadn't yet appeared to try to stop them, and Theodora doubted there was a small army of angels hiding inside the mausoleum. That meant he was the only thing standing between them and the fifth seal. Still, he didn't move. "Whatever your plans, I cannot allow them."

She stared at him. Jesus fucking Christ. The man was in his seventies at least. A strong gust of wind might have knocked him over. He was as intimidating as Santa Claus. What was he going to do to stop them? Lecture them about retirement benefits?

"Please, Father," Annabeth said. "Billions of innocent people will die if we don't at least try to stop the Apocalypse. You don't want that. I know you don't. If you would just—"

His eyes went to her as his mouth twitched into a deeper frown. "Annabeth, where is your faith?"

Theodora growled. She didn't like how he was trying to guilt and manipulate her friend. It was time to stop being polite. "We're getting to that seal whether you like it or not. So step aside or I swear to God I will punt you halfway across this cemetery."

In response to the threat, the priest took a step back. But it was no gesture of fearful retreat. He hunched over as he reached into his pocket. When he withdrew his hand, he was holding a small silver ball topped by a gold cross.

"Do not come any closer," he warned, waving it in front of him like a weapon.

Theodora squinted at it, mystified. "What...?"

"Whatever that is, it's something celestial," Annabeth said sharply, seeing details her companions couldn't.

"If you try to enter this mausoleum with force, you will be turning your back on God. You will be denied His grace and forever barred from Heaven. You will be cast down with the demons into Hell, where you will burn eternally." Passion made the priest's voice quiver. Or possibly fear. Theodora wasn't kidding about punting him, and he knew it.

She licked her lips, anticipating the whoop-ass she was about to dish out. Whatever trinket Father Domenico was holding wasn't going to do shit to save him. Out of respect to Annabeth, she might not kill him in front of her, but that didn't mean she couldn't dislocate both his elbows and obliterate the bones of his nose on her way through him.

"Damned to Hell?" she repeated. "Oh well."

She had always assumed she'd end up in Hell anyway. It wasn't just all the morally gray things she'd done. It was the fact that up until recently, she thought she was half-demon. And they didn't let demons into Heaven. So being told now she was going to Hell wasn't exactly the threat Father Domenico thought it was.

His hand drooped, letting the orb fall a few inches as he guessed some of what she was thinking. Still, he tried to rally, raising his voice to give himself courage. "If this is the path you choose, then it is for nothing. You cannot open the seal without God's grace."

Theodora had thought there was nothing he could say that would stop her. She was wrong. She flinched as though struck. If God deemed her fallen, her blood couldn't open the fifth seal, just as Harriet could no longer open the fourth. No. Her mind rebelled against this new wall that had been thrown in her way. This couldn't be the end, not like this. They couldn't have lost their only opportunity to stop the Apocalypse without so much as a single punch thrown.

And what about her father? If she couldn't finish what he'd started, then he had died in vain. She couldn't accept that. As though he were standing next to her, speaking in her ear, she heard his voice. *"Demons can be martyrs too, Theo. Remember that."* It was the last thing he had said to her, and therefore it must have been deeply important to him. He had wanted her to do something with that information, but what?

She thought about her father taking her around the city, trying to find the seal that had once been his. He must have planned to use her blood to open the seal and then take control of it. But what did a demon martyr have to do with that? Was the martyr a specific demon? If only she could remember…

"Why don't I remember the day Michael killed my father?"

She didn't know if she had intended to ask the question aloud or whether the tortured, anguished words had tumbled out without her consent, but regardless, now they hung in the air, a rhetorical question with no answer.

Or was it?

Without warning, the priest answered. "It was better you not remember. You were only a child, and the sins of your father were not yours. We had hoped you would not follow in his footsteps, that you could be saved." Contempt tickled at his nostrils, making them twitch. "But you are just like him."

She stared at him, so bewildered she barely registered his insults. Her tongue had turned thick and heavy, too torpid to move. He… what?

Annabeth asked the question Theodora was too stupefied to. "What did you do to her, Father?" She spoke slowly, her voice saturated by horror and suspicion.

Father Domenico hadn't betrayed only Theodora. Annabeth, too, was a victim. She had loved and respected him for decades. Now she was starting to realize he wasn't the man he had presented himself as. It was no coincidence he had come into her life exactly when she had needed help. As the only half-human seal guardians, he must have been tasked by the angels to keep track of them. He had known when she was most vulnerable, and he had taken advantage.

Why he had only groomed Annabeth, Theodora didn't know. Perhaps the angels had wanted to influence her to stay away from her father, the high lord of the Daemonium. Perhaps the priest had only had time for one child and had decided Annabeth would be the easiest to control. But if he thought Annabeth would be unquestioningly loyal to him, he was wrong. Theodora could see it in Annabeth's eyes. For the first time, she was seeing him for who he was, and she didn't like that man.

Father Domenico didn't acknowledge Annabeth's question. Instead, he hoisted the orb once more, trying to regain control over the situation. "This is your last chance. Obey, or by the power vested in me I—"

The chain of the kusarigama flew gracefully through the air, the links flashing like the scales of a silver fish in a stream, and wrapped tightly around his wrist. When Theodora yanked sharply, it pulled his hand down, causing the orb to spill to the ground before he even knew what was happening. It bounced down the stairs, coming to rest in front of the mausoleum with the cross leaning like a kickstand. Whatever talisman it had been for him, whatever its angelic power, it was out of reach now.

The righteousness disappeared from his face in an instant, replaced by fear. He was an aging human priest with indigestion and a sedentary lifestyle. She, on the other hand, was a half-celestial who had spent two decades revoking the worst of the worst demons using any weapon she could get her hands on. For a beat, she drank his panic in greedily, savoring it with malicious glee. For all the times he'd judged her and cut at her with snide remarks, finally she was getting payback.

Hauling on the chain, she jerked him off his feet, sending him sprawling down the stairs just as she'd imagined. He landed heavily, limbs akimbo, then scrabbled to his knees.

"No, Theodora. Please, wait. You are condemning your immortal soul," he cried.

His glasses had been jostled askew, the temple tip pushed over his left ear. The hand he extended toward her was wrinkled, with brown liver spots. Had he not gone into the priesthood, he could have been a grandfather, handing out butterscotch to rambunctious children out of a glass jar. But he hadn't. He had made his bed half a century or more ago. He had chosen to collaborate with the angels and keep information from her, Annabeth, and Harriet. He had lied, manipulated, and who knew what else? He had signed on to the extermination of billions of humans wholesale and without question. It was time to lie in that bed.

Crouching beside him, she used the chain to quickly bind his hands together. Then she looped the rest of the chain around his neck, drawing it so tight his hands were pinned to his chest. The metal bit into his skin. It wasn't tight enough to kill him, but it was more than tight enough to make him extremely uncomfortable. She grabbed his chin, digging her bright red nails in so hard they almost broke the skin, and forced him to look into her eyes.

"I am *nothing* like my father," she hissed. "My father was a kind, compassionate man who believed in the goodness of the world. I'd rather pull out all your fingernails and listen to you scream." Was she exaggerating for effect or not? She no longer knew.

She paused, letting the words sink in. Perhaps one day he might realize the mistake he'd made. If the world lasted long enough. She continued, "I can't be like my father because you took that man away from me. In a sick and twisted way, you *made* me. So if you want to see a real demon—"

Abruptly, she stopped. The demon martyr. Her father had known what would happen. He had known the angels would one day turn against his daughter, just as they had him. When he had whispered one last secret in her ear before he died, he had been trying to tell her that she could open the seal anyway. *She* was the demon martyr.

As soon as she thought it, the last remaining pieces of the puzzle started to come together. It *wasn't* only angelic blood that could open the seals; otherwise there would have been no reason to move the seals after their guardians fell. Relocating them only made sense if the seals remained keyed to their guardians' blood—regardless of whether they were angels or demons. After he had fallen, her father had lost the ability to hear his seal's call, but he had been planning to open it himself. His blood would act as the equivalent of a spare key.

She let go of the priest and looked back at her companions. This was no run-of-the-mill revocation. By opening the seal, they would be setting themselves against God Himself. They were putting the kind of target on their back that would never go away. But the alternative was to let the world burn.

"I know what to do," she said.

She noted the fatigue in Harriet's face, the worry in Annabeth's eyes. They didn't have to come with her for this part. Maybe God would forgive them if only Theodora opened the seal. Hell was a terrible place. It would be better if only she went.

"You should stay," she told them. She meant it.

Harriet frowned. "What are you talking about?"

"We don't all have to go. If you don't, then maybe—"

"You're not going in alone." Annabeth's tone said there would be no arguing with her.

Theodora shook her head. "Okay. Then let's roll."

She strode forward, fired by determination. It wasn't until she was halfway up the stairs that she realized the seal had stopped calling to her. She paused midstep, surprised. The thread that connected her to it had been severed permanently and she hadn't even felt it happen. There was no earthquake, no solar eclipse to mark the moment. It had just happened. Like Harriet, she was officially fallen.

She pressed onward, past the weeping angels. What did she care if she was no longer half-angel? What good had it ever done her? She was happier to have no connection to the angels anyway. Her father had been fallen and it didn't make him any less of a man. Now the two of them were connected by more than just blood. And it was time to finish what he had started.

Theodora couldn't see anything at first when she stepped into the mausoleum, temporarily blinded by the transition from sunlight to darkness. But when her eyes adjusted, she saw that the inside of the mausoleum was spartan and unadorned, with bare concrete walls and a thick layer of dust covering the floor. She looked around, confused. There was nothing there; it was just an empty room.

"Where is it?" she asked.

"There." Annabeth pointed. Against the far wall was a massive, round stained-glass window. A kaleidoscope of blue, red, and yellow, it depicted the Virgin Mary holding a baby Jesus, surrounded by a crowd of adoring angels. It let in so little light, covered by years of dirt and grime as it was, that Theodora had barely noticed it.

"You're sure?" The question might as well have been rhetorical. Of course Annabeth was sure. As one of the fallen, Theodora could no longer see her seal, but Annabeth could.

Annabeth nodded.

"Okay." It didn't matter where the seal was, so long as Theodora could reach it and smear some blood over it.

As she walked the few short steps to the window, she pulled her last weapon, pricking her finger with the knife's sharp tip. As a drop of blood welled to the surface, she thought how ironic it was that her blood—her polluted, half-human blood—was the key to either stopping or furthering one of the angels' most important plans. A half-human was the key to the future of humanity.

Things could have turned out differently. The angels could have prepared her since childhood to fulfill her angelic duty. They could have turned her into their mindless minion, a younger version of Father Domenico. But they'd ignored her until it was too late, and so her allegiance was to herself and humanity, not to them. They could fuck themselves.

Reaching up, she touched the glass with her finger. She didn't have time to wonder what it would be like when the seal opened. Or how long it would take. The second her blood made contact with it, the portal blew open.

"*Oh shit!*" she yelled as a blast of air struck her full-on. It was so hot it sucked the breath out of her lungs, filling them instead with burning steam.

Unconsciously influenced as she was by Christian iconography, she had imagined the scene on the other side of the fifth seal would be a bucolic diorama of white-robed old men strolling peacefully through a garden, singing hallelujah and reading books and all that. Instead, what awaited her was a hellscape of molten, raging fire, billowing black clouds that obscured huge swathes of the sky, and smoldering, toppled stone structures. The caustic smell of brimstone filled her nostrils, making the sensitive mucous membranes there burn. Her body recoiled with instinctive fear. Theodora had no doubt what she was seeing. Somehow, she had opened a door directly into Hell.

Before she could move, an invisible force grabbed her and sucked her through the portal, depositing her on what might have been a pile of decaying entrails. The matter oozed beneath her feet, making a slick squishing noise. As she watched with horror, black skeletons with glowing red eyes emerged from the shadows, crawling over the devastation like terrible, obscene spiders. She couldn't move. Her muscles were completely rigid.

The skin of the demons around her sloughed off in burned, black flakes, then regenerated in time to fall again. Her mind screamed. She had to get out of here. She had to get back to Earth. A passing demon turned his head to gape at her, his eyes a sallow yellow, and she realized with a jolt that she recognized him. She had revoked him years ago.

In that moment, that awful moment, she realized she had misunderstood her father's words. He hadn't been offering her the key to success. He had been delivering a warning. A demon opening the fifth seal would open the door to all the demons that had been killed outside of Hell—the *demon martyrs*. All the demons she, Harriet, and Annabeth had revoked were there. And not just them. Any demon the angels had killed were somewhere in this inferno too. She had made a terrible mistake.

Lost in their private miseries, few of the demons around her had immediately noticed when the seal opened. Now, as the cool air from the mausoleum wafted through from the portal behind her and provided them the first breath of relief in half an eternity, they did. Dozens if not hundreds of heads raised, sniffing the air and the hope it represented. Yellow eyes turned upon her, piercing her like spears. Assessing. Then understanding.

As one writhing, surging mass, the damned began to move. A door to Earth had been opened, an escape hatch after untold years of misery. The only thing between them and freedom from the endless agony of Hell was Theodora.

Even as they shambled closer, she couldn't move. Her mind was no longer connected to her body, which had turned to stone. Faces with unhinged jaws leered at her. Charred hands reached toward her. But her limbs still refused to move. All she could do was watch with helpless horror as more and more appeared.

They were going to spill back out onto the Earth, thousands of monsters from a nightmare. They moved closer, limping, crawling, dragging themselves. She stopped breathing.

A hand closed over her wrist. It was so hot the leather of her jacket immediately burned and curled away. Moving slowly, as though through molasses, she turned her head to stare into a too-familiar face. As her face went slack, the hand let go.

"Theo." The voice creaked, the breath pushed through vocal cords that hadn't been used in decades. The creature's body was half gone, nothing left of its torso but a rib cage charred black by fire. Skin hung from the monster's cheekbones like tattered banners. "Stop them." Reedy as it was, there was urgency in the creature's voice.

"Daddy..." Theodora could barely say the word past the lump in her throat. She was simultaneously repulsed and desperate for the monster beside her, caught between wanting to shove it away and hug it tightly. Although it had lost almost all of its human features, she would have known those brown eyes anywhere.

"Tell them the time hasn't come yet. Complete the prophecy or they'll escape into the world...Protect...the humans." His voice was barely a whisper. She had to strain to hear it.

It was hard to look at the gaunt, decaying monstrosity her father had become. But she couldn't look away, either. He was still her father, and she still loved him. "I—"

She choked, helpless. She wanted to do what he commanded, but she couldn't move an inch. And how could she close the Pandora's box she'd opened? She hadn't even been certain she could open it.

"You can do it," he said. "The seal is yours. *They* are yours now. They will obey you."

Whoever opens the seals controls what lies within. Was she really now the master of the demon martyrs? What did that even mean? But she trusted her father. If he said she was, she believed it. He would never lie to her.

The monsters continued to move toward her, writhing shapes with terrible, tortured faces. Heat battered her face like a dragon's breath and broiled her lungs. She could hardly have been in Hell for more than a minute, but sweat already had started to pour down her forehead and back, making her skin slick. Fighting to pull herself together, Theodora threw out her hand in as firm a gesture of command as she could manage. "Stop!"

As one, the demons before her stopped. The faces looking to her turned curious, waiting to hear what their new master would say next. The magnitude of what was happening hit her like a wrecking ball. These pathetic creatures were hers to control now. It was an army of the damned, but it was an army. And it was hers... if she wanted it.

She looked into her father's eyes, drawing from his strength, then addressed her army again. "It's not yet time for revenge."

An unexpected thrill danced down her spine. The demons were listening to her, hanging on her words. She had outplayed Michael, and now the tables had turned a little. With this army, she could take on the heavenly host and punish it for what it had done to her father. To her.

Stillness followed her words, punctuated only by the hiss of geysers of fire in the distance. Then, with slow, pained movements, the demons began to move away. The tide of bodies around her ebbed. She watched the demons go with a mixture of revulsion, excitement, and pity. She had done it. She had taken control of the seal. Still...

"What happens if Michael keeps opening seals?"

"So long as you control the fifth seal, the Apocalypse can go no further."

"What about—"

"Theo," her father interrupted. "Your mortal body can't exist here much longer. You must go."

She was only half-celestial, and nowhere near to being immune to the heat. Already, her body felt as though it might catch fire at any moment...and perhaps it would. When she looked down, blisters were forming on the backs of her hands. She didn't want to think about what her face must look like.

"You must leave and close the seal."

"Come with me."

She was more than happy to leave Hell, but she couldn't bear the thought of leaving him there. She envisioned the two of them departing the inferno together, Orpheus leading home a freed Eurydice. This was the opportunity of a lifetime. She could save her father from an eternity of torture.

Kasdeja shook his head. "This is my place for now; I can't leave it. Go without me and don't return. And remember, you only control this seal so long as you're alive. The angels will come for you. They won't stop until they've retaken the seal."

Theodora was prepared to argue for as long as it took to get him to accompany her. She would stand there until her skin caught fire if she had to—it would grow back. But he didn't give her the opportunity. Putting his smoldering, skeletal hand on her chest so firmly that the mark burned even through her jacket, he pushed. Surprised, she toppled backward out of the seal, landing on her seat on the stone floor of the mausoleum.

"Close the seal now!" he commanded, his voice carrying all the wild, chaotic force of Hell.

Theodora was the master of the fifth seal, the new commander of the army of demon martyrs, and a grown-ass adult, but he was her father, and she obeyed automatically, without thinking. The seal closed like a door slamming in front of her, hiding Hell from view. In an instant, it was like nothing had happened. She was in a dark, empty mausoleum. Hands lifted her to her feet, helping her stand as she blinked, dazed.

"What happened?" Harriet asked.

"Are you okay?"

Theodora stared at Annabeth and then Harriet blankly, trying to find her voice. Her throat was parched and raw. "You...didn't see any of it?"

Harriet shook her head. "No. When the seal sucked you in, you just...disappeared. All I could see was the glass."

Annabeth nodded, agreeing. "And I could only see the seal, not what's beyond it."

Theodora leaned against Harriet, unsteady in more ways than one. Her companions hadn't seen what she had. They had no idea what lay behind the fifth seal. She alone knew about the army waiting there. Her army. By claiming the fifth seal, she had stopped the Apocalypse. But what now?

EPILOGUE

Harriet yanked hard on the hellhound's chain, trying to force the creature to sit and stop its loud snuffling. It was a lost cause. Four feet tall at the shoulder and more than two hundred pounds of muscle, he was ill-tempered and obstinate even in the best of circumstances. As he began to whine loudly, the sound like a car's broken serpentine belt, she cast a frustrated look at Annabeth, who was standing far enough down the hall to be out of reach of the beast, watching her struggle to control the creature with misgivings. The dog sometimes obeyed Theodora and—although without any obvious pattern to when or why—occasionally Harriet, but he was too dangerous to let near Annabeth. He was relentlessly aggressive toward her, and the one time he got within arm's reach, he tried to tear her to pieces. The wounds had healed, but since then, she'd kept her distance.

"Shut him up," Theodora hissed as the hound—which she had named Muffin in what could only be described as a pique of facetiousness—started to dig at the bottom of the door in front of them.

Harriet made a face that indicated she was trying and that if Theodora thought she could do any better, she was welcome to try. Not for the first time, Annabeth wondered if Muffin was worth the effort they had put into tracking and trapping him once they realized Merihem had succeeded in summoning him to Earth after all. Apart from his deep and incorrigible behavioral issues, his breath smelled like a sewage overflow mixed with rotting meat and was enough to trigger involuntary retching in anyone who made the mistake of getting too close. And the amount of excrement he produced was positively unreal. But she had to admit he had many highly effective uses. One of which was providing advance warning when an angel was nearby.

Theodora raised her new shotgun to her shoulder, aiming the barrel at the smooth white door. The hallway around them was spotless, polished to peak shine. It was not a place for people like them. It had been built specifically to keep the lower socio-economic strata out. Annabeth knew it therefore gave Theodora pleasure to breach those walls.

"I bet he tries to run," Harriet said.

Technically, the correct verb was "fly." Uriel lived in the penthouse apartment, so his only options once the four of them burst through his door would be to fight, jump out the window, or parley. They hoped he would choose the latter, but it was as likely or more that he would try to fight instead, in which case they might see his legendary flaming sword in action. Annabeth was fine with just reading about it instead.

"If he does, I'll fucking catch his ass and drag him back," Theodora growled.

Annabeth had a vision of Theodora blowing through the window, black wings spread like Hell's angel as she caught up to him and the two engaged in a dogfight high above the city. But... it would be too dangerous for Theodora to challenge Uriel that way. A fallen half-angel stood little chance against a full archangel.

"Don't," she warned.

It had taken them a week to hunt him down, but they had done it. If he ran, they would be able to find him again. So long as he remained on Earth.

Theodora shoved Muffin's black head aside—he shifted his weight with a mournful growl but didn't try to rip her arm off—and kicked the door a few times, leaving a brown scuff mark several inches from the bottom. The sound was muffled, absorbed by the thick wood.

"Maybe he's not home," Annabeth suggested after a long, silent minute. She clutched her morning star in her hands, her cardigan sleeves rolled up to three-quarters length. Although the weapon was satisfyingly heavy in her hands, she couldn't imagine using it against Uriel. In this case, it was more for her own comfort than anything else.

"Muffin thinks he's home," Harriet said, nodding at the creature.

"Plus, it's two in the morning," Theodora added. "Where the fuck else would he be? It's not like he's at a strip club."

They waited. After another few seconds, the gold door handle moved, pressed on the other side by an invisible hand. Annabeth's muscles clenched in anticipation. She shifted her weight onto the balls of her feet.

The door didn't have a peephole. It was an aesthetic decision that was about to come back to bite Uriel. He had no idea what was waiting for him on the other side. Theodora looked at Harriet and nodded, tacitly confirming the plan they had made back at the pawnshop. Harriet nodded back.

As the door cracked open, Harriet let go of Muffin's chain. In response to the sudden absence of restraint, the hellhound hit the door like a cannonball, barreling through and into the person behind it like a freight train. There was a flash of color and movement, then a shout followed by the clattering sound of limbs striking marble. Drawing her katana, Harriet hastened to follow, Theodora on her heels and Annabeth several steps behind her. They needed to get to Muffin quickly. Given the extreme malice he seemed to bear angels, he might try to rip Uriel's throat out before they had the opportunity to talk to him. Then they would have to hang around the apartment while they waited for him to heal. Better they stop him before that happened.

"Get it off me," Uriel was screeching as Annabeth slipped through the door.

The angel was on his back, Muffin sitting on his stomach and thighs with his paws on Uriel's chest. The hellhound's face was mere inches from his. Muffin's excessive saliva dripped onto the angel's chin and ran down to soak into his crushed red velvet dressing gown. In response to the angel's cry, Muffin growled, fierce and savage and terrifying. It made the hairs on the back of Annabeth's neck stand up with a primal fear. She took a step back.

Even Harriet made no move to approach the dog, standing a safe distance away with the metal leash dangling from her right hand.

"What are you doing? Get it away!" Uriel shrieked.

Annabeth looked to Theodora. The other woman's face was perfectly blank. Realizing Muffin was a much more compelling threat for the moment than her shotgun, Theodora pointed the weapon down at the floor and looked around, taking in the smooth white walls, the large oval mirror over a minimalist entryway table, and an abstract chandelier that hung from a soaring ceiling. She snorted. "Shit, Uriel, you live in a damn museum." She picked up the thin taupe vase that was on the table and admired it. "Is this from Etsy?"

"Why have you come here?" Uriel snarled.

He squirmed under Muffin's weight, uncomfortable yet clearly afraid to try to displace the hellhound. Angels might be immortal, but they still felt pain. He didn't want to anger the creature, a wise approach. Muffin growled again, unleashing another waterfall of thick saliva that dripped down the angel's neck and into his long hair. Uriel was going to need to shower later. Muffin's saliva didn't go away like normal water. As Annabeth knew too well, it was like a dog slobber loogie.

Theodora put the vase down and raised her eyebrows at Uriel, cradling her shotgun in her arms. "I'm surprised Muffin hasn't eaten your face off yet. He must like you." She paused. "Although also he eats literal shit, so...he doesn't have the greatest taste."

Uriel glared at her, his dark brown eyes almost black. He looked like he'd just taken a big bite of what he thought was cake but was actually a lemon. Now he was furious, insulted, disappointed, and his mouth was full of sour rind. Annabeth was short on sympathy for his situation. He might have been an archangel and the once guardian of Eden, but she lost all respect for him when he exposed himself as an angel supremacist. He deserved a dog drooling in his hair.

"Okay, okay, I'll tell you why we're here," Theodora said graciously. Reaching into the pocket of her new black jacket, she withdrew a single feather, longer and more brilliantly white than that of any bird on Earth. She placed it beside the vase on the table, where it rested weightlessly, concave side up as though artfully posed for a photo.

"What is that?" Uriel asked, craning his neck to see. In response to the movement, Muffin snarled, reminding the angel how close his long yellow fangs were to his face. Uriel froze instantly.

"I didn't catch his name," Theodora said.

Annabeth shivered at the memory of what they'd done and didn't look at the feather. Michael had made a mistake. In the course of pontificating to Harriet, he had accidentally told them exactly how to revoke an angel back to Heaven. And destroying the corporeal body of the angel that had been sent to assassinate Theodora had been surprisingly easy, if still deeply uncomfortable for Annabeth. Theodora and Harriet had felt much less ambivalent about the job.

Uriel realized what he was seeing and gaped at Theodora, horrified by her implication. "You—"

"Revoked him, yeah. As I will anyone you send after him." She gazed fondly at Muffin. "Hellhounds are a fuck-ton of work, but they're great at letting you know when some sneaky angel bastard is trying to creep in and murder you."

She took a few steps around the foyer, shaking out her shoulders lazily before she returned to face him. With her feet planted and her chin high, she was just as intimidating as any archangel. She was vengeance made flesh. Annabeth pitied anyone who crossed her. Angels included. "Anyway, enough chitchat. It's time to talk business. You're trying to kill me."

"You opened the fifth seal!" Uriel's hiss was a mixture of indignance and anger.

Theodora shrugged the accusation off. "Yeah, yeah, water under the bridge now. What I'm saying is that I don't want to spend the rest of my life wondering if some angel is going to pop up like a jack-in-a-box every time I turn the light on in a dark room."

"So long as you live, we will pursue you."

To his credit, Uriel's threat almost sounded ominous. But the effect was immediately destroyed by Muffin roaring furiously and biting into his shoulder. Uriel screamed, a high-pitched wail of shock and pain, and bucked, trying futilely to fight him off, but the demonic creature only growled and clamped down harder, red eyes glowing with a supernatural brilliance. As he shook the angel's shoulder viciously, neither Harriet nor Theodora moved to help him. Annabeth put her hand to her mouth, queasy, but she, too, rendered no aid to the beleaguered angel.

After Theodora watched Uriel struggle for a few moments, she tapped Muffin gently on the shoulder. "Let him go, sweetheart. Momma has to finish talking."

The creature surveyed her out of the corner of his eye rebelliously, calculating whether to resist or obey, then with one final, brutal shake, let go.

Theodora examined her red fingernails, pointedly ignoring the angel's agony. "Now, about your plan to hunt me until I'm dead. You're going to go back to Michael and you're going to tell him to leave us the fuck alone, do you understand me?" She let a beat pass. "Because if you don't, and you angels keep trying to goddamn ninja into my apartment..." She dropped her hand and stared intensely at the archangel, dropping the act. "Do you know what happens when a demon opens the fifth seal?"

"Hell," he gasped, tears of pain trickling down the sides of his cheeks. "You entered Hell."

"Yes, I did," Theodora agreed. "And you know what else? Now I have my own little doorway to Hell that not even you angels can open or close. Just me. And you know what that means?"

She waited another dramatic beat, then dropped her voice. "If I choose to, I can let Lucifer through at any time." She snapped her fingers. "Just like that, the Devil himself back on Earth. Crazy, how easy it would be, isn't it? John the Revelator didn't see that future, did he? But Michael Psellus did."

Uriel's eyes went wide. "No. You wouldn't." If there was one thing that terrified the angels, it was Lucifer. Uriel couldn't even pretend to be calm about the prospect of the Prince of Darkness's return and what it meant for the future of the angels.

Theodora smiled. It was a genuine smile, full of amusement. And something dark and sinister. "Of course I would."

She crouched down next to him again, her face only a few feet from his. "You know what your problem is? You angels think you're the ones holding all the cards. But God didn't write the future in stone, did He? And He didn't give you all the cards. He likes a little twist, a surprise. If I let Lucifer through the seal, that's it for you all. He and his demons climb to Heaven and it's game over, isn't it?"

It was Annabeth who had made the connection. Lucifer appearing on Earth before all seven seals were opened would mean John the Revelator's prediction for the future was wrong. Like a train switching tracks, the future would move in a new direction. Theodora threatening to trigger the future Psellus saw was the trump card to end all trump cards. The angels couldn't afford that future.

Theodora straightened and took a step back, putting space between herself and Uriel, whose bright red blood was starting to spread over his white marble floor. "This is the only warning you're going to get. Tell Michael to send his Horsemen back to wherever they came from. And if I ever see another angel, even if he's just fucking in line buying coffee, I'm opening the seal and every demon in Hell is welcome to walk right out and take a little vacation to Heaven." She waited, letting the threat sink in, then picked up the vase on the table. "And I'm taking this Etsy shit too."

"You will burn in Hell for all eternity for this," Uriel gasped. "You haven't done anything but delayed the inevitable. You can't stop the Apocalypse forever." He looked past Muffin's bulk to Annabeth. "And you, sister? Will you not stop her?"

Theodora tucked the vase under her left arm. "Don't bother. She's not on your side, buddy." She raised her chin and looked down at him. "And for your information, I have no intention of going to Hell. I figure I've got about fifty years to figure out how to avoid it and permanently stop the Apocalypse." And rescue her father, Kasdeja, Annabeth knew. "Half a century may be nothing to you angels, but it's a long fucking time for us humans."

She gave a sharp whistle. "Come on, Muffin, let's go home. Those pesky angels won't be bothering you anymore."

Reluctantly, the hellhound shifted his weight off Uriel, slipping to the floor and obediently rejoining his mistress. As Theodora made for the door, Annabeth's attention was caught by her eyes. For the first time, there was a fleck of yellow there.

Bella Books, Inc.

Women. Books. Even Better Together.

P.O. Box 10543
Tallahassee, FL 32302
Phone: (800) 729-4992
www.BellaBooks.com

More Titles from Bella Books